HARLEQUIN SMALL TOWN CHRISTMAS COLLECTION

It's a wonderful time of year! A time when friends and family gather to celebrate the joy of the season with good food and beautiful gifts.

And where better to meet than in a small town? The warmth of community adds extra delight to Christmas. Even the hardest of hearts is warmed by the sight of Main Street wearing its festive finery. Seeing the town square decked out in bows, lights and holly brings a smile to every face.

There is even the possibility of romance for the unsuspecting beneath those sprigs of mistletoe!

So join us in this special 2-in-1 collection as we bring romance and good cheer to this special holiday.

If you enjoy these two classic stories, be sure to look for more books set in small towns in Harlequin Special Edition and Harlequin Superromance.

VICTORIA PADE

is a *USA TODAY* bestselling author of multiple romance novels. She has two daughters and is a native of Colorado, where she lives and writes. A devoted chocolate-lover, she's in search of the perfect chocolate chip cookie recipe. Readers can find information about her latest and upcoming releases by logging on to vikkipade.com.

Look for more books from Victoria Pade in Harlequin Special Edition—the ultimate destination for life, love and family! There are six new Harlequin Special Edition titles available every month. Check one out today!

USA TODAY Bestselling Author

Victoria Pade
and
Kristi Gold

THEIR HOLIDAY
TOGETHER

 HARLEQUIN® SMALL TOWN CHRISTMAS

Recycling programs
for this product may
not exist in your area.

ISBN-13: 978-0-373-60964-2

Their Holiday Together

Copyright © 2014 by Harlequin Books S.A.

The publisher acknowledges the copyright holder
of the individual works as follows:

The Bachelor's Christmas Bride
Copyright © 2010 by Victoria Pade

The Son He Never Knew
Copyright © 2011 by Kristi Goldberg

HARLEQUIN®
www.Harlequin.com

Printed in U.S.A.

CONTENTS

THE BACHELOR'S CHRISTMAS BRIDE   7
Victoria Pade

THE SON HE NEVER KNEW   225
Kristi Gold

THE BACHELOR'S CHRISTMAS BRIDE

Victoria Pade

Chapter 1

"Ho! Ho! Ho! What good skaters you are!"

Shannon Duffy smiled a little at what she saw and heard in the distance when she got out of her car.

After a long drive from Billings, she'd just arrived in the small town of Northbridge, Montana. At the end of Main Street, she'd spotted a parking space near the town square and pulled into it so she could get out and stretch for a minute.

Not far from the parking area was an open-air ice skating rink and it was there that a group of preschool-age children were apparently being taught—by Santa Claus—how to skate. Or at least they were being taught by a man dressed in a Santa suit, using the *ho-ho-hos* to encourage them.

Christmas was a little more than a week away and Shannon was anything but sorry to have it herald the close of the past year. It had been a rough year for her.

Very rough…

But as she breathed in the cold, clear air of the country town, as she watched the joy of kids slip-sliding around the ice rink that was surrounded by a pine-bough-and-red-ribbon-adorned railing, she was glad she'd come. She already felt just a tiny bit less disconnected than she had, just a tiny bit less alone, almost as if the small town her late grandmother had loved was holding out its arms to welcome her.

Shannon had suffered three losses this year. Four, if she counted Wes.

She'd lost her dad at the beginning of January, and her mom just three months after that. Their deaths hadn't come as a surprise; both of her parents had been ill most of their lives. But when, in August, her grandmother had suddenly and unexpectedly had a heart attack and died, too, that had been a shock. And it had meant that her entire family was gone in just a matter of months.

Then her relationship with Wes Rumson had ended on top of it all.…

But now her trip to Northbridge was twofold. Primarily, she was there to attend the wedding of and spend the holiday with the people she'd come to think of as her New Wave of family.

Two months earlier she'd been contacted by a man named Chase Mackey. Out of the blue he'd made the announcement that he was one of three brothers and a sister she'd been separated from when she was barely eighteen months old, when they'd lost their parents to a car accident and—with no other family—had been put into the system and up for adoption.

Shannon had known that she was adopted. She just

hadn't known—before Chase Mackey's call—that she had biological siblings out in the world.

And not even too far out in the world at that since Chase Mackey had been calling her from Northbridge where her grandmother had lived and owned the small farm that Shannon had inherited at the end of the summer.

The farm was the second reason she was in Northbridge. Today she was to attend the closing on the sale of the property that she had no inclination to keep.

"Ooh, Tim! You okay?"

One of the little boy skaters had fallen soundly on his rump and Shannon heard Santa's question as she watched him race impressively to the child, clearly not inhibited by the bulky red suit and what was obviously padding around his middle.

Tim was a trouper, though. He fought the tears that his puffed-out lower lip threatened, let Santa help him up and get him steadied on his feet again. Then, casting nothing but a glance in the direction of the adults who looked on from the sidelines, the child let Santa ease him back to the group without making a bigger deal of the fall than it had called for.

Shannon silently approved of how the whole thing had played out.

Not that she had any reason to approve or disapprove, it was just that she was missing her job and some of that kicked in as she watched the scene.

She'd taught kindergarten since she'd graduated from college. It was a job she loved, but she was currently on sabbatical. Her grandmother's death had just been one blow too many and she'd needed to take some time.

It was a job she loved but might not be going back to.

At least not exactly the way she'd done it before, not if she accepted her old friend's offer and moved to Beverly Hills instead....

But that possibility was in the mulling stages and for the next week and two days she was just going to get to know her new brother, and her new nephew, and try to enjoy this first holiday without the only family she'd ever known.

She looked away from Santa and the skaters and took her cell phone from her coat pocket. She'd lost service just before getting to Northbridge and she wondered if she was back within range or if she was going to have a problem while she was here.

No problem, she had service again.

And a message...

The message was from Wes's secretary, informing her that Wes wanted to know when she arrived safely at her destination.

Shannon appreciated the concern the same way she'd appreciated it when Wes had inquired about her plans for the holidays to make sure she wasn't spending them alone.

But merely the fact that it was Wes's secretary calling now rather than Wes himself was a glaring reminder of why she'd turned down the proposal of the man she'd been involved with for the last three years.

Wes Rumson. The Hope-For-The-Future of the Rumson family political machine that had provided a long history of Montana's district attorneys, senators, representatives, mayors and now—if Wes's campaign was successful—a governor.

The man who would have definitely provided her with

the bigger life she'd always wanted, always dreamed of having. If she'd just said yes to his on-camera proposal.

But she hadn't. Regardless of how it had appeared, she hadn't. She'd said no.

Of course the general public didn't know that yet, only a select few insiders did. But still, she'd said no.

And she wasn't going to call and talk to Wes's secretary now, so she sent only a text message that yes, she had arrived safely in Northbridge. Then she added a cheery *Merry Christmas!*

Maybe just being near a jolly old Saint Nick was giving her some much-needed Christmas spirit.

Although when she returned her phone to the pocket of the knee-length navy blue wool coat she was wearing, and glanced at the skating teacher again, it struck her that this particular Saint Nick wasn't old at all. That behind the fake beard and mustache, under the red hat that he wore at a jaunty angle, was a much younger man with broad shoulders and impressively muscled legs that powered those skates expertly.

No, he was definitely not old. He was fit and trim and strong and...

And she didn't know what she was doing standing there ogling him. Especially when she knew she should be on her way.

Taking one more deep breath of the clear air and a last glance at the snow-covered town square, at the festively decorated octagonal-shaped gazebo at its center, and finally at the tiny skaters enthralled with the somehow-sexy-seeming Santa, Shannon got back into her sedan.

The fact that she would be seeing her new brother again made her want to make sure she didn't look too much the worse for wear from the drive, so she pulled down the visor above her and peered into the mirror on the underside of it.

She'd tied back her long, dark, walnut-colored hair into a ponytail in order to keep it neat. The plan had been a success because it looked the same as it had that morning. She wasn't sure she liked the new mascara she'd used to accentuate her blue-green eyes, but at least it had stayed on. So had the blush that dusted her cheekbones to add some pink to her pale skin and give her oval face some definition. But her glossy lipstick needed refreshing so she took the tube from her purse and did that.

Otherwise, she decided she was presentable enough to meet Chase Mackey where he lived with Hadley—the woman he was marrying on Saturday.

Take a left on South Street. Pass three mailboxes outside of town. Turn right at the fourth.

Shannon read her directions again to make sure she had the number of mailboxes correct.

She'd met Chase twice since he'd made contact with her, but he'd come to Billings each of those times—much the way her grandmother had over the years. This was Shannon's first trip to Northbridge since she was barely twelve.

According to Chase, he and his business partner Logan McKendrick had bought a section of an old farm that they had converted to meet their private and business needs. Logan lived in the original farmhouse. There was work space and a showroom for Mackey and McKendrick Furniture Designs as well as a loft where Chase lived, and a separate apartment he'd offered to Shannon for the holidays. So she wouldn't merely be visiting her newfound brother and the woman who would be his bride, she would apparently also be having a lot of contact with Logan and his family.

And with her nephew, Cody.

Cody was the fifteen-month-old son of Shannon and Chase's oldest sister. The death of Cody's mother was the reason Chase was now raising Cody, and what had revealed the far-reaching family ties that had brought Shannon and Chase together. Chase had brought the baby on both trips to Billings so Shannon had had the opportunity to meet the adorable baby and she couldn't wait to see him again.

She flipped the visor back up, and when she did she saw that the skating lesson had apparently ended because Santa and his not-quite-elves were all taking off their skates.

Thinking to leave before the parking lot got busy, Shannon buckled her seat belt and turned the key in the ignition.

Click, click, click. Nothing.

"How can that be, you just got me all the way to Northbridge?" she said to the thirteen-year-old car as she tried again.

But the same thing happened—a few clicks and nothing.

Not that time, not the next time, not the fourth time. The car just wouldn't start again.

And the only thing Shannon knew about a car was how to drive it.

"Great," she muttered.

As if something might have changed in the few minutes since she'd tried, she tried again, just as Santa was headed in her direction.

Still the engine wouldn't turn over. And then there

Santa was, at the window right beside her, bent over so that a pair of thick-lashed, smoldering, coal-black eyes could peer in at her.

"Need help?"

He'd tied his black ice skates together by their laces and was wearing them slung over one shoulder as if having them there was second nature to him. The beard remained in place, but even from what she could see of his face she knew she'd been right in thinking that he wasn't *old* Saint Nick. The man appeared to be about her own age.

Shannon rolled down the window. "It won't start. There was no problem when I drove in. I stopped for two minutes and now it won't start again."

"Pop the hood and let me take a look," he suggested in a deep, deep voice.

Shannon had no idea if her roadside service could provide a rescue all the way in Northbridge, so this seemed like the next best thing. She pulled the lever that unlocked the hood and then got out of the car to join Santa in front of it.

He was tall. Of course he'd seemed tall compared to the kids who had surrounded him in the distance minutes earlier, but when Shannon stepped up beside him, she was surprised by just how tall he was—over six feet to her five-four. He was also much more massively muscled within that Santa suit than she'd realized.

And she had no idea why she was taking note of things like that...

He slipped his skates off his shoulder and set them on the ground. Then he found the latch that still held down the hood, released it and raised the heavy front cover of her car to expose the engine.

Shannon looked at it along with him even though she didn't have the foggiest idea what they were looking for.

"Your battery is new so it isn't that, and a jump won't get you going."

Oh, the wicked places her mind wandered to when he said that!

And again, she didn't know why. She didn't ordinarily have sex on the brain.

Silently scolding herself, she curbed her thoughts just as he said, "Let me try a couple of things. Get back in and turn it on when I holler for you to."

Shannon did as she was told but after several more attempts to get the engine to start whenever Santa told her to turn the key, it just didn't happen.

"I think you have something more going on than I can fix," he finally called to her.

Stepping out from behind the hood, he bent over, scooped up as much snow as he could and used it to clean his hands.

Shannon got out of the car and handed him several tissues she'd taken from her glove box.

"Well, thanks for trying," she said as he took the tissues to dry his hands. She nodded toward Main Street. "I saw a gas station up there—do you know if they have a mechanic?"

"Absolutely. The best—and only—one around here. I can give him a call for you, have him come down and take a look. He has a tow truck, too, if he needs to take it back to the station."

Shannon checked the time on her cell phone. The closing on her grandmother's property was in little more than an hour.

"I guess that would be good," she said tentatively. "Do

you think the mechanic could come right down? I'm kind of in a hurry to get somewhere...."

"Even if he can't, you can just leave the keys under the seat and Roy—he's the mechanic—will take care of it. And if you need a lift somewhere, I can probably get you there."

Nice eyes or not, she wasn't getting into a car with a complete stranger.

"Thanks, but I can call my brother—"

"Who's your brother? It's a small town, I probably know him."

"Chase Mackey?"

"Shannon? Are you Shannon Duffy?" Santa asked.

"I am. How—"

"I'm Dag McKendrick—I'm the one you sold the farm to. Chase's partner, Logan, is my half brother."

The local Realtor had handled the sale. Shannon knew the name of her buyer, and that there was a family connection with her brother's partner, but they'd never met.

"Wow, this *is* a small town," she said, thinking about the coincidence.

"And I'm staying at Logan's place until I finish remodeling your grandmother's house. You're set to stay in the apartment above Logan's garage, right? So that must be where you're headed."

"Right."

"So we can call Roy and have him take a look at your car while you just go home with me."

Oh.

He made that sound as if everything had worked out perfectly. But Shannon still couldn't help being uncomfortable with the thought of taking everything this man said at face value and totally trusting him.

"Uhh…thanks, but—"

"Come on, it's fine. I even have candy.…" he cajoled, taking a tiny candy cane from his pocket.

"You're a stranger masquerading as Santa Claus trying to lure me into a car with candy?" she said.

He laughed and while it wasn't a Santa-like *ho-ho-ho,* it was a great laugh.

"I guess that does sound bad, doesn't it?" he admitted. "Okay, how about this…"

He reached into one of the skates that he'd again slung over his shoulder and pulled out a wallet.

"Look—I'll prove who I am," he said, showing her his driver's license.

Shannon took a close look at it, particularly at the picture. For the kind of photograph that had a reputation for being notoriously bad, his was the exception. Not only were those eyes remarkable, but so was the rest of his face.

Roller-coaster-shaped lips. A slightly long, not-too-thin, not-too-thick nose that suited him. The shadow of a beard even though he was clean shaven, accentuating a sharp jawline and a squarish chin that dented upward in the center ever so alluringly.

And his hair—like the full eyebrows she could see for herself—was the color of espresso. It was so dark a brown it was just one shade shy of black, and he wore it short on the sides, a little long on top and disheveled to perfection.

And yes, the name on the license was, indeed, Daegal Pierson McKendrick.

"Daegal?" Shannon said as she read the unusual name.

"My mother had visions of glory. She thought it sounded European and sophisticated. My sisters are Isadora, Theodora and Zeli. But you can see that I am who I say I am. And in an hour and a half we'll be sitting across a table at the bank for the closing on your grandmother's property. Plus, tonight we're having a family dinner together, and we'll actually be living within spitting distance of each other even when we aren't together. I think you can risk a five-minute ride in my car."

Shannon had no idea why, but she couldn't resist giving him a hard time despite the abundance of reasons why she could trust him.

"How do I know that the person behind that beard is the person on this driver's license?"

He looked to his right, to his left, over his shoulder, making sure none of the children he'd been teaching to skate were around to see. Then he eased the beard down just enough for her to realize that in reality he was even better looking than in the photograph.

It was only a split-second glimpse, however, before he released the fluffy white disguise that must have been held on by elastic because it snapped back into place.

Then he waved a finger between the driver's license in her hand and himself and said, "Him, me, same guy. Not somebody who's gonna drive you out into the woods and ravage you."

Why did *that* make her smile? And maybe sound a little tantalizing?

She again had no answer to her own question but she did finally concede. "Okay. Let's call the mechanic and then I guess I'll *have* to trust you."

Dag McKendrick took a turn at smiling at her—a great smile that flashed flawlessly white teeth. "You don't *have* to trust me. You can walk—it's about four miles straight down South Street—five minutes by car, maybe an hour or more on foot, your choice..."

"I'll take the ride. But remember, the mechanic will know who I left with."

"And the possible future-Governor of Montana will track me down and have me shot if anything happens to his soon-to-be wife."

So the news had even reached Northbridge. Shannon had been hoping that somehow the media coverage might have bypassed the small, secluded town during the two weeks since Wes's on-camera proposal.

But while she *wasn't* Wes Rumson's soon-to-be any-thing, she'd agreed not to refute it in public. She'd agreed to let Wes's press people handle it in a way that saved face for him, that didn't harm his bid for governor. And she couldn't blurt out the truth now, on the street, to some-one she didn't know.

Even if she suddenly wanted to more than she had at any moment in the last two weeks.

Because, as she looked into Dag McKendrick's coal-black eyes, she hated the idea that he thought she was engaged when she wasn't.

And she didn't understand *that* any more than she'd understood any of the rest of her response to this man.

But that was what she'd agreed to and she had to stick to it.

She had to.

So she bit her tongue on the subject and merely said, "I'll get my suitcase out of the trunk while you call the mechanic. If you would, please."

"Already sounding gubernatorial," he teased.

Shannon merely rolled her eyes at him and reached

beside the driver's seat to release the lever that opened the sedan's trunk.

"Just leave your suitcase, I'll get it," Dag McKendrick commanded as she headed for the rear of the car. "We can't have the future First Lady toting her own luggage."

Shannon ignored him and went for her suitcase anyway.

But as she was standing behind the car, she couldn't keep herself from peeking around the raised trunk cover at him, telling herself it was to make sure he was using the cell phone he'd taken from the inside of that same skate his wallet had been in, and not just to get another look at him.

Dag McKendrick.

Why on earth would she care if he thought she was engaged? she asked herself.

She still didn't have an answer.

But what she did have about five minutes later was a ride in a truck with Santa Claus behind the wheel, honking his horn and boisterously hollering *ho-ho-hos* to every child he drove by.

Chapter 2

On Thursday evening, in the upstairs guest room of his half brother's home, Dag set the packet of papers for the property he now owned in the top dresser drawer. As he did, the sounds of more and more voices began to rise up to him from the kitchen.

A family dinner to welcome Shannon Duffy and celebrate his new path in life as a land- and homeowner— that was what tonight was, what was beginning to happen downstairs.

It was a nice sound and he sat on the edge of the bed to give himself a minute to just listen to it from a distance.

And to stretch his knee and rub some of the ache out of it.

He should have used the elastic support brace on the ice today but he hadn't thought that teaching preschoolers to skate would put as much strain on his knee as it had. Plus he knew he was sloughing off when it came to things like that because on the whole, the knee was fine and didn't need any bracing. It had been that quick rush to the kid who had fallen—that's when he'd jimmied things up a little.

But just a little. The pain lotion he'd rubbed into it after his shower this afternoon had helped, the massage was helping, too, and he thought it would be fine by tomorrow. Every now and then it just liked to let him know that the doctors, the trainers, the coaches, the physical therapists had all been right—there was no way he could have gone on to play hockey again.

And he wasn't going to. After returning to Northbridge in late September he'd done some house-hunting, and he was now the owner of his own forty-seven acres of farm and ranch land, of a house that was going to be really nice once he was finished remodeling and updating it. He was on that new path that was being celebrated tonight and he'd be damned if he was going to do any more mourning of what wasn't to be.

He'd had a decent run in professional hockey. Hockey and the endorsements that went with a successful career had set him up financially. And even if it hadn't been his choice to move on, even if moving on had happened a lot earlier than he'd hoped it would, a lot earlier than he'd expected it would, he was still glad to be back in Northbridge.

The positives were the things he was going to concentrate on—the new path, getting back to his hometown and the fact that it was Christmastime. The fact that this was the first Christmas in years that he was home well in advance of the holiday, with family. The fact that he didn't have to rush in after a Christmas Eve game or rush out for a December twenty-sixth game. The fact that he wasn't in a hospital or a physical therapy rehab center the way he had been the last two Christmases.

So things might not be exactly the way he'd planned, but they were still good. And he still considered himself a pretty lucky guy. A little older, a little wiser, but still pretty lucky. Lucky enough to have been able to go on.

The sound of a woman's laughter drifted up to him then and he listened more intently.

Had Shannon Duffy come across the backyard from the garage apartment?

And why should he care whether she had or not?

He shouldn't.

He didn't.

But when he heard the laugh again and recognized it as his half sister Hadley's laugh, he stayed put, continuing to rub his knee rather than go down the way he might have otherwise.

It was just good manners, he told himself. They were sort of the co-guests-of-honor. If Shannon was here, he should go down. If she wasn't here yet, there was no rush.

Yeah, right, it's just manners...

Okay, maybe he didn't hate the idea that he was going to get to see her again. But only because she made for a pleasant view.

Dark, thick, silky, walnut-colored hair around that pale peaches-and-cream skin. A thin, straight nose that came to a slight point on the end that turned up just a touch. Lips that were soft and shiny and too damn kissable to bear. Rosy cheeks that made her look healthy and glowing from the inside out. Eyes that at first had seemed blue—a pale, luminous blue—and then had somehow taken on a green hue, too, to blend them into the color of sea and sky together. And a compact little body that was just tight enough, just round enough, just right...

A beauty—that's what Shannon Duffy was. No doubt about it. So much of a beauty that he hadn't been able to get the image of her out of his head even after he'd left her to her brother this afternoon when he'd come up here to shower.

So much of a beauty that he'd had to rein in the urge to stare at her every time he'd had the opportunity to see her today.

No wonder she'd snagged herself a Rumson....

Wes Rumson, the newest Golden Boy of the Montana clan that had forever been the biggest name in politics in the state. It had been all over the news a couple weeks ago that not only was he going to run for governor, he was also engaged to Shannon Duffy. When Dag had heard that, he'd figured that was the reason she was selling her grandmother's property.

It was also one of the reasons that no matter how great-looking she was, he would be keeping his distance from her.

Engaged, dating, separated—even flirting with someone else—any woman with the faintest hint of involvement or connection or ties to another guy and there was no way Dag would get anywhere near her. And not only because he wasn't a woman-poacher—which he wasn't.

He'd learned painfully and at the wrong end of a crowbar that if a woman wasn't completely and totally free and available, having anything whatsoever to do with her could be disastrous.

So, beautiful, not beautiful, he wouldn't go anywhere near Shannon Duffy.

At least not anywhere nearer than anyone else who

was about to share the holiday with her as part of a larger group.

Nope, Shannon Duffy was absolutely the same as the decorations on the Christmas tree, as the lights and holly and pine boughs and ribbons all over this house, all over town—she was something pretty to look at and nothing more.

But damn, no one could say she wasn't pretty to look at....

"A neckruss goes on your neck, a brace-a-let goes on your wristle."

"Right," Shannon confirmed with a smile at three-year-old Tia McKendrick's pronunciation of things.

After a lovely dinner of game hen, wild rice, roasted vegetables and salad, followed by a dessert of fruit cobbler and ice cream, everyone was still sitting around the table in the dining room of Logan and Meg McKendrick's home.

Wine had also been in abundance and had left Shannon more relaxed than when she'd arrived this evening. She assumed the same was true for her dinner companions because no one seemed in any hurry to get up and clear the remainder of the dishes.

Tia, on the other hand, had ventured from her seat to sit on Shannon's lap and explore the simple circle bracelet and plain gold chain necklace that Shannon had worn with her sweater set and slacks tonight.

"Can I see the brace-a-let?" Tia requested.

"You can," Shannon granted, taking it off and handing it to the small curly-haired girl.

Looking on from Shannon's right were Meg and Logan—Tia's stepmother and father.

To Shannon's left were Chase and his soon-to-be bride, Hadley—who also happened to be Logan's sister.

On Hadley's lap was fifteen-month-old Cody, and directly across from Shannon was Dag.

Which made it difficult for her not to look at him in all his glory dressed in jeans and a fisherman's knit sweater, his well-defined jaw clean shaven and yet still slightly shadowed with the heaviness of his beard.

Their positioning at the table apparently made it difficult for him not to look at her, too, because his dark eyes seemed to have been on her most of the night.

"I think that brace-a-let is kind of big for you, Miss Tia," Dag said then. "You can get both of your wristles in it."

Tia tried that, putting her tiny hands through the hoop from opposite directions as if it were a muff. Then, giggling and holding up her arms for everyone to see, she said, "Look it, I can!"

That caught Cody's interest and the infant leaned far forward to try to take the bracelet for himself. Luckily Shannon had worn two, so she took off the other one and handed it to the baby. Who promptly put it in his mouth.

"So, Shannon, you're pretty much a stranger to Northbridge even though your grandmother lived here?" Logan asked then.

"I am. I only visited here a few times growing up and that was all before I was twelve. Between my parents' business and their health, there was just no getting away."

"What was their business?" Hadley asked.

"They owned a small shoe repair and leather shop, and the building it was in. We lived above the shop and they couldn't afford help—they worked the shop themselves six days a week—so in order to leave town, they had to close down and that was too costly for them. Gramma would come to visit us—even for holidays. Plus with my parents' health problems they were both sort of doing the best they could just to get downstairs, put in a day's work and go back up to the apartment."

"Did they have serious health problems long before they died?" Chase asked.

"My mom and dad's health problems were definitely serious and started *long* before they died," Shannon confirmed. "As a young man, my dad was in an accident that cost him one kidney and damaged his other—the damaged one continued to deteriorate from the injury, though, and he eventually had to go on dialysis. My mom had had rheumatic fever as a kid and it took a toll on her heart, which also made her lungs weak and caused her to be just generally unwell."

"I'm a little surprised that people in that kind of physical shape were allowed to adopt a child," Meg observed.

"The situation at the time helped that," Shannon said. "What I was told was that my birth parents were killed in a car accident—"

"True," Chase confirmed.

"There wasn't anything about other kids in the story," Shannon continued. "I didn't know there was an older sister who had a different father to take her, or that there was an older brother and twin younger brothers, that's for sure. What my parents said was just that there wasn't any family to take me, that the reverend here had put out feelers for someone else to. When my parents asked if that could be them, the reverend helped persuade the authorities to let them have me despite their health issues—which weren't as bad at the time, anyway."

"I don't know if you know or not, but that reverend is my grandfather," Meg said.

"Really? No, I didn't know that."

"And sick or not, your folks must have wanted a child a lot," Hadley concluded.

"A lot," Shannon confirmed. "But having one of their own just wasn't possible."

"Did you have a good life with them?" Chase asked.

Despite the two occasions when she and Chase had met in Billings and the few phone calls and emails they'd exchanged, they'd barely scratched the surface of getting to know each other. And while she was aware that Chase's upbringing in foster care had been somewhat dour, Shannon hadn't gotten into what her own growing-up years had been like.

"I didn't have a lot of material things," she told him now. "But no one was more loved than I was. My parents were wonderful people who adored each other and who thought I was just a gift from heaven," she said with a small laugh to hide the tears that the memory brought to her eyes. She also glanced downward at Tia still playing with the bracelet in her lap and smoothed the little girl's hair.

When the tears were under control and she glanced up again, she once more found Dag watching her, this time with a warmth that inexplicably wrapped around her and comforted her before she told herself that she had to be imagining it.

"It must have been so hard for you to lose them," Meg said, interrupting that split-second moment.

"It was," Shannon answered, forcing herself to look away from Dag. "But at the same time, they had both gotten so sick. That's why my grandmother left Northbridge a few years ago—to help me take care of them when it was just more than I could do on my own—"

"You took care of them?" Dag asked in a voice that sounded almost as if it was for her ears only.

"I did—happily, and they made it as easy as they could, but I still had to work, too, and do what I could to help the man I'd hired to keep the business running. Plus my parents needed someone with them during the day, as well, so Gramma came to stay. By the time my dad died last January I couldn't wish him another day of suffering just so I could go on having him with me. And he and my mom were so close that she just couldn't go on without him. I think her heart really did break then, so it was no shock when she died just months later. And to tell you the truth, after spending every day of their adult lives together—working together, going up to the apartment together, never being without each other—it sort of seemed as if they belonged together in whatever afterlife there might be, too."

"And then there was just you and your grandmother?" Dag asked, his eyes still on her in that penetrating gaze.

"Right, Gramma was still with me. And she seemed healthy as ever. She helped me go through all my parents' things—personal and financial and business. She helped me find an apartment so we could sell the business and the building it was in. She helped me move. She was just about to come back to Northbridge—which was what she really wanted to do for herself—when she had a heart attack in August. She didn't make it through that...."

This time Shannon shrugged her shoulders to draw attention away from the moisture gathering in her eyes. When she could, she said, "Strange as it may sound, my grandmother's death was actually the shock."

"And just like that—within a matter of eight months—you lost your whole family?" Hadley marveled sadly. "Chase said you had taken some time off from teaching kindergarten then, and it's no wonder!"

"But now she has Chase and two more brothers out there somewhere who she and Chase are going to find," Meg reminded, obviously attempting to inject something lighter into the conversation.

Shannon looked at her newly discovered brother. "Whatever I can do on that score..." she said to him.

"I've hit a wall trying to find the twins," Chase said. "I'm thinking about hiring a private investigator after the first of the year. But we can talk about that later."

To change the subject completely then, Shannon said, "So I know Chase and Logan grew up together as best friends and then traveled the country and ended up starting Mackey and McKendrick Furniture Designs, but were you all friends in school?"

"Actually, no," Meg answered. "I know—small town, you'd think we would have lived in each other's back pockets. But I was younger than Chase and Logan, so I was barely aware of who they were and they say the same thing about me. I knew Hadley a little better, but again, we weren't the same age, so we didn't hang out together."

"But, Hadley, if Logan and Chase were close, you must have known Chase," Shannon observed.

"Oh, she knew him all right," Dag said, goading his half sister.

Hadley didn't rise to the bait beyond throwing her cloth napkin at him before she said, "I knew Chase. I had the biggest crush on him *ever*. But we didn't get together until this past September when he moved back here—"

"When I really got to know her," Chase contributed,

putting his arm around the back of Hadley's chair and leaning in to kiss her.

And why, when Shannon averted her eyes, her gaze landed instead on Dag, she didn't know. But there they were, suddenly sharing a glance while the soon-to-be-married couple shared a kiss. And to Shannon it almost seemed as if something couple-ish passed between them, too.

Which, of course, couldn't possibly have been the case and she again questioned what was going on with her.

Wanting whatever it was interrupted, she focused on Logan to say, "And there are three more McKendrick sisters with unusual names, right?"

"And another McKendrick brother—Tucker," Logan answered. "You'll meet them all tomorrow night at the rehearsal and dinner."

Cody threw Shannon's bracelet then, letting everyone know that he was no longer content.

"Oh-oh, I think it's past a couple of bedtimes," Meg said.

"Not me!" Tia insisted. She was still on Shannon's lap but now she'd taken off her shoes and was trying unsuccessfully to put both of her feet through Shannon's bracelet.

"Yes, you, too," Logan interjected.

"And that's our cue for dish duty," Chase added with a grimace tossed at his friend.

"That was the deal," Hadley reminded. "Meg and I will put kids to bed, Logan and Chase get to show what they learned as dishwashers on their grand tour of the country, and Dag and Shannon are off the hook because the dinner was for them."

"I don't mind helping with clean-up," Shannon said.

"Shhh," Dag put in. "Don't ruin a good thing."

"Besides," Meg added. "You've had a long day, Shannon. You drove the whole way in from Billings and had the closing, and all of us plying you with questions tonight. You have to be worn out. I know I would be."

"How about if I walk you out to the apartment?" Dag offered before she could respond to what Meg had said.

"Oh. You don't have to do that," Shannon demurred, not because she didn't want him to, but because the minute he suggested it she wanted him to *too* much.…

"I think that's a great idea—Dag *should* walk Shannon to the apartment so she doesn't just have to trudge out there alone," Meg agreed.

"Really—"

"Go on," Hadley urged. "I'd walk with you but I have to get all of Cody's gear ready to take with me to our place."

The spacious, luxurious loft was what Hadley was referring to. It was in the building beside the apartment over the garage where Shannon was staying. The same building that housed the work space and showroom for Mackey and McKendrick Furniture Designs on the ground floor.

Hadley's urging seemed to have ended the discussion because everyone got up from the table and Meg came to take Tia from Shannon's lap.

"Give back Shannon's bracelet and tell her thank you for letting you play with it," Meg told the three-year-old.

"I could keep it.…" Tia whispered to Shannon.

"No, you can't keep it," Meg said before Shannon had the chance to answer, taking the bracelet from Tia and the other one from where Cody had thrown it, and giving them both to Shannon just before she picked up Tia.

Shannon said her good-nights while Dag ran upstairs for a jacket. A brown leather motorcycle jacket that made him look every inch a bad boy when he returned with it on.

But Shannon told herself that wasn't anything she should be noticing. Or appreciating. And she curbed it.

She had her own coat on by that time, too, and the next thing she knew, they were out the back door and into the cold, crisp night.

"It's so quiet here," she said softly when Dag had closed the door behind them.

"A nice change from inside?"

"It wasn't that dinner wasn't nice," she was quick to say as they headed for the garage in the distance, not wanting him to think there was anything about the evening that she hadn't enjoyed. "I guess it's just that I'm not used to having so much family around."

"Because there was always just your mother, father and grandmother?" Dag said as they fell easily into step with each other.

"Yes. And really, until the last few years, it was just my parents and me. But here I am now with a brother and a nephew and Hadley will be my sister-in-law, and there's all of you McKendricks, too, who seem to be like family to Chase—"

"Not to mention two more brothers if and when you find them," Dag reminded.

"It's a lot for someone who's always been part of a small group, a small life."

"A small life?" Dag repeated with a laugh. "What exactly does that mean?"

"You know, just a small, simple, workaday life. Certainly no living in Italy and France the way Hadley did.

Or even the kind of travel Chase and Logan did around the country for years. Teaching kindergarten isn't a high-powered career. I've been to a few fancy parties with Wes, and there was a trip to Europe, but I haven't done anything that would qualify as a *big* life."

"So far," Dag amended. "But marrying into a rich and powerful family and possibly becoming the First Lady of Montana? That ought to pump up the volume considerably."

Shannon hoped that dropping her head when he said that only seemed to be because she was watching her first step up the outer wooden staircase alongside the garage to the apartment. But really she was hiding her expression so she didn't give away that she wasn't going to *pump up the volume* of her life by marrying Wes Rumson.

"Becoming the First Lady of Montana would be a bigger life all right," she muttered noncommitally. "And a bigger life is always what I've wanted. But we were talking about what I'm used to and neither a bigger life nor a lot of large family gatherings like tonight are it."

"So you'll have some adjusting to do and tonight was good practice," Dag said as he followed her up the stairs.

"Tonight was just nice," she said quietly again.

They reached the landing and she unlocked the apartment door, reaching inside to turn on the light and wondering suddenly if she should invite Dag in. She couldn't think of any reason why she should. And yet she felt some inclination to do it anyway.

"Want to hide out here until the dishes are done?" she asked with a nod in the direction of the main house where Chase and Logan were visible through the window over the sink.

Dag glanced in that direction, too, but then brought

his gaze back to her, accompanied by a grin that was disarmingly handsome. And made her think that he was tempted to accept her invitation to stay.

But after a moment he seemed to fight the urge and said, "I might not have been able to hold my own with those two when I was eight and they were making me pick up their smelly socks, but now? They don't get anything over on me."

Still, he didn't seem in any hurry to go and Shannon wasn't sure what to do about that. Standing there facing him, staring up into features any movie star could have used to advantage, wasn't giving her answers.

Then Dag said, "Those movers you hired to pack everything and clear out your grandmother's house missed a few things. Nothing big—just some odds and ends I've come across working on the place—"

"Like?"

"Like some clothes and a blanket that were stuffed up high in a closet. Some kitchen things. A couple pictures that had fallen behind a drawer. An old jewelry box—I can't even remember what all. I've been putting them in boxes when I come across them because I didn't know if there was anything you might want—"

"Most of what the movers brought to Billings I sold in a yard sale at a friend's house. There was so much of it that I can't imagine that they missed anything."

"Like I said, I don't think there's anything important. It's stuff that was probably jammed somewhere because not even your grandmother needed or wanted it. But still, I don't want to be the one to throw out anything that isn't mine. There's only two boxes and I can bring them home, but I thought you might want to see what I'm doing to the place. Maybe have one more walk through it for old time's sake..."

Was that what was appealing to her about his suggestion?

Or was it the thought of going out to the ranch and seeing him?

It had to be the nostalgia—the house *had* been her grandmother's after all. And she had spent some time there with her grandmother when she was a child.

Plus there *was* some curiosity to see what Dag was doing to the place, she told herself. That had to be what was behind her wanting to take him up on his offer.

"I think I might like to walk through the place one more time," she said. "Just tell me when it's convenient for you."

His grin returned even bigger than it had been before, but Shannon refused to allow herself to read anything into it—like the fact that maybe he wanted the visit from her just to see her, too....

"Tomorrow? I'll be working out there all day. You can swing by anytime."

"Shall I take your cell phone number and call first?"

"Nah. Anytime. Sleep in in the morning, unpack, do whatever you had planned and when it works out for you, just drive over."

"Okay."

And why did they go on standing there, looking at each other as if there should be more to say?

Shannon didn't know but that's what they were doing—she was just looking up into those black, black eyes of his, lost a little in them....

Then he finally broke their stare. "Great. I'll see you tomorrow, then."

"Sometime tomorrow," she reiterated, thinking that the minute it came out of her mouth it sounded stupid.

But it didn't seem to affect Dag because he just tossed her another thousand-watt smile and turned on his heels on the landing. Then he called a good-night over one of those broad shoulders and went back down the steps.

Which was when Shannon stepped into the warmth of the apartment and closed the door.

And realized that she was suddenly eager to get to bed, to get to sleep, to get tomorrow to come.

Chapter 3

"Yes, I got here, I did the closing on Gramma's farm yesterday, and it's nice to be spending time with Chase and Cody—I had breakfast and lunch with them and Hadley, and then Hadley took me to have my bridesmaid's dress fitted so it will be ready for the wedding tomorrow. And tonight is the rehearsal and the rehearsal dinner," Shannon said into the phone.

"Doesn't sound like you're missing me at all," Wes Rumson said on the other end.

"Wes..."

"I know, there's no reason you should be missing me— even if we *were* engaged you were used to not having me around for most things. It's the curse of the Rumson men."

And of his own parents' marriage and one of the reasons Shannon had turned down his proposal.

But she didn't say that.

Instead she said, "I appreciate that you called, though." Which was true. She honestly did hope they could remain friends.

"It feels a little weird to be so included in this wedding," she admitted then. "Hadley told me it was important to her and to Chase that the family he's found be a part of everything. But as nice as they all are—and they all are wonderfully nice people—they're still basically strangers to me."

Wes made no comment and she had the sense that he was at least half occupied with something other than their conversation.

Still, she felt the need to fill the silence he'd left and she said, "How are things going on your end?"

"Great!" Wes said in his most enthusiastic politician's voice. "We're looking good in the polls, we'll likely have the endorsements we need, even the President has promised to stop here sometime in the spring to throw his weight behind me."

"So maybe this would be a good time to make the announcement that there isn't any engagement...."

"I keep hoping we might not have to make that announcement."

"Wes—"

"The voters love you, Shannon. They love the idea of a little romance in the wings, of a wedding. And you know how I feel...."

That what the voters loved was of first and foremost importance to him? That how he felt about her was merely an afterthought?

But Shannon didn't say what ran through her mind.

Instead she said, "You have to make the announcement, Wes."

"The First Lady of Montana—that would be the Bigger Life you've always wanted," he said as if he were dangling a carrot in front of a donkey's nose. *Bigger Life* was the way he'd come to refer to her desire—as if it were an entity of its own. "No tiny apartment above a shoe repair shop—you'd live in the Governor's mansion. And this is only the start—you know we're shooting for the White House. You can't get a *Bigger Life* than that."

"I couldn't marry you just to have a bigger life, Wes. Any more than you should marry me to win votes."

"That's not fair—we talked about getting married before—"

And even then Shannon had had doubts about it. Yes, she'd always wanted a life that was bigger than the very small, limited life her parents had lived and Wes knew that. But when it came to a relationship, to marriage, she wanted exactly what her parents had had. And that wasn't the way she felt about Wes. She knew that wasn't the way Wes felt about her. Which was the *real* reason she'd said no.

"You don't really want to go over this again, do you?" she cajoled.

This time rather than silence giving away the fact that Wes's attention was split, he proved it by saying something away from the phone to someone else.

And since he never did answer her question, Shannon let it drop so she could persist with what she needed to get through to him. "I'm sorry, Wes, but you need to break the news publicly. And isn't sooner better than later? Don't you want to get it out there and get it over with so it will be genuinely old news and forgotten by election day?"

"Rumsons aren't quitters, Shannon. If there's any chance—"

"But there isn't," she said as kindly as she could. "I'm not an undecided voter who needs to be swayed, Wes. This really is just a no."

"Because of that Beverly Hills deal," he accused. "When it comes to a Bigger Life, Shannon, wiping the noses of movie stars' and moguls' kids can't compare to being—"

The hanger-on to Wes's Bigger Life?

Shannon thought that but she didn't say it. What she said was, "The *Beverly Hills deal* was also not the reason I said no—I told you that, too. It's just a new avenue I may take. But no matter what, Wes, you need to have your public relations group get on the announcement that there isn't any engagement. Even people in the boonies of Northbridge think I'm going to marry you."

"Then let's not disappoint them."

Shannon closed her eyes, dropped her face forward and shook her head. "Wes…"

"All right, I have to hang up, too," he said as if their exchange had involved something different than it had. "I'll check with you in a couple of days to make sure you're still okay. But if you need anything—anything at all, day or night—"

"I know I can call you. I appreciate that." Even though she also knew that rather than reach him, her call would automatically be rerouted to his voice mail or his secretary or his campaign manager—depending on how many numbers she tried—and that there would never be an immediate callback. Like when her grandmother had died so suddenly…

They said their goodbyes and Shannon hung up.

With a quick glance at the time, she grabbed her car keys and went out the apartment's door and down the steps to her car—freshly back from the local garage where it had required a new starter.

Wes's call was making her late. Dag had said she could come by her grandmother's house anytime to see what he was doing with the place and to pick up what remained of her grandmother's things, but it was already after four and she was afraid he would give up on her. And she didn't want that.

Behind the wheel, she turned the key in the ignition and was pleased to see that the repair had been a good one—the engine started on the first try.

On her way to what was formerly her grandmother's place, she kept an eye out for Dag's big electric-blue truck coming in the opposite direction, just in case, and that was all it took to replace thoughts of Wes with thoughts of Dag.

Until she turned onto the road that led to her grandmother's house and it came into view.

The two-story wedding cake–shaped farmhouse was the home her grandmother had come to as a bride. Shannon's eyes filled with tears when she suddenly pictured her grandmother sitting on the big front porch, snapping green beans fresh from the garden.

She missed her so much.…

She missed them all so much.…

But even though the memories of being at that house brought on some pain as Shannon parked in front of it, she wasn't sorry she'd come. To her this was still her grandmother's house no matter who owned it on paper and she did want to touch base with it one last time.

Then the front door opened and Dag McKendrick appeared behind the screen. And somehow seeing him bolstered her and made it easier for her to actually go through with it.

As she turned off the engine, Dag shouldered his way out onto the porch. He was wearing jeans that Wes wouldn't have considered owning—low-slung and faded. Wes also would have had no use for the equally antique chambray shirt that Dag wore over a white T-shirt peeking above the unfastened top two buttons.

Shannon wasn't sure why she was mentally comparing the two men but she couldn't seem to stop herself as she took in the sight of Dag's shirtsleeves rolled midway up his massive forearms. Drying his hands on a small towel, he tossed her a smile that wasn't at all the kind of practiced-in-case-a-photographer-might-be-nearby smile she knew she would have received from Wes.

Both men were handsome, she admitted, but in different ways. There was never a hair out of place on Wes's dusty blond head while disarray was part of the style for Dag's dark locks. Wes was lean and wiry and stiff backed where Dag was muscular and powerful looking, his posture relaxed—as if his confidence came from knowing he could handle himself rather than from the entitlement that came with being a Rumson.

Rugged versus refined—that's what Shannon concluded. Dag's good looks were rough and earthy, while Wes's were polished and sophisticated.

"Hey there! I was beginning to give up on you," Dag called to her as he came down off the porch.

And that was when it struck Shannon that it wasn't only their looks that were different.

Wes would have waited for her within the shelter of the house. He wouldn't have come out into the cold December afternoon to greet her. But that was what Dag did. Because their styles were entirely different. While Wes was known for his charisma, what she'd already seen from Dag just in the brief time since they'd met was a special brand of charm that—while equally as smooth—was more natural than slick.

And when it came to sex appeal?

When it came to sex appeal, Shannon had no idea why anything like *that* had even popped into her mind as Dag opened her door.

She recalled belatedly that he'd said something a split second earlier that she'd heard through her closed window.

What was it…?

Ah, that he'd just about given up on her.…

"I'm sorry I'm so late. It took longer with the seamstress than I expected it to and then I had a phone call I had to take. I kept an eye out for your truck the whole way here in case I passed you on the road."

"Another ten minutes or so and you would have."

And the sound of his voice—there was absolutely no reason why she liked the deeper timbres of Dag McKendrick's voice better than the slightly higher octave of Wes's but in that instant it struck her that she did.

Then she told herself to stop this right now! She had no interest in this man. He was nothing but a friend of her brother's and the buyer of her grandmother's house and someone she just happened to be acquainted with for the time being. Her relationship with Wes was barely cold—

not even cold enough for anyone else to know about. Her entire life had changed in the last year, she could very well be headed to a new life in Beverly Hills, and in all of that there was no room, no time, no reason, for her to be even remotely interested in this man.

And she wasn't.

She wasn't…

"Is it too late? Do you need to get home?" she asked then, stiffening her spine a bit to resist his appeal.

"Nah. We can have a little time here and still get back for a shower before the rehearsal."

Had he meant to say that as if they'd be showering together? Or was this just another of those crazy blips that made her mind wander into territory where it had no business going?

"Not that *we'll* be showering. What I meant was that *I'll* still be able to get back to take a shower," he amended then, letting her know that she hadn't misheard him. But the cocky grin that went with the amendment told her that the slip of tongue didn't embarrass him at all.

Mischief and teasing—two more things Wes never indulged in. Not even with her, let alone with someone he barely knew.

"Yeah, I think I'll leave you alone to shower," Shannon answered the way she would have addressed a kindergartner who had said something inappropriate, even if she couldn't help smiling at their exchange.

"Probably for the best," he said, undaunted by her tone.

"I didn't realize the outside of the house needed painting so badly," Shannon said as she got out of the car, staring at the farmhouse in order to avoid looking at Dag and obviously changing the subject.

"Yep. I don't know when your grandmother had it done last but it has to have been decades ago. It'll all have to be scraped and power-washed then re-primed. What do you think about the color when I get around to painting? Back to the yellow or shall I go with white?"

"I know I don't really get a vote, but I always liked it yellow—it looked warm and homey and sunny to me that way."

"Trimmed in white?"

"I would, but it's your house now."

Dag motioned for her to go ahead of him up the porch steps and when they reached the house, he held the screen door open for her.

There were no signs of her grandmother in what Shannon stepped into. The inside of the house was empty of furniture and all the rooms she could see from the entry were in various stages of repair, remodel or renovation with the necessary tools and supplies littering them.

"Wow, you're really gutting the place," Shannon observed. "I know the appraiser said it needed work—that was why I reduced the price—but I had no idea it was this extensive."

"How long has it been since you were here?"

"The summer just before I turned twelve, so almost eighteen years...."

"Things were pretty run-down."

"My grandfather died the year before I was here last, I guess Gramma must not have kept up with things as well on her own. I didn't realize."

"From what you said about your folks last night, it sounded like you had enough to deal with."

"And it wasn't as if my dad could come here and help her out, or send money for her to hire someone," Shannon added as they pieced together why her grandmother must have let the place fall into such disrepair. "But I'm sorry if you came in on a big mess—I had no idea.…"

"It was just an old house. I would have wanted to update it anyway. No big deal. And there are some pluses to the place—the crown molding everywhere, the hardwood floors and just the way the whole house is built makes it more sound and sturdy than newer construction. It gives me a good foundation to work from. Come on, I'll walk you through what I have planned."

They spent the next half hour going room to room, with Dag explaining a complete plumbing overhaul that would leave all three bathrooms like new, a kitchen that sounded like it would be a chef's dream come true, and even ideas for accent colors of paint here and there that left Shannon surprised by his good taste.

When they reached the upstairs bedroom where she'd stayed on her visits here, Shannon said, "Have you found the secret cubby?"

Dag's eyebrows shot up in curiosity. "There's a secret cubby? Whatever that is…"

"I'll show you."

Shannon knelt down in front of a section of flowered wallpaper a few feet to the right of the closet. It didn't look any different than the rest of the loud pink tea-rose print but when she pressed inward and then did a quick release, that particular section popped open to reveal a two-foot-by-two-foot hole in the wall.

Dag laughed. "I'm sure I would have found that when I stripped off the wallpaper, but I had no idea it was there."

"It makes a great hiding place," Shannon said, peering inside to see if the things she'd hidden in it long, long ago could still be there.

They were.

"Let's see," she said as she began pulling them out.

Dag hunkered down on his haunches beside her to have a closer look.

"This is the notebook I brought with me on my last trip—I was going to write a novel in it. An entire novel that I would write in secret and then surprise everyone with when I was finished."

"At eleven?"

"Uh-huh. I believe I wrote about two paragraphs…" she said as she turned the notebook upright and unveiled the first page. "Yep, two paragraphs. That was as far as my career as a great American novelist went. And I think it's for the best," she added with a laugh after glancing at what she'd written.

Then she set the notebook down and reached back into the cubby.

"Let me guess—those were from your great American artist period?" Dag teased when she pulled out several pages cut from a coloring book.

Shannon flipped through the sheets. "Not a single stroke outside the lines—I was proud of being so meticulous. I think I was six."

"And this? You were going to be a chess master?" Dag said, picking up a carved horse's head chess piece that had come out with the coloring book pages.

Shannon grimaced. "*That* was me being a brat."

"You were a brat?" he said as if the idea delighted him.

"I was five," she said. "You have to understand, my parents were so close, so devoted to each other, so happy just to be together, that sometimes I felt a little left out. Not that I actually was," she defended them in a hurry. "I was actually about as spoiled as I could be with their limited resources. But at five, when they were talking and laughing over a chess game…" Shannon shrugged. "One of those times I tried to interfere by—"

"Stealing one of their chessmen so they couldn't play?"

"And hiding it," Shannon confessed. "I was leaving to come here the next day and I stuck it in my suitcase, so I ended up bringing it with me. By the time I was supposed to go home, I didn't want to bring it back and admit I'd taken it and get into trouble, so I put it in the cubby."

"Shame on you," Dag pretended to reprimand, but it came with a laugh.

"I know. Of course as I got older, the kind of relationship my parents had was what I realized I wanted for myself, but as a very little kid, there were times when I resented it because they were just so content being together no matter what they were doing—watching their favorite TV show or movie, or doing puzzles, or just talking or—"

"Playing chess?"

"Or playing chess. *I* wanted to be the center of their universe—and I was—but they were also the center of each other's universe, if that makes any sense…" Another shrug. "I think maybe I was a little jealous—it wasn't rational, I was a kid."

"And now have you found that kind of relationship for yourself with the potential future-Governor?"

There was no way she could answer that and luckily at about that same moment, she spotted one more thing in the cubby and reached in to retrieve a very ragged stuffed dog.

"Oh, Poppy! I'd forgotten all about you," she said as if she hadn't heard Dag's question.

She didn't know if he recognized that she didn't want to answer him or just went with the flow, but he didn't push it. Instead he said, "That is one ratty-looking toy."

"I know. I carried him around with me, slept with him, played with him—he was my constant companion. When I got too old for that I couldn't stand the thought that he might get thrown away, so I brought him here with me and put him in the cubby for safekeeping."

She checked out the old toy, saying as she did, "Poor Poppy, I never sucked my thumb, but I chewed off both of his ears, he lost an eye and his nose, and my mom had to sew the holes. His tail is gone, and his seams split and had to be fixed more times than I can remember—he's kind of a mess."

"He looks well loved," Dag decreed, and Shannon appreciated that that was the perspective he took when she knew that Wes would have been impatient with her sentimentality over it.

But Dag even waited while she hugged it for a moment before she set it down and took the last few items out of the cubby.

"Love notes," she confided as if they were a deep, dark secret. "This was from the summer I was ten—I was at camp just before I came to see Gramma and I had a sizzling romance with one of the boys there...."

"How sizzling could it have been at ten?"

"Hot, hot, hot!" Shannon said with a laugh. "He sat next to me on movie night and held my hand when the lights went out. And look at these notes—he thought I had nice teeth. And my woven pot holder was the best in the whole class. And he liked my eyes because they match! How much more sizzling do you want it?"

"Oh, yeah, it doesn't get better than that!" Dag agreed facetiously. "This cubby-thing is a treasure trove."

"Ah, but it looks like that's it," Shannon complained after poking her head into the cubby to make sure. "Now the place is all yours."

Which struck her with a sudden, unexpected sadness that made her think that maybe she had a few more attachments to her grandmother's house than she'd originally thought.

But it was done and she knew from the way Dag had talked about his plans for the remodel that he loved the place, so she comforted herself with that—and by petting her old stuffed dog the way she had when she'd needed solace as a kid.

"I'll get a box for this stuff," Dag suggested then, as if he knew she could use a minute alone with her things, with the cubby, with the house. She was grateful for that, and once he'd gotten to his feet and left the room, she swiveled around to take one last glance at it.

The wallpaper was gaudy and overwhelming but she still had fond memories of being here with her grandmother on those few visits, of the fact that despite not spending much time here, it had still felt like an extension of home.

"I think he'll take good care of your house, though, Gramma," she whispered as if her grandmother might be listening.

Then Dag came back with a cardboard box.

"It must be late—it's starting to get dark," Shannon said with a glance out the window as she accepted the box from Dag. "We should probably be going."

"Probably," Dag confirmed, holding out a hand to help her to her feet once everything was in the box.

She could have stood without aid but she didn't want to offend him by refusing, so she accepted the hand up.

"Thanks," she said, wishing she wasn't quite so aware of how big and strong and warm his hand was. And how well hers fit into it.

But wishing didn't make that awareness go away and as soon as she could, she took her hand back. Somehow regretting it when she had—another of those crazy blips, she decided.

Dag seemed completely oblivious to the odd effects he could have on her and once she was on her own again, he bent over and picked up the box. He tucked it neatly under one arm and motioned for her to lead the way out.

"I have a favor to ask you," Shannon said as they went back downstairs.

"Sure," Dag responded without hesitation as he set the box from upstairs on top of the two boxes of things he'd been keeping for her in the entryway and picked up all three as if they weighed nothing.

"I can take one of those," she said before saying more about the favor.

"They aren't heavy. Just lock the door and pull it closed behind us."

Shannon did, returning to the subject of the favor as they went toward her car.

"What if the favor I have to ask is something you'll hate? Shouldn't you hear what it is before you say *sure?*" she teased him, having no idea where the flirtatious tone in her voice had come from.

"I think I can handle whatever you dish out," he flirted back. "What is it?"

As Shannon unlocked the trunk of her car, she said, "When the wedding is over, could you spare some time to go Christmas shopping with me? I bought Chase and Hadley's wedding gift at a store in Billings where they'd registered, but Christmas gifts are different. I thought I might get an idea what to buy after being with them, and then it occurred to me that since you're here and you know everyone better than I do, you'd also know what they might like."

"I could probably do that," Dag said as he put the boxes in the trunk. "We can go on Sunday—ordinarily not all the shops in town are open on Sundays, but this close to Christmas everything is."

"I would be eternally grateful."

"No problem."

And there would be no scheduling conflicts or meetings or public appearances or other obligations that prevented him from accommodating her request—the things that would have kept Wes from doing it at all. Shannon had become so accustomed to Wes putting her off if she did ask something of him that Dag's ready agreement seemed unusual to her.

But she didn't say that. Instead she closed the trunk and headed for the driver's side of the car. Dag managed to reach it at the same time and leaned around her to open her door.

Again she thanked him.

"I'll see you back at Chase and Logan's place," she said then.

"Right behind you," he answered, closing her door with that same big hand pressed to the panel that had been wrapped around hers a few minutes earlier.

That same big hand that her eyes stuck to when he waved it at her and even as it dropped to his jean pocket to dig out his keys.

It had felt so good....

Shannon yanked her thoughts back in line and started her engine, putting her car into gear and heading for the road that led away from the house just ahead of Dag.

Dag, who did stay right behind her all the way home, making it difficult for her to keep from watching him in her rearview mirror.

Dag, who she was thinking about seeing again tonight during the rehearsal dinner.

Dag, who she knew she shouldn't let cloud her thinking at all.

And yet somehow he seemed to be anyway.

Chapter 4

After the wedding rehearsal Friday evening, the dinner was in the poolroom section of a local restaurant and pub called Adz. The pool table had been removed and replaced by dining tables to accommodate what was a large wedding party. The lighting was dim and provided mainly by the candles on each table and there was a roaring fire in a corner fireplace made of rustic stone. The entire place reminded Shannon of an English pub she'd visited on a recent trip to London.

Shannon knew very few people there, and those she did know—Chase and Hadley, Logan and Meg—were busy mingling. Dag was the only other person she knew and he ended up being a godsend because while he was not her formal date to the event, he stayed by her side as if he were, as if he recognized that she was an outsider and had taken it upon himself to make sure she didn't feel that way.

Not that Shannon hadn't become accustomed to being in rooms full of strangers during the past three years. Dating a politician made that a common occurrence and she'd frequently been either expected to stand beside Wes, smile and say nothing, or had been left alone among strangers while Wes glad-handed and networked and basically scoured the crowd for votes or endorsements or funds. But still she appreciated that Dag kept her company. It was a nice change.

And it came in particularly handy when Dag's other brother and sisters headed their way.

"Oh, I'm not going to remember which of your sisters is which," she said quietly to Dag as they approached the spot in front of the fire where Dag and Shannon stood.

"We just wanted to tell you how happy we are that Chase found family," Tucker said as he and his sisters joined them.

Tucker was easy—he was the only other McKendrick male. But even though Shannon had been introduced to the sisters earlier, she'd been introduced to so many people tonight that she couldn't remember which was which.

"I'm happy about it, too," Shannon answered the third McKendrick brother.

"I was just telling Shannon about our names," Dag lied then. "About how with me and the girls, Mom filled in the birth certificates and chose the names when Dad wasn't at the hospital so he wouldn't have a say. How Dad knew the game by the time Tucker was born and made sure he got to pick Tucker's name. But the rest of us—" Dag pointed to each sister as he explained "—Isadora, Theodora and Zeli—those were all Mom."

Shannon was so grateful to him for making that easy for her that she could have hugged him. Instead she just cast him a smile and went along with the ruse that they'd been discussing the names before. "I like unique names, and they give you all something to talk about right off the bat."

"That's true," Zeli agreed with a wry laugh that insinuated that she never got away without talking about her name the minute it was mentioned.

"We all saw you on the news, Shannon," Issa said then. "You looked so shocked—you must not have had any idea that you were going to be proposed to."

"It was a surprise," Shannon agreed, hating that Wes hadn't yet taken her off this hot seat.

"What about a ring, though? You don't have one," Tessa contributed.

"I noticed that, too," Dag commented.

"I'm not a big jewelry person," Shannon said as if the lack of an engagement ring were nothing. Then, desperate not to talk about this, she said, "Speaking of jewelry, Tucker, you did get your cuff links for tomorrow, right? I don't know how they got mixed in with my wedding things, but Chase said he'd get them to you."

"Got 'em," he confirmed. Then, to Dag, he said, "So there was a last-minute change and now I'm walking Tessa down the aisle tomorrow and you're walking Shannon?"

It was news to Shannon that Tucker had ever been set to walk with her and she glanced at Dag to find an expression on his face that said he wasn't pleased that his brother had mentioned this.

"Yeah, I guess it was something to do with height or something," Dag obviously hedged.

"I'm half an inch shorter than you are—how much difference can that make?"

Dag shrugged. "There must be a reason. Maybe for pictures or something. What do I know?"

Shannon couldn't help wondering if Dag had done some backstage rearranging in order to walk with her.

Then with an enormous grin and in a tone that goaded his brother, Tucker said, "Is this another Dag-gets-a-dress-for-Christmas?"

"Oh, cheap shot!" Dag muttered with a laugh.

But that was as far as the confusing exchange went because just then three waitresses bearing dessert trays came into the room and all eyes turned toward them.

"Chocolate Crème Brûlée," Dag announced rather than saying any more to his brother. "Hadley says we're all gonna love this. And you know Hadley knows chocolate."

"She really does," Issa assured Shannon just before Tucker and the sisters moved back to the table they'd all been sharing so they could be served the dessert.

"Looks like that tiny corner booth is empty—what do you say?" Dag suggested then.

They'd had dinner at Hadley and Chase's table, after which everyone had begun to mingle and table-hop. Now some—like Tucker, Issa, Zeli and Tessa—were returning to their original spots, some remained standing and some were taking new seats.

Shannon had no problem with the idea of taking a new seat. In the corner. With Dag.

Not because she wanted to be alone with him, she told herself. But merely because talking to Dag always seemed to come easily, and after a long evening of trying to remember names and relationships and make conversation with a whole lot of people she didn't know, she was more than ready to sit back and relax a little.

"The tiny corner booth it is," she agreed, moving the few steps required to get there and sliding in from one side just as Dag was waylaid before he could slide in from the other.

Shannon had been introduced to the man who had stopped to talk to Dag and thought she remembered him to be Noah Perry, Meg's brother. He was intent on talking hockey with Dag—a subject that had cropped up several times tonight. Shannon didn't know much about Dag beyond the fact that he was Logan's half brother, but she had gathered here and there that for some reason he had a serious interest in the sport.

But rather than eavesdropping on the conversation the two men were having tableside, Shannon instead fell into studying Dag.

Dress had been decreed casual for the rehearsal and the dinner, so she was wearing charcoal gray pinstripe wool slacks and a white fitted shirt she'd left untucked.

But Dag had gone more casual still. He—and several other men—had on jeans. Dressier jeans than Shannon had seen him in before, jeans that fitted him to a tee, but jeans nonetheless.

And with the jeans he wore a bright pink shirt that he'd taken some ribbing for from Logan and Chase before they'd all left home. But if any man was masculine enough to wear a pink shirt, it was Dag. In fact, somehow the pink shirt topped off by a dark sport coat seemed to lend even more depth to his nearly black eyes, and both shirt and jacket were so expertly tailored that they accentuated the pure massiveness of his shoulders, leaving nothing at all feminine about the way he looked.

Noah Perry didn't keep Dag long and about the time one of the waitresses came to the corner table with the crème brûlées, Dag slid into the booth the way he'd initially intended.

"We need three, Peggy," he told the waitress.

If the teenager wondered why, she didn't ask, she merely left them three of the confections with three spoons and fresh napkins to go with them.

"Hadley isn't the only McKendrick who likes chocolate?" Shannon guessed.

"Maybe I got the extra for you."

"Or maybe you got the extra for you," Shannon countered with a laugh.

"I'll share," he tempted.

"I think I'll be fine with one."

Shannon had cause to rethink that after her first bite of the rich, creamy delicacy lying beneath a crusty shell of caramelized sugar. But she kept her second thoughts to herself even as they agreed that Hadley had made an excellent choice of desserts.

Then Shannon opted for giving Dag a tad more grief and said, "So, between the Dag-gets-a-dress-for-Christmas and the pink shirt, I'm beginning to wonder if there's something I should know about you...."

That made him laugh boisterously. "The shirt is salmon-colored—that's what the sales guy said. Salmon, *not* pink."

Shannon leaned slightly in his direction. "The sales guy lied, it's all pink."

Dag just laughed again. "Hey, I like this shirt."

Shannon did, too, but she didn't tell him that. Or that Wes could never have worn it or been able to look the way Dag did in it.

"And the Dag-gets-a-dress-for-Christmas?" she prompted only because she was curious about his brother's earlier comment. And because she was enjoying giving Dag a hard time.

"That was *me* being a brat as a kid," he answered, referring to her remark that afternoon about herself. "The Christmas I was eight I asked for a fancy dump truck. It had all the bells and whistles—lights that lit up, a switch that made the bed of the truck rise on its own, it even beeped when it backed up. It was great!"

"Uh-huh," Shannon said indulgently.

"I'd been asking for that truck since Thanksgiving and two days before Christmas, Tucker started saying he wanted it, too."

"And you were afraid he would get it and you wouldn't?"

Dag pointed a long, thick index finger at her. "Exactly! My mother was always making me hand something over to Tucker when he asked for it because he was *The Baby*. I figured the truck could be another one of those things, only she'd just give it to him herself."

"You didn't believe in Santa Claus and that Santa would come up with two of them?"

"I was on the fence about Santa by then—you know, hoping he was real, but skeptical. And with the dump truck, I didn't think I could take any chances. It was just that cool," he continued to gush, making Shannon smile as she finished her crème brûlée.

"So what did you do?" she asked, inviting a confession.

Dag had finished his first brûlée, too, and he replaced it with the second, pointing to it with his spoon before he answered her or dug in. "Want to share?"

It was tempting. But Shannon shook her head. "It's so rich—I don't know how you can eat two of them."

"Nothin' to it," he assured.

Then, after cracking the sugar shell to begin his second helping, he went on with his story. "Here's how Christmas was done—presents from Santa weren't wrapped, they were set up and waiting for us. Presents from our parents and other relatives were wrapped. But the presents from our parents never had tags on them. So when we came out in the morning there was a pile for each of us, some with tags from the relatives letting us know which pile was ours."

"And in each pile there were some untagged gifts—I think I'm getting the picture," Shannon said.

"So I snuck out of bed before dawn Christmas morning that year, before any of the other kids, hoping the truck would be set out like a Santa present. But no luck—Tucker and I both had some building blocks and a couple of puzzles—I think—from Santa. Then I checked out all the wrapped packages for Tucker and for me but I couldn't tell what was what—"

"No two were the same?"

"Hey, I was eight, there was no logic to this. Anyway, I found a package in Tucker's pile that I was convinced was the truck. So I took it. Then, in my pea-sized eight-year-old brain, I got the brilliant idea that if I mixed up a few more packages, no one would know I was the one who did it. So I did some of that, never paying any attention to what I was putting where or if I was only switching girls to girls, boys to boys—"

"Oh what a tangled web we weave..." Shannon said with yet another laugh.

"Right."

"And somewhere along the way you ended up with a dress," Shannon concluded, laughing yet again.

Dag made a face. "I think it was called a jumper—it was kind of like a plaid apron with a frilly blouse that went underneath it. Logan encouraged the folks to make me wear it but luckily my dad didn't think that was such a good idea."

Once more Shannon laughed. "Did you get the truck?" she asked sympathetically.

"Tucker and I both got them—in packages I hadn't switched at all. But that was what he was talking about— it's been known ever since as the Dag-gets-a-dress-for-Christmas Christmas."

Funny how Tucker was drawing a comparison between Dag making this secret switch and the change in who was walking her down the aisle tomorrow. So Dag must have done some manipulating to make sure he was her groomsman....

Shannon had no desire to tease him about that. Maybe because she was just pleased that he had done it. Although there certainly wouldn't have been anything wrong with walking with Tucker, she told herself. She was just more familiar now with Dag.

At the head of the room, Logan stood up then to draw everyone's attention. He made a toast to the last night of single life for both Chase and Hadley, joking at their expense before he wished them well and suggested that everyone get home to bed so they could all be well-rested for the wedding the next day.

His advice was unanimously taken and the party broke up.

Shannon had ridden to the church with Chase and Hadley, while Dag had driven his own truck. But because Chase and Hadley were the center of things, when Shannon was ready to go, Chase and Hadley were still saying good-night to people.

"Why don't you just ride with me?" Dag asked with a nod toward the exit after they'd both put on their coats.

It was late, Shannon was tired and wanted to get things organized for the next day, so she accepted the invitation, ignoring the fact that she just plain liked the idea.

There were still a number of good-nights that had to be said on the way out but they eventually made it to Dag's truck. It was already running and warm when he opened the passenger door to let her in.

"You never left—when did you start this to warm it up?" Shannon marveled.

Dag held up his key ring. "Remote," he said simply. "I did it before we ever stepped foot outside."

"Fancy," Shannon said as she got in, luxuriating in the warmth.

When Dag rounded the rear of the truck and slipped in behind the wheel, she said, "You don't worry about somebody stealing your car when they walk by and see it running with no one in it?"

"First of all, the doors have to be locked for the remote to work, and I have to have another key to open them. But even if that wasn't true, we're in Northbridge—everybody knows everybody, everybody knows everybody's car or truck—no one could drive off in something they didn't own and get away with it."

"There *is* a lot of everybody-knows-everybody, isn't there?" Shannon said as Dag headed for home. "I couldn't keep all the Perrys and Pratts and Walkers and Grants and Graysons straight."

"The Graysons are actually new to Northbridge, but since they married the Perrys and a Pratt, I can see where it would still get confusing. It's good, though, like being one big—for the most part happy—family."

"And you know them all?"

"Eventually you get to know them all, even the ones who move in. It's just that kind of community."

"Did you like growing up here?" she asked because she could tell that he honestly was happy in his old hometown.

"I know—you grew up in Billings and still felt like your life was small, so you figure growing up in a small town must have been *ree-eally* claustrophobic. But it wasn't. I loved it. I mean, my mom was kind of a pain, but other than that? I had more freedom than you probably did growing up in the city. I pretty much came and went as I pleased as long as I checked in every couple of hours."

Shannon glanced over at his profile, finding it impossible not to admire despite a slight bump on the bridge of his nose that she'd never noticed before. "What did you do with that freedom?" she asked.

"Anything I could think of," he said with a nostalgic shake of his head, as if the mere memory transported him to the heart of the fun he'd had. "Summers I'd hop on my bike—even after dark—find my friends and we'd just hang out or walk Main Street or play baseball or go to whatever event was happening at the town square, or have ice cream or swim or get into mischief—"

"Innocent mischief?"

He shot her a sideways glance that went with a grin full of devilry. "Sure," he said as if there was no chance that he would admit to anything else.

Then he went on with his answer about what he'd done with his freedom as a kid. "In the fall there was Halloween, and Northbridge loves its holidays. The whole town gets into the act, so that was great. Trick or treating was an endurance sport because the only boundaries were the city limits. It's beautiful around here when the leaves fall—we'd rake them up and jump in them or have bonfires. Sometimes we'd go hunting—"

"Mischief-makers with guns?" Shannon said in mock horror.

He just smiled at her again and went on. "Winter was ice skating and sledding and skiing and snowball fights and snow forts. And spring—well, not only is school gonna end and summer is coming, but before that there's mud-month. For a kid, sliding through it, sloshing around in it, wrestling in it, having tugs-of-war over the worst puddles of it? Heaven..."

Shannon laughed at his rapture. "It does sound like you had a good time."

"The best," he confirmed as he pulled off the main road and drove past Logan and Meg's house to come to a stop at the garage below the apartment where Shannon was staying.

Shannon didn't wait for him to come around and open her door, and they both got out of the truck at the same time. But while she was reminding herself that this was merely one person giving another person a ride home, that it was *not* a date, still when she headed for the stairs on the side of the garage, Dag tagged along to walk her to her door as if it were.

"Am I wrong or for you is tomorrow an all-day-getting-ready-for-this-thing thing?" Dag asked along the way.

"A group hair appointment will go from early in the morning until early in the afternoon. Then there's makeup and dressing, and getting to the church for the seven o'clock ceremony. So you're right, for those of us on the female side of the wedding, tomorrow is an all-day-getting-ready-for-this-thing thing. It takes a lot to do a big wedding."

"For the guys, not so much. My day looks like the way today was—I'm working at the house, I'll come home, shower, shave and dress. The only difference will be the tux. And I think tomorrow night we're all meeting for a better pre-festivities drink—tonight we had a beer. I understand Chase has some premium scotch we're breaking out tomorrow night to kick things off."

"Oh, yeah, much easier to be a guy," Shannon said as she opened the apartment door.

She didn't go in, however; she stayed on the landing as Dag said, "So I guess the next time I see you it will be at the church."

"I will not be the one in the white dress," Shannon joked because there was an odd tone to Dag's voice that almost made it seem as if he thought not seeing her again until the next evening was too long a time to wait. And even though she told herself she must be mistaken, she wasn't quite sure how to respond.

"Oh, I think I'll be able to pick you out of the crowd anyway," he said in a completely different tone of voice— that one somehow intimate and tantalizing.

They were facing each other and Dag was peering intently down at her, but Shannon took a more concentrated look at him to try to tell if she was imagining things. What she found was a small smile curling the corners of his mouth. And she felt her own gaze inexplicably drawn to that mouth, to those sexy roller-coaster lips that she suddenly couldn't help yearning to feel pressed to hers...

Would they be as soft and warm as they looked? As supple? What kind of kisser was he? Not pinch-lipped the way Wes sometimes was, she thought. Relaxed, confident, natural—that was Dag and probably how Dag kissed....

But that wasn't anything she should be thinking about! she reprimanded herself.

She jerked her eyes away from their study of his mouth just about the time Dag said more to himself than to her, "Engaged...to a Rumson..."

Would he have kissed her otherwise? Shannon wondered. Was that what he'd been thinking about, too?

Her strongest sense was that it was.

But that still didn't make it okay, she told herself. She was moving on with her life after this holiday and that could well mean Beverly Hills. She couldn't start anything with Dag that would only end when Christmas was over.

Which meant that maybe Dag believing that she was engaged was sort of a safety net for her.

"Okay, then," he said suddenly, firmly, taking the top step backward. "I guess I'll see you tomorrow night."

"Thanks for the ride home," Shannon answered as if nothing else at all had passed between them. Because it actually hadn't, regardless of the fact that it felt as if something had.

"No problem," he assured, turning to descend the rest of the steps with his back to her. "Night."

"Night," Shannon called as she went into the apartment and closed the door between them.

But as she deflated against it, she couldn't help feeling a tiny bit more perturbed with Wes than she had been.

Because if Wes had publicly set her free before tonight, Dag might have kissed her.

And while she knew it was better that that hadn't happened, she was still dying to know what it might have been like if he had.

Chapter 5

Shannon ended up enjoying Saturday's wedding preparations more than she'd anticipated. Although she was a
stranger among the other women who made up the bridal
party and had the lifelong connection of Northbridge,
there was nothing in the way they treated her that would
indicate otherwise. They made her feel like one of the
group—one of the family, actually—and it turned out to
be a lot of fun to be included in the hair and makeup ses-
sions, and in the general preparations for the wedding.

The seven o'clock ceremony was held at the local
church that served all denominations. Hadley had kept
with a Christmas theme. White candles and tiny white
lights illuminated the church, which was adorned with
red roses, sprigs of holly and holly berries intermingled
with baby's breath flowers.

Because Hadley was a seamstress with a background

in dress design, and had worked in haute couture in both Italy and France for many years, she'd designed her own gown and those of her bridesmaids and flower girl. With the help of a local seamstress, she had also made the dresses. Hadley's wedding gown was simple white satin with a fitted, strapless bodice and a full floor-length skirt in front that gracefully elongated in back to a five-foot train. A red sash marked her waist and tied in a large bow at the base of her spine, then fell in two long streamers that matched the length of the train.

Tia was the flower girl and her dress was similar to the bride's—it was also white, though white organza rather than satin. It had short puffy sleeves like two clouds billowing from each shoulder, and an empire waist wrapped with a red-and-white polka-dot sash and a bow that tied in front.

Each of the seven bridesmaids' dresses were fashioned in styles to make the women who would wear them feel comfortable and to best accentuate their own personal body sizes and shapes. But all were made of red organza and dropped to just below knee-length.

Shannon's dress was a formfitting halter with a deceptively high collar that wrapped her neck but completely exposed her back. For the ceremony she wore a matching shrug that made the ensemble seem more conservative. But for the reception she had the option of removing the short jacket and exposing a dress that looked classic from the front and sexy from behind.

The wedding ceremony itself was traditional and touching, especially when Chase and Hadley had their turn at saying a few words about what they meant to the other and how happy they were to have come full circle from their childhood acquaintance to find each other now. And when their vows had been exchanged and they were pronounced man and wife, the church bells were rung.

Then the reception was held in the showroom portion of Mackey and McKendrick Furniture Designs. The furniture showcases had been emptied for the occasion, allowing room for the buffet table, the eight-man band, a dance floor and dozens of red-and-white-linen covered dining tables and chairs along the perimeter.

In the center of each dining table was a pyramid of small, festively wrapped boxes that each held a piece of Belgian chocolate in the shape of a wedding cake as special treats for all the guests.

Shannon had volunteered to care for her nephew during the reception and to babysit overnight, as well, when Chase and Hadley would take their one-night honeymoon in a countryside cabin far on the outskirts of Northbridge. Also, since she hadn't thought there would be much mingling to do, she'd offered to watch Logan and Meg's three-year-old daughter, Tia, in thanks for their hospitality. When Tia had learned that Shannon was spending the night with Cody, Tia hadn't wanted to be left out, so as a result, the three-year-old was sleeping over at Chase and Hadley's loft tonight, too.

All of which Shannon had felt just fine about. But what she hadn't considered was that although she was a virtual stranger to Northbridge, her grandmother had lived all of her adult life there, and that everyone who had known Carol Duffy might choose the wedding as an opportunity to say hello, to give their condolences to Shannon, to talk a little about her grandmother. So Shannon found herself juggling a fifteen-month-old who had only recently discovered his own mobility and wanted to exercise it rather than be contained and a precocious three-year-old, while doing far more socializing than she'd bargained for.

Had Dag not taken it upon himself to stay by her side the entire time, it might have been far worse. But as it was, not only had he apparently assigned himself to be her groomsman when it came to walking her down the aisle, but he stayed with her and the kids for the reception, as well. Which also helped tremendously when other guests approached her about her grandmother because Dag knew them all, introduced them and filled any gaps.

"I am sooo going to owe you," Shannon told him after he'd provided that service for about the dozenth time.

"Yeah, you are," he agreed before he said, "For what?"

"I thought I'd be sitting alone in a corner so I might as well take Cody and Tia just for company. But tonight hasn't been anything like that. I don't think I could have done it without you."

And to prove her point, Cody chose that moment to climb from Shannon's lap onto the table and very nearly knock over a full glass of water. But Dag caught the glass just in time.

"*I* thought I might get at least one dance with you," Dag countered. "But it doesn't look like that's gonna happen, so I was thinking that now that the cake is cut, maybe we ought to snag a few pieces, take these two upstairs to the loft to eat it—so we don't end up with cake on the floor, too—and then put them to bed."

A dish of appetizers and Tia's chicken had been knocked off the table by the kids and, like Dag, Shannon wasn't looking forward to cake being the next course to hit the floor. And it was more than an hour after Tia's bedtime and more than two hours later than Cody usually went down for the night. Plus Shannon had not thought she would have any help getting the duo to bed, but if Dag was volunteering…

Still, she felt obligated to give him an out. "I'm the one who signed on for babysitting duty. Are you sure you don't want to stay down here and enjoy the rest of the night the way everyone else is?"

He smiled. "Who says I won't enjoy the rest of the night if I go upstairs?"

There was a lascivious sound to that that Dag must have realized only after he'd said it because his smile stretched into a grin and he added, "I've had about enough of the wedding stuff anyway. Getting out of this noise, away from all these people to eat cake in some peace and quiet, and then listen to you read Tia *Goodnight Moon*—what could be better than that? Besides, if I stay down here I'll just end up dancing with my sisters."

"Okay, then, I'm not dumb enough to turn down an offer of help with these two," Shannon said, knowing she probably should just because she liked the idea of Dag's continued help and company more than she had any business liking it.

But that was all the encouragement he needed to stand and say, "I'll get the cake and we can go."

Chase and Hadley were occupied, but while Dag was gone Shannon caught Meg's attention and motioned her to the table to tell Meg the plan.

Meg agreed that it was long past the bedtimes of both kids. She asked Shannon if Shannon was sure she didn't mind leaving, and when Shannon insisted she didn't, Meg kissed both children good-night, said she'd let Logan, Chase and Hadley know what was going on, and turned to leave just as Dag came back to the table with the slices of cake.

"Thanks for lending Shannon a hand," Meg said as they crossed paths.

"Glad to do it," Dag assured, and something about that made Meg smile knowingly as she moved off to rejoin the festivities.

"All set?" Dag asked then.

"All set," Shannon answered.

Tia was tired and beginning to be cranky and uncooperative so she let it be known she didn't want to leave. Shannon used the promise of cake to lure her into compliance, and with Cody slung on one of Shannon's hips, the three-year-old finally accepted Shannon's free hand and allowed herself to be led through the celebration to the workroom and up the stairs that led from there to Chase and Hadley's loft.

"Let's do pajamas first and then have cake—cake always tastes better in pajamas," Shannon said when they were upstairs.

"Are you and Uncle Dag gonna put on your 'jamas, too?" Tia asked.

"Good question," Dag said under his breath, laughing at what Shannon had unwittingly walked into.

"No, cake just tastes better for kids when the kids are in their pajamas," Shannon improvised.

Tia frowned as if that didn't make sense but before she could pursue anything more along those lines, Dag again saved the day and said, "So, shall we split up boys and girls? I'll get Cody ready for bed and Shannon, you can get Tia out of that dress she looked so pretty in tonight."

As if on cue, Tia swirled around to make the skirt billow out—something she'd done numerous times during the evening.

"Cody will need a diaper change, you know…" Shannon reminded Dag.

"Yeah, no big deal. I've done it before."

"Then it's boys with boys, girls with girls," Shannon agreed. "Tia's things are in Chase and Hadley's room with mine so you and Cody can have the nursery to yourselves, and we'll meet back here for cake when we're finished."

"Deal," Dag decreed, setting the plates full of cake on the island counter and taking Cody from Shannon's arms. "Come on, little man, you don't look like you're gonna last too much longer."

In the end, Cody didn't stay awake long enough for the cake—when Dag joined Shannon and the pajama-clad Tia in the kitchen portion of the loft again, he announced that Cody had fallen asleep on the changing table. "So I just put him in his crib."

"Tha's cuz Cody's a big baby—he can't stay awake and he gots to sleep in a crib, and he calls his moose *oose*," Tia said as if she were far above that.

"You call your gorilla *grilla*. And before you know it, Cody will be keeping up with you just fine, Miss Tia. He's no better or worse than you, and you're no better or worse than he is," Dag said as Shannon poured the little girl a glass of milk.

Shannon studied the frown that went with the gentle reprimand from Dag as she returned to the island counter where Tia was sitting with her cake in front of her.

"A lecture on equality?" Shannon said quietly to him.

"Sore point with me."

Shannon didn't push it with Tia there and Tia didn't

seem to notice anything because she was more interested in why Shannon and Dag had opted to have their cake later.

When Tia was finished with her piece—and indulged by her uncle with a few bites of Cody's piece—Shannon washed Tia's face, helped Tia brush her teeth and together she and Dag read the bedtime story Tia required before she slipped off to sleep in Chase and Hadley's big bed.

But when Shannon and Dag returned to the island counter to stand on opposite sides of it and eat their cake, Shannon said, "Tia's pseudo-sibling-rivalry with Cody bothers you?"

"It isn't that. It's that hint of superiority that came with it tonight. After years of my mother thinking she was better than everybody and putting on airs, it sort of pushes my buttons when anyone does it."

"The putting-on-airs thing—you really didn't like that about her...."

"I really didn't. Don't get me wrong, I loved my mother, she was a decent enough mom...well, not to Logan and Hadley, she resented having stepkids and let them know it—"

"Chase told me a little about that—Hadley found comfort in food and ended up being very overweight until she got away from your mother, is the way I understood it."

"That's true—poor Hadley took the brunt of my mother's mean streak."

"But to you, Tucker, Issa, Zeli and Tessa—"

"She was okay. She kind of left us alone while she put all her energy into trying to dress fancier than everyone else, trying to talk more formally, trying to make sure our house, our car, everything about us put other people to shame. Not that any of it made her happy, because it didn't—"

"It seems like it would have made her isolated."

"Exactly! She alienated everyone with her I'm-better-than-you-are attitude. She wouldn't *lower herself to the level of the peons*—as she said—but that meant she didn't have any friends, any outlets, she never enjoyed anything because it didn't meet her high standards. It made her difficult to like and there was no living with it without being affected by it."

"Did she just not want to be in Northbridge?"

"She said that it was too dull and ordinary for her. But there wasn't anywhere else she wanted to be, either—my father killed himself trying to find any way to please her and there were half a dozen times when he said he'd pack us all up and move anywhere she wanted to go—"

"*That* must have been scary—moves are so unsettling for kids."

"Oh, yeah, it worried me every time that she was going to take him up on it and we'd all have to leave our friends, our school, our home—"

"But she didn't."

"To tell you the truth, I think Northbridge was tailor-made for her. Finding fault in the simplicity of the town, in the fact that the people who live here are so down-to-earth, was how she elevated herself. So no, she didn't ever take my dad up on his offer to leave. I think here she could think of herself as the big fish in the little pond, and she definitely didn't want to be the little fish in the big pond."

"So you don't think she just wanted more out of life?"

"Like you do?"

"Do I *put on airs?*" Shannon asked, alarmed that he might think that of her.

He smiled as if her concern entertained him. "Not that I've noticed. But you did say you've always wanted a bigger life than your parents had."

"True. But it's the life I want to be bigger. I still want to be me."

"I hope so, because you're pretty good," he complimented with another smile—this one appreciative enough to send a warm rush through her as she finished her cake and watched Dag polish off what was left of the piece Cody hadn't eaten.

Then Dag continued with what they were talking about. "I think there's something to be said for people who can be happy with who they are, with what they have, who can make the best of the cards life deals them. It sounds like that's what your parents did and you admired them for it."

"I guess that's true—that was how my parents were and I did admire them for it," Shannon agreed. "But maybe some people need more and there's nothing wrong with trying to achieve that, either."

Shannon couldn't be sure whether the music from the reception downstairs suddenly got louder, or with the kids asleep and the silence that followed that last statement, it just seemed that way.

Dag must have noticed it, too. He'd been leaning on the island counter and just then he straightened up, looking as if something had just occurred to him. "Hey, maybe I can have that dance with you after all."

"Here? Now?"

"Why not? There's music—not loud, but there's still music. There's an open area, there's a hardwood floor…"

The loft did have a lot of open areas, particularly just a few feet from where they were, in front of an entire wall of windows where stars sparkled in the sky overhead and the main house in the distance was brilliantly and colorfully illuminated with Christmas lights.

"Come on, dance with me—you would if we were downstairs, wouldn't you?"

She probably would have, yes. Just to be polite...

"Come on," Dag repeated, clasping her hand in his to bring her out from behind the counter and with him to that spot near the windows.

When they got there he used a bit of a flourish to spin her into his arms where his other hand landed on her bare back and sent a wholly pleasant little shiver up her spine.

It's just a dance, she told herself. *An innocent little dance like everyone downstairs is doing...*

And yet this seemed so much more intimate. Especially since she was ultra-aware of the feel of Dag's skin pressed to hers.

She tried not to focus on that, though, as she fell into step with him.

"You're a good dancer," she said with some surprise. And with a secret wish that he wasn't quite as good as he was—if he hadn't been, maybe he wouldn't have been able to keep such a respectable space between them. "I haven't run into many men who can dance at all, let alone well."

"You can't be talking about your Rumson—"

"Wes can dance—all the Rumsons learn how early because dancing at fancy dress balls and parties and at their country club makes for good photo opportunities," she said, reiterating what Wes had told her. "But when it comes to non-Rumsons—"

"I didn't have to learn to dance for photo opportunities, but it *was* part of my mother's notions of high society—she said that all people of class knew how to dance. And the girls had to wear party dresses and the boys had to be in a suit and tie so we learned the *correct comportment*."

That explained the respectable space between them.

But once the wedding pictures had all been taken, Dag had removed his bow tie and cummerbund. His tuxedo jacket had come off by the time dinner was served. The collar button of his pleated white shirt was unfastened, and he was definitely looking like himself—in what was left of the tux, he'd managed to combine refined and relaxed. So Shannon wouldn't have minded it if he had eased up a little on that comportment, too, to hold her closer.

But instead he displayed what he'd probably also been taught—to make polite conversation while dancing.

"So, kindergarten, huh? You start at the ground floor with the kiddos?"

"Actually, for most kids the ground floor is preschool now. But yes, I teach kindergarten."

"Kindergarten for me was more playtime than learning."

"Playtime teaches kids social skills and to share and to cooperate with other kids—there's value in it. But there are academics now, too—work on reading and writing, numbers, the basics."

"Ah, I'm underestimating the kindergarten teacher of today—it's not just sing-alongs and reading stories and breaking up fights over toys?"

"There's all that, too, but there's also definitely more to it than that."

"And why did you pick the beginners rather than say… fourth grade?"

Had he just adjusted his hand on her back and brought her the tiniest bit nearer?

Shannon had to tip up her head slightly more to peer into that handsome face, so she thought he might have.

Not that she was inclined to complain...

"I'm licensed to teach K through sixth, but I like the really little kids," she answered his question. "They're so full of life and so unjaded. They truly believe the world is their oyster, that anything—and everything—is possible. I guess I like to believe that, too. And seeing things through a kindergartner's eyes helps."

Dag was looking down into *her* eyes and that explanation seemed to please him because he smiled an appreciative smile. "You're good with Tia and Cody. And Tia is crazy about you. So I'm betting that teaching is what you're cut out for."

"I never doubted it. Even now, when I've needed time off and appreciated having it, I've still missed my job."

"Are you going back to work after Christmas break?"

"No, actually I'm going to Beverly Hills."

"California?" he said with an arch of his eyebrows.

"I have a good friend there—Dani Bond. She's been my best friend since first grade, we were college roommates. She married a businessman from Beverly Hills and she's building her own private school...well, with the help of her husband's funding. The Early Childhood Development Center."

"Fancy. And private, I'll bet."

"Yes, private. And intended to attract the Beverly Hills elite. Dani will make sure that it also provides the best possible early education and academic foundation for kids from pre-kindergarten through sixth grade." Without thinking, Shannon added, "She wants me in on it with her. She's invited me to invest the money from selling my parents' business and the building it was in, and from Gramma's house, to be a partner in the school. I could head the pre-K and kindergarten portion and teach, too."

"Wow. That sounds exciting. But how does that fit in with marrying Wes Rumson and potentially becoming Montana's First Lady?"

Oh, for a minute she'd forgotten.

Shannon could have kicked herself.

It was just *too* easy to talk to this man.

And too easy to forget herself and everything else she should be remembering.

"Well, sure…I mean…I couldn't do both…at least not the work parts. I could still invest in Dani's school," she said haltingly as she stumbled to keep the secret of her nonexistent engagement. "Anyway, you asked if I was going back to work after Christmas and I'm not. I have plans to visit Dani, to check things out, to see what I think. Right now I'm just considering what to do."

Dag went on studying her for a long moment as they continued to dance, and Shannon had the sense that she was being read like a book.

Then he proved her right when he said, "So, really, you have your choice of two lives bigger than what you've known. You're engaged to a Rumson who will likely be the next Governor. Or you could invest in your friend's school, be instrumental in setting the educational foundation of kids of the rich and famous, and make your own flashier life—"

Dag definitely saw things too clearly.

"Wes says I'd just be wiping their noses," Shannon heard herself say before she even knew she was going to, appreciating that Dag's view of her opportunity was not so pompous.

But she knew she'd ventured further than she should have already and she needed to rectify it, so she shrugged and said, "It's just the investment opportunity I'm checking out after Christmas."

Dag nodded but she didn't think he completely believed her.

Before he could pursue it, though, the bandleader's voice came over the muffled strains of music to announce that the next song would be the last.

"We better make this good," Dag said as the band segued into a romantic ballad.

That was when comportment finally went out the window.

In keeping with custom, Shannon's right hand was in Dag's left. He raised her hand to his shoulder and let it rest there in order to clasp both of his hands at the small of her back in a very informal—and even more intimate—dance posture. He also closed that respectable space between them completely by pulling her near enough for their bodies to touch, for Shannon to have no choice but to put her cheek to the rock-hard wall of his chest while her other hand pressed to the expanse of his broad shoulders.

"Wouldn't your mother be upset with your *comportment?*" Shannon whispered.

She half expected him to say *Wouldn't your fiancé have a fit if he knew you were letting me do this?*

But the only sound Dag made was a soft response into her hair. "Shhh…I won't tell if you won't."

Shannon knew that if she truly had been engaged, she probably shouldn't have gone along with this. But his arms were strong around her, bracketing hers like muscular parentheses. He smelled of a fresh, citrusy cologne. His body was big and warm and powerful. And it was just all too nice to deny herself what she continued to insist was nothing more than a dance. A simple, harmless dance…

A dance that really just amounted to swaying in place now…

Then the music ended and the distant voice from below congratulated Chase and Hadley one last time and wished them well.

And while Shannon regretted it, Dag stopped their dancing on cue, too, and released his hold of her enough for there to be a separation between them again. Enough for his arms to only be loosely around her still as he smiled down at her.

"Sooo much better than dancing with my sisters," he said in a deep, quiet voice.

Shannon returned his smile, looking up into his thickly lashed, almost-black eyes as they peered down into hers.

And for no reason it just seemed like a moment for him to kiss her.

Go ahead…she silently urged, wanting him to, unable to convince herself it was a bad idea even though she tried.

And she thought he might do it because his chin tipped downward just slightly, because his gaze went from her eyes to her lips, because she even found her own chin raising a fraction of an inch to encourage him.

But then those brawny shoulders of his drew back enough to break the spell that dancing seemed to have cast, and as he pulled his arms from around her, he instead caught her hand again.

It was that hand that he brought up to his lips, pressing them to the back of it, kissing it very gallantly before he released it and said, "I suppose I should go see if I'm needed to get things wrapped up down there."

Shannon nodded her agreement with that and walked him to the top of the stairs that would take him back to the workroom, silently swearing to herself that the kiss on the hand had been more than sufficient....

"Thanks for everything tonight," she said when they reached the doorway that opened to the steps.

"Don't mention it. And tomorrow we're going Christmas shopping, right?"

"I feel kind of guilty asking more of you after all this."

"I'm looking forward to it," he said sincerely. Then he leaned forward and added, "Just don't tell your Rumson and get my butt kicked."

"Believe me, you don't have to worry about that," she said wryly.

"I'll see you tomorrow, then."

Can't wait, she thought.

But she didn't say it.

She merely nodded and, after exchanging good-nights, watched him go down the stairs.

Then she turned and headed for the bedrooms to check on the kids.

And somehow along the way she discovered herself staring at the back of that hand Dag had kissed.

And recalling every detail of how his lips had felt there.

And really, really wishing—in spite of everything—that she'd felt those lips on her own instead.

Chapter 6

Shannon spent Sunday morning with Cody and Tia, and it started her day off just right. Her hiatus from teaching had left a shortage of kid contact in her life and since that was something that genuinely uplifted her, she drank in every moment with the duo until Meg and Logan came to the apartment to take Tia off her hands, and—a while after that—Chase and Hadley returned from their one-night honeymoon to get Cody.

Then Shannon and Dag were off to shop down Northbridge's Main Street.

Prior to that afternoon, Shannon hadn't taken full notice of just how thoroughly—and splendidly—the small town celebrated the Christmas holiday. But there was no overlooking it in the heart of things on the last weekend before Christmas.

In the cold, crisp winter air every building front was

outlined in lights that were turned on to brighten the overcast threat of the storm that was coming. Every eave had both real and decorative icicles hanging from them like glittery crystal spears. Every door had a wreath, and every display window had a Christmas scene or Christmas wares exhibited.

Lining the sidewalk were Victorian-style wrought iron streetlights all wrapped in tiny white lights, pine boughs and red ribbons that were also strung between them like a canopy.

At the corners of each of the three cross streets, there were decorated Christmas trees. And for Sunday there were numerous carts selling ornaments, trinkets and gift items; warm, salty pretzels; mulled cider and hot chocolate; sugar-and-spice almonds; popcorn; roasted chestnuts; and cookies, fudge and divinity aplenty.

There were also carolers outside the general merchandise store whose songs echoed the full length of Main, and a Santa Claus—who *wasn't* Dag—set up at the end of a candy-cane-lined walkway that led to the courthouse doors. He sat on a red velvet throne waiting to hear children's requests.

All in all, Shannon thought it was like a scene from a Dickens novel except there wasn't a Scrooge to be seen, and she again found only warmth and welcome and people who seemed to feel she was one of the local family even though she was basically a stranger to them.

Dag came through for her with gift suggestions. For Meg and Hadley she bought copies of a book he said they were both dying to read. For Logan there was an autographed baseball that Dag said his brother had been admiring in a store window since it had appeared there. And Chase's gift was also a gift to herself and the other brothers she still hadn't found—four family albums and Shannon's promise to fill them with photographs that would give the separated siblings a sense of their years growing up apart and then continue with photos from now.

"I know you probably haven't had time yet to go through the stuff from the house—"

"I haven't even taken the boxes out of the trunk of my car," Shannon told Dag when he recommended the albums.

"—but there are about five old pictures I came across stuck in the back of a drawer and four of them are of you as a kid. If you can part with three of them, you could start the albums with those."

Shannon thought it was a great idea.

Gifts for Tia and Cody were more plentiful just because Shannon couldn't resist a few indulgences during their hour in the toy store. Plus the kids were also getting books, though Dag said he'd yet to hear of Tia sitting still for anything but *Goodnight Moon*.

During the course of the afternoon, Dag also finished his Christmas shopping and for a short while at the end of the day, they parted at Shannon's request so she could retrace her steps slightly and buy Dag a sweater he'd considered buying himself and then hadn't.

It was cashmere and probably more than she should have spent on him. But she rationalized that besides being something she knew he liked, she owed him for all he'd done to keep her company through the wedding, for shopping with her today and for sharing gift ideas that were insightful and had made for presents that she was looking forward to giving on Christmas morning.

And when he'd held up the sweater in front of him, the deep charcoal-gray color had emphasized his dark coloring and made him look indescribably dashing, and she'd known at that moment that she just had to see him wearing it. Extravagant or not.

As dusk fell they could have gone home but Dag had a better idea—a dinner of pizza and beer to get them off their feet for a little while, then some ice skating in the town square where Shannon had first seen him.

"I'll call home and tell them to eat without us," he said, and like his other suggestions, it had too much appeal for her to reject.

So pizza and beer it was, sitting at the front window of the local pizzeria.

"Look at that," Dag said as he peered out at the beauty of Main Street while they ate.

Shannon was looking at something, but it wasn't out the window. She was looking at him, dressed in jeans and a plaid flannel shirt over a Henley T-shirt—all outdoorsy and wintery, his heavy five o'clock shadow making him look very rugged and handsome.

"It's like a postcard out there," Dag added, forcing Shannon to amend her gaze to take in what he was marveling at.

He was right, but it was his awe-filled admiration of his hometown that made Shannon smile. Well, that and just how much she liked the way his face was lined with pleasure.

"You really love it here," she said.

"There's nowhere else I want to be."

"I don't really know much about your background," she said then, when his appreciation for Northbridge struck her as somewhat curious. "I know you grew up here, but it seems like you've moved around as an adult. And since you just bought Gramma's house, I guess I assumed you've lived somewhere else until now, that you're just moving back. If you love Northbridge so much, why *haven't* you always lived here?"

"It was the hockey—no team in Northbridge," he said simply. And as if she should know what he was talking about.

"I've figured out that you *like* hockey," she said, confused. "But you wouldn't live here just because there isn't a team?"

Something seemed to strike him suddenly and he smiled a wide smile. "I played hockey. I played hockey to get me through college and then I played it professionally in Detroit."

It took a moment for that to sink in, for Shannon to put two and two together. In all the mentions of Dag and hockey, there had never been anything about him playing *professionally*. She'd thought that it was a passion of his, that he'd probably played in school, that maybe he played recreationally, the way Wes golfed. It had never occurred to her that hockey had been Dag's *career*.

"Seriously?" she said. "You were a professional hockey player?"

"Past tense. I suppose I thought you knew because everyone around here does. Everyone who knows me knows. And…well, a lot of people know—it's the kind of thing that's…well…known…."

"You're a celebrity and I completely missed it?" Shannon exclaimed with a laugh.

Dag grimaced. "Not really a *celebrity*. But making a living at a professional sport is kind of a public occupation. And my career ended with a splash, so most of the time, people know I played hockey for a living without my telling them."

"I didn't," Shannon confessed. "I've never been interested in any sport. Or who plays. I completely stop paying attention to anything that comes up that has to do with sports. I'm sorry."

"Nothing to be sorry about."

"When did you stop playing?"

"About this time two years ago." But rather than go on with that, he returned to the original topic. "So, no, I haven't lived in Northbridge since I left for college—"

"Where you also played hockey—"

"On a full scholarship to the University of North Dakota—go Fighting Sioux!" he said in a joking cheer. "Then the Red Wings signed me so I moved to Michigan. I came back to Northbridge for extended visits whenever I could during the off-season, but that's all it's been— visits."

"And you missed it?"

"Oh, yeah! Not only is Northbridge home, but there's just something about it that you don't find in other places. It's like this secret safe haven from the rest of the world."

"Bad things never happen here?" Shannon teased him because he was so over-the-top about this place.

"Sure, bad things happen everywhere. But when they happen here, you're never alone with it. Everyone jumps in and does whatever they can to help. You're a prime example of that—when your folks were killed in that car wreck, the cops brought you to Meg's grandfather, the reverend. He let word out that there were kids who needed homes and slam-bam-thank-you-ma'am, you got homes."

"Chase didn't."

"No, Chase sort of fell through the cracks on that score. But he did grow up here and even though his fos-

ter father was a jerk, Chase still came away from Northbridge liking it enough to move back."

There was no disputing that.

"Northbridge is..." Dag shrugged as if it was difficult to sum up. "It's the kind of place where I know when
I first start to farm, to ranch this spring, every other
farmer, every other rancher around here will be willing
to lend me a hand if I need it, to share his or her secrets—
well, most of them anyway. Butch Butler will never tell
anybody what he's feeding that prize pig of his. But you
get the picture. Plus there's this—"

He motioned toward the window.

"Every city and town decorates for Christmas," Shannon pointed out.

"It isn't the decorations, it's everything that goes with
it—the spirit of things, the way everyone gets into this
holiday and all the rest. The way a wedding or a new
baby is happy, important news no matter whose family
it is. The way people around here just *care*. I like that."

"Family, team sports, this town—I think there's a
theme with you," Shannon said.

Dag laughed. "I hadn't thought about it like that, but
you're right—I am *not* a loner. I like being a part of a
close-knit group that's working and playing together."

Once they'd finished eating, their waitress appeared
tableside to ask if they'd like anything else. When they
said no, she set down the bill and two complimentary
cookies that looked like small frosted knots.

"The owner's aunt makes these cookies at Christmas—
they're Italian anise knots. I love them, they taste like
licorice," Dag explained as he paid the bill.

They ate the cookies as they moved on to the town
square where the gazebo was completely lit by tiny white

lights. All the fir trees were decorated and lit up, too. More Victorian-style streetlights lined the outer perimeter of the square and had strings of the bough-and-ribbon-wrapped lights draped between them to illuminate the entire area.

Before dinner they had stopped at Dag's truck to leave their day's purchases and to get his ice skates. Now Shannon rented a pair for herself from a stand by the rink.

"It doesn't matter—because I can teach you—but do you ice skate?" Dag asked as they sat on the benches that lined the ice just inside the decorated railing.

"I used to," Shannon said. "I haven't since I was a teenager, and even then I preferred wheels to blades."

"You'll have to come back in the summer, then—when the ice melts, there's roller skating and skateboarding here."

Shannon was perplexed by why that should have any appeal at all, but it did. She didn't respond, though, and once their skates were in place, Dag got up onto his first. Then he spun around to face her and hold out his hands to help her get to her feet.

"You're just assuming I'm going to be a klutz?" she joked.

His only answer was an engaging grin while his hands remained outstretched to her, waiting to be taken.

They both had on gloves so she thought it was safe enough to accept his help. But even through two layers of knitted wool just the meeting of their hands sent a warmth all through her.

But it only lasted a moment because she had to concentrate on maintaining her precarious balance.

"It's been a *very* long time since I was on skates," she said, stating the obvious.

"Yeah, you're a little wobbly, but you'll get the feel for it again," Dag said as he steadied her and began to skate backward to tow her out onto the ice at a snail's pace.

He was right, it didn't take Shannon long to regain the knack of ice skating. But once that happened, even when Dag let go of her and turned to skate at her side, she was no match for him. He glided so effortlessly across the ice that there were times as they circled the rink with the rest of the skaters that Shannon glanced down to make sure he wasn't just floating.

But she didn't mind that he was better than she was. There was Christmas music playing over a speaker system, there were lots of people laughing and enjoying themselves—despite a few spills on the ice here and there—and there were kids galore.

And if Shannon hadn't just found out over dinner that Dag had played professional hockey, she would have discovered it then because many of those kids—as well as a few of the adults—seemed awestruck to be seeing Dag on the ice. They mentioned games and plays in which he'd apparently dazzled them.

But in spite of the friendliness and the adulation, Dag was all hers. He answered whatever greeting or question or comment was aimed at him, he introduced her whenever the opportunity arose, but nothing and no one ever took him from her side or kept his primary focus from her.

They skated for about an hour before the cold seeped through Shannon's wool coat and earmuffs, through the crewneck sweater she was wearing, through the turtleneck that was underneath the sweater, even through her jeans.

Dag didn't appear as affected as she was, but before

she had found the words to tell him that she was freezing, he said, "Home?" as if he'd read her mind. And Shannon jumped at the suggestion.

Shannon was grateful when they finally reached it that Dag's truck was already running again—thanks to his remote starter—so he could instantly push the heat to full blast. Then he left her there to warm up while he ran into the Groceries and Sundries without telling her why.

"The fixings for my famous hot chocolate!" he announced when he returned to the truck and got in, holding a bag in the air as if it were a prize of war. "I'll build you a fire, fix you a cup of that and you'll forget all about being frozen."

"Who says I'm frozen?" Shannon said defensively.

"Not who, what—those two bright red cheeks and that even brighter red nose." He flipped down the visor on the passenger side and pointed to the mirror there. "See for yourself, Rudolph," he teased as he put the truck into gear and pulled away from the curb. "There I was, skating along, looking at where we were going instead of at you, and then I catch a glimpse of your face and you're all lit up!"

Shannon didn't know whether to laugh or cry at the way she looked, but she *was* a sight—her nose and cheeks were beet-red.

Before she'd reacted in any way, Dag said, "Why didn't you tell me that you were cold?"

"And let you think I'm a sissy?" she challenged. "Besides, I shouldn't have been any colder than you."

"*Ice* hockey, remember? I'm used to it. Apparently they heat kindergarten rooms, huh?" he added with a wry glance in her direction.

Shannon just laughed, glad that they'd reached the garage apartment.

While Dag built a fire, Shannon went to do some damage control. First—following his orders—she removed the socks she had on and replaced them with two pairs of dry, heavier ones she'd snatched from a drawer and brought into the studio apartment's bathroom with her. After that she focused on what she was most concerned with and went to the mirror above the sink.

She was glad to discover that her nose was no longer bright red and that her cheeks had calmed to merely a rosy glow. The knit cap she'd worn and now removed had mussed her hair, so she put a brush through it and then applied a little lip gloss.

Despite the calming of her coloring, she was still feeling chilled when she left the bathroom, so she made a beeline for the fireplace.

"Fire is definitely more my speed than ice," she said with one last shiver.

"You *are* a sissy," he teased, bringing two steaming cups with him when he joined her.

Shannon took one of the mugs he offered, first encircling it with both hands to warm them and then tasting the rich, frothy brew that it held. "Oh, wow, you and chocolate must be a match made in heaven—this is *not* everyday stuff."

"It's my special blend," he said, not offering exactly what that special blend was.

But all Shannon cared about was chasing away the chill and enjoying her hot chocolate, and to that end she sat on the hearth and sipped.

Dag sat beside her, leaving a few inches between them. Not too many inches, but enough so that there was no touching—except in Shannon's mind where she was imagining his thigh running the length of her thigh, and his upper body close enough for her to snuggle against....

Trying to ignore that image, she glanced sideways at his oh-so-handsome, slightly beard-shadowed face with its rugged appeal, and said, "Professional hockey, huh?"

"Guilty."

"Playing professional sports of any kind is the dream of a lot of little boys."

"Playing pro-hockey was mine, that's for sure. It was already something I was fantasizing about and acting out with my friends when I asked for my first pair of skates."

"Which was when?" Shannon probed to learn more about him.

"I was four. There was a pond near our house that froze solid every winter. All the kids skated there and the bigger guys played hockey. I was itching to get in on the action. So I asked for the skates for Christmas and the minute I put them on they just felt right. I knew I was going to be able to fly in them—"

"That seems so young," Shannon marveled.

Dag laughed. "I know guys who think if their kid can walk, he can skate, to get a head start in the game."

"And you were a natural?"

"Let's just say I was a quick learner. But I was right about the skates—once I learned how to get around on them, I could move as if my feet had wings."

"And because of the older guys playing hockey, rather than figure skating, you went in that direction?" Shannon asked after another sip of her hot chocolate.

"I didn't even know what figure skating was as a kid. But hockey was everywhere around here. I played in the amateur league, I spent two summers in Canada at hockey camp, and I played one season of midget before I finally started high school and could play there—"

"And then through college," she contributed, recalling that he'd said he'd had a scholarship, "before you went pro."

"Right," he confirmed, drinking his own hot chocolate quicker than she was.

"You must have been really good."

"Good enough," he said.

But this evening someone had marveled at Dag being twice-named MVP, so she knew he was being humble.

"Was it all you'd hoped it would be?" she asked, wondering why he wasn't still doing it.

"Oh, God, yes," he answered heartily. "Making a living doing something you love? Being treated like a king by fans? By women—"

Shannon laughed at that. "Groupies?"

"Some…" he said the same way he'd refrained from bragging about his skills. But rather than elaborating on that, he went on talking about how hockey had been everything he'd hoped it would be.

"But it doesn't make for a long career?" she said to encourage him to tell her why he wasn't still playing.

Dag shrugged. "Some guys make it into their forties. One guy played until he was fifty-two."

"But you…"

"I'm definitely not forty or fifty-two," he said wryly.

"But you're not still playing the game you love," she persisted.

"Nope, now I'm a land- and homeowner," he said.

Shannon sensed that his positive attitude about this change was some sort of spin, that he wasn't actually happy to have stopped playing hockey.

And her feeling grew stronger when he abruptly changed the subject. "So, your face is back to its normal color. How about your hands and feet—any pain? Can you feel all of your fingers and toes?"

"I'm fine."

"I can stop worrying about frostbite and hypothermia?"

Shannon smiled. "*Were* you worrying about me having frostbite and hypothermia?"

"A little," he admitted.

She knew it shouldn't matter, but it felt good that he'd been concerned, that he cared. Not that it meant anything, she told herself in order to keep from reading more into it than she should.

She did, however, sorely regret it when Dag stood then and said, "I should probably get going."

She wanted to say, *Do you have to?*

But she didn't. She just stood, too, and walked him to the door.

"I can't thank you enough for today…and tonight—"

"Don't thank me at all," he said as they reached the door and he was shrugging into his coat. "I got my own Christmas shopping finished, too."

But once his coat was in place, he turned to face her and added in a quieter tone, "Besides, I had a great time. Getting into town, having pizza, an hour on the ice, hot chocolate in front of a fire—all of it with you—there's no chore in any of that." Then he smiled a slow, sexy smile. "Actually, now that I think about it, maybe *I* should be thanking *you*."

Even knowing nothing about hockey or its players, Shannon connected the sport with bruisers, not with charmers. But as she smiled up at Dag, it was his charm that was getting to her.

And his dark eyes.

And his chiseled features.

And everything else about him...

And it all suddenly bowled her over and left her unable to recall another time, another man, she'd ever wanted to have kiss her quite as much as she wanted that man to kiss her at that moment.

It was so potent tonight that it seemed impossible to hide what was on her mind and she felt her chin tip upward with a will of its own, silently sending a message.

Dag smiled a small, knowing smile and grasped her upper arm, sliding down to catch her hand, to enclose it in his and hold it tight.

Don't just hold my hand...and please don't just kiss that again tonight...

But that's what he did.

And despite the fact that the kiss lingered longer than it had the night before, despite the fact that his thumb did a sexy massage on the top of her wrist, Shannon couldn't help wishing that chivalry was dead and buried!

But he thinks you're engaged, a little voice in the back of her head reminded her.

And she'd given her word that she wouldn't tell anyone otherwise....

Then Dag squeezed her hand and lingered at that, too, as if he were having trouble giving her up.

And no matter how much Shannon willed him not to, he still did, saying, "G'night," in a tone that seemed to shout, *If only things were different...*

And it was so tempting to tell him that they were!

But she didn't. She merely whispered back, "Good

night," trying to keep the disappointment from her voice as she watched him flip up the collar on his coat and slip outside into snow that had begun to fall since they'd arrived home.

Then she closed the door and pressed her forehead to it, sighing a deep sigh of regret.

But Dag was right in practicing restraint, she told herself. Right to be respectful of her supposed engagement.

And she was wrong, wrong, wrong to want him not to.

It was just that wrong, wrong, wrong or not, she still couldn't help wishing that he *would* have kissed her until she begged not to be kissed any more.

On the mouth!

Chapter 7

A blizzard struck overnight and Shannon woke up Monday morning to a winter wonderland. And to two and a half feet of snow separating the garage apartment, Chase's loft and the main house.

The snow was still falling in big, fluffy potato-chip-size flakes as Chase shoveled a path between the loft and the garage, and Dag shoveled one from the rear entrance of the main house to the garage. By lunchtime the two connecting paths provided a way for Chase, Hadley, Cody and Shannon to join Meg, Logan, Tia and Dag for a snow day all together in the big farmhouse.

The Christmas lights were lit and Logan made sure the fire never got too low in the fireplace. They spent the early part of the afternoon munching on an abundance of fresh popcorn and drinking mulled cider while watching a Christmas movie.

When it was time for the kids to take naps, Chase and Logan were dispatched to bed them down while Shannon, Hadley and Meg began cooking a roast for dinner, started dough to rise for homemade bread and made an apple pie that would go into the oven when the roast came out.

Then Meg and Hadley joined their mates for naps, too—Meg and Logan on the sofa, and Chase and Hadley in the overstuffed recliner—leaving Shannon and Dag on their own.

That was when Dag said to Shannon, "Why don't we go through the boxes of your grandmother's things from the house and find those pictures of you as a kid? We can do it in the kitchen without disturbing anybody and then you'll have them to start the photo albums."

Shannon jumped at the idea and while she cleared space on the big, country-kitchen table, Dag put on his fleece-lined suede coat.

He had to reshovel the path to the garage where her car was parked to get to it. Shannon watched from the window over the sink, enjoying the sight of the burly man cutting a swath through the pristine white powder. She was looking forward to a little time alone with him. More than she should be, she knew, but it didn't matter.

Should I tell him now or wait? she wondered as she watched.

She'd had a phone call from Wes's secretary before she'd even gotten out of bed this morning telling her to watch the evening news. The press had been invited to the Rumson compound for the arrival of all the Rumsons for their Christmas holiday. The secretary hadn't said that Wes would be announcing that the engagement was off, but Shannon couldn't think of any other reason why she would be encouraged to watch.

And if Wes was finally going to go public with the news, then it didn't seem like it would do any harm for her to tell Dag only a few hours earlier, when they were snowbound and it wasn't likely for her secret to get beyond the walls of the house.

Except that again she thought of the vow she'd made not to tell anyone, and decided she could probably wait those few hours herself.

But she was definitely going to be glad when she didn't have to continue this charade.

The frustration of wanting Dag to kiss her good-night the last few evenings and not having it happen came to mind just then, accompanied by the fleeting idea that this could change once he knew she was free.

She pushed those thoughts away and reminded herself that the illusion of an engagement was not the only reason she shouldn't be kissing Dag McKendrick, that her life was in flux, that her time with him was just a brief interlude, and that she couldn't allow herself to be swept up in the cozy comfort she was experiencing here, with him.

But a tiny, secret part of her, deep down inside, was still excited at the prospect of finally having it known that she wasn't engaged to Wes Rumson. And seeing what happened...

"I didn't bring the box with the blankets and clothes in it," Dag said when he returned to the warmth of the kitchen with only one of the two cardboard boxes he'd filled for her at her grandmother's house. "The pictures should be in this one—I put them in the jewelry box so they wouldn't get any more worn than they already are."

Shannon rummaged through the box of odds and ends until she found an old jewelry box she remembered playing with as a child—it was cream colored with an inlay of flowers on top, and when the lid was lifted, a tiny ballerina sprang up from the center of the top tier of velvet-lined compartments.

"I loved this as a kid," she told Dag. "When you wind it up—" which she did, using the turnkey hidden on the back "—it plays music and the ballerina dances."

Surprisingly, it still worked, and for a moment Shannon watched the ballerina turn on her pedestal just like she had as a child.

Then the music ran out, the ballerina came to a stop, and Dag said, "The pictures are in the bottom. Oh, and there's a ring, too—that was in the jewelry box when I found it. I forgot about that until just now."

Shannon retrieved the ring first, remembering it, too. "This was my grandmother's—she got it when she turned sixteen," she explained of the delicate gold band with three small amethyst stones set in it. "It only has sentimental value, but I'm glad it wasn't lost."

She slipped it on her left ring finger. "I used to pretend it was my wedding ring," she confided with a laugh, holding out her hand, fingers splayed upward the way she had done many times in her young life on visits to her grandmother.

"I suppose you could use it for that now, but I'm betting the wife of a Rumson is supposed to have something flashier."

Letting his remark pass, Shannon said, "I think I'll get a chain for it and wear it as a necklace, instead."

She took off the ring and set it in the top tier of the jewelry box beside the ballerina. Then she reached into the lower portion for the photographs she'd spotted there.

They were a little ragged from age and the wear and

tear of wherever they'd been hiding until Dag found them, but Shannon thought they were still usable.

She set them all out on the table.

"There's six," Dag said. "I thought there were five."

"Five of me," Shannon said, looking over four photographs of her taken the summer she was nine, all of them from a Fourth of July picnic she remembered. The fifth snapshot was from her last visit to Northbridge when she was not quite twelve—looking gangly and awkward.

"Oh, this one is bad!" she said with a laugh. "My mom gave me a perm just before I came here and it was sooo awful!"

Dag picked up that picture to take a closer look at it and laughed, too. "That *is* pretty bad. You look like you're wearing a fright wig."

"I don't think that one is going into albums."

"Ah, come on, Chase would get a kick out of it. Give him that one *and* one of the others—he should get two since it's his Christmas present."

"I'll have to think about that..." was the most Shannon would concede to.

Dag replaced the fright-wig photo on the table and studied the others.

"These are good, though," he decreed. "You just look like a happy kid."

"Probably because that's what I was."

"So that's something to share with the brothers who weren't there to know you then."

"What's this other one?" Shannon said as she picked up the sixth picture.

Sitting next to her at the oval table, he stretched an arm across the top of her high-backed chair to lean over and peer at the photograph, too.

He was wearing a plaid flannel shirt with a white thermal T-shirt visible underneath it, and a pair of jeans. He had a fresh, woodsy smell to him that seemed warm and cozy, and between that and having his big body only inches away, something inside of Shannon went a little weak.

She made a conscious effort not to lean in even nearer to him, but it did take some forethought because she felt an almost magnetic pull toward him.

Just look at the picture, she told herself sternly, forcing herself to do that.

"It's Gramma," she said as she did. "And me, I think— that looks like me in the pictures my parents took when they first got me. I don't recognize that other woman, though, or those two really small babies she's holding…"

"I didn't look at these when I found them, but now that I am…if I'm not mistaken, that other woman is a young Liz Rudolph," Dag said. "Turn it over, I think there's something written on the back."

Shannon did as he'd suggested, reading what was there along with the date. *"Liz and me with the new members of our families."*

Shannon flipped the picture over again to study it even more closely. "It's the right year, the year I was adopted. And those babies are twins—they look just alike. Could this be a picture of my twin brothers?"

"The new members of our families," Dag repeated what was scribbled on the back of the photo. "You were the new member of Carol's family. The twins were what—two months old—when they were adopted?"

"Yes."

"I don't know much about babies but those are some pretty small ones. And you're right—they do look alike, so I'd guess they were twins, too. I'd say it's possible they're your brothers."

Shannon continued to stare at the photograph as if she might see something else in it if she looked long enough. "You know this Liz person?"

"Liz Rudolph. She's your grandmother's age. Of course my earliest memory of her is long after this. But maybe she and your grandmother were friends."

"Was she related to that couple Chase said adopted the twins—Lila and Tony Bruno?"

"I've never heard those names other than from Chase. The reverend told him that he placed the twins with the Brunos. But Liz could be related to the president and I wouldn't know it. I only know Liz because when I was a teenager I mowed her lawn a few summers after her husband died. It wasn't as if we talked or anything."

"Is she still living? And around here?"

"Actually, she moved out of town to be nearer to her sister after my third summer of mowing. But you're in luck because rather than sell her house, she rented it all this time and she moved back into it this summer—I met her at the post office about a week after I got here in September. We were both picking up forwarded mail."

"So Chase and I could talk to her…"

"She's a nice lady, I don't know why not. Chase may or may not remember her, but when the snow clears I can take you over there and introduce the two of you. We could bring the picture with us and ask her about it."

The old photograph was the topic of conversation all through dinner. Meg, Logan, Hadley and Chase all knew Liz Rudolph by name—as an older woman who had lived in Northbridge when they were all kids. But none of them knew anything more about her or were even aware that she'd returned to Northbridge.

Both Shannon and Chase were encouraged by the possibility that the infants in the picture could be their lost siblings, though, and that they might suddenly have a way of garnering some information about what had happened to them. But Shannon's general excitement over that and the pleasure she was finding in the day both ebbed slightly after the family had all watched the evening news at her prompting.

Wes's secretary was right—there was a report on Wes arriving with the rest of his extended family at the Rumson compound, which was decorated in Christmas splendor. But even when one reporter asked where Wes's fiancée was, he merely said Shannon was spending Christmas with her own family this year. No announcement was made that he did not actually have a fiancée.

Shannon was still steaming over that fact when she placed a call to Wes after dinner and left him the curt message to please call her back.

Of course he didn't do that immediately so she silently simmered all through the evening of board games.

Then the power went out and while both couples decided the best thing to do was just get the kids and themselves into nice warm beds for the night, Dag volunteered to go out to the garage apartment with Shannon, build a fire for her for heat, and set her up with candles and flashlights so she would be prepared should the power not be restored until morning.

It wasn't an offer Shannon could make herself refuse, and so she and Dag bundled up and she followed behind him as he reshoveled the path between mounting walls of snow to the garage apartment.

Dag had just lit two candles for light and begun to put the logs in the fireplace when Wes finally returned Shannon's call.

"I have to take this," she told Dag when she checked to see who her caller was.

"Want me to make myself scarce and come back in a little while?"

A scarcity of Dag was the last thing she wanted, especially in a blackout, and she could not, in good conscience, make him leave and come back.

"No, it's okay," she said, moving across the small studio apartment to the kitchen section to talk with her back to Dag while he went on laying the fire.

"Wes," she said into the phone when she answered it, keeping her voice low even though she knew Dag probably still couldn't help overhearing it.

"Can you hold on just a minute?" was Wes Rumson's response.

He didn't wait for her to answer before she could hear him talking to his campaign manager—who also happened to be his cousin—about the photo opportunities that would be provided by Christmas shopping in Butte the following day.

Then Wes came back on the line. "Sorry. You know how it is."

Too well.

"How are you? Is everything all right?" Wes asked then.

"No, it isn't," Shannon said tightly to keep her voice from rising the way it was inclined to do. "When your secretary called this morning to tell me to watch the news tonight I thought it was because you were making the announcement."

"She didn't tell you that, did she?"

"No, it was what I assumed because it needs to be done, you said you would do it and it should have been done long before now," Shannon said a bit heatedly.

Wes ignored that and said, "I was just thinking about how much you liked it here when you visited that one time—remember? It occurred to me that maybe if you saw the place again on TV and pictured yourself here with me next Christmas—the way you could be—you might change your mind."

So his secretary calling to make sure she watched the news had been a manipulation. Much like the trip they'd taken to Europe a few months earlier.

Shannon shook her head despite the fact that Wes couldn't see how much that irked her.

"I saw it all on the news," she said curtly. "It didn't change my mind. You *need* to make the announcement."

"Everywhere I go, every hand I shake, people want to know when the wedding is. Yesterday Bill Muny and I were both at the same event—"

Bill Muny was the gubernatorial candidate for the other party.

"—and every reporter flocked to me, all wanting to know about you and the wedding. Bill Muny couldn't get the time of day from any one of them! Plus it's Christmas, Shannon. No one wants to hear about breakups now."

"In other words, you aren't going to announce it until when?"

Silence.

"Wes…" Shannon said through clenched teeth. "You need to do this."

"When the time is right—you left it to me, remember? Are you going back on that?"

"It's getting more and more difficult for me," she said, thinking of Dag, knowing he shouldn't be a factor and reasoning that she also didn't like having to pretend with Chase and Hadley and Logan and Meg, either. Or with any of the other people she was meeting in Northbridge now who all believed she was engaged.

"I just don't think it can be done before the holidays," Wes said then. "It could kill my momentum and I might not be able to pick up speed again. If we release the story in January, there could be some sympathy and that could carry us over."

"Sympathy? Are you going to make me the villain in this? I thought we agreed that you would say it was a mutual decision!"

Okay, that time her voice *had* gotten a little louder and she knew Dag must have heard. But she couldn't help it. She didn't want to have to face public scorn for rejecting one of Montana's favorite sons any more than she liked having to pretend she was engaged.

"Sure, yes, right—we'll say it was a mutual decision," Wes said insincerely.

"And that you didn't want to be distracted from your dedication to the constituents—that's what you said you would say so it sounded like you were doing it for the good of your voters," she reminded insistently because she'd thought that if he took that tack neither of them would come out the worse for wear.

"We can't have it sound as if I dumped you—no one votes for a heel," Wes countered.

"Which is why I agreed to make at least one public appearance with you after you make the announcement so everyone can see that there are no hard feelings."

"Still…"

Shannon knew at that moment that she was likely to come out of this looking like the bad guy. But at this point, she was even willing to accept that to have it over with.

"Just do it, Wes," she said definitively then. "Just do it!" she repeated before hanging up on him.

For a moment she remained where she was, leaning against the island counter, keeping her back to Dag, considering what to say to him.

After the phone call, she thought that he might well have guessed that the engagement was off. And if that was the case, then it seemed better to come clean so she could impress upon him the importance of keeping her secret.

Having made her decision, she turned around. Dag was adjusting the fireplace screen, his suede coat still on.

"You could take off your coat and stay awhile…" she said softly, removing her own coat now that the fire was roaring and providing enough heat so that she didn't need more than the jeans and heavy cable-knit sweater she was wearing.

"Okay," he agreed without the need for more persuasion.

He removed his coat, too, tossing it on the sofa where Shannon had placed hers. Then they each sat on a bar stool at the island counter, sitting at angles to face each other.

"I'm sure you heard some of that call," Shannon said then, opting to cut to the chase.

"I tried not to listen," he said with a smile full of mischief. "But this *is* a pretty small place…"

"If I tell you the truth, you have to make a solemn promise that it stays just between you and me."

"Things are not what they appear with you and the potential future-Governor," Dag guessed.

"You have to make a solemn promise," Shannon repeated.

"Cross my heart," he joked, using a long index finger to draw an *X* over one side of that impressively massive chest of his.

"I'm not joking," Shannon said when she'd forced herself not to feast her eyes for too long on that portion of his body and looked at his ruggedly gorgeous face again. "I gave my word that this wouldn't get out until Wes's public relations people have found exactly the right time, exactly the right spin to put on it."

"And you think I might rush out of here, put in a call to the newspapers and news stations, and tell them whatever you tell me? Come on," he cajoled. "I wouldn't do that to you."

She was aware that she barely knew this man, and yet she somehow did believe that he wouldn't do anything to bring harm to her.

"Okay, I'm trusting you…" she said anyway before she confided, "I'm not engaged to Wes Rumson."

Dag grinned a grin so big it was clear he wasn't sorry to hear that. And he didn't pretend to be. But he did say, "So explain, because I saw it myself—nobody could have missed it since the news stations played it over and over again. First Rumson announced he was running for governor, then he took you by the hand to stand next to him at the microphone and said if you'd have him, he wanted to introduce you as the future Mrs. Wesley Rumson."

Shannon remembered the moment vividly. The crowd of Wes's supporters and the bevy of reporters had cheered, Wes had raised her hand into the air as a gesture of victory, and what else could she do but smile even as panic had rushed through her?

And of course the assumption had been that she was accepting his proposal…

"I know it looked as if I said yes," she said. "But if you'll recall, I didn't say anything at all. In fact, I had already made up my mind to break things off with Wes before that. I just hadn't found a minute alone with him to do it—which was part of why I *wouldn't* marry him."

"Take me back to square one—how did you get together with Wes Rumson in the first place?"

"Three years ago my friend Dani and her husband treated me to a ski trip to Aspen for New Year's. Dani's husband is…well, he's rich, so everything we did—where we stayed, where we skied, where we ate—was top-of-the-line, among a whole lot of bigwigs. Wes and his cousin were some of those bigwigs. Wes noticed that I was the third wheel with Dani and her husband, and since he was the third wheel with his cousin and his cousin's wife—"

"You formed your own couple?"

"It actually started as a running joke, something he used to flirt with me. Then he asked me for a drink. We started staying in the bar after the couples went up to their rooms for the night. We were both from Montana, so we had that in common. He lives primarily in Billings, I live in Billings. He asked if I'd go out with him once we were both home again, and I…" Shannon shrugged. "I did say yes to that."

"And it went from there."

"Wes called soon after we were both in Billings again, and yes, it went from there. We started dating and eventually we were serious enough to talk marriage."

"But…"

"Dating a Rumson is not like dating someone else. Wes is the Rumson family's hope for the future in politics. He's the center of their political machine. *That's* his priority and the priority of everyone around him— his personal life doesn't really exist. His personal life is more a tool used to make him look good to voters, it isn't something he actually indulges in much."

"No seeing more and more of each other until you became an inseparable couple?"

"Dating Wes meant we saw each other when it worked out—and that definitely didn't make us inseparable. But until about six months ago, that was okay with me. I liked Wes. I grew to care about him—I still care about him. He's a decent man. But I was swamped myself. I was working and taking care of my parents, so I didn't really have any more time for Wes than he had for me."

"Until six months ago," Dag repeated what she'd said.

"Actually, I began to have doubts about the relationship when my Dad died. I would have liked to have had Wes be there for me more than he was."

"But he wasn't?"

"He made it to the funeral, he sent flowers and condolences, he had his secretary check with me every day for a while, but no. Things were the same with him—he was busy. And it really hit home for me then that I wasn't his top priority, even when there was a reason I should be."

"But you didn't break it off with him then?"

Shannon shrugged again. "I still had Mom to take care of and Gramma was with us, so I didn't make a big deal out of it, but I did start considering whether or not I wanted to go through life never being who or what came first with Wes."

"Then your mom passed away—did he step up any better for that?"

Shannon shook her head. "It was about the same and then out of the blue, Gramma died…"

"Which was a shock," Dag recalled.

She didn't know why it touched her that he remembered how difficult it had been. But it did touch her and suddenly tears threatened. She looked at the fire for a moment to blink them away before she brought her gaze back to his chiseled features.

"I just couldn't believe I'd lost Gramma, too," she confirmed. "And I really didn't know where to turn, so Wes was the first person I called. But I got his cousin—"

"The campaign manager?"

"Right—Mose Rumson. Mose said Wes was having a drink with an important contributor and I couldn't talk to him. I said it was an emergency, that my grandmother had had a heart attack. Mose still wouldn't put Wes on, he said he'd have him call me back, and Wes didn't even do that until the next day—"

"You have to be kidding me?"

"Mose held off telling him, so it wasn't really Wes's fault—"

"Still! Did he deck that guy when he found out?"

Shannon shook her head. "Wes made excuses for him."

"He took the cousin's side?" Dag said, sounding outraged on her behalf.

"Basically. And when it came to the funeral I thought—I was hoping—that since I really was alone for that one, Wes would do more—"

"But he didn't."

"He sent his mother. And she was great, she stayed with me, she went through all the arrangements with me,

I couldn't have done it without her. But no, Wes came to the funeral, he paid for a catered luncheon after the burial, but he didn't show up for it, and after spending so much time with his mother and talking to her about her own marriage and how this was life as the wife of a Rumson, I was just about done."

"*Just about,* but *still* not completely?"

"I was so…*alone* then," she said. "And Wes was always apologetic about how little we saw each other, about his distractions and all the interference. When Gramma died and he didn't do more, he promised to make it up to me with a month in Europe. Just the two of us. I thought there might be some hope for us…I guess I was *hoping* there might be some hope for us."

"I heard that Chase tried to get hold of you but couldn't for a long time because you were in Europe, so Rumson must have come through on the trip?"

"He did. We did go to Europe. But not by ourselves. We went with Mose and his wife, and it ended up being Wes and Mose working on the campaign while Mose's wife was dispatched to take me sightseeing. And that was when I'd really had it," Shannon said conclusively. "I wanted—want—a bigger life, and being the woman-behind-Wes, being Mrs. Wes Rumson, could have been that. But I also want the kind of relationship my parents had with each other and I knew then that that would never be what I had with Wes."

"Plus, maybe I'm wrong," Dag ventured, "but it doesn't sound like you had the kind of feelings for him that your parents had for each other, either."

Shannon couldn't deny that. "I kept thinking that might come with time, but no, I finally admitted that to myself, too."

"So you were going to end it with him," Dag prompted.

"But again, once we got back, I kept trying to get a minute with him and never could. I didn't want to break up over the phone, but I *had* told him that I needed to see him alone, that we needed to talk—which seemed like it should have been a clue as to what I was going to do—"

"It would have been to me," Dag agreed.

"But Wes couldn't fit me in before the announcement that he was running for governor. He said he wanted me there with him for that and I said I would come, but only if he swore that afterward we could talk. The next thing I knew, I was by his side in front of all those people and there was that public proposal and the assumption that of course I would marry him. The minute we were behind closed doors after that I told him I wouldn't. That cleared the room, let me tell you…"

Dag laughed. "I'll bet."

"So there never actually was an engagement," Shannon concluded.

"But that was almost a month ago and—"

"I know! Since it *looked* as if I'd said yes, it became a big deal how it was presented that we *aren't* getting married. I agreed to let Wes's public relations people handle making that announcement in a way that won't damage Wes's run for governor. But it keeps not happening! When his secretary called to tell me to watch the news tonight, I thought for sure it was because they were finally going to say it—"

"But they didn't…"

Why had Dag's tone turned so ominous when he said that?

"Is that because Rumson is hanging on, hoping you'll change your mind?" Dag asked.

"There's a little of that," Shannon admitted.

"Maybe he has deeper feelings for you than you think."

"It isn't that I don't think Wes has feelings for me. But I don't believe that's what's really causing the delay. He keeps talking about how much attention the engagement is getting his campaign. He doesn't want to lose that more than he doesn't want to lose me. And he certainly doesn't want to lose any of the votes that a wedding might have gotten him."

Dag didn't say anything to that, he just looked slightly skeptical.

"But the bottom line is that I am *not* engaged to Wes Rumson," Shannon said firmly. "You just can't tell anyone."

"Chase and Logan and Hadley and Meg would keep the secret," Dag said then.

"I know they probably would, but I said I wouldn't say anything until Wes's people handled it the best way possible and I'm trying to stick to that…"

"Well, I won't tell anyone. But if you decide to, you could. Without worrying about it."

The power came on then—light from outside could suddenly be seen through the windows and the sound of the refrigerator running again alerted them to it.

Dag got up and turned on the lamp beside the sofa. "Looks like we're back in business," he said.

But it was so nice sitting here in the fire glow—come back…

Apparently he couldn't hear her thoughts because rather than rejoining her, Dag snatched his coat from the couch and said, "And it's late so I should let you get to bed and turn in myself—if I get an early start shoveling us out tomorrow, we might be able to make it to see Liz Rudolph in the afternoon."

Disappointed, Shannon stood up to walk him to the door.

It was there that he put his coat on, leaving it unbuttoned but jamming his hands into the pockets.

And out of the blue Shannon wanted to snake her hands inside the fleece-lined suede and snuggle between its open ends, up against that broad chest...

She chased away the urge and the image, and glanced up at Dag's face. But that didn't help much since the man was so heart-stoppingly handsome and he was standing so close in front of her, peering down at her with those piercing black eyes.

"*Not* engaged, huh?" he said in a voice that was quiet and deeper than it had been.

"*Not* engaged. Not now. Not ever. Never have been."

"That changes things, doesn't it?" he mused. "That means you're a free agent..."

"I guess I am," she said.

"And *I* am..."

"Are you? We haven't really talked about that..."

"Oh, I am! Believe me, I am!"

His enthusiasm made her curious. But all she did was smile because quizzing him on his romantic past wasn't what she was really interested in doing at that moment. Not when, once again, thoughts of kissing him were tiptoeing around the edges of her mind. And hope had a new hold on her...

Then Dag took one hand from his coat pocket and raised it to the side of her face. Her cheek, her jaw, fit into the sturdy palm he laid there.

He went on looking into her eyes and even though

he still wasn't kissing her, she was at least glad that he hadn't gone for a peck on her hand again.

Then he used a gentle pressure to tip her head slightly back. He came forward, and after what seemed like an eternity of hovering a scant inch from his target, he pressed his mouth to hers.

She couldn't help the tiny sigh that escaped when that finally happened. But if Dag noticed it, it didn't make any difference because he merely went on kissing her.

His lips were tender and adept and parted just slightly. His breath was warm. And there was a sweet sway to his head that Shannon was caught up in as she answered every bit of that kiss, letting it—helping it—grow and deepen and go on long enough for her to savor it and wish with all her might that it would go on and on…

For a little while it did just that. It went on as if Dag didn't want it to end any more than she did. But eventually it had to, and when it did Shannon found herself light-headed.

"Not engaged," Dag repeated in a husky voice for her ears alone.

"Not engaged," Shannon echoed.

Then he opened the door and went out into the cold winter night, calling over his shoulder, "I'll see you tomorrow," and disappearing down the stairs.

But Shannon ignored the chilly air and craned her head out the door so she could watch him go, still feeling the heat he'd left behind on her lips, in her blood.

And thinking that that kiss had just added one more thing that Wes couldn't compare to.

Chapter 8

As Dag shoveled snow the next day, his mind was in turmoil and not even the quiet of the winter countryside or the rhythmic repetition of the work could stop it.

So Shannon was not engaged, he kept thinking.

But she still wanted a bigger life.

She wasn't engaged.

But she still had Wes Rumson hot on her trail.

She wasn't engaged.

But even if she stuck to her guns about Rumson, she was probably headed for a bigger life with that school in Beverly Hills.

So if anything, he should give her a wider berth now than he had before, he told himself. Because before, he was just struggling with his attraction to someone who was engaged to someone else and completely off-limits to him. But now?

Now what made her off-limits to him was less concrete. No less valid. But a whole lot more wobbly a barrier to protect him from himself and his own inclinations when it came to Shannon.

Inclinations like the one to kiss her.

He'd managed to control that when he'd believed she was engaged to another guy. But last night? Last night he'd kissed her. And wanted to kiss her again and again and again...

Jeez, he thought he'd learned his lesson about staying away from a woman who had another man on the hook in any way. He thought he knew, inside and out, to avoid women who weren't satisfied with who they were or what they had.

But maybe he didn't know anything, maybe he hadn't learned anything, because what was he doing now?

He was panting after a woman who had her sights set on greater things than a small ranch in a small town—whether it was being a politician's wife or owning a school in Beverly Hills. A woman who might be saying that her relationship with Wes Rumson was over, but who was still having contact with him, still admitting that she cared for him, still not *completely* finished with him.

Dag just didn't seem to be able to stop himself.

Yes, she was beautiful and maybe if that was all there was to it, it would be easier to maintain some control. But he also liked her. A lot. She was nice, she was kind, she was calm, she was good with the kids, she was funny and easy to talk to. She wasn't judgmental, she was sexier than she seemed to know, and more down-to-earth than she might want to be. And every minute he was with her was so good he didn't want it to end.

But it was going to end! One way or another, when Christmas was over, Shannon Duffy was gone.

And if he was in too deep with her, it was going to be his own tough luck, he told himself when he'd finished the path from the front porch out to the drive that ran along the house.

But as he turned the corner to shovel from the side of the house to the garage—where Logan was starting an old tractor he and Chase had bought with a blade attached to the front of it to deal with the driveway snow removal—Dag's perspective suddenly took a turn, too.

Wasn't he getting ahead of himself when it came to Shannon? Wasn't he thinking about things on too large a scale?

There wasn't actually much time at stake. Christmas was in a few days. How deep could he get in just a few days? Especially knowing that that was all the time he was going to have with her? Why was he thinking about her in an all-or-nothing way?

Traveling for hockey—to training camp, to tournaments, on publicity tours—there had been plenty of times when he'd known he was only going to be in a city for a short time. But if he'd met someone he was interested in, attracted to, that hadn't kept him from asking them out.

Brief was better than nothing, and that hadn't meant a string of one-night stands. Sure there had been those, too. But sometimes nothing had come of things but a dinner or two, some clubbing, maybe an afternoon at a museum or a zoo. Just some relaxation, some fun, some entertainment, some company. Why was he thinking this thing with Shannon was any different?

Sure, after the fiasco with Sandra, after the end of hockey, after settling in Northbridge again, he'd been doing more thinking about settling down with one particular woman. But who said Shannon was that one particular woman? Or that he couldn't have this time with her the way he'd had short-lived times with other women—knowing it would come to an end—before he moved on to looking for that one particular woman?

It was no big deal. He would just do what he'd done on those other occasions—go with the flow. He'd done it in the past, why couldn't he do that now?

Shannon *wasn't* engaged so it wouldn't be cheating on her part, or anything sleazy on his. True, he had vowed to steer clear of any situation that even resembled his last one. But the last relationship had gotten serious. And this one wouldn't. So that made it different.

And it was Shannon who was moving on after Christmas, Shannon who would be leaving him behind. If she was willing to see him before that, to let him kiss her, why was he sweating it?

Just don't take it for anything more than it is, he advised himself.

And he thought he could do that. That he could be okay with a casual holiday hook up—if it went that far. He could be okay with going with the flow as long as he kept in mind that things with Shannon would end.

And he would definitely keep that in mind, he decided. But in the meantime he could have a few days, he could have Christmas, with Shannon.

Then she'd go her way, he'd go his.

And as for kissing her?

He knew he was likely to do that again because he couldn't even stop thinking about it.

As long as he didn't lose sight of the fact that there was an end to whatever it was that was between them, it would keep him from getting too attached and he could just enjoy the ride and be happy for whatever time he got with her and however far it went.

But the end *would* come, he reminded himself.

Time with Shannon was like Christmas cookies—they were around now, he enjoyed them, indulged in them, but when Christmas was over, that was it for the treats.

And after Christmas was over this year, that would be it for his time with Shannon, too.

But at least he'd have had this time with her, and in the same way he wouldn't deny himself the cookies just because they weren't around forever, he couldn't deny himself these few days with her, either...

It was midafternoon before the snow-shoveling was complete, before Dag and Chase decided they could probably make it into Northbridge to visit Liz Rudolph.

Shannon was curious about what had happened to her other brothers and eager to get any information. But Monday's snow day had been so nice she wouldn't have minded putting off the visit until Wednesday and having a second snow day today.

Or was it just a second day secluded with Dag that she wouldn't have minded having? she wondered as she sat close beside him on the bench seat of his truck with Chase on the passenger's side.

She decided that it might be wiser not to delve too deeply into that possibility, but she certainly didn't have any complaints about the tight quarters that had her sitting right up next to Dag as he drove.

Unfortunately when he was forced to plow the truck through a mound of snow to get onto Liz Rudolph's driveway, sitting so snugly next to him caused Shannon's shoulder to jab into Dag's rib cage.

"Sorry," she said.

Dag grinned down at her. "For what, that tiny body-check? I've taken a little worse," he joked as he turned off the engine.

A well-dressed elderly woman was standing in the open doorway by the time the threesome maneuvered the narrow path of cleared cement to get up to the house. Petite, she stood straight and unbowed by time. Her silver hair was in a perfect bob around her lined face and she looked very much just like an older version of the woman in the picture—unlike Shannon's grandmother who had gathered many pounds over the years and had not aged quite so gracefully.

Liz Rudolph greeted Dag warmly as she ushered them inside and closed the door behind them.

"I don't know if you remember Chase—" Dag said as they all accepted her invitation to take off their coats.

"I do. While I still lived here I was curious to watch you grow, knowing you were the twins' brother," she said as she draped each coat over a branch of a hall tree. "I was always praying that a nice family would take you but... Well, Alma Pritick was good to you as a foster mother, wasn't she?"

"She was," Chase assured.

Shannon noted that there was no mention of Chase's foster father, Homer, who Shannon knew hadn't abused Chase but had also not been a loving caregiver by any stretch of the imagination.

Then Liz Rudolph turned her attention to Shannon. "And you're Shannon," she said affectionately. "I was so, so sorry to hear about your mother and father. And then Carol…she and I were close all the years we both lived in Northbridge, and kept up with each other through Christmas cards when I moved away. I wanted to go to her funeral but I'd just had a pacemaker put in when I heard and I couldn't travel. I can't tell you how surprised and sorry I was…"

"It was very sudden and unexpected—it took me by surprise, too," Shannon said.

The older woman offered tea but when they all declined, she led them into her spotless living room where Shannon, Dag and Chase sat on the sofa facing the overstuffed chair Liz took. That was when Chase got to the point, showing her the photograph Shannon had found.

"We wondered if the babies in the picture are our brothers," he said.

"They are," the elderly woman answered without hesitation.

She repeated what they already knew about how they'd come to be in need of new homes.

"My sister's son and his wife wanted children and couldn't have them," she went on from there. "As tragic as the whole situation was—a young couple losing their lives, children orphaned—to Lila and Tony it was…well, it was a blessing. They were willing to take the twins so the twins wouldn't be separated from each other at least, and that went a long way in persuading Human Services to allow them to adopt the boys. And of course, Shannon, your mom and dad took you."

"Do you know why they—or Gramma—never told me there were other kids?" Shannon asked a question that had been on her mind since Chase had first contacted her.

"Oh, everyone just wanted to make their own little family. They didn't want it all spread out. Your grandmother and I were so close and we imagined that everyone might become one big happy family, but we were naive. Your parents wanted you to just be their little girl, without outside ties to anyone else. And Lila and Tony felt that way, too. Maybe it was sort of selfish, but in a way I understood—sometimes I think there's some insecurity connected to adoptions. Getting the twins away from here was actually part of why Lila and Tony left town when the babies were just six months old—they wanted to be somewhere where no one knew the twins as anything but their sons."

The older woman cast a guilty-looking glance at Chase and said, "Plus everyone felt bad about you, Chase. No one thought they could take on more, but being in the same small town with you, knowing you were at the boys' home all alone…"

Shannon saw Chase nod his understanding. But that seemed to be as much as Liz Rudolph wanted to say about the touchy subject because then she went right back to speaking mainly to Shannon as if they had more of a connection than she had with Chase.

"And then Lila and Tony's little family didn't even stay together," Liz informed her.

"They didn't?" Shannon asked.

The silver head shook. Liz pursed her lips disapprovingly for a moment before she said, "A year after Lila and Tony left, they divorced. Lila got custody of the twins and when my sister died, I lost contact with my nephew—"

"So, are you saying that you don't know what happened to the twins?" Shannon asked.

"I do know that by then my nephew Tony had been persuaded to give up his rights to the boys—they were barely two years old. But Lila had found a new husband

and her new husband wanted to officially be their father since he'd be raising them. Tony was a housepainter and what he could provide for them just couldn't compare, so for their sake, he relinquished his paternity."

"What do you mean that what he could provide couldn't compare?" Chase asked.

"Lila married Morgan Kincaid," Liz Rudolph said with some awe in her voice.

"Morgan Kincaid the football player?" Shannon said to verify because while she didn't follow sports of any kind, Morgan Kincaid—and what he'd parlayed his football fame and fortune into—was well known in Montana.

"Morgan Kincaid," the elderly woman confirmed, "the football player, the owner of The Kincaid Corporation and all those restaurants and buildings and hotels and car dealerships and who knows what else," the elderly woman confirmed. "Those boys—Ian and Hutch they were called—ended up Kincaids."

Chapter 9

"Why don't you guys go and I'll stay with the kids?" Shannon offered as dinner ended on Tuesday evening.

The plans for the night had been for them to drive into Northbridge for the Christmas Bazaar being held at the town square. But when Dag, Shannon and Chase had returned home from visiting Liz Rudolph that afternoon, both Tia and Cody seemed to be a little under the weather. After discussing that fact over another communal meal, the two couples decided that the kids shouldn't be taken out into the cold. That prompted Shannon to volunteer babysitting services so everyone else could go anyway.

"To tell you the truth, I think we all actually want to stay in tonight, don't we?" Meg insisted, looking around the rest of the group for support.

Hadley and Chase assured Shannon that they would rather watch TV tonight. Logan said he'd had enough of the snow for today and wanted nothing but to sit in front of a fire.

"I don't know," Dag piped up then. "It still sounds good to me. If it still sounds good to you, Shannon, why don't you and I go?"

And much to Shannon's dismay, *that* had more appeal than any of the other options.

So when the rest of the group chimed in with their encouragements, Shannon took up Dag on his counteroffer and the next thing she knew, she was in his truck again, headed for Northbridge and looking forward to seeing what else the small town did for the holiday.

And to once more spending the evening with Dag…

"So…proposed to by a Rumson, now related to Kincaids—maybe you not only *want* a bigger life, maybe you're destined to have one," Dag said as they turned from the driveway onto the road leading to Northbridge for the second time today. "How does it feel to be related to the Kincaid dynasty?"

Shannon laughed. "It feels exactly the same as it felt *not* being related to anyone in the *Kincaid dynasty*."

"What did you and Chase decide about contacting the twins after I dropped you off this afternoon?"

"We're trying to locate them," Shannon said. "We looked them up on the internet—there's a lot about Morgan Kincaid and The Kincaid Corporation, but less on Ian Kincaid or Hutch Kincaid. It looks like Ian works with something called an expansion football team…"

"Morgan Kincaid is bringing a pro-football team to Montana—it's been in all the papers and on the news. You must have heard about that…"

"I told you, I honestly don't pay any attention to

sports," Shannon said. "It could have been on the front page of the newspaper—"

"It has been—more than once."

"Even then, if it had to do with sports, I would have just turned to page two."

Dag laughed in disbelief and glanced at her. "I mean, it may not be hockey…" he said facetiously, "but football is pretty big, too. There's that whole Super Bowl thing and all."

"Still, I know nothing about sports and don't keep up with anything about them," Shannon said.

"Well, it's a big deal to get a new NFL franchise— a *huge* deal," he said, dumbfounded by how lightly she was taking that fact.

But all Shannon could do was shrug and say, "Okay."

Dag laughed again and shook his head in dismay. Then he went on with what Shannon actually did have an interest in. "But Ian Kincaid's name shows up in connection with the football team?"

"Right, he's listed on the website as the Chief Operating Officer so I guess that means he's on the business end of things. But we couldn't find anything recent on Hutch Kincaid at all. Apparently he played a lot of football himself a while ago, and was a star quarterback, but there's nothing current about him and he doesn't show up working for The Kincaid Corporation anywhere, so we're thinking the only way to reach him will be through Ian."

"But it sounds like you might be able to reach Ian."

"I hope so," Shannon said. "But sometimes the more public people are, the harder it is to get through to them."

"Like Wes Rumson, who can't even be reached by people he should be close to."

"Let alone by strangers with a story about long-lost

siblings that the twins were probably never told they had," Shannon said. "There wasn't a way to email Ian Kincaid through the new football team, so we sent one through The Kincaid Corporation—we used a *Contact Us* tab on that website. We'll just have to see if the email gets to him."

"And if he answers it even if it does."

"True. I can tell you from my own experience with Chase that this whole thing comes as a shock and it's hard to believe. And I'm nobody—"

"Hey!"

"You know what I mean. I'm a kindergarten teacher, nothing high profile—"

"You were connected to a Rumson," he reminded.

"But until the public proposal, no one knew my name—in the few pictures of Wes and me at some charity function or another, if I wasn't cut out of the shot when it was printed, I was never included in the caption. It wasn't me who anyone cared to know. But for high-profile people, someone coming out of the woodwork with a weird claim—"

"Yeah, even if you're not high-profile but just in the public eye, sometimes people *do* come out of the woodwork with some crazy claim to get to you," Dag said as if he'd had experience with that. "And you're right, if it was me, I would probably think it was a prank or scam or something."

"And from what Liz said, I doubt if the twins were ever told anything about us. So I wouldn't be surprised if it takes more than an email to get through to them."

"Still, it's a start," Dag said optimistically.

They'd made it safely into town by then, and as he pulled into a parking spot near the ice skating rink, there didn't seem to be more to say on the situation. Plus there was so much going on in the town square that that was where their attention naturally turned.

"After that blizzard yesterday, I can't believe this is all still going on and so many people showed up," Shannon observed.

"One of the advantages of a small town—there aren't a lot of streets to clean so the plow can take care of most of them in a day, and no one has to go too far to get around."

Before they left the heat of the truck's interior, Shannon buttoned the top of her wool coat, tied her knitted scarf around her neck and put on her earmuffs and then her gloves.

Dag fastened a few of his suede coat's buttons and added fleece-lined gloves, but that was as far as he went in bundling up.

Then they got out of the truck.

"According to the schedule in the newspaper this morning," Dag said, "we have a little while before the ice-sculpting competition—I understand there will be chain saws for that so we don't want to miss it—"

Shannon laughed at his enthusiasm for the chain saws. "No, we definitely wouldn't want to miss that!" she agreed, as if it were of the utmost importance.

Dag took the teasing in stride and merely grinned at her. "So we can either wander through the booths before that and then take the sleigh ride, or we can take the sleigh ride before the contest and walk through the booths after—your choice."

"Well, since I'm still warm from the truck, let's do the sleigh ride first. Then we can get under some of the heat lights to watch the chain saw ice massacre and walk through the booths."

"Good choice," Dag decreed.

Shannon had put both of her hands into her coat pockets and without warning, Dag hooked his arm through one of her elbows as if he'd done it a million times before.

And that was all it took for her to feel an instant sense that all was right with the world. Especially when he used their entwined arms to tug her close to his side as they headed for the line of sleighs waiting for passengers.

Confused and somewhat in awe of the phenomena, she glanced up at him, wondering exactly what was going on with her when it came to this man.

But there were no answers in the profile of his handsome face above the turned-up collar of his coat. She just felt another wave of gladness to be there with him.

Maybe it's only the spirit of the holiday, she told herself.

But despite making a valiant attempt to believe that, she still had the sneaking suspicion that it was the man himself.

"We want that one," Dag announced to the teenagers waiting to drive the sleighs that were different in size, shape and ornateness, but all painted white and decorated festively with red ribbons and wreaths on the backsides.

Dag's pick was a simple, plain-sided, old-fashioned country sleigh with a thick plaid wool blanket waiting in its plush red velvet interior.

Once they were situated side by side behind the driver, Dag tucked the blanket around their laps and the driver gently tapped the reins to put the big roan into motion, setting off the jangle of small golden bells on the harness's girth.

The sleigh ride took them in a big circle around the

town square and the connecting grounds of the small private college that was closed for winter break.

Dag explained that two other contests had been held—one for the best decorated evergreen tree in the square or on the campus, and another for the best snow sculpture.

"It's no wonder they're offering sleigh rides to see it all," Shannon said in astonishment at what the small town had produced.

Businesses, clubs and organizations had sponsored the decoration of the trees and each one was more elaborate than the other. The tree done by the local beauty salon had won first prize with bedazzled ribbons tied around almost every branch, bright lights and hair accessories all turned into sparkling tree ornaments.

Between the trees done up in festive finery there were snow forts, a snow village, snow families, snow spaceships, snow cathedrals and so many other snow-erected marvels that Shannon lost track of them all.

"This town is just its own little oasis, isn't it?" she said when their sleigh ride tour came to an end.

"Ya gotta love Northbridge," Dag agreed, heading them for the ice-sculpting contest that was getting under way.

Huge blocks of ice had been set up near the gazebo. The contestants went three at a time with a goal of producing the best sculpture in the shortest amount of time.

The expertise in the wielding of the chain saws was something to see all on its own but the little wonderland of ice sculptures that resulted from it was an added bonus. The sculptures went from simple—a Christmas tree and a snowman—all the way to a complicated castle and even a five-foot-high lumberjack, complete with his dog at his feet.

It was the lumberjack that won and, along with the applause and cheers of the onlookers, the other sculptors did a good-natured chain saw salute to the winner before Shannon and Dag moved on to the booths.

Food, drinks, gifts, ornaments—the bazaar had a different tone than what they'd seen on Main Street on Sunday. Of course there was the hot chocolate and hot cider booth, but there was also a booth that offered Christmas Treats from Around The World—different cookies, desserts and sweets that were traditional to assorted countries and cultures.

There was a booth selling beautiful gingerbread houses for those without the time or inclination to make their own, there was a booth selling hand-carved and painted nativities and another offering all sizes of Moravian stars. There were two stands selling handmade candles, one offering adult-size rocking horses, and several others where hand-knit sweaters and scarves could be had.

All in all, Shannon continued to admire the talents and what seemed like the unlimited energy of the people who lived in Northbridge. But after a few hours, not even the heat lamps were enough to keep away the cold and she was ready to go home.

The problem with that was the thought of saying good-night to Dag—which she wasn't ready to do yet despite all the reasoning she did with herself about why she should be.

So, hoping she wasn't being too transparent, she developed a sudden enthusiasm for the mulled wine being sold at one stand, bought a bottle and used it as the excuse to invite Dag back to the apartment—for the third night in a row—in order not to have this evening end yet.

And if Dag saw through it?

Shannon couldn't have cared less because he jumped at the idea, looping his arm through hers as he took her back to his truck to drive them home.

"Sooo, I'm not engaged and you said last night that that makes me a free agent," Shannon said forty-five minutes later when she and Dag were sitting on the apartment's sofa, in front of a blazing fire in the fireplace, sipping mulled wine.

"Uh-huh," Dag said, an amused but confused frown pulling his brows together since she had said that out of the blue.

Shannon was sitting in the middle of the couch, her feet tucked to one side and underneath her so she could look at him. Dag was sitting next to her, angled in her direction, one long arm stretched across the top of the sofa back.

"And you also said last night that you're a free agent, too…" she added.

"Did I?"

She might have been more concerned about that question except that the look of mischief in his expression let her know he was just giving her a hard time.

"You did," she confirmed. "With some conviction behind it—I believe you said, *Oh, I am! Believe me, I am!*" Although Shannon put even more oomph into his words than he had and made him laugh.

"Like that? Did I really say it like that?"

"You did," she claimed. "Which is why it has me wondering—was that *too* much of a protest? Is it not true?"

He laughed. "Oh, it's true. When it comes to women,

I am definitely a free agent. And I have been for about two years."

"Two years? Wow, the last one must have really made you gun-shy."

"Actually, it made me crowbar-shy," he said wryly but with an ominous undertone.

Shannon was curious about why a man who looked like Dag did, who was as charming and funny and nice and fun to be with, was without a girlfriend or fiancée or wife. It hadn't occurred to her that by prying a little into the subject she might be opening a can of worms. But she was too curious not to lift the lid anyway.

"I told you about my fiasco with Wes—even though I wasn't supposed to," she said. "You can trust me with yours…"

"Mine was a fiasco but it was no secret—it made a splash, remember?"

"I remember you saying that the end of your hockey career made a splash. What does that have to do with your last relationship?"

"Everything. And it all made the news. But there *was* a sports element to it, so if you came across anything about it you probably didn't pay any attention to it."

"Sorry," she said unapologetically. "But your love life made the sports page? You must have *really* gotten around!"

Dag's laugh this time was wry as he shook his head in denial. "My *love life* was not a sporting event. It made the sports page because I was a name in hockey at the time and so was the jerk who blindsided me."

"That doesn't sound good," Shannon said more seriously.

"Yeah, you could say it wasn't good," he said with

enough of an edge to let her know this subject was even more sobering than she'd imagined.

"If you don't want to talk about it, you don't have to," she said, feeling obligated to offer him the option even though her curiosity was growing by the minute.

"Nah, I can talk about it," he said. "I told you, mine *isn't* a secret, it's just not for the faint of heart."

"I'm not faint of heart," she assured.

"Okay, but don't say you weren't warned...." Dag took a drink of his wine. Then he said, "A little short of three years ago I got involved with a woman named Sandra Pierce."

"A hockey groupie?"

"A hockey wife."

Shannon was midsip of her own wine when he said that and her eyes widened over the rim of her glass. She stared at him in shock. "You were involved with someone else's wife?" she said when she'd swallowed her wine.

"No," he answered instantly and firmly. "I would never get involved with anyone else's wife. I'm not even completely comfortable being here drinking wine with you knowing that you're as fresh out of a relationship as you are."

Shannon opted not to address that in favor of hearing his story. "So how was this Sandra person a hockey wife?"

"She was a former hockey wife. I actually met her the night she was out with friends celebrating that her divorce had become final that day."

"Her divorce from another hockey player," Shannon guessed.

"Exactly. She hadn't been married to anyone on my team, she'd divorced a defenseman on the team we had come into town to play the night before. We'd won our game and were out clubbing to celebrate, too."

"And one celebration overlapped the other?"

"A bunch of rowdy hockey players out on the town, a bunch of already-tipsy women cutting loose—paths crossed, we were buying drinks, you know how it goes."

Shannon's social life had always leaned toward moderation, but there had been a few evenings out with friends when she'd witnessed what he was talking about even if she'd shied away from it herself. So she said, "Sure."

"As the night wore on, I sort of paired up with Sandra. I liked her—she was kind of wild and brash, but she was beautiful and smart, too, and we hit it off. The game we'd played and won the night before had been an exhibition game in Canada but Sandra was from Detroit and she was moving back. We arranged to have dinner when she got there."

"Which you did," Shannon said.

"Which we did. And I still liked her even when she was sober, so we started dating."

"Because you were a free agent then, too, and since she was divorced, so was she."

"That's what I thought. Divorce seems pretty final to me. But I didn't factor in that while things might be over on paper, that doesn't necessarily mean they're *over-over*...."

"Oh-oh…"

"She kept *saying* it was over. But he still called her and she still called him. She'd always tell me whenever they talked so I thought that proved she didn't have anything to hide. I figured it was just an amiable divorce. I didn't think they were talking because they weren't really done with each other—"

"But they weren't."

"I learned later that the calls were mostly about how her ex wanted her back. And that she was torn and actually thinking about it. I was six months into things when she let that slip. If I'd had any brains I would have said goodbye on the spot."

"But you didn't?"

"I didn't," he answered with self-disgust. "I had feelings for her by then. And much to my regret, my competitive streak came right to the surface. Instead of bowing out, I did everything I could think of to win. To get her to pick me over the ex."

The low, disgusted tone of his voice, the way his brows almost met in a frown, let Shannon see how much he damned that choice.

"It didn't work? She picked the ex anyway?" she asked gently.

He shook his head again. He let out a mirthless laugh. He took a drink of his wine and stared at the fire for a moment before he looked Shannon in the eye again and said, "Yeah, she picked the ex anyway, but not until after he and four of his teammates jumped me one night."

Shannon hadn't realized until that moment just how literal he'd meant his comment about crowbars and being blindsided. "Were you alone? Against five other hockey players?"

"I was alone. Coming home after a game, figuring to shower and go over to Sandra's place. Then out of the shadows came these guys..." He shook his head again and he looked more angry than anything as he went on. "I can take a beating with the best of them, and I've dished out plenty of my own on the ice—I played hockey, after all. But these guys took me by surprise—"

"And you were *alone* against *five* of them? With *crowbars?*"

"Sandra's ex-husband was the only one with a crowbar. His four friends held me down while he broke my knee and my leg in three places."

Shannon felt her own eyes widen and the color drain from her face, and she wondered if she might be more fainthearted than she'd thought. "Oh, my god…"

"Luckily a neighbor heard the attack and called the cops—they were there before Sandra's ex got started on the other leg. The cops arrested him and got an ambulance there right away—"

"But the damage he'd already done—"

"Ended my career."

"And hurt you!"

"Five surgeries to put pins in bones and rebuild my knee almost from the ground up. In and out of the hospital, then in and out of rehab each time to make sure the leg would go back to working. I got hit on Christmas Eve the Christmas before last, so I was in the hospital for that one, and I was in rehab after a surgery last Christmas—he definitely did damage."

"No wonder you're so happy to be here this year!"

"And walking."

"But that was it for hockey," Shannon said, referring to his end-of-his-career comment.

"I worked like crazy in rehab every time, thinking I could get back to where I was if I did it with the same intensity I used to train for hockey. But all the doctors, the physical therapists, and then the coaches and trainers and the team doc agreed—there was no way the leg or the knee wouldn't crumble with a good hard hit on the ice. So I had to retire."

He seemed determined not to make it sound like a tragedy, but Shannon knew it had to have been devastating. Still, his refusal to feel sorry for himself reminded her of her parents and all the times she'd watched them put a happy face on their failing health, and she couldn't help being impressed by that in Dag, too.

"What about the creep who did it?" she asked.

"He got eighteen months in jail for assault, his cohorts did a few months each. There was also a civil lawsuit that I filed against them. And won."

"And Sandra?"

"She took the whole thing as some kind of grand romantic gesture," Dag said with disbelief. "It was actually the other guy's winning goal—they remarried the week he was released from jail."

"And you thought that woman was smart?" Shannon said, her own outrage sounding.

"Apparently not when it came to relationships," he admitted.

Shannon glanced at his legs—one of them bent at the knee, his foot on the floor, the other stretched out to the coffee table. She'd never seen him so much as limp and had no idea which leg had ever been hurt.

"It's that one," he said as if he knew what she was thinking, pointing to the leg stretched onto the coffee table.

"How about now—are you okay?"

"For everything but hockey, I'm fine. So I've moved on to the next stage of my life—back to Northbridge and new things here."

And he sounded as if he'd genuinely accepted that without bitterness.

"You're kind of something, you know that?" she heard

herself say as she gazed at the face that hockey playing hadn't scarred, as she saw more of the depth of the man and admired his inner strength as much as his outer, his spirit and his ability to take something awful that had happened to him and make the best of it.

"*Kind of something* what?" he asked with a dash of devilry to his voice and to the one eyebrow he raised rakishly at her.

It made Shannon smile. "Just kind of something," she hedged, setting her glass on the coffee table.

Dag did the same with his as he persisted, "Kind of something wonderful? Kind of something brave and heroic? Kind of something too hot to resist?"

All of the above, Shannon thought.

But she didn't say it. She just laughed at him because it was obvious he was joking. "I'll give you brave—because even after that you're still here with me when I'm as fresh out of a relationship as I am," she said, reiterating his earlier words.

"Well, yeah, that *is* brave," he deadpanned. "Facing down five hockey thugs is one thing, but a politician? I could end up with my taxes raised or an IRS audit—that's *really* terrifying!"

Shannon laughed again, also appreciating his sense of humor.

Then he said, "You're not going to offer to kiss it and make it better?"

"Your knee? No. Have you had a lot of offers to do that?"

"One or two—nurses can be hockey fans, too, you know."

"Then you don't need me to do it, do you?"

"Need? Maybe not..." he said, bringing his hand up

from the sofa back to cup the side of her face. "But want? That's another subject…"

"Even under threat of higher taxes and audits?" she asked, her voice somehow just barely above an inviting whisper as she lost herself a little in black eyes that were delving into hers.

"Even then…" he said, coming forward enough to kiss her—but so lightly it was more like the kiss he'd pressed to her hand than the one they'd shared the night before and she wondered if he was a little leery after all.

If he was, it didn't last, though, because after a moment he deepened the kiss, parting his lips and hers, and slipping his hand to the back of her head, into her hair while his other hand came to the other side of her neck, inside the collar of the blouse she wore under a V-necked sweater.

He had the warmest hands. And a touch that only hinted at the power they contained as his lips parted wider still and his tongue came to meet hers.

Shannon's own hands rose to his solid chest, once again encased in a plaid flannel shirt over a thermal T-shirt. She wished there were fewer layers between them as their kiss rapidly escalated, mouths opening wider and tongues courting and cavorting.

Dag's arms came around her then, pulling her so close she was nearly lying across his lap, held by those massive arms as he took that kiss to yet another level. A level that was so thoroughly intimate it was almost an act of love all on its own.

It most definitely awakened things in Shannon that no mere kiss ever had. She was suddenly aware of every inch of her skin, of a craving to be set free of her shirt, her sweater, her jeans. Her breasts seemed to swell, testing the confines of her bra, begging for the touch of more than lace. Her knees pressed together to contain the desires that sprang to life in places that should have been sleeping. And until they were already there, she didn't even realize that her arms had gone around Dag's broad shoulders or that her fingers were digging into his back.

And that ravaging kiss just fed it all like fuel. She gave as good as she got—plundering his mouth as surely as he plundered hers, with an abandon that would have shocked the politician even after years together. An abandon that the hockey player took in stride.

But it was that abandon that actually gave Shannon pause, that gave her the sense that she was somehow not herself, that warned her to slow down, to think, to stop before things went too far...

She slid her hands from Dag's back to his muscle-wrapped rib cage, then to his chest again. But instead of pushing him away, she continued caressing those perfect pectorals for a while, almost forgetting herself all over again. Until she realized what was about to happen and then she put some effort into taming the kiss, finally managing to begin a retreat.

Dag got the message, although he showed no eagerness to end anything and even after tongues had parted ways, he still kissed her and kissed her again. And kissed her once more on the side of her neck where he flicked the tip of his tongue just a little.

After another moment of nuzzling her neck, he rose up enough to rest his chin atop her head and sigh. "Okay," he said as if she'd spoken. "I s'pose we should call it a night."

"I think it's late..." Shannon said by way of agreement.

Another sigh. "Yeah, probably is..."

Still they stayed the way they were—his arms wrapping her, cradling her, her head against his shoulder.

"I know you hate sports," Dag said then. "But tomorrow night the local men's team plays their Christmas basketball game, and the school choir is singing carols at halftime. From what I hear nearly everyone in town is going. Can I persuade you—even if Logan and Meg and Chase and Hadley decide not to?"

At that moment Shannon thought he could persuade her to go to the moon with him.

"While I'm here I might as well get the full Northbridge experience," she said as if that was the only reason.

"You might as well."

He kissed the top of her head, and Shannon closed her eyes, drinking in the feel of his breath in her hair before she sat up to really let him go.

Then they both got off the couch and Dag shrugged back into his coat as they headed for the door.

There didn't seem to be anything to say but goodnight, and that's what they did. Afterward Dag stood there for a moment looking down at her.

She thought he was considering kissing her again. Or maybe fighting not to. But either way, he didn't. He merely repeated his good-night and left.

Which was for the best, Shannon told herself.

Because the kissing they'd already done had gotten a little out of control and she wasn't sure if even a simple kiss at the door might have started it all over again.

And if a part of her wished it might have? Wished it had started all over again and gone so, so much further?

That was the part of her that she hadn't really known existed until tonight.

A part of her that she found unnerving, unsettling...

And maybe a little more exciting than she knew what to do with.

Chapter 10

"Three shopping days until Christmas and I haven't even *started* yet!"

"Then what are you doing on the phone with me instead of hitting the mall?" Shannon responded, when she answered her friend Danica Bond's call early Wednesday morning. She followed it with a belated, "Hi, Dani."

"Hi, Shan. I haven't talked to you since you left for Northbridge. I just wanted to check in, see how you're doing—*then* I'm hitting the mall."

"I'm doing really well," Shannon said. "Much better than I expected, actually. It's like something out of a Christmas movie here and it's nice spending time with Chase and Hadley and Cody. Chase and I have even found out what family the twins ended up with...." She went on to explain how her younger brothers were part of the Kincaid family.

"And why haven't I heard a public announcement yet that you and Wes aren't engaged?" Dani asked then.

Dani was the one person on Shannon's side—before Dag—who was aware that there wasn't an engagement. Shannon had told Dani in advance that she was going to break up with Wes so Dani hadn't ever believed that Shannon had accepted the proposal. Plus she and Shannon had talked several times since then and Dani knew exactly what was going on. But she, too, had sworn to keep quiet.

"Wes is dragging his feet," Shannon said.

"But he hasn't worn you down, has he?"

"No, he hasn't worn me down. He's trying, but not nearly hard enough. Every reason he gives me to marry him is still about votes and voters. He can be really clueless sometimes."

But Wes was the last thing that Shannon wanted to talk about so she said, "What about you—have you honestly not even started Christmas shopping yet?"

"I honestly haven't. I've been too swamped with the school—there's even a temporary sign up now that says Coming Soon: The Early Childhood Development Center. I can't wait for you to get here after Christmas and see everything. We're about three-quarters finished with construction so it's easy to envision the way it will look in the end—just like the drawing I sent you from the architect. Only in real life it's much more impressive. You're going to love it! You're going to love California, too, and never want to leave—I just know it! I can't wait for you to *finally* get here!"

Dani's enthusiasm was infectious and it made Shannon smile. She missed her friend. Because of her own job and caring for her parents, she hadn't been able to visit Dani in Beverly Hills, and Dani hadn't come back to Montana nearly often enough since marrying Ronald Bond two years before and leaving. She had come back for all three funerals during the last year but each of those trips had had to be quick and she and Shannon hadn't spent any real time together.

"I have your room ready," Dani went on, "and it would be fine with me if you got here, decided to come on board with the school and just never left."

Shannon laughed. "I would still have to come back to Billings and move my stuff."

"Okay, one trip and that's all," Dani said. "Because nobody can tell me that once I get you here it isn't going to hit you that *this* is how you can break out and move on to bigger and better things—the way we talked about when we were kids, the way we dreamed about, the way I have."

It never failed that when she talked to Dani about moving to Beverly Hills, about going in on the school with her old friend, Shannon was always tempted to just say *Sign me up!*

But even without the possibility of a future with Wes holding her back, she still didn't do that. Her parents had lived a cautious life—financially and otherwise—and she supposed they'd passed on the need for caution to her. As a result, despite the lure of what Dani was offering, Shannon knew she had to see things for herself, get a feel for the school, for California and Beverly Hills, and seriously consider everything before she committed to anything. Even if Dani was involved.

So she merely said, "I can't wait to see you."

"But you're really doing okay? I mean…the first Christmas without everybody…"

"I'm a little blue here and there." She admitted to her friend what she hadn't said to anyone else. "But everyone is so nice and the whole town is—"

"Don't let it suck you in!" Dani ordered.

"Did I say it was sucking me in?"

"I can hear something in your voice—you like it there. Or have you met someone…"

Dani knew her much, much too well. "My brother's partner's brother—Dag—is helping to show me around, but it isn't as if I've *met someone*, no," Shannon insisted.

Although that somehow felt like a lie. Especially when the image of Dag came so vividly to mind suddenly and sent a wave of warmth all through her. Warmth and the same eagerness to be with him again that she felt every minute they were apart…

"Well, don't let him suck you in, either," Dani said. "This is your time and don't let anyone keep you from having it."

Ah, but Dani hadn't met Dag.

And she certainly hadn't been kissed by him the way he'd kissed Shannon the night before.…

"You know my coming out there after Christmas doesn't make this a done deal," Shannon felt obligated to remind her friend then. "As much as I hate that you moved away and as much as I'd like us to be near each other again—"

"I know," Dani interrupted her. "I won't blame you if investing in the school seems too scary—without Ron I wouldn't be brave enough… Well, without Ron I wouldn't be able to do it at all since most of the capital is his. But I've been thinking and even if you don't want to jump in right away, you can still think about just giving me a year—"

"A year?"

"You could set up the pre-K and kindergarten section, and when school starts in the fall, you could teach here instead of in Montana. It would give you a chance to try it all out. You wouldn't even have to get a place, you could stay with Ron and me and just settle in temporarily to make up your mind. You can even invest after that, if you want to. Once you see that we can make a go of it, it will ease your mind."

It was an offer too good to refuse.

Yet Shannon still said, "We'll talk about it when I get there."

"Oh, believe me, I'm talking about it until I get you to say yes!"

Shannon laughed at her friend. "Now *that's* the kind of determination Wes should have had."

"Isn't that the truth!" Dani agreed.

"Anyway," Shannon said then, "for now I'm due to bake and decorate Christmas cookies with Hadley, Meg and Tia. And you'd better go shopping."

"That's where I'm headed. I probably won't bother you again until Christmas day. But if you get too blue—day or night—you call me, okay?"

Shannon knew Dani meant that. The same way she would always be available to Dani day or night. "Okay," Shannon agreed. "But go on—shop. And happy hunting."

"At this point there's no time for hunting—I'm rushing in, buying and rushing on to the next store!"

While Chase and Logan helped Dag with some woodwork at Dag's place that afternoon, Shannon went to the main house to pitch in with the Christmas cookie making, and to lend Meg and Hadley a hand with Tia and Cody.

There was discussion between Meg and Hadley about whether or not to attend the evening's basketball game that Dag had asked Shannon to, but in the end the other two women decided on another quiet evening in.

Obviously since Chase and Hadley were newlyweds, and Meg and Logan had only been married a few months, at that point nothing was quite as compelling for either of the two couples as time alone.

Meg and Hadley did encourage Shannon to go, however, and Shannon told herself she should do it for the sake of her brother and his bride, to give them that time alone.

Which seemed like a much better reason than that she might just want to be with Dag the same way Hadley and Meg wanted to be with Chase and Logan.

So after a quick dinner with Chase, Hadley and Cody at the loft, Shannon rushed back to the apartment to change into her best butt-hugging tan slacks. Gambling that it might not be warm enough, she nonetheless put on a U-necked T-shirt over a tight camisole top that gave her enough lift to form the hint of cleavage. Then she freshened her blush and mascara before she took her hair out of the ponytail it had been in all day and brushed it to fall free around her shoulders.

But again she swore to herself that sprucing up wasn't for Dag, that it was only because she was going out for the evening.

As planned, at six forty-five, she heard Dag drive his truck around to the garage to get her. She was just putting on her coat and tying a matching scarf around her neck when he knocked on the door.

Opening it to him, she could tell that he'd put a little extra thought into his own attire tonight, too. He had on a very dashing-looking calf-length black wool coat over a pair of charcoal-colored slacks that fit him so well they had to have been specially made to accommodate his hockey player thighs. He also had on a cashmere polo-style sweater that caressed his upper body in a way that made Shannon's hands want to do the same thing.

He was freshly shaven, his almost-black hair was shiny-clean and artfully disarrayed, and all in all, he had more of an air of a take-charge corporate raider than a jock or a cowboy. And were Shannon to hazard a guess, she would have said that that was how he had dressed to go out clubbing after hockey games when groupies had gathered and—no doubt—swooned at the transformation he was capable of making. She, herself, certainly had to put a whole lot of effort into not swooning....

"This is a good look for you," she mentioned casually when she realized she was staring and mentally kicked herself.

Dag merely smiled, gave her an up-and-down glance and said, "I haven't seen a look that isn't good on you yet."

Then he swiveled away from blocking the door and with a sweep of his arm, he invited her to go ahead of him out of the apartment.

The basketball game was being played in the school gymnasium by the local men's team that played baseball, basketball and football against each other year-round. But despite the loud and jocular participation of the crowd, despite the humor and festiveness exhibited by the players in the holly crowns, the bell-adorned wristbands, and the red-and-white or green-and-white striped knee socks they wore to designate teams, Shannon was no more enthralled with this sport than with any other.

She liked the choir concert of Christmas carols sung by the school children at halftime, but she was glad when Dag suggested they leave after that.

"I'm sorry if I was a drag," she apologized as they left the school. "I just can't begin to tell you how sports-stupid I am and it's hard to get into something when I honestly don't have any idea what I'm watching."

Dag leaned sideways and said, "To tell you the truth, I didn't make it back to Logan's for dinner tonight and I'm starving. I thought I might be able to persuade you to grab some takeout with me and go back to your place for a bite to eat. That's what I was fantasizing about through "Silent Night"—you, me, another fire and a burger."

Shannon had to laugh at the rapture with which he'd said *burger*. "Even though I came first on that list, why do I still get the feeling that the hamburger is the biggest draw?" she teased him.

He grinned. "Low self-esteem?"

"That must be it," Shannon said facetiously before she agreed to his suggestion.

A quick stop at the Tastee Dog's new drive-through window and within fifteen minutes they were back at Shannon's place with Shannon taking a turn at building a fire while Dag ate.

Then they were once again where Shannon secretly most wanted to be—sitting on the center of the sofa in front of that fire. Alone, together...

"So what did you think of our school, Ms. Kinder-garten Teacher?" Dag asked as they began to share the brownie-mint ice cream sundae that was the dessert Shannon had agreed to partake in.

"I didn't see much of it," Shannon said.

There were three buildings that housed it—one each

for the elementary, middle and high school grade levels—
and Shannon had only seen the gym. Since that was also
the site for the elementary grades, she *had* seen the kindergarten classroom.

"It looks like a nice school, though," she said. "For
such a small area I'm kind of surprised by how nice it is."

"It probably doesn't compare to whatever is going on
in Beverly Hills with your friend's school, but still—"

"It gets the job done," Shannon finished for him. Then
she said, "I actually talked to my friend Dani this morning. She says her school is shaping up."

"And that it could all be yours?"

"Not all of it, no. But a small piece of the pie."

"So I'm curious," Dag said as they finished the sundae, set the container on the coffee table and moved on to
the spicy tea Shannon had brewed for them. "This Dani
is your best friend, right? You're not marrying the Rumson. You've sold your parents' business and the building
that was home to you all. You've sold your grandmother's house here. It seems like you've cut all the ties in
Montana in order to move on and that you kind of like
the idea of going out to California with your friend. But
you haven't actually made that decision?"

"I didn't sell anything to *cut ties*," Shannon amended
his assumption. "I had to sell the business and the building it was in to pay off the last of my parents' medical
bills. I wasn't going to move to Northbridge to live, so
there wasn't a reason to keep Gramma's house—especially since I couldn't afford any kind of upkeep or the
taxes or insurance on it. And between what little was
left of my parents' assets after the bills and the sale of
Gramma's place, that still only gave me a small nest egg."

"But now you have that nest egg and it gives you the

money to invest," Dag said, putting his mug of tea on the coffee table after a few sips.

Shannon went on warming her hands around her cup. "Yes. But if I invest the nest egg, then no nest egg," she said reasonably. "And if the investment doesn't pay off, I won't have anything. Nothing. No job to go back to—because right now I'm on sabbatical and slated to return to work next fall, but if I don't do that, I'm giving up my job. Also if I move to California and The Early Childhood Development Center doesn't succeed, it isn't as if I have parents to help out or come back to."

"But it isn't as if you're alone in the world—you have Chase, he's your brother," Dag reminded.

And Shannon didn't doubt that if she needed Chase's help, he would give it. But still their relationship was in the infant stages and asking him for help—especially financial—wasn't something she actually felt she could do. It was certainly something she wouldn't want to do.

"And I'd still have Dani," she pointed out, thinking aloud, sorting through the pros and cons with Dag and wondering at the fact that she *did* feel comfortable doing that with him.

"Unless owning a business together and working together put a strain on the friendship," he said. "Or doesn't that worry you?"

"It does…" she said, but she hadn't had anyone to talk to about it and now that Dag had brought it up, she appreciated the chance to air her feelings.

"Dani and I have been friends since we were kids," Shannon said. "We're as close as I imagine sisters are. I'd do anything for her and I know she would do anything for me—"

"Why do I hear a *but* coming?"

"But we're different, Dani and I. We have different ways of doing things, different temperaments, different opinions. It's never mattered before because we always went our own directions—even though Dani's a teacher, too, she's taught fourth, fifth or sixth grade because she says the ages below that are too immature for her. We've always shared what we had in common and supported each other when either of us did something the other one didn't, but—"

"If you invest in the school—"

"And/or go to work there, that's something we've never done before."

"It might be fine—"

"Or it might mess up our friendship. And I don't know if anything is worth that," Shannon confided.

Dag nodded his understanding. Before he'd said anything, however, she went on with her list of pros and cons.

"Plus there's Dani's husband..." she whispered as if someone else might hear as she finished her tea and set the mug on the coffee table beside Dag's.

"You don't like him?"

"He's..." She shrugged while she chose her words, not wanting to say too much against her best friend's spouse. "He's kind of full of himself and maybe just a little...slick. He needs to be the center of attention—the smartest, most successful person in the room. And he's the major investor in the school—which still makes it Dani's school since she's his wife, but I know that everything has to have his okay on it. I don't know if that's just for now—in terms of construction—or if it's going to influence the way things are done with the kids, with the educational programs. I just don't know how far his input and influence are going to go."

"That seems like something to find out before you get in," Dag counseled.

"There's also the fact that it will be a private school in *Beverly Hills*," Shannon went on because now that she'd started this, she thought she might as well get it all out. "I've only worked in public school. I don't know if I'll fit in, if I'll feel uncomfortable or out of my element there. I don't know if a schoolteacher—even in a private school—is a respected part of a community like that or not. I just don't know if I'll like it. And if I don't and all my money is tied up in it, then what? Then I'm back to the financial issues and having no one...."

"Or then maybe you just cash in on your investment and make another change," he suggested. "You could even come back here. I could keep a room for you, if you want. I'll put a plaque on the door that says The Just-In-Case Room of Shannon Duffy. Would that help?"

Shannon laughed. "You're kidding, but I might take you up on it."

"Who says I'm kidding?" he asked with a kind smile. "I can keep the cubbyhole room for you."

"Why do I think you actually might do that if I asked you to?"

"Because I would?"

Maybe he wasn't joking.

"I'm sure the future Mrs. Dag McKendrick would love that!" Shannon said.

"*Future* is the key word—if there *is* a future Mrs. Dag McKendrick, then we can make adjustments. But until then? I'll be your safety net if you'd feel better knowing you literally have a place to come back to if Beverly Hills doesn't work out."

"You're serious..." Shannon said when she began to believe he was.

"I am," he answered as if he'd made the decision on the spot but was willing to run with it. "Let me sign on to be your safety net."

Oddly enough, that had an appeal because she somehow did feel safe with this man. Among so many other things she felt about him and with him...

But she tried not to think too much about those feelings and to stick to reality.

"It would be weird to go to Chase for help," she said then, "but you think it would be less weird to go to the brother of my brother's partner for it?"

"Why is it weird if I'm volunteering? It can be like a pact we make, one free agent to another free agent—if I get sick of Northbridge and long for the Hills of Beverly, I'll come to you—"

"We both know that isn't going to happen, you *love* it here."

He shrugged that off and went on with the terms of his pact. "And if things don't work out for you there, you'll come to me. I sort of like the idea of being someone you'd turn to if you needed to."

She sort of liked that idea, too. But she wasn't sure why. "Thanks, but—"

Dag took her hand, holding it, rubbing the back of it with his thumb in a way that was an enticement all its own. "Just factor it into your thinking," he said then. "Maybe it'll help you make your decision—if Beverly Hills still seems too risky even when you have a backup plan, then you may realize that isn't the way to go. If you feel more free to jump in *because* you have a backup plan, then maybe you should give it a try. I've heard that sometimes just having the safety net in place makes the high-wire walker less likely to fall."

"You dated a circus performer?" she joked to hide how touched she was by his willingness to make things easier for her.

His smile was simple and sweet and endearing. "Only for a little while," he said, his voice deeper, more quiet suddenly as he went on rubbing her hand with his thumb, watching himself do it, unaware of the tiny electrical charges it was sending up her arm.

Then he raised her hand to kiss it much the way he had those other nights. Except unlike those other nights, once he'd kissed it, he let go of it and raised his palm to the side of her neck, and met her gaze with his dark, smoldering eyes.

"Not that I'm advocating for you to leave," he said just before he closed the distance between them and took her mouth with his.

Why that kiss was like coming home, Shannon had no idea. But there was such warm familiarity in lips parted instantly to perfection, in mouths that seemed to fit together as if one had been carved from the other, and she just melted into that kiss.

Her palms rose to his cashmere-covered chest the way they'd been aching to do since the minute she'd laid eyes on him tonight. His other arm came around her, pulling her closer, repositioning them both so they were facing each other on the sofa.

The kiss deepened, reawakening that part of her that she'd discovered the night before, inviting it to come out to play again.

She could feel that slightly wilder streak rising, gaining ground, with each circle and thrust of Dag's talented tongue, with each time her own met and matched it. And when his hand went to the back of her head to brace it for the deepening of that kiss, when he held her tighter, she didn't think she could have contained herself even if she'd wanted to.

The man just brought things to life in her! As if every sense was on high alert—but only in the best way. With Dag, kissing wasn't merely kissing, it was an indulgence in something decadent, and every movement, every placement of his hands in her hair, on her back, between her shoulder blades, only made her want to feel them everywhere else, too.

Her nipples grew taut behind the binding knit of the camisole that held them confined and thoughts of those big hands on her breasts suddenly became inescapable. Those big, strong hands...

She massaged the muscles of his broad back, which barely gave way beneath her fingers digging ardently through his sweater. The sweater that—regardless of how soft and fine it felt—stood between her and his bare flesh.

The new, more daring Shannon found the bottom of his sweater and slipped her hands underneath it, sliding them up sleek skin over honed muscle as Dag came slightly more atop her, his mouth pillaging hers as his hand found her breast, surprising and delighting her at once.

But both the surprise and the delight were short-lived because Shannon wanted so much to feel his hand on her bare flesh that she could have ripped her shirts off herself.

Dag always seemed somehow in tune with her and no sooner had that thought flitted through her mind than he snaked his hand under both shirts and found her naked breasts.

First one, then the other, giving them both equal time, equal opportunity to know the magic of a touch that was, by turns, light and firm, playful and serious, teasing and tormenting.

It felt so wonderful that Shannon's breath caught in a tiny gasp and all new desires made themselves known, causing her to slip one of her legs over his.

Desires that only mounted when his mouth left hers, kissing, nibbling a trail down her neck, to her side, to her belly and then up to take her breast into that sweet haven.

The wild streak in her took full hold then and thrust her forward without inhibition, begging for more of that hot, wet wonder of mouth and tongue and teeth that stole her breath and left her weak with all the more wanting.

Because yes, she did want this man more than she'd ever wanted any man!

So much more that again it was a little alarming...

What if this was just some kind of rebound thing? What if it was some kind of insanity that had come from so much loss? What if it was some kind of seizing-of-life after so many encounters with death?

But it might just be Dag, she thought as he drew her breast more deeply into his mouth, as his tongue did a twirl around her nipple and it seemed as if it was Dag and Dag alone that she wanted.

It might just be Dag...

And how special, how cared for, he made her feel. How free...

But freedom was one of the things she'd always thought came with a bigger life. That brought Beverly Hills to mind to add to her qualms.

Beverly Hills and a bigger life and the fact that living

in Northbridge—the way Dag did and was determined to do from here on—was not a life she had ever dreamed of.

Which screamed for her to keep things cool with him.

Too late for that, she thought because she was already on fire for him.

But still once the reasonable, rational side of her recognized that she should cool this off, it wouldn't leave her alone. And as amazing as kissing him was, as amazing as it was to have his hands on her, to have his mouth on her breast, she didn't think she could let it go on...

No matter how much she wanted it to.

And oh, did she want it to!

But other than what was happening at that moment, they wanted different, different things. So wanting him, wanting what he was doing to her, had to be sacrificed.

Yes, the small groan that echoed from her throat then was in response to a tiny flick of his tongue to the very tip of her nipple and how good it felt. But it was also to her own decision that she couldn't have more of that. Of Dag. And it was that decision that made her draw back just enough to let him know not to go on. That decision that dropped her head to the top of the couch cushion as Dag got the hint and stopped.

His audible exhalation was disappointed but resolved. He pulled her shirts down and then her head to rest on his chest so that he could lower his cheek to it.

And this time it seemed as if she had an inkling of what he was thinking even before he whispered in a gravely voice, "Yeah, you're right, we shouldn't."

Shannon had no explanation whatsoever for why Dag thinking that, too, should disappoint her. But she wrote it off to the confusion of emotions that were all running rampant through her at that moment, and agreed. "No, we shouldn't."

Yet they stayed the way they were for a while longer, holding each other, in no hurry to part.

But it had to be done and eventually it was Dag who did it—sending another wave of regret through Shannon.

Dag raised his head from hers, loosening his arms from around her, sitting up straighter. She sat up, too.

He kissed her again. Briefly. As if he just couldn't stop himself. Then he stood, swiped his coat from the arm of the nearby chair and put it on while Shannon got to her feet to walk him to the door.

He kissed her yet again there—his hands were shoved into his coat pockets so he didn't touch her, but the kiss was still long and lingering and open mouthed, a sexy farewell that made Shannon hate that there was any farewell being said at all.

But just when she was fighting the inclination to ask him to stay, he ended that kiss, too, straightened up again and glanced over her head at the apartment.

"I think tomorrow we need to get a little Christmas cheer into this place," he decreed. "What do you say we cut you a tree and decorate it?"

The man just always made her smile....

"Isn't that a lot of work for just a couple of days until it's all over?"

"A couple of days is still a couple of days that you'll get to have it," he said, looking at her again and making her think that it wasn't only a Christmas tree on his mind when he said that.

But one way or another, what he was suggesting would give her more time with him and even though she told herself she shouldn't do it, that he was just too hard for her to resist and that she was tempting fate, she heard herself say, "I've never cut my own Christmas tree...."

"So tomorrow it is?"

"If you don't have anything else to do..."

"I don't have anything else I'd rather do."

He held her eyes with his for another moment. He kissed her again—this time a quick buss. And then he said, "Tomorrow it is," in a husky voice, before he opened the door and went out into the cold.

And not even the blast of winter air that shocked Shannon as she watched him go could cool her off.

Instead, hours and hours after she'd closed the door, changed into her pajamas and gone to bed, she was still feeling the heat of Dag.

And still wanting him every bit as badly as she had when she'd been in his arms.

Chapter 11

Cutting down a Christmas tree for the apartment was delayed on Thursday when Chase received an answer to the email he and Shannon had sent to Ian Kincaid.

Shannon ended up spending the morning with Chase, using the phone number in the return email to try to reach Ian.

That eventually happened, leading to a lengthy conference call during which Ian let them know that he and Hutch also had no idea there were other siblings, that he had thought Chase and Shannon's email was some sort of scam until he'd spoken to his mother. Reluctantly, his mother had admitted that there had been another brother and two sisters.

Ian—like Shannon and Chase before him—was thunderstruck. But he had agreed to arrange a time to meet Chase and Shannon after the first of the year.

The second twin—Hutch—was another matter.

Hutch was apparently not on good terms with the Kincaid family. They had not been in touch in several years.

"This is the last email address I have for him, but I haven't used it in so long, I can't tell you that it will get you through to him," Ian said, giving them the address but not offering to relay the news of newfound family himself. And also, Shannon noted, not explaining why a rift existed.

When the phone call ended, Shannon went from Chase's loft to the main house in search of Dag. But Dag had gone into town and left word for her that he would be back soon.

Soon was just after lunch and that was when Shannon bundled up in borrowed heavy-weather gear to go out into the countryside to finally cut her Christmas tree.

The sun was shining, the sky was blue, but it was only three degrees. Shannon wouldn't have blamed Dag if he had backed out of the tree-cutting with the temperature that low, but he was good-natured, full of energy and enthusiasm, and—as usual—game for anything. The only thing he would concede to was not going too far to find a tree.

Luckily there was a stand of evergreens a mere two miles from the barn on Chase and Logan's land, so that was where Dag and Shannon went. Dag parked as near as he could to the small forest but they still had to hike through knee-high snow to reach the trees.

Shannon was grateful when they located one that was a mere four feet high not far into the cluster.

"This one! This is the one," she decreed, breathing warm air into her gloved hands. "Cut it down and let's get out of this cold!"

Dag grinned at her, seeming amused by her chattering teeth. But he didn't hesitate to use a chain saw at the base of the low-lying fir while Shannon stood back and watched.

And that actually helped with the cold.

The mere sight of the big man, dressed like a burly lumberjack, wielding the saw with expertise, was enough to chase away some of Shannon's chill. Or maybe it was just the fact that she was so enthralled with him that she forgot about the frigid temperature. Instead—as she had so many times since she'd put a stop to it—she relived in vivid detail all that had happened between them the night before. And that was like a little ray of private sunshine heating her from the inside out...

When the tree toppled, Dag bent over, picked it up with one hand and held it in the air as if it were a trophy. "Another brother and a Christmas tree for Shannon Duffy all in one day!" he shouted in victory.

"Let's just get the tree home where there's heat!" Shannon said in response, pretending that Dag didn't generate that for her all on his own.

The remainder of the afternoon went into building a stand for the tree, after which Shannon and Dag joined everyone else at the loft where Hadley had made a dinner of beef stew.

And as much as Shannon enjoyed having so many people around her and being included in the large extended family, tonight she was eager to get away from them all, to get back to the apartment.

Only to put up her Christmas tree, she told herself. It wasn't merely another evening alone with Dag that had her antsy.

Except that visions of Christmas decorations weren't dancing through her head.

Regardless of how much she denied it, it was still Dag who was firmly on her mind....

"That's what you were doing in town—buying lights and tinsel and ornaments for my tree? I thought I was just using whatever Logan and Chase had left over," Shannon said when she and Dag finally got to the apartment Thursday evening and Dag brought in two sacks full of Christmas decorations that he'd purchased that morning.

"It isn't much. But while you and Chase were talking to Ian Kincaid, I got the bug to go pick up a few things. This stuff will all get used somewhere again next year, so what's the harm?"

There wasn't any harm. In fact it was another nice thing he'd done for her. Another nice, thoughtful thing.

"Let me at least pay for them," she offered.

"Nah. This close to the big day everything was on closeout. Consider it part of your Christmas gift."

"*Part* of my Christmas gift? You got me a Christmas gift?" Shannon couldn't resist saying.

Dag grinned. "Santa brings everybody a Christmas gift," he answered with a wink as he hunkered down to make a fire before they got started.

Try to keep a lid on it, Shannon warned herself when her eyes followed him to the hearth, devouring the sight of him much the way she had that afternoon.

But she wasn't sure she could.

After cutting down the tree and making the stand for it, they'd gone their separate ways to get ready for the evening. For Shannon that had meant a shower and shampoo to get the sawdust off her.

It had also meant some special attention to curling her hair into loose waves around her face, into applying fresh makeup and into opting for her tightest jeans and a teal-green turtleneck that also conformed to her curves. A turtleneck sweater that she'd buttoned up all the way to her chin but that stopped at the exact spot the jean's waistband began so that if she raised her arms the slightest bit, she flashed a hint of skin—unless she wore a tank top underneath it, which she usually did. Except tonight…

Dag had showered, as well. He'd also changed into clean jeans that were low on his hips. And tonight, rather than wearing one of the thermal T-shirts underneath a second shirt, Dag had on the thermal T-shirt alone—a white crewnecked thermal knit that fit like a second skin and left no question that his V-shaped torso was all lean muscle and sinew.

And the fact that he had the long sleeves pushed to his elbows and she could see his forearms? Who would ever believe that one look at those forearms could send a tiny tingle along the surface of her own skin? But it did.

He'd also shaved again before dinner, and combed his hair, and he smelled of that cologne that she attributed to him and him alone. And altogether Shannon knew it was not going to be easy to keep a lid on anything when it came to Dag.

Once the fire was made they went to work on the tree, using an end table to elevate it. All the while they did the job, Dag sang in a surprisingly good voice, making Shannon laugh because his own made-up versions of the old favorite Christmas carols were sometimes a little raunchy and always irreverent.

And when the tree was finished he brought out a bottle

of wine he'd also gotten in town that morning, opened it and poured them each a glass.

Then he turned off all the lights so the apartment was illuminated only by the fire's glow and the tiny twinkling white lights on the tree.

They'd taken off their wet shoes when they'd come in and they sat together in the center of the sofa again, only tonight they were slumped down, both pairs of stockinged feet on the coffee table, heads resting on the back of the couch—to sip wine and look at their handiwork.

"Sooo…I've been wondering about something," Dag said then.

"What?"

"Well, you've mentioned wanting a bigger life a couple of times, but it occurred to me that I'm not quite sure what exactly makes up your idea of that. Is it traveling around the world in a hot air balloon? Climbing Mount Everest? Wiping out illiteracy for all time?"

Shannon laughed. "Traveling, yes—but not necessarily around the *whole* world, just the parts I'd like to see with my own eyes. And definitely not in a hot air balloon, a plane would be just fine. And forget Mount Everest, Montana is cold enough for me. Sure, I'd like to wipe out illiteracy for all time, but I'm happy sending one kindergarten class a year on to first grade with the basics. It isn't as if I have grandiose visions."

"What, then?"

"I guess I mean *bigger* as in broader—not isolated, with more options, more choices for everything. I don't want to always be the person looking at other people's pictures and hearing other people's stories, I want pictures of my own to show, stories of my own to tell. I don't dream of being the first woman to walk on Mars, but I want to be *having* experiences, not just watching them on TV."

"You want more freedom than your parents had, more than you had, since you had to take care of them. Up until very recently, your life was bound to theirs."

Shannon hadn't thought of herself as *bound* to her parents' life, but now that Dag put it into that perspective, she knew she had been.

"You're right," she said. "And in a lot of ways, to me, I guess having a bigger life means the kind of freedom most people have and take for granted. It doesn't necessarily have to be full of fanfare, it just has to be…I don't know, life not lived in a cocoon."

"Like the cocoon of a small town."

"A small town does seem cocoonlike," she agreed.

And she knew that appealed to Dag. But for some reason, tonight, highlighting where they differed seemed depressing. Thinking beyond what they had right then, alone together, talking, enjoying the wine and the fire and the tree, brought her down. So she changed the subject.

"Now, what *I've* been wondering about is if you really did date a circus performer…."

Dag laughed out loud, heartily, happily, with that barrel-chested laugh he had. And just the sound of it made her smile and chased away any doldrums that had threatened.

"You're wondering if I really dated a circus performer because of my safety-net-tightrope-walker crack last night?" he clarified. "As a matter of fact, I *did* date a circus performer, and she *was* a tightrope walker. And a contortionist."

"Oh, dear…" Shannon said, thinking that that was a lot to compete with. If she were competing… "Isn't that every man's dream?" she asked. "Being with a contortionist?"

"I don't know about every man's dream, but I know it got me some high-fives in the locker room. I just didn't admit that I never got her into bed."

"That's not an image I want to think about," Shannon confessed, laughing herself. Then she persisted with what she'd actually been curious about. "But what about serious relationships other than the last one that got you battered—have you had any?"

"Serious? Two, I guess. If serious means thinking and talking about marriage but not actually getting to the engaged phase."

"But close to it?"

"Both times were after a long while of dating—one for a year, the other for almost two—when the women I was involved with decided that was enough of the dating—"

"They proposed to you?"

"Proposed? No, it was more like ultimatums—marry me or we're done."

"So you were done?"

Dag shrugged. "I didn't have marrying kinds of feelings for them. I was sorry about it, sorry to have the relationships end because I liked both Steph and Trish and I enjoyed my time with them. But that's just the way it was—when I tried to picture myself with them forever, I couldn't do it. What about you? Anybody before the Rumson?"

"Two for me, too. But mine were both proposals."

"Really..." he said, raising his eyebrows at her. "And assuming you said no both of those times, too, the Rumson made it *three* guys you turned down? Are you allergic to marriage?"

"No. The first one was my high school sweetheart— he didn't have plans to go to college, he'd already gone through a mechanics training program and was going to work repairing cars as soon as we graduated. He wanted to get married then, too, thought having an apartment over a garage—like our apartment over the shoe repair shop—was the perfect setup and that was his goal—"

"Minus your parents' poor health, he was inviting you to have the same life you had."

"Except without the feelings my parents had for each other—I liked Trip, but that was as far as it went. And I wanted to go to college, and he didn't want me to do that, so there was no way I was marrying him."

"And the second guy?"

"I dated him in college. Lou. His family owns a factory that manufactures and sells some sort of cog that almost every piece of machinery uses. When he finished college he was set to be trained to take over for his father to run things—"

"Another bigwig?"

"Not on the level of the Rumsons, but Lou's family is definitely well-off, so yes, I guess you could say he was another bigwig-in-the-making at least."

"Offering another bigger life."

"In Texas."

"But your family needed you in Billings so you said no?" Dag guessed.

"My family needed me in Billings *and* I also didn't have strong enough feelings for Lou to marry him—same as you and the contortionist."

"The contortionist wasn't one of my two other serious relationships. I told you that didn't go anywhere."

Shannon merely smiled. She'd just been giving him a hard time.

She finished her wine then and did a sit-up to put her glass on the coffee table before settling comfortably back alongside Dag again.

He did the same thing but when he sat back he turned slightly to his side so he could look at her. He also stretched an arm along the sofa behind her head.

"So let me see if I have this straight. Three proposals—two of them offering bigger lives—but what made you turn them all down was—"

"The same thing that made you turn down the two women you dated for long periods of time but didn't want to make a commitment to—the way I felt about them. Or, actually, the way I *didn't* feel about them. There was nothing really *wrong* with any of them. But with every one of them, if I went a week or two without seeing them, I was okay with it."

And yet with Dag she didn't seem to be okay with even a few hours without seeing him or talking to him…

She couldn't let that mean anything, she told herself.

"And the bottom line," Dag summarized, "is that bigger life or not—in any form—you won't accept less than what your folks had together."

Shannon shrugged. "My parents truly, truly loved each other. And as sappy as it may sound, after seeing that, after witnessing with my own two eyes that that kind of love does exist, it's something I have to hold out for."

Dag nodded his understanding but Shannon had the impression that there was something he wanted to say yet wasn't.

"What?" she asked. "You don't believe that kind of love exists?"

"I'm just wondering…"

"About?"

"Well, we can't count the high school kid because he wasn't offering the feelings or a bigger life. But with the other two guys you haven't had much trouble turning down the bigger life because the feelings weren't there. What happens if the feelings come without the bigger life?"

How had they gotten back on this subject she hadn't wanted to talk about?

"I don't know," she said. "But you're kind of harshing my buzz—"

Dag laughed again. "*That's* not what I had in mind!"

"I know. But here we are, with the Christmas tree and the fire and the wine and—"

"Maybe you'd rather hear more about the contortionist," he said, obviously getting the message. "Shall I tell you how she once got me out of a speeding ticket by dislocating her toes and telling the cop I was rushing her to the hospital because she'd broken her foot?"

"Oh, no! Stop!" Shannon said in horror, closing her eyes as if to block out the vision.

When she opened them again it was to Dag studying her and smiling a small, secret smile. Then he said, "What does it mean if I hate not seeing you for even a few hours?" he asked then, echoing her own thought of moments earlier.

"That you're really, really bored and need a hobby?"

He shook his handsome head as if he'd considered that, but then he said, "Nope, I don't think so.…"

She knew that her own craving to be with him didn't come out of boredom, either, but she was afraid to think about what it might mean that every minute she was away from him was spent wishing she wasn't.

Then he came nearer and kissed her. And she recognized one of the reasons she craved being with him—because for the second time, the moment their lips met she felt an overwhelming sense of well-being, of euphoria, of just plain gladness that still didn't dampen the sheer excitement that kissing him flooded her with.

Shannon raised a hand to the side of his chiseled face as she answered his kiss, parting her lips, kissing him in return, welcoming his tongue when it came.

He was braced on his side, on one elbow, but with that hand he took hers where it rested on the sofa cushion, holding it while he wrapped his other arm around her and turned her more toward him.

And while Shannon knew it was probably not wise, her knee bent and her leg drifted over his.

That definitely lit a match to the kiss—mouths opened wider and tongues played with more fervor, more daring and audacity.

Shannon's hand went from the side of Dag's face along the unyielding column of his neck to his shoulder, to his chest, encased in the waffly weave of that thermal shirt.

Had his nipple grown slightly hard at her touch? The idea made her smile inside. And it made her own nipples tighten into much more adept little knots in memory of his hands on them last night. His mouth...

And if her own mouth opened a bit wider beneath his at just that thought? If her tongue met his more boldly? If a new hunger erupted in that kiss? She couldn't help it.

Not that Dag seemed to mind—he gave as good as he got in the joust they were toying at, and then he did her one better still, and brought his hand from her back to the side of her waist where it took nothing to find his way under that short sweater to bare skin.

His hand was warm, slightly calloused, so, so strong. He did a light massage of her side, racking her with memories of what he could do to more sensitive parts of her. Parts of her that were straining against her bra, her sweater, pining for his attention.

She demonstrated, pressing her fingers into his pectoral, releasing only to press again, inspiring a throaty chuckle from him.

Then his tongue changed to playful, instigating a little cat and mouse before he ended that kiss altogether and said, "I can't go home in the state I was in last night."

Her own unmet yearnings of the previous evening had been all she'd thought about. She hadn't considered what condition he might have been left in.

But now here they were again, and the choice was clear-cut—either they stopped before this went any further, or they didn't stop at all.…

And stopping the previous evening had been bad enough.

Shannon kissed him again, a long, lingering, sensuous-but-not-sexy kiss, while her mind spun.

Before, she'd been worried and unsettled by the primal, out-of-control side he'd unveiled in her. The side that she could feel fighting to be unleashed again.

Before, she'd found willpower in reminding herself that they wanted different things.

But tonight…

Tonight she couldn't find the inclination to summon any kind of control.

Tonight she just kept kissing him and thinking that this wasn't her entire future or her whole life. That it wasn't his entire future or his whole life, either. That this was just now. One night. Christmastime. With a man who made her feel things she'd never felt before. Things she didn't want to leave behind without exploring them all…

"Maybe you just shouldn't go home…" she whispered in a moment's pause between kissing him and having him kiss her back—but with some reserve. A reserve that remained even as she felt his lips stretch into a smile.

Then his head reared away from that kiss altogether and he peered down into her eyes. "Are you sure about that?" he asked skeptically in a low, husky voice.

"I am," she confirmed, rubbing her foot against his calf.

Dag continued to study her, to read her expression as if real assurance could only be there.

And maybe he found what he was looking for, because after a moment he smiled a small smile and said, "And Rumson—you're sure you're done with him? It's over? Finished? History for you?"

"All of that."

He did more looking into her eyes, more of what she thought of as soul-searching, although it seemed as if it wasn't so much her soul he was searching now, but his own.

After another moment his smile grew and turned devilish. "If you change your mind, I'm gonna have to run naked through the snow to cool off."

She wanted him naked all right, but not in the snow.…

And her answer was to pull free the back half of his shirttails from his waistband and kiss him again, marveling at just how far her newly discovered wild side would go. Because she'd never taken any steps whatsoever to seduce another man and yet here she was…

With her thigh riding higher and higher on Dag's...

He was returning her kiss again but still cautiously. At least for a few minutes—maybe while he made up his own mind about the wisdom in this.

But then his mouth opened wide over hers once more, his tongue reclaimed hers with a vengeance, and that hand at her side went straight up to cup her breast, sending a tingle of delight to skitter across the surface of her skin.

That was when inhibitions flew out the window.

Shannon yanked the remainder of his shirt from his jeans and both of her hands crawled up the widening expanse of his back, pressing her palms to follow the highs and lows of muscle and bone and sinew.

When she reached his shoulders he broke away from kissing her long enough for her to pull his shirt off, and for one brief moment before he returned to that kiss, she got to see the glory that was a professional athlete's shoulders and biceps and broad, broad chest.

And even when he'd blocked her view, even when he'd drawn her into another wildly wet and wicked kiss, she could still run her hands all over that naked torso, glorying in the feel.

She hadn't had quite enough of that when, without warning, Dag tore his mouth from hers to do a quick repositioning that turned him to lie flat on his back on the sofa, lifting Shannon to sit atop him, straddling that portion of him that had apparently caused him problems last night and tonight offered only promise.

He unfastened the buttons of her sweater while she feasted on her second view of his bare chest and flat, honed stomach, running her hands from its center to his sides to absorb the sight and feel of him all at once, provoking him to arch his waist off the couch just enough that the hard ridge of him tantalized her even further.

Then off came her sweater, leaving her lacy, demi-cup bra and the upper swell of her breasts exposed to him.

She thought she would feel more shy than she did at that first loss of her own clothes but instead that wilder side took over once again. She basked in the heat of his dark eyes as they took their turn at feasting on her with an appreciation that brought a smile to his oh-so-ruggedly-handsome face.

But looking wasn't nearly as good as touching and with a little laugh, Dag pulled her down to kiss her again, rolling them both to their sides.

Somewhere along the way her bra had come unhooked and he tossed that aside, as well, giving himself free access. Free access that he used to best advantage as one mighty hand closed around her now-naked breast, kneading, caressing, massaging, causing a fresh wave of desire to erupt in her that was relayed in the pinpoint pebble her nipple became in his palm.

But last night there had been even more...

Even better...

And when his mouth abandoned hers so he could kiss a moist trail downward to take her breast that way again, she couldn't keep from greeting him with an arch of her spine and a soft moan.

Circling, flicking, nipping at her. Teasing her nipple with the faint tip of his tongue. Sucking hard, then soft, he brought things to life in her that were sweeter and more intense than she'd ever known.

His hands went to the button on her jeans, opening that, too, unzipping the zipper. He pulled her pants off, taking her stockings with them, while his tongue twirled around the outer edge of her navel, before his mouth found her other breast and occupied it with the same wonders.

That was when it occurred to her that she could have more of him, too. That his jeans could go the same way hers had.

She reached for his waistband button, finding so much more than she'd bargained for in the burgeoning behind that zipper that almost parted on its own when the button was undone.

With a little help from him, off went his jeans and socks, as well, and then he clasped her rear end in one hand big enough to cradle it and pulled her tight up against him.

But not so tight that she couldn't fit her hand between them to find that steely shaft and enclose it in her grip to make him groan with pleasure and pulse into her palm.

He abandoned her breast again and rediscovered her mouth with his, kissing her with a wide-open, seeking kiss as he shed her lacy panties.

Then he reached to the floor, fumbling among their discarded clothes until he found his jeans and took protection from his pocket. He returned to kissing her with a sexy playfulness while he put on the condom.

Once he had, he was moving her again. This time to lie on her back so he could come over her, between her legs that parted in invitation.

But it was more kisses that came first. Beginning at her knees, going up one thigh. He dropped a kiss at a spot just below her belly button and proceeded to leave a trail of them up her middle to her breasts again.

One after the other, he drew her straining, arousal-engorged breasts into his mouth, flicking his tongue to her nipples, using tender teeth to drive her to the brink of insanity with wanting so much more that she would be writhing beneath him.

And when she was, the body kisses began again, this time traveling up her breastbone to her throat, to her chin, to her mouth...

And at the same moment his tongue made an impertinent entrance, he slid into her down below, too, in one smooth movement that joined them as if there were no other, more perfect fit.

Shannon's body answered all on its own. Her spine arched from its lowest point, pulling her shoulders, her neck off the sofa in turn, before the full ripple washed through her and the pure force of having him inside her became a reality.

An incredible reality...

Only then did he begin to move—slowly at first, making it easy for her to follow his lead, building desire, anticipation, increasing speed and intensity until their mouths separated and just their bodies moved in perfect rhythm, perfect harmony, perfect communication. Faster and faster. Shannon clung to Dag's massive shoulders. His big hands were on either side of her head. His long, strong arms braced him above her. And with each thrust of his hips, each meeting of hers to his, each pitch that took him to the very core of her, passion mounted and grew. And grew...

Until things sprang to life in her that had never known life before, taking over, taking *her* over, embracing her to lift her higher and higher and higher still.

She could feel her own heartbeat racing. She could feel the power and strength in every muscle of Dag's body. She watched his own passion mounting in the tense lines of his sexy, sexy face until she couldn't keep her eyes open to see it as she reached that peak he was taking her to, a peak better than she'd known was possible. A peak that held her in an explosion of ecstasy that she'd never experienced the same way, with the same astounding, astonishing, breathtaking splendor that seemed to freeze her in time and space for that one blissful moment...

That one blissful moment that Dag suddenly burst into himself, plunging so deeply into her that it was more than a meeting, a matching, it was a union, a melding together of spirits and souls, a bonding that Shannon had also never experienced, that left her not only spent, not only satisfied and satiated, but a little dazed and dumbfounded by just how profound it had been...

Then Dag lowered himself to lie fully atop her, to kiss the side of her neck, to breathe warmth there and bring her back to earth, to herself, to a place where she could catch her own breath and tell herself it had just been some phenomenon of rapture...

"Wow..." Dag whispered in awe.

"Wow..." Shannon echoed the word and the sentiment. "That was something..."

Something she still couldn't fully fathom.

And maybe neither could he because for a brief while they just stayed the way they were, basking in the afterglow before he slipped out of her, rolled to his side and half covered her with his big body while he insinuated one arm under her, wrapped the other over her, and held her to him.

"Tell me I didn't hurt you," he asked then.

"You didn't," she answered, looking up at him, savoring the sight of his hair mussed more than usual, of the tiny lines that formed around the corners of his mouth when he smiled. A smile so sweet she couldn't keep from raising a hand to his cheek.

"Now tell me you want me to stay the night," he commanded.

"I want you to stay the night." She had no problem saying it because she couldn't imagine having him get up, dress and go. She couldn't imagine losing the warmth of his amazing body and getting into her bed tonight without him.

But now that neither of them was going to have to face that, Dag settled his chin on top of her head. She could feel fatigue weighing him down as he muttered, "Good. So good…and if you give me just a catnap, it can be good again…" he tantalized.

Shannon nuzzled into his neck and closed her eyes. "I guess we'll see," she taunted him.

"Oh, yeah, we'll see all right," he said as if he were accepting the challenge.

But accepting it or not, the arm that was across her stomach suddenly became slack enough to let her know that he'd fallen asleep, and Shannon closed her eyes, too.

She was warm and oh-so-comfortable there on the sofa, with Dag's big body partially her blanket, the fire still roaring and the Christmas lights shining down on them.

And in that moment that had its own special kind of perfection, she fell asleep, too.

Chapter 12

Every Christmas Eve, Northbridge held a non-denominational service at the church followed by a pot-luck supper in the church basement. Year after year, much of the town chose to spend that evening dressed in their finest, attending the event with their whole family. This year the Mackeys and the McKendricks planned to be among them.

To Dag that meant that he was going to be with Shannon again. But in advance of that, he slipped out of her apartment well before dawn and went to his house to work all day.

Had it been up to him, he would have spent the day the way he'd spent the previous night—with Shannon, making love, napping, making love again and again and again.

But he'd also seen the merit to Shannon's wish to keep

things private. So it wasn't until everyone was dressed and ready to leave for the Christmas Eve service that evening that he saw her again. And by then it had already been arranged that she would drive into town with Hadley, Chase and Cody.

Saying that he wanted his own vehicle at the church to allow himself the freedom to leave whenever he chose, Dag was left to follow behind Chase's car, watching Shannon through his windshield.

At the church they all filed into a pew—with Shannon separated from him by Chase and Hadley—and the most Dag could do was steal a few glimpses of Shannon during the service.

The service that spoke of gratitude and caused Dag to think how grateful he was to have met Shannon, to have had the night together that they'd had.

The service that spoke of counting blessings and making the best of every gift, and also brought Shannon to Dag's mind.

The service that spoke of rejoicing and celebrating and holding close what was most dear—and again it was only Shannon who Dag could think of in those terms.

When the service was over, they went into the church basement where there were so many people that Dag still didn't get a minute alone with Shannon. A minute to pull her into his arms the way he was itching to. To kiss her, to feel her body against his like he had so many times last night.

And now that the meal was finished, while everyone else mingled, Dag was sitting alone at the cafeteria table, nursing a glass of eggnog and watching Shannon.

Three-year-old Tia had taken her to the Christmas tree to show her the ornaments that Tia's preschool class had made. But when desserts were laid out on the buffet table, Tia abandoned Shannon to an elderly couple who Dag thought were likely talking to her about her late grandmother.

And all Dag could think was how beautiful Shannon was and that he wanted her so much it was almost driving him out of his mind...

She'd twisted her hair into a knot at the crown of her head and left the ends of it to spring out like a geyser. She was wearing a simple, long-sleeved white mohair knit dress that skimmed her curves and wrapped the column of her neck in a high-standing turtleneck. The hem of her dress ended just above her knees and from there Dag's gaze followed shapely legs to the three-inch high heels that he couldn't help picturing her wearing with nothing else at all—something he thought he might be able to persuade her to actually do now that he'd discovered a hint of a daring streak in her. A hint of a daring streak that he took great pleasure in bringing out in her.

But then there were so many things he took great pleasure in bringing out in her. So many things he just took pleasure in when he was with her.

Everything, in fact...

Gratitude and counting blessings and cherishing gifts and rejoicing and celebrating and holding close what was most dear...

The sentiments of the service came back to him then, making him recall that it had been Shannon he'd counted as a blessing, Shannon he'd been grateful for, cherished and rejoiced and celebrated in. Shannon he'd mentally held close and dear...

And it struck him that the things he'd felt making love to Shannon had been unlike anything he'd ever come across with anyone else. What he'd felt since then, what he'd felt all through the church service, what he felt at that moment, wasn't anything he'd ever felt before, either. Not even with Sandra. Not with anyone.

But the day after Christmas, Shannon was leaving...

And suddenly that became an unbearable thought.

How the hell had he come to that? he asked himself as it struck him just how unbearable a thought her leaving was. How had he gone from believing she was engaged, from knowing to steer clear of her not only because of the other guy in her life but also because she wanted bigger and better things than he could offer, to this? To wanting her so much he would have gladly faced another five men—all of them with crowbars this time—if it meant he could end up with her?

Now *that* was crazy!

But somehow it was true.

And as that fact sunk in, Dag had to face it.

He wanted Shannon Duffy.

And not just in bed.

He wanted Shannon Duffy in his life. Constantly and continuously. Permanently. In his life, by his side, as close as he could get her every minute from now until the end of time...

That beautiful woman in white...

Who was more recently out of a relationship with another man than Sandra had been—a man Sandra had ended up with after all.

That beautiful woman in white who wanted a bigger life—much like his mother had always wanted more...

Maybe I'm just the dumbest idiot who ever lived, he thought as he reminded himself of the two reasons he'd known from the beginning not to get involved with Shannon.

Two penalties, he told himself, in a game he swore had to be squeaky-clean for him to ever play again…

And yet something caused him to balk at thinking of Shannon in terms of infractions—hockey or otherwise. Shannon was too good for that. She was generous and kind and funny and sweet and caring.

Did she want a life that had more to offer than she'd known growing up? Than she'd known through the course of taking care of ailing parents?

She did, but Dag understood that. And he couldn't fault her for it. He'd wanted to play hockey and he hadn't let anything hold him back. Good parents or not, Shannon could well have done the same thing. But she hadn't. And now that she was free to do more, to have more of the kind of life she wanted? He couldn't hold it against her that she was determined to do that.

Plus there wasn't anything in what she wanted, anything about Shannon that was really like his mother—it wasn't as if Shannon put on airs or thought she was better than anyone, she just wanted a bigger bite of life. And he thought she deserved that. If anyone deserved that, it was someone who had done as much caring for and sacrificing for other people as Shannon had.

But if he thought that she deserved a bigger bite of life, he couldn't be the one to ask her not to take it, he told himself.

Because that's what it would cost her if he tried to keep her by his side, in his life, as close as he could get her every minute until the end of time.

It meant asking her to sacrifice what she wanted again.

Unless he did the sacrificing…

It took him a moment to accept that as potentially another way to go. And another, longer moment to consider it.

He could change his own course for her...

Surprisingly, that wasn't so difficult a thing to imagine once it had occurred to him. It was a lot easier to think about that than about her walking away the day after tomorrow and his never seeing her again.

But here he was, thinking about throwing his own plans out the window, about making a significant—a *huge*—alteration in his own life, without knowing how she felt.

And that was a very big deal.

Because it was the feelings that really mattered, he reminded himself. Shannon had turned down three proposals because her feelings for those other guys weren't strong enough, because they hadn't matched up to what her parents had felt for each other. If she wasn't feeling anything for him that was as strong as what he was feeling for her...

Dag stalled. He couldn't think beyond that.

He couldn't entertain *any* thought beyond that one, now that that one had come into his head—*did* Shannon have feelings for him? And if she did, were they the kind of feelings he had for her? The kind her parents had shared that had made them content to live any sort of life as long as they lived it together?

Until he knew what was going on with Shannon, where he stood, everything else was inconsequential. He *had* to know....

And he had to know now!

He got up from the table and crossed the room to her, grateful that when he reached her the conversation she was having with the elderly couple was ending with them wishing her a merry Christmas and moving on.

Grateful, too, that when she saw him, when her luminous blue-green eyes met his, her expression seemed to light up.

"Any chance we might slip out of here?" he asked without segue.

Shannon seemed more intrigued than surprised by that idea—which he was glad to see. "Think anyone will notice?" she asked.

"I don't care if they do," he confessed, hearing the note of urgency in his own voice but not caring about that, either.

"Okay," Shannon said with a smile he'd seen several times the night before, a smile that let him know she thought it was something other than talk that he had in mind for them.

But if all went well, talking could only be the beginning, so he didn't elaborate. Instead he nodded in the direction of the doors and that was where they went.

No one noticed them as Dag helped Shannon on with her coat, threw his on, too, and then ushered her out into the cold where a light, fluffy snow had started to fall.

He was parked in a nearby spot in the church lot and they hurried to it.

"This was a long day," Shannon said as he held the passenger door open for her and helped her into the truck.

"Way, way too long," he agreed emphatically, not sure she meant what he did—that the day had dragged by because he hadn't been with her...

Once Shannon was settled, he shut the door and rushed around the front end of the truck, nearly bounding behind the wheel and starting the engine. Then he put it into gear and headed out, deciding as he did that he wasn't going to beat around the bush.

So, with a glance in her direction, he said, "I missed you so much today that I screwed up everything I tried to do. I nearly ran into the back of Chase's car tonight following you here because I was looking at you instead of the taillights. I haven't been able to take my eyes off you all night and while I was doing that I figured something out. I figured out what I want for Christmas."

"I hope it's what I got you, because I don't think there's any twenty-four-hour shopping in Northbridge," Shannon joked.

But Dag merely looked over at her and said, "I want you, Shannon."

Her eyebrows formed two perfect arches over her eyes and he could see that she didn't know what to say. But that was okay. He'd known this would shock her. It shocked him. But that didn't deter him. In fact he liked that he knew her well enough already to have predicted this response and it just made him smile.

"How long did your parents know each other before they realized what they had together?" he asked.

"My father said it was love-at-first-sight for him. My mother said it took her ten or fifteen minutes. But I think that was a joke…"

"Maybe it wasn't…"

Dag had to look back at the road, but he went on talking. "Here's how it is for me—I love Northbridge, I really do. I love Northbridge as much as I loved hockey. Knowing the end of my career would put me back here was the only thing that got me through. But now there's you and I have to tell you that when I think about being anywhere in the world—including Northbridge—*without* you, it isn't where I want to be."

Another glance at her showed him the perplexed expression on her face, but still he was undaunted.

"What we've had since we met hasn't been like anything I've ever had with anyone else—there's never been this kind of instant connection, as if I've stumbled into the one person I was honestly intended to be with. You know what you said about the guys in your life? About how part of what told you they were wrong for you was that you didn't care when you *didn't* see them?"

"I remember..."

"Well, I never realized it before, but the same has been true for me with every other woman in my life. Until you."

He had to brake for a stop sign and, despite the fact that there wasn't any traffic to keep him there, he stayed so he could look at her again to say, "I wasn't kidding when I said I hate not seeing you for even an hour—I *hate* it. There's never been this... I'm not even sure how to put it... This feeling like nothing really matters unless I'm doing it with you. Or for you. And then there was last night...last night was off the Richter scale."

He watched her smile just barely, as if the memory of their night together was so remarkable for her, too, that she couldn't help it. And that gave him the courage to say, "I think it's been the same for you..."

He finally drove on, giving her a moment to tell him that he was wrong, that she didn't have feelings that were anything like what he was describing.

But instead, in a quiet voice, she said, "It has been different for me than anything has ever been with anyone else. But—"

"I know," he said to stop her, guessing what she was going to say. "You want a bigger life than Northbridge has to offer. And you should have it. So I've been thinking, and if you want to be the first woman on Mars, I'm willing to be the first man—if that's what it takes to be with you. If you decide to invest in your friend's school and live and work in Beverly Hills, I'll see if I can coach hockey somewhere there—"

"You just bought my grandmother's house!"

"And I'll turn around and sell it. The point is, Shannon, what I realized tonight is that the only thing that matters to me—that truly matters—is that I want you. I want to be with you. I want to live whatever kind of life makes you happy, because the only thing that's going to make me honestly, genuinely happy, too, is you. Anywhere. Living with wild monkeys, if that's what you want. As long as I'm with you…"

The words were hanging in the air as Dag turned onto the road that led to Logan and Meg's place. But that was when both Dag and Shannon spotted a black limousine up ahead, already parked beside the big farmhouse. A black limousine that certainly didn't belong there. And abruptly put everything else on hold.

Dag hit the brakes purely out of reflex, knowing instantly that there was only one person who was likely to have come to Northbridge in a limousine on Christmas Eve.

"That can't be…" he muttered darkly to himself.

"Wes," Shannon said, giving voice to Dag's worst thoughts.

Wes Rumson.

In what Dag had no doubt was a grand gesture.

And even if this one didn't come with a crowbar, Dag thought it couldn't have hit him any harder.

The other guy from Shannon's so-recent past.

The guy Shannon had said she was finished with.

And Dag couldn't help wondering if it was possible that he'd made the same mistake twice—that Shannon wasn't as finished with Rumson as she'd said. That a grand gesture from the rich politician might sway her still...

"Can I turn us around and go the other way?" Dag joked feebly.

"If it's Wes, I'll have to see him."

"*If?* Who else is it gonna be?"

And what else is the politician going to do but pull out all the stops to get you to say you'll marry him...

Dag really was tempted to jam his truck into Reverse and back the hell out of that drive. Sweep Shannon away. Make *that* grand gesture.

But he resisted the urge, knowing if she was determined to hear out the other guy, there was no stopping it.

He took his foot off the brake and went the rest of the way up the drive, reaching the limo right about the time Wes Rumson got out the back of it—tall and straight, dressed in a suit and tie underneath a custom-tailored overcoat, looking as if he were ready to take the governor's chair right then.

Dag pulled to a second stop beside him and Shannon rolled down her window.

"What are you doing here, Wes?" she asked, not sounding thrilled to see him, but also not perturbed or angry—the way Dag would have preferred. And probably not knowing that that alone was like a sucker punch.

"I came to talk to you," the politician said as if he'd

just driven around the block rather than from his family's estate in Billings.

Shannon didn't jump at that and Dag took some comfort in what he interpreted as hesitancy. But then she said, "I'm staying in the apartment around back. You can follow us."

"Right behind you," Wes Rumson said as if it had been an engraved invitation he was expecting and entitled to. Then he ducked into the limo's rear seat and Shannon rolled up the window again.

And Dag just sat there, fighting so many inclinations that he knew he couldn't act on.

But Shannon was looking at him again, her brow furrowed once more, and rather than reassuring him, she said a simple, "I'm sorry."

That Rumson is here? That you're dropping me flat to talk to him? Or that you can't say yes to me, either...

Dag didn't know. And there was no time to ask. And even if there was, was this really the best moment to force her into a corner?

Dag knew it wasn't, so he merely raised his chin in answer to her apology—whatever it was for—and drove around to the garage, followed by that damn black limousine.

Without another word, Shannon got out of the truck at the foot of the apartment steps, and Dag watched her lead the politician up those same stairs he'd been climbing with her every other night. The politician—the man—who wanted her, too. Who could offer her more than he could. Who she must have had feelings for in one way or another. Who she might still have feelings enough for to take what he was offering after all...

And that was when Dag felt something that hit him harder than any beating he'd ever taken. On the ice or off.

Dazed and confused—that was how Shannon felt as she turned on the apartment's lights and took off her coat. First there had been all that Dag had stunned her by saying. Now Wes. She was having trouble gathering her wits.

But Wes was standing just inside the door, taking off his own coat as if she'd asked him to, and she had to deal with him. So she pushed aside what Dag had said and turned to face her former non-fiancé.

"It's Christmas Eve and you drove all the way to Northbridge?" she said when Wes hadn't taken the lead.

"I wanted to see you. To talk to you."

"And you had Herbert drive you? Didn't he want to be with his family—his *kids*—tonight?"

"I'm paying him well. If I'd driven myself I would have wasted the time. Instead I was able to work on my next speech while he drove—that is his job."

Shannon was thinking about the three kids the driver had shown her pictures of and of them not having their father with them tonight of all nights because Wes's work came first. For Wes at least.

Not to mention that even as he'd been coming to see her, she hadn't been what he was actually focusing on.

"I'm still not sure why you're here, Wes," Shannon said.

The tall, impressive politician stepped nearer and took a velvet ring box from his pocket. "I thought maybe a private Christmas Eve proposal might be welcomed with a little more favor," he said, opening the box to reveal the biggest diamond Shannon had ever seen.

But even dazzled by the diamond, Shannon thought

that this was nothing but another tack he was taking. A retry that had the earmarks of a new strategy he and his cousin had devised.

Or maybe coming after what Dag had just said to her—full of so much emotion, so much passion—this just sounded rehearsed and superficial. Either way, it wouldn't have swayed her even before all that Dag had said on the drive home.

She shook her head, wondering how many times she was going to have to turn this man down to get him to accept that she wouldn't marry him. "The *way* you propose, the timing, whether it's public or private—those aren't the reasons I won't marry you, Wes. I told you—"

"Yes, you did tell me. But I think you're mistaken, Shannon. We may not have the mirror image of what your parents had, but we're not so bad together. I know people who have much less to build on than we do and they make perfectly successful pairings. We get along, we can always find something to talk about, we have things in common, we both want to make our mark—"

"You want to make your mark. I just want—"

"I know what you want. But how much bigger can your life be than as the wife of the governor? As maybe the wife of a president some day? And you can make your mark, too. You can push education—*I'll* push education, it's a popular topic and with you being a teacher, you can do great things for the state, for the country. We make a good team."

"And you love me so much you can't live without me," she said facetiously, as if she were feeding him the line he should have used.

"I do love you, Shannon," he contended. "You know

that. Maybe not the way you think your father loved your mother—"

"It isn't something *I think,* it's something I know."

"Still, I care for you. The same way any normal husband cares for his wife. We could have a lifelong, fruitful marriage. Kids. And you'd never again have to spend a Christmas Eve, a Christmas, alone like this, without family."

"That's why you're really here now, isn't it?" Shannon said as it dawned on her. "You came because you thought I'd be at a particularly low point tonight, tomorrow. That I'd be vulnerable…" Not because he wanted to make this first holiday after the loss of her family easier for her, not because he wanted to make sure she was all right. But to use what he'd hoped might be a weak moment to his own advantage.

She considered telling him just how not-alone she'd been since arriving in Northbridge, or tonight, how not-alone she would be tomorrow with Chase and Hadley and Cody and Meg and Logan and Tia. And Dag… But it didn't seem worth it, so she merely repeated, "No, Wes, I won't marry you."

"I just don't understand you, Shannon," he said curtly, sounding frustrated and aggravated that this play still hadn't accomplished his goal. "We've been involved for a long time. We've talked about marriage. Your parents are gone so there's not that holding you back. You've said you want more out of life and I'm here offering that. Get your head out of the clouds and let's be realistic—you idealized your parents' relationship. You made it some sort of storybook love that nothing can live up to—"

"In all the time we've known each other, Wes, you

only met my parents twice. You don't know what kind of relationship they had."

And Shannon knew that he was right when he'd said he didn't understand her because he genuinely didn't. He didn't understand why there was absolutely no temptation, no appeal in this passionless *Bigger Life* that he was offering.

But she wasn't even slightly tempted by it. Despite the fact that he was Wes Rumson, that he was impeccably dressed, handsome, cultured, intelligent, wealthy, well respected. Despite the fact that they *had* had a pleasant-enough, enjoyable-enough relationship that had met some of her needs.

It just didn't matter to her because she hadn't had even the tiniest thrill when she'd first seen his limousine, the tiniest thrill at thinking that he'd come all the way from Billings on Christmas Eve just for her. She certainly didn't want to run into his arms. She wasn't aching to have him touch her, kiss her—everything that came instantly with every thought, every glimpse of Dag.

Dag, whom she'd had to leave hanging…

"Go home, Wes," she advised then. "Go back to Billings to be with your own family, let Herbert get to his. This—you and I—just wasn't meant to be. I might vote for you, but I won't marry you."

Wes snapped closed the ring box like the jaws of an alligator and put it back in his jacket pocket. "I don't think you know what you want."

He was right about that, too, because it wasn't as if she was ready to rush to Dag and accept all he'd laid out for her either…

"But I know what I *don't* want," she said quietly.

Wes remained with his pale brown eyes boring into

her from beneath a fierce frown, shaking his head. Then he put his coat back on, all the while watching her as if he thought she'd gone out of her mind.

"Once I announce this publicly we're through—you know that?" he warned. "The polls may like you now, but yo-yoing would cost me votes."

And she wasn't worth the loss to him.

"I know, Wes. Just make the announcement and get it over with."

"We could have had a good thing, Shannon. I hope you don't regret this."

"I'm sorry, Wes," was her only response, the second apology she'd made in the last half hour.

And it brought back to mind the first one she'd made as Wes cast her a final glare and walked out of the apartment—it brought Dag back to mind.

And all he'd said.

And all she really needed to think about.

Chapter 13

Almost the moment that Wes Rumson was out of sight, he was out of Shannon's mind, replaced with thoughts of Dag. And the things Dag had been in the process of saying to her on the way home from the church.

Because those things had been monumental.

Dag was willing to give up everything for her....

She hadn't fully grasped it at the time but as she re-hashed it all in her head, she began to realize that that really was what he'd been saying. Offering.

He was willing to live any life she wanted to live. Anywhere. He was even willing to sell the house he'd just bought from her, to follow her to Beverly Hills, if she decided that was what she wanted.

Her grandmother had left her own life behind to help Shannon care for her parents. But other than that, no one else—certainly no man—had ever been willing to do anything that big for her. All three of the other men who had proposed to her had wanted her on their terms and their terms alone.

Because Dag had been so convincing, because his words had been so heartfelt, she didn't doubt that he'd meant what he'd said, that he *would* give up his house, Northbridge, his plans for his future, for her.

The way she knew her dad would have given up anything and everything for her mom…

And after Wes had stood there only moments before, basically telling her that she was a dreamer to think she could ever find something like that, that she should just settle and accept what Wes believed most people had, Dag's sacrifice stood out as even greater.

But he hadn't said it was any sacrifice at all. Dag had said only that he was willing to do whatever it took to be with her because she was what he wanted.

Which *was* the way her parents had felt.

And maybe it was time to stop ignoring her own feelings, she told herself. To stop locking them up and keeping them at bay, stop telling herself that everything that was going on with Dag was a lark, and take a look at what she actually did feel for him.

Realizing she was still standing in the middle of the living room, Shannon went to sit down. She looked at the sofa, at the floor between the sofa and the fireplace. At the hearth. At the spots where she and Dag had ended up so many evenings since they'd met. Talking. Joking. Laughing. Kissing. Making love…

Seeing it all in her mind somehow helped to set free her feelings for him. To experience them with a clear head rather than in the uncontrollable bursts that had come in the heat of the moment. Uncontrollable bursts that she'd followed by hiding those feelings from herself again as soon as she could get them back under control.

And the power of those feelings was a little startling when they washed over her unrestricted, and undistracted.

Yes, she'd been aware of the fact that every minute she hadn't been with him she'd been thinking about him, watching the clock, counting the hours that would have to pass before she could see him again and wishing the time would go faster.

Yes, she'd been aware of a sense of contentment, of completion, of safety and security whenever she'd been with him.

Yes, she'd been aware that everything she'd done, everything she'd experienced, every food she'd eaten, every Christmas song she'd heard when she was with him had seemed to have a special, improved quality to it.

Yes, she'd been aware that she'd just felt happier whenever she was with him. Happier than she ever remembered feeling before. That she'd even been able to deal better with the moments when grief had paid her a return visit, she'd been able to talk about her parents and her grandmother with Dag without feeling as devastated by the loss. She'd been able to visit her grandmother's house and remember mainly good things.

But for some reason she hadn't associated any of that with having *feelings* for Dag.

And now she knew that—of course—that was where it had all come from.

Knowing that now, when she thought again about what he'd said on the way home, she suddenly couldn't deny that she felt all the same things he'd said he felt. That nothing seemed more important than being with him.

That anything and everything seemed more manageable if she had him by her side. That there wasn't a single thing she could think of that she didn't want to share with him.

The way her parents had felt about each other...

Her jaw actually dropped a little when that struck her.

Was it possible that she actually *had* found with Dag what her parents had had?

Maybe a small part of her had worried that what Wes had said tonight might be true—that she was searching for, holding out for, something unrealistic or idealized. Or at least, unattainable. But suddenly she knew that wasn't true. Because what she felt for Dag was exactly what she'd seen in her parents' feelings for each other. It *did* exist. And she was in the throes of it.

She was in the throes of it so firmly, so deeply, so intensely that she understood Dag's willingness to give up Northbridge, his house, his plans, to be with her.

The problem was, she was too firmly, too deeply, too intensely in the throes of it to feel as if she could let him do that...

But if she didn't?

If she said yes to Dag but didn't let him give up everything for her, then she was saying yes to Northbridge, too. To living in her grandmother's house. To a life that might have more open air than an apartment over a shoe repair shop, but that would be lived in a place that wasn't even as big as Billings.

She'd be saying yes to a life that was, in some ways, even smaller than the life she'd known before.

And then what?

Would she end up feeling the way Dag's mother had? Isolated and unfulfilled and as if she was missing out?

That gave her some pause.

But then she began to think about Northbridge and what she'd discovered here. What she could have here over and above Dag.

She'd come to the small town feeling sad and alone, feeling disconnected. But all of that had gone away, because while Northbridge might not be large, it still had so much to offer. Such warm and caring and kind and fun-loving people who had embraced her, who had made her feel a part of things as well as a stronger connection with her grandmother's memory.

And in Northbridge she had a brother, a sister-in-law, a nephew. She had the beginnings of a tenuous relationship with her other two brothers. The thought of staying to cultivate all of that actually felt better to her than any of the thoughts she'd had about Beverly Hills, about risking her friendship with Dani by becoming business partners.

The plain truth, she finally realized, was exactly what Dag had said he felt about her. The most important thing to her was him. Being with him. But being with him in Northbridge had an appeal all its own and she knew deep down that she could be okay with that. With a lifetime of living here. If she always had Dag….

Which was what she suddenly knew without a doubt that she wanted. What she had to have. Right now!

But it hadn't been early when she and Dag had left the church. Topping that off with Wes's visit and then with all the thinking she'd just done since, and the evening was gone—it was very late and she knew that Dag couldn't be alone anymore, that Logan, Meg and Tia had to have come home a while ago.

She went to the window that looked onto the back of the main house. The room Dag was staying in faced the front, so she had no way of knowing if he was still awake or not, but in the rear of the house the only light on was in Meg and Logan's bedroom upstairs. And that went out a few seconds later, warning her that it was likely that by now everyone was in bed.

She hated that she'd left Dag the way she had, after the things he'd said to her, without anything but an apology for Wes's unwelcome appearance. And she couldn't imagine that Dag was thinking anything good or he would have been watching for Wes to leave and would have come to the apartment.

She could try his cell phone but she didn't want to do that. She wanted to see him. To see his face when she told him what she had to tell him. To have him wrap his arms around her and let her know he forgave her for running out on the most important thing he might ever have to say to her.

The doors to Logan and Meg's house all had keyless locks and she had the combination to the one on the back door—Meg had given it to her just in case she'd needed to get in at some point when they were gone. And even though Meg and Logan weren't gone, Shannon decided that she definitely needed to get in.

So without bothering with her coat, Shannon went out the apartment door, into the gently falling snow and across the yard.

The combination to the lock was easy and she punched it in quickly, instantly gaining access to the dark, silent house and feeling like a cat burglar as she went through the kitchen to the staircase that took her up to the bedrooms.

The bedrooms formed a semicircle around a large landing at the top of the stairs and Shannon forgot that there was a table just to the left of the steps. So when she turned in that direction she hit it, shoving it with a bang against the wooden railing.

She caught hold of it in a hurry to keep it from toppling over or making any more noise but apparently that had been noise enough, because just then from Tia's room came the three-year-old's voice.

"Santa?" she exclaimed.

In a panic, Shannon was about to dash back down the stairs to get out of sight when the door to the guest room opened. A surprised Dag registered that she was there, grabbed her wrist to pull her into his room, and—in his deep Santa voice—said, "Ho, ho, ho, little girls have to be asleep to get presents…"

Then he softly closed the door again.

He'd spun Shannon into the center of the bedroom and she watched him listen with his ear to the door for a moment to make sure his niece didn't take it any further. She couldn't help smiling at his quick thinking and impromptu acting. And at the sight of him shirtless, in a pair of sweatpants that dipped below his navel and made her shiver just a little with how sexy he looked.

But she wasn't sure if any of that was appropriate under the circumstances, so she forced a sober expression onto her face as Dag turned to her.

And the questioning challenge in his raised eyebrows let her know there were, indeed, more solemn things to deal with.

"I wondered if you were still here," he said.

"Where else would I be?"

"On your way to Christmas with the Rumsons?"

Shannon shook her head. "There was never a chance of that," she assured.

"There was if the guy had convinced you to marry him after all."

"There was never a chance of that, either. But at least I think Wes has accepted it now and he'll finally make the announcement that we aren't engaged." She paused a moment and then said, "Are you and I?"

That made Dag laugh involuntarily. And slightly forlornly. "Engaged? I don't know. I did a lot of talking. All I got from you was an *I'm sorry* before you hopped out of my truck to run off with that other guy."

"I don't remember any hopping or running," she pointed out.

"It must have just seemed like it to me."

"And you weren't even watching to see if I went off with him?"

"Couldn't. I knew I wouldn't be able to stand it if I had to see that."

"So you were just up here, going to bed?"

"I was just up here pacing and wondering and worrying and hating the hell out of the fact that there *was* another guy...."

"Maybe this time you should be glad there was," she told him then. "I've been comparing the two of you since we met. Not on purpose, it just seemed to keep happening. And Wes Rumson came up short every single time."

"Even with all the money and power and a *much* bigger life to offer you?"

"None of that matters. And neither do a lot of other things—like Beverly Hills..."

She watched his expression turn curious. And maybe cautiously optimistic. But before he could say anything she told him what she'd been thinking about since Wes had left tonight, the realizations she'd had, the decisions and conclusions she'd come to.

When she'd said her piece, she added, "So I don't know if what you were saying on the way home tonight was a proposal—"

"That's where it was headed. Number four for you."

"Well, I think this is the one I can say yes to...."

He frowned.

Shannon hadn't expected that and felt some uncertainty herself suddenly.

Then Dag said, "I just want to be clear—you're saying yes to me, but no to Beverly Hills with or without me?"

"I told you when we talked about it that I had my doubts. I've told Dani that. I still had doubts about it, even thinking that you would come with me, that I wouldn't be doing it alone. But Northbridge? It's sort of grown on me, and I don't have any doubts about living here, maybe teaching kindergarten here if I can...."

"And you're okay living in your grandmother's house?"

"We can make it our house, can't we?"

He finally smiled. "Yellow paint it is—warm and homey and sunny," he said, repeating her words from when she'd visited the house and they'd talked about whether he should paint the outside of the place white or return it to its original yellow.

And as if that settled everything, he pulled her into his arms then, kissing her the way she'd been craving to have him kiss her all day, all evening, certainly since finding him shirtless.

But the kiss didn't last long before he let go of her, yanked on a pullover hooded sweatshirt and then took her hand.

"Let's go where we don't have to worry about waking anybody," he suggested as he led her out of the guest room.

They moved quietly through the dark house—with Dag making one quick stop to snatch a present from under the tree—before they retraced Shannon's path to put them back at the apartment. There, Dag crossed his arms over his middle and instantly peeled off the sweatshirt.

And once he had, he pulled her to him again, kissing her a second time as if he'd been too long away from her lips.

Shannon had no resistance to him and let her hands do as they pleased, pressing to his naked chest, up and over his shoulders to his broad, hard back.

Everything else fell away then, along with Shannon's clothes and those sweatpants that Dag had on. Still kissing her, Dag picked her up and carried her to the bed where they made love with an urgency that said even mere hours of separation had been too much.

An urgency to reclaim what they'd discovered the night before, to stake a new and permanent claim now, with hands that caressed and teased and delighted, with mouths that clung together or broke apart to do amazing things elsewhere, with every inch of their bodies coming together as seamlessly as if one was split apart from the other long ago and had finally been reunited with its mate.

Together they reached an even more profound pinnacle that left Shannon drained and weak and limp in Dag's powerful arms as he rolled them both to their sides, cradling her, brushing her hair away from her face so he could look down into her eyes.

"I love you," he said then, for the first time.

"I love you, too," Shannon could answer without the slightest hesitancy. "With all my heart and soul."

"I want you to know that I won't let our life be small, even if we do live it here. I'll make sure it's a full one, and that you are always the biggest part of it for me—if that matters."

It mattered enough to bring moisture to her eyes that she had to blink back.

"We can still go to Beverly Hills, visit your friend, see her school, you know," he offered then, obviously again thinking of her, putting her ahead of himself.

"I'd like that. I'd like for Dani to meet you. And you to meet Dani."

"And if you change your mind and want to stay—"

"I won't," she said without the shadow of a doubt. "I really did fall in love with this place and the people here."

"Are you just using me to get your house back so you can move to Northbridge?" he joked.

"Yep," she answered glibly, tightening her muscles around him. "I'm just using you."

He slipped out of her then and left the bed long enough to retrieve the small package he'd taken from beneath Meg and Logan's tree.

Bringing it back, he kept hold of it until he was lying with Shannon beside him, in his arms again.

Only then did he hand it to her.

"Merry Christmas."

"You want me to open it now?"

"I do."

It wasn't easy in that position, but Shannon managed, opening a box that contained a very delicate chain.

"It's for your grandmother's ring," Dag explained. "You said—"

"That I would get a chain for it and wear it around my neck. And you remembered that?"

"It was part of what I went into town for yesterday."

She really did love this man....

"Thank you," Shannon said.

"Thank *you*."

"For?"

"For my Christmas gift."

"I haven't given it to you yet," she reminded, thinking of the cashmere sweater that was still under Meg and Logan's tree since that was where gift-opening was slated to occur in the morning.

"You gave me my gift," Dag insisted, taking the box that held the necklace and setting it on the nightstand. "I told you it was you I wanted."

"Oh, *that* Christmas gift," Shannon said. "I guess you're welcome, then."

"You don't ever have to give me anything else," he whispered in a husky voice. "Well, except maybe a couple of kids?"

"I can't promise them for Christmas, but I'll see what I can do."

He chuckled just a little, but Shannon saw his eyes drift closed as if they were too heavy to keep open, and she could feel him relaxing, falling asleep.

"I know—you need a nap," she said, guessing what he was about to tell her.

"Somebody kept me up almost the whole night last night."

"And you didn't get much sleep, either..."

He laughed, but he really was fading, and Shannon opted for giving in to her own fatigue.

She settled her head on his bare chest and closed her eyes, too, snuggling into Dag, knowing from the previous night that she would only nap for an hour or so before he would wake her with feathery kisses and everything would start again.

And just the prospect of that made her smile against him and marvel at how very, very much she loved him.

So much that she knew without question that living whatever kind of life, whatever size of life they ended up living, would be perfect as long as they were together.

Because now that her feelings for him were unbound, they were boundless, and that was what really mattered— not the life she led or where she led it, but who she got to share it with.

Just the way it had been for her parents.

Just the way she'd always wanted for herself.

And just what she'd found with Dag.

* * * * *

KRISTI GOLD

Since her first venture into novel writing in the
midnineties, Kristi Gold has greatly enjoyed
weaving stories of love and commitment. She's
an avid fan of baseball, beaches and bridal
reality shows. During her career, Kristi has been
a National Readers' Choice Award winner, an
RT Book Reviews Award winner and a three-time
Romance Writers of America RITA® Award
finalist. She resides in central Texas and can be
reached through her website at kristigold.com.

Be sure to look for more Harlequin books from
Kristi Gold!

THE SON HE NEVER KNEW
Kristi Gold

To all the men and women in the armed forces
who sacrifice daily to keep the world safe.

And to those who have made the ultimate
sacrifice—giving their lives.

Prologue

He was the last person she expected to see at her dorm room doorstep.

As soon as the initial shock disappeared, Jessica Keller squealed with delight, hurled herself into Chase Reed's arms and hugged him hard. But when his frame went stiff as steel, she stepped back to assess her best friend's mood.

In the eight months since she'd seen him, he hadn't changed at all, at least when it came to his appearance. He still wore his golden hair in close-cropped military style, still wore sand-colored camouflage fatigues and heavy boots. Six-feet-three-inches of prime fourth-generation soldier, exactly what he'd always wanted to be and now was. Yet something in his brown eyes seemed different, maybe a little more intense, but definitely different. Then again, after the Towers fell three months ago, the whole world had changed forever.

"What are you doing here this time of night?" she asked when he failed to speak or smile.

"We have to talk."

Chase sounded so serious, Jess's anxiety took a major leap right behind her imagination. "Is something wrong with Mom and Dad? Your mom and dad? Or is it—"

"Calm down, Jess," he said in the reassuring tone she'd grown to expect and sometimes resent. "Everyone's fine. If you'll let me in, I'll explain." He leaned to his right and looked behind her. "Unless I'm interrupting."

She frowned at his assumption. "My roommate's already gone home for the holidays, so there's no one here but little old me."

"Are you sure you're not hiding your boyfriend in the closet?" Chase followed the query with a visual sweep down her body and back up again, much the same as she'd done to him a few minutes earlier.

A second passed before Jess realized why he might think he'd intruded on an intimate interlude. She'd answered the door wearing a tattered white terry robe, her favorite furry pink slippers and not much else.

She twisted her damp hair in a knot at her neck and sent him a dirty look. "I finished a shift at the coffee shop an hour ago and I just took a shower, so get your mind out of the sewer. Besides, the university doesn't take too kindly to boys visiting girls in their rooms after 9:00 p.m."

He looked totally skeptical. "You mean to tell me Dalton hasn't been up here after hours?"

Her long-time boyfriend happened to be a sore subject she didn't care to discuss with Chase, especially under the current circumstances. "Let's leave him out of this, okay?"

"Not a problem. He's my least favorite topic of conversation anyway. And if you're worried about breaking the rules, we can go somewhere else to talk."

"Don't be ridiculous, Chase," she said. "It's almost eleven, it's cold outside and my hair's wet. Besides, the place is pretty much cleared out. However, if you'd called me in advance, I could have saved you the trip. I planned to be back in Placid tomorrow after work."

"This couldn't wait until tomorrow."

In order to unravel the mystery, Jess stepped aside and made a sweeping gesture with one arm. "Welcome to my humble abode, heavy emphasis on *humble*."

Chase breezed past her and after Jess closed the door, she turned to find that he made her tiny room seem even tinier. She tightened the robe's sash, feeling somewhat naked even though she was sufficiently covered. "Now tell me what couldn't wait until tomorrow, Mr. Army Man."

Chase strolled between the two twin beds and picked up a photo of Dalton from the nightstand. "Where's the demon tonight?"

The "pet" name Chase had given her high school sweetheart grated on Jess's nerves. "I have no idea where he is because right now we're taking a break."

His gaze snapped to hers. "Permanent break, I hope."

She wasn't the least bit surprised by his comment. Chase and Dalton had been embroiled in one-upmanship since elementary school. "Right now I don't know what's going to happen."

His scowl returned. "So you didn't get engaged?"

Suddenly it became all too clear to her why Chase had shown up unannounced. "You've been talking to Rachel."

He set the frame down carefully though he looked as

if he wanted to hurl it. "Yeah. I ran into her yesterday at the diner. She told me the Big D proposed and I figured since she's his sister, she should know."

Dalton had done more than simply propose. He'd offered to whisk her away to Vegas over the Christmas holidays for a quickie wedding. She opted to keep that little tidbit to herself. "I told him I wasn't sure I was ready to get married, and he said to let him know when I made up my mind. In the meantime, he doesn't want to see me."

Chase gave her a champion smirk. "You mean he's blackmailing you into saying yes."

Jess gritted her teeth and spoke through them. "Would you cut him some slack, Chase? We're not kids anymore and this whole competition thing between you and Dalton is getting old."

"Maybe we aren't kids, but my guess is Dalton hasn't changed, Jess. You haven't always seen the side of him that we have."

We as in him. Same song, fiftieth verse. "I know Dalton better than anyone. I also know he'd never do anything to hurt me."

He stared at the ceiling for a moment before bringing his attention back to her. "Fine. I'll drop it for now. But I need you to promise me something."

Jess hugged her arms close to her middle. "That depends on the promise."

"First, I want you to sit." He dropped down on the edge of her bed and patted the space beside him.

Jess claimed the spot and prepared for a promise she wasn't certain she wanted to hear, much less make, especially if it involved Dalton. "I'm all ears, so talk."

Chase studied the industrial tile beneath his boots.

"Promise me you won't do anything stupid. I can't leave here tonight unless I know you're going to be okay."

She found his sullen attitude disturbing. "I'm not going to do anything stupid."

Finally he looked at her. "Are you sure? You've always been a jumper first and a thinker later."

She rolled her eyes at his dig over her impulsive nature. "Yes, I'm sure. If you don't believe me, then I guess you'll just have to wait and see if I have a ring on my finger Christmas morning."

His gaze slid away again. "I won't be here on Christmas."

"Let me guess. You and the guys are going on your annual hunting trip, leaving the women home for the holidays to fend for themselves. That must thrill your mother—"

"I received my orders today to head back to the base in the morning."

Jess swallowed hard to clear the fear from her throat. "Why so soon?"

He took her hands into his and shifted to face her. "I'm shipping out tomorrow night."

"To where?" She worried she already knew the answer.

"Afghanistan."

The word sounded like a gunshot in the small space and Jess felt it land straight in her heart. She yanked away from his grasp and came to her feet to face him. "You can't go, Chase. You have to find some way not to go."

"I have to go, Jess," he said. "I don't have a choice, and even if I did, I'd still go."

She was caught somewhere between panic and fury. "What are you going to do over there?"

"That's classified."

"You mean dangerous," she said as she sat on the opposite bed.

"Look, Jess, I've been training for almost three years to serve my country, just like my father and his father—"

"And your great-grandfather," she interjected. "I know the story." And she did—that story and several others pertaining to war. She recalled how her dad used to speak in an almost reverent tone about the boys who went to Vietnam and never came back. About how he'd been lucky to survive. Still, she'd never really understood the sacrifice her father and so many others had made...until now.

Chase raked a hand over his jaw and sighed. "You don't have to worry about me, Jess. I'm a damn good soldier."

Of course he was. He'd always been good at everything, from sports to school and reportedly sex—if she chose to put stock in the rumors spread over at least three counties. All that aside, when they were growing up, he'd been consumed by video games involving battles and espionage. But this wasn't a game. Not even close.

She couldn't seem to control the need to lash out. "Great. Go be a soldier. Forget about your family and all the people who love you."

"I won't forget you," he said quietly. "And I can't forget that it's my duty to keep you and my family safe."

Jess wanted to scream, to bargain, to beg him to stay. But all the pleading in the world would be futile. She couldn't change his mind and in reality, she wouldn't want him to be anything less than he was—her hero. He always had been.

As her anger began to dissolve and the sorrow set in,

Jess lowered her face in her hands and sobbed from abject fear. Fear for him. Fear for herself.

Chase joined her and pulled her close to his side, holding her tightly while she dampened the front of his field jacket with her tears. They stayed that way for a time until she felt composed enough to speak. "What am I going to do while you're off battling the bad guys, Chase?"

He thumbed away a tear from her cheek. "You're going to go on with your life as usual, just like you have since I signed up for this gig after graduation."

She leaned over and grabbed a tissue from the box on the nightstand. "Just so you know, if you die, I'm going to have to kill you. You have to come back and get married and make a bunch of little Chases."

He released a cynical laugh. "You know I'm not the settling down kind, Jess."

She'd heard him say that more than once. "You might change your mind when you get over there, Chase. You might even wish you had a girlfriend back home waiting for you."

He took her right hand and laced their fingers together. "Just knowing I have your support is enough. You can send me an email every now and then."

She tried to smile but it fell flat. "I'm going to write you the old-fashioned way, with a pen and paper. I'll make sure you know all the trashy gossip from home. Heaven knows someone's bound to do something newsworthy sooner or later."

"As long as it's not you."

"I'll try not to run naked through the town square."

He grinned, flashing his to-die-for dimples that had dropped many a woman in their tracks. "I'll get you an address as soon as I have it. Feel free to send me some of your mom's oatmeal raisin cookies, too."

"I'll make the cookies."

"I thought you didn't want me to die."

She sent him her best sneer. "I take back every nice thing I've ever said about you, Chase Reed."

"You know you love me, Gertrude." He followed the use of her horrid middle name with a winning grin.

She'd forgive him anything tonight. She'd also carry the image of that smile close to her heart until he came back home again. "And you're going to miss me."

His features turned somber again. "Yeah, I am. Just don't forget me while I'm gone."

How could she ever forget him or what they'd meant to each other for most of their lives?

Chase pulled her into a bear hug and when he released her, Jess resisted the urge to cling to him. "What time does your bus leave?"

He took a glance at his watch. "6:00 a.m. sharp."

She saw an opportunity and went for it. "Do you mind staying a little while longer? Just another hour or two. We can watch some corny sitcom and make up our own lines, which no doubt will be much funnier." Anything to spend a little more time in his presence, until Jess was ready to let him go. Like she'd ever be ready to let him go.

Chase hesitated a moment. "I have to get Dad's truck back to him and I really need some sleep. Haven't had a whole lot of that lately."

Jess suspected she'd be in the same boat after he left. "You can take a nap before you head back."

"I don't know, Jess. If I fell asleep, I might not wake up in time to catch the bus."

All the more reason for him to stay. "I'll make sure

you don't sleep that long. Besides, you can't march in here, announce you're about to head off to a war zone and then just leave me all by myself to deal with it."

Jess could tell by his expression she'd worn him down. She confirmed that when he said, "Okay, but only an hour or so."

"Great." She hopped onto her bed, scooted as close to the wall as she could to reserve a place for him. "Take off your shoes and stay awhile, sailor."

"I'm not a sailor," he grumbled as he unlaced his boots and then toed out of them. "U.S. Army, Special Forces, and don't forget it."

Not much chance in that, thanks to the obvious reminders.

After Chase settled in beside her, Jess flipped on the TV with the remote and chose an ancient rerun. He slid his arm beneath her shoulder, she rested her cheek against his chest, like they'd done a thousand times before.

A span of silence passed before Jess said, "I wish we could go back to those summers when we used to hang out at the pond. We had some great times."

"Before you started dating the jerk," he muttered.

"He's really a good guy, Chase."

He kept his gaze fixed on the ceiling. "Being born to a father who owns half the state of Mississippi doesn't make him a good guy."

"And being rich doesn't make him bad, either."

He nailed her with a serious stare. "Are you going to marry him, Jess?"

She'd asked herself that question many times during the month she and Dalton had been apart. So far, no solid answer. "I could do worse."

"You could do better."

"He's going to take good care of me, Chase. He'll make sure I have a great life."

"Sounds to me like you've made up your mind."

Not exactly. "If I do decide to go through with it, I'll wait until you're home so you can be my man of honor."

His frown returned. "Thanks, but no thanks. I don't see myself being front and center when I believe you'll be making the biggest mistake of your life."

That stung Jess to the core. "I wish you'd give me some credit. I'm not a complete airhead."

He shifted to his side and surveyed her face. "I just want you to be happy, Jess. I want to leave here knowing you're going to have a solid future with someone who deserves you." He sounded and looked so sincere, so sweet, that Jess started to cry again.

Chase held her securely in his strong arms. "It's going to be okay," he told her in a soft, even tone.

"Nothing's okay," she said. "It won't ever be okay if you go."

He pressed a kiss on her forehead, brushed a kiss across one cheek, then the other. "I'll be back. I promise."

"You better."

As the time ticked away, they simply stared at each other, caught in a place they'd never been before. And then in one unexpected, defining moment, Chase kissed Jess on the lips. Not an innocent kiss. A deep, insistent kiss that made her head spin out of control.

In all the years they'd known each other—practically since birth—not once had they ever ventured beyond a platonic bond. Not once had Chase ever made a move on her. For years Jess had told herself she'd never wanted more from him. She'd rejected the fantasies that crept in on occasion as she wondered what it would be like to kiss him. What it would be like if he saw her as a woman, not a surrogate sister.

Chase tipped his forehead against hers. "Tell me to leave, Jess."

That was the last thing she planned to tell him. "I want you to stay." And she did, right or wrong.

He framed her face in his palms, forced her to look right into his eyes. "If I don't go, I don't know what might happen. Right now I just need…"

"To be with someone," she finished for him, knowing she risked becoming only another of his meaningless hook-ups if she let this continue. But she couldn't—wouldn't—let the chance go by, consequences be damned. "You need to feel alive, Chase, and I need that, too. Whatever happens from this point forward, nothing will change between us. We'll still be friends and no one will have to know."

"But I'll know, Jess. And I can't give you—"

Jess pressed a fingertip against his lips to silence him. "You've given me more than you know." She lifted her finger and pressed her lips against his. "Now no more talk." She took his hand and slid it beneath the robe's opening above her breasts. "Just touch."

That seemed to unleash something in Chase, something uncontrolled but unbelievably sexy as he skimmed his palms down her body. Somehow she'd managed to bring them past the turn-back point, but she honestly didn't care. She only cared about the prospect of being with him completely.

Maybe this was the reason she'd held back committing to Dalton. Maybe subconsciously she'd always loved Chase a little more than she'd cared to admit. More than the way he loved her as a friend.

Regardless, this could be the last opportunity to know what she'd been missing. The last chance to explore the feelings for Chase that had suddenly surfaced. Possibly the last time she ever saw him again.

She'd been caught between two men for years—the one who treated her like a queen, and the one who'd viewed her as only a best friend. The one who could give her the world, and the other who could only give her this one night.

She wanted this one night…even if it proved to be a life-altering mistake.

Chapter 1

Placid, Mississippi
Ten years later

There had to be some mistake.

As he pulled out of the sheriff's station parking lot, Chase Reed requested the dispatcher repeat the address one more time.

1101 Oakwood Lane.

No mistake, and no time to waste.

Chase flipped on his emergency lights and siren as he sped through downtown, concerned over what he might be facing when he arrived at his destination on the out-skirts of Placid—the recently-divorced Jessica Keller Wainwright's home. He only knew that a domestic dis-pute call had been placed by a hysterical woman and an ambulance had been dispatched. He didn't know who had been injured or how. One thing was certain. If Dalton Wainwright had laid a finger on Jess, he'd kill him.

In the six months since he'd returned to Placid, he'd only spoken to Jess once by phone, a tense conversation that involved generalities—her new job teaching second grade, his new job as deputy sheriff and briefly about her divorce, like they were only acquaintances. Even though they'd corresponded through the years, they'd never talked about the night before he left for his first tour of duty.

He hated that he'd obviously hurt her with his careless behavior. Hated that she'd run off and married Wainwright two weeks later. Hated that he'd somehow driven her to that decision and in turn, set a course that had ultimately led to this moment.

Chase's mind continued to reel with the possibilities as he whipped into the lengthy drive leading to the massive redbrick mansion. He barely had the car stopped before he slid out of the driver's side and his feet hit the pavement. A gust of unseasonably cold, bitter wind sent a spiral of leaves across the stone walkway as he strode past the for sale sign toward the planked porch. The white holiday lights hanging from the eaves and the huge artificial Christmas tree filling the entry window gave the appearance of normalcy. But when he found the front door partially ajar, he prepared for anything but a normal situation.

Chase poised his hand on the Glock holstered at his hip as he moved into the foyer, an automatic reaction resulting from hour upon hour of military training. But in this instance, he wasn't the soldier navigating war-torn territory. He was the deputy sheriff doing his duty no matter what he might encounter.

Senses on high alert, he cocked his head to listen as he walked past the ornate staircase and down the tiled corridor. The sound of harsh sobs caused him to quicken his pace, his heart keeping an equally rapid tempo. The minute he entered the great room, he pulled up short to survey the scene.

To his left, Jess sat on the floor, her back to a white leather sofa, hugging her knees to her chest as she rocked back and forth like a lost child. Chase instinctively started toward her until something caught his immediate attention from the corner of his eye. He turned to see a figure crumpled near the stone hearth—only to discover it was Dalton Wainwright.

When he noticed the blood pooling around Dalton's head, images of war zipped through Chase's brain. Fallen comrades, chaos and confusion. Death and destruction. A fatal error he'd made that couldn't be rectified...

Chase again forced the memories away as he walked to his long-time nemesis, crouched down, pressed his fingertips against Dalton's neck and fortunately for Jess, found a pulse.

"He's dead, isn't he?" she asked in a tone strangely absent of emotion.

"He's alive but unconscious," he assured her, although right then he wasn't sure of anything.

When he heard the wail of sirens, Chase immediately went to Jess, knelt and took her by the shoulders. "Are you okay?" he asked, even though he could tell she wasn't from the undeniable shock in her eyes.

"It was an accident," she muttered as her gaze slid away. "No one's fault."

Chase couldn't imagine Jess would intentionally injure her ex-husband, but he wasn't fool enough to deny

anything was possible when it came to volatile relationships. "Look at me, Jess." Once he finally had her attention, he added, "When the paramedics get here, don't say
anything about what happened."

"But I didn't mean—"

"Don't talk about it," he cautioned again. "You have
to remember who you're dealing with here, even if it
was an accident."

Realization dawned in her expression. "Edwin," she
said in a whisper.

"Yeah. Your ex-father-in-law could make this tough
on you. And anything you tell me could be used against
you in court if it comes to that."

Her eyes went wide with terror. "Court?"

Before Chase had a chance to reassure her, the sound
of gurney wheels echoing through the foyer interrupted
his train of thought. He straightened and met the EMTs as
soon as they entered the room. "He's still alive," he told
a fifty-something paramedic named Joe. "But it looks
like he has a pretty serious head injury."

"We'll take it from here," Joe said before he and his
partner went to work on Dalton.

Chase helped Jess to her feet and guided her down the
hall to the formal dining room he found nearby. After he
had her seated in a chair at the polished mahogany table,
he asked, "Where's your son?"

"Upstairs."

Chase wondered exactly what the boy had witnessed
during the last few minutes. "I want you to stay right here
while I go check on him."

She nodded like she needed complete guidance. Chase
understood that all too well.

He strode back into the great room in time to find the

crew loading Dalton onto the stretcher, but he didn't stop to check on his status. Instead, he took the stairs two at a time. When he reached the top landing, he discovered Danny Wainwright, dressed in a pair of race-car pajamas, standing against the wall with his gaze focused on the hardwood floor.

After Danny finally looked up, Chase was amazed over how much he resembled Jess, with the exception of his blond hair. Fortunately he couldn't see a scrap of Dalton in him, but he did see the same vacant stare his mother had exhibited a few moments ago.

More recollections of another time, another foreign place and another child intruded into Chase's thoughts. He had to get a grip on the present and stay out of the past for both Jess and her son's sake.

Chase swept his cowboy hat from his head and kept a safe distance. "Hey, Danny. I'm Deputy Reed, a friend of your mom's."

The boy blinked but remained silent.

He decided tackling Danny's immediate worry might help. "The paramedics are taking your dad to the hospital, so he's in good hands."

Still no response, and Chase wasn't real sure how to proceed. "Do you want to go see your mom?"

This time Danny shook his head, which fueled Chase's concerns. If the kid had witnessed Jess injuring Dalton, inadvertent or not, he could have a damn hard time forgiving his mother. He wasn't too keen on leaving the boy alone, but he didn't want to push him, either. "Why don't you wait in your room and I'll have your mother come up to talk to you."

Without any reply or hesitation, the boy headed down the hall and walked through a door to his right. Chase followed behind and entered a bedroom decked out in dark blue walls and baseball memorabilia. A typical kid's room that reminded him of his own when he'd been about Danny's age, only he'd been more inclined to collect football souvenirs.

When Danny curled up on the bed facing the wall, Chase felt the need to say something else, to offer some words of comfort, but he had no real experience dealing with childhood trauma. "I'll be back in a few minutes with your mom, okay?"

Danny didn't respond, didn't even shrug his shoulders to acknowledge the suggestion. With any luck, reuniting him with Jess would be the key to his comfort. Then again, maybe not, but Chase felt he had no choice in the matter.

As he sprinted back down the stairs, Chase heard the sound of an all-too-familiar voice coming from somewhere in the house. A booming voice that belonged to his father, the sheriff. No surprise that Buck would have been summoned, considering the nature of the crime. Correction. Accident. Chase refused to believe anything else until proof landed in front of his nose. Even then he'd have a hard time buying Jess flying into a homicidal rage.

He made his way back to the dining room where he'd left Jess and arrived just in time to hear his dad say, "You're going to have to give me more details than that."

Furious over Buck's tone, Chase stepped inside the opening, hands fisted at his sides. "Can I have a word with you?"

Buck turned to him and scowled. "I'm taking Jess's statement, son, so you'll need to wait a minute."

Chase was tempted to remind his father that he should call him by his proper name, not *son*. "It's important."

Buck forked his fingers through his silver hair and sighed. "Fine," he said before turning to Jess. "Don't go anywhere."

As soon as Buck joined him at the front door out of Jess's earshot, Chase turned his fury on his father. "What in the hell are you doing?"

"My job, exactly what you should be doing, too. She told me you hadn't questioned her about Dalton's injuries."

"She said it was an accident and that's all I needed to know."

Buck hooked his thumbs in his pockets and stared him down like he was thirteen, not thirty-one. "Doesn't matter what she said, boy. You have to get all the facts to put into the report."

Chase pointed in the direction of the dining room. "That's Jess in there, Dad. The same girl who used to come with her folks to our house for Sunday dinner and dominoes."

"Yeah, and you're too close to the situation. That's why I called in Barkley to assist me. He should be here in about five minutes."

That only increased Chase's wrath. "Barkley can't find his way out of a feed sack. He'll arrest Jess first and ask questions later."

Buck raised a brow. "Any reason why you think Jess should be arrested?"

He reflected on Danny's reaction and decided to keep his mouth shut for now. "Like I said, she claims it was an accident, and I have no reason to believe it wasn't."

"You know the procedure," Buck said. "I still have to take an official statement."

"Then do it in the morning after she's had some time to recover."

"That's not the way it works, son."

"Make it work, Dad. Right now she needs to rest."

"She can't stay here, Chase. We'll need to gather evidence in case Dalton dies during the night."

On one hand, he didn't give a rat's ass if Dalton died. On the other, he had to consider what that might mean for Jess. "She can stay with me tonight and I'll have her at the department first thing in the morning."

"She can get a room at the motel."

He had no intention of sticking Jess in some seedy, pay-by-the-hour dive on the outskirts of town. "She's in shock and so is her kid. She needs to be in a place where she's comfortable."

Chase could see Buck's frustration beginning to build. "And you think that's with you? Best I recall, she hasn't come around once since you've been home."

Understandable why they'd been avoiding each other, but he'd be damned if he let his father in on a ten-year-old secret. "She's been busy getting rid of Dalton."

Chase realized how questionable that sounded when Buck said, "Maybe that's what she did tonight, got rid of him once and for all."

He couldn't quite understand why his father was bent on treating Jess like some black widow lying in wait to off her former husband. Buck might be one of the good guys, but he could be an obsessed hard-ass when it came to the job. If serving as sheriff for thirty some odd years did that to a man, Chase wanted no part of it, even if that's exactly what was expected of him.

"Tell you what, Sheriff," he said. "If you'll stop jumping to conclusions, then I'll have Jess to you bright and early. But if you're not going to stick to the innocent until proven guilty clause, then I'll be damned if I'm going to continue to work for you."

Chase could see the cogs spinning fast in Buck's head. Placid had suffered a deputy shortage for years, and there sure as hell wasn't a long line waiting to sign on. If he up and resigned, he'd leave his dad high and dry and working longer hours again, which sure wouldn't set well with the missus.

Buck took on a look of reluctant submission. "Okay, you bring her home and have her in my office no later than 8:00 a.m. And have her boy there, too. Maybe between the two of them, we can shed some light on this thing."

As far as Chase was concerned, having Danny put through the wringer was entirely up to Jess, at least for now. "Fine. You can go. I'll handle it from here."

"I'll go outside to wait for Barkley until you leave with Jess." Buck turned toward the door then stopped and pointed at Chase. "8:00 a.m. sharp or I'll come down to the cabin and get her myself."

"I'll have her there, Sheriff." And he would, right on time. He didn't sleep much these days anyway. Too much on his mind. Too many nightmares to count.

After his dad had finally left the immediate premises, Chase made his way to the dining room, only to find it deserted. Jess would've had to walk past him to go up the stairs, which made him wonder if she'd headed out the back door. With that major dilemma in mind, he strode to the back of the house and came upon a rear staircase adjacent to the top-of-the-line kitchen. Hopefully that had been her escape route, if in fact she felt the need to escape.

He opted to give Jess the benefit of the doubt and headed to the second floor. As suspected, he discovered her in Danny's room, perched on the edge of the bed, sifting her hands through her son's hair.

Chase paused a moment to take in the subtle alterations in Jess's appearance. She'd cut her long auburn hair to her shoulders and she wore the kind of loose-fitting clothes designed to hide her figure. At five-foot-three, she'd always been small in stature but tough as barbwire. But the most noticeable change could be found in her light amber eyes when she leveled her gaze on him. The former outgoing cheerleader, who could talk the bark off a tree, looked lost and defeated. He damned Dalton Wainwright for that. Damned him for sucking the life out of Jess. Damned himself for staying away from her because of his own guilt.

Chase remained in the doorway and in a low tone said, "Pack a bag for you and your son. You're going to stay with me for a few days."

"Why?"

"According to procedure, you have to leave the premises until you give your statement. And even if you could stay, do you really think that's a good idea?" He nodded toward Danny.

"No," she said, her voice barely above a whisper. "But I don't want to put you out, Chase. I can call around and find somewhere to stay. Maybe with Sam and Savannah or Matt and Rachel."

He prepared to shoot down her protest with logic. "First of all, Savannah and Sam are in Hawaii and won't be back for a couple of days. Secondly, I figure Rachel's on her way to the hospital to see about Dalton by now." Blood ties trumped friendship any day of the week, even if Rachel and Jess had been friends for years and Rachel's brother was about as sorry as they came.

"As far as the rest of the town goes," he continued, "do you want this getting out any sooner than it has to?"

She shook her head. "No, I don't."

"Then it's settled," he said. "I'll wait downstairs while you get your things together."

She twisted the ruby ring that once belonged to her grandmother round and round her right ring finger, a habit she'd developed long ago. "I appreciate your hospitality, but we'll only stay until I can make other arrangements."

Funny, they spoke to each other like they were strangers. Like they'd met for the first time tonight when in reality they'd known each other for a lifetime. "You're welcome to stay as long as you need to, but we'll work it out tomorrow."

Before she could make up another excuse to refuse the offer, Chase walked out of the room and went back downstairs to wait.

He needed to hear the truth from Jess, but he also feared what that truth might be. Feared that he would have to testify against her if she'd attacked Dalton for whatever reason. Justified or not, her cold-blooded father-in-law would see to it that she paid dearly, and he had the political pull and financial means to do it.

When Chase had signed up for the job, both as a soldier and deputy sheriff, he'd sworn to uphold the law. But experience had taught him sometimes justice could be bought by the highest bidder. This was one of those situations.

Regardless, he vowed to stand by Jess, come hell or

high water. After what he'd done to her all those years ago, it was the least he could do for her now.

Alone with her child in Chase's sparsely furnished guestroom, Jess claimed a space next to Danny on the twin bed. She pulled the covers over his thin shoulders and whisked a kiss across his cheek. And when he turned away from her, she felt her heart shatter one painful fissure at a time.

Still, she rested her face on the pillow, hoping that he found a measure of comfort in her presence. But since the moment they'd arrived at Chase's house, he'd refused to look at her, refused to speak a word. She couldn't really blame him after what he'd endured, both tonight and throughout his nine years on earth.

She smiled at the slight curl at the nape of his neck, remembered how she'd been terrified to hold him after he was born and then soon found it hard to put him down. She recalled his baby-soft smell, how little time it had taken to bond with him. He'd been such a joy from the beginning, the brightest part of her day.

Jess's life had been littered with what-ifs and regrets, of foolish decisions she'd wished she could take back, but having her son had never been one of them. She should have left Dalton a long time ago, when Danny had been too young to understand the ongoing battle between his mother and father. Before Dalton had begun to demean both son and wife.

Her precious baby, who'd been quick with a grin and fast on his feet, had become withdrawn and doubted himself, just as she had since the day she'd married Dalton Wainwright. Yet over the past two months since the divorce, he'd begun to smile more often, talk more freely and even his grades had improved. Now this horrible, horrible incident could scar him beyond repair.

Jess leaned over to see if Danny was sleeping, only to determine he still seemed wide awake. "Do you want some water?" she asked.

He shook his head no.

"Do you want me to stay in here with you tonight?"

Again, another negative response.

She couldn't blame him for his anger. After all, what had happened tonight had been entirely her fault, and he was going to suffer the brunt of her decisions for years, if not forever. Mothers were supposed to protect their children, and she'd failed miserably.

Jess was torn between staying a little longer with Danny and having a serious talk with Chase. She didn't dare discuss all the details with him. She wouldn't involve him more than she already had. But she could attempt to reestablish their friendship that had been damaged a decade ago, thanks to another error in judgment. That could be asking too much, but she had to try. Like it or not, she needed Chase's support more than she ever had before.

She pressed a kiss against his cheek. "It's going to be all right, honey. Everything's going to be fine. I'll take care of you."

If only she could believe her assertions. As it now stood, if Dalton didn't survive his injuries, nothing would ever be fine again. Danny might never be fine again.

But for now, it might be best if Danny wasn't talking, at least until Jess could come up with a plan. Otherwise, her beloved son's words could destroy them both.

Chapter 2

Seated at the small dining table, Chase glanced up from the mug of coffee when he heard the sound of footsteps. Jess approached him slowly, and considering the way her shoulders sagged, the fatigue in her eyes, she looked liked she'd been ambushed.

He shoved the chair across from him with his boot. "Sit before you drop in your tracks."

After she slid onto the seat, Jess crossed her arms around her middle like she was cold. He'd made a point to turn up the heat soon after they'd walked in the door even though he'd felt like his skin had caught fire.

Chase lifted his mug. "Want a cup?"

"No, thank you." She eyed his gun resting on the table where he'd unloaded it a few moments before.

He hooked a thumb over his shoulder toward the guest room. "How's he doing?"

"As well as can be expected, I guess. He's not saying much but I'm sure he's still in shock. I know I am."

Chase really wanted to ask Jess how Dalton's injuries had come about. She could either clear things up, or incriminate herself. He wasn't willing to take that chance because he'd be damned if he'd speak one word against her.

"You look like you could use some sleep," he said when she yawned.

Jess folded her hands together and rested them on top of the pine table. "I'm not sure I could sleep if I wanted to. Every time I close my eyes, I see these awful images."

Chase could seriously relate to that scenario. He couldn't remember a time in the past few years when he drifted peacefully off to sleep. Couldn't remember the last time he had any real peace.

"If you decide to try and rest, you can take my room. I'll sleep on the couch."

She brought her attention back to him. "I'm not going to put you out of your bed. I'll sleep on the sofa."

No point in arguing with Jess. He'd learned that a long time ago. But he'd also learned how to skirt her objections. "You sure you don't want some coffee? Maybe a beer? I'm fresh out of whiskey but I could sneak into the main house and see if Dad still has that seventy-year-old bottle that belonged to my great-grandpa."

Jess shuddered. "I can't even stand the smell of whiskey, much less drink it. I have Dalton to thank for that."

"He always did like his booze." And women. Chase had heard from friends that the demon had been scouring the bars and cheating on Jess for years.

When Jess continued to stare blankly across the room,

Chase scraped his mind for some way to lift her spirits as much as possible. "Do you want to call your folks?"

Her gaze snapped to his. "No. They just left two days ago on a cruise with Gary, Becca and the kids for the holidays. I don't see any reason to bother them while they're on their first real vacation in years."

Chase could think of one reason—giving her family advance notice in case Jess wound up in jail. "Fine. Is there anyone else I can call for you?"

She drummed her fingertips on the table, a purely nervous gesture. "Yes. I need you to call the hospital and find out how Dalton's doing."

He'd like to think she wanted to know because of Danny, but he wondered if there might be more to it. Either she still cared for the jerk, or she felt responsible for his wounds. Maybe both. "I could call but I won't get anywhere. The hospital won't release any information unless you're a family member or the family gives permission. I doubt that holds true for either of us."

She rubbed her temples like she had one hell of a headache. "You're right. I'd just hate to read about it in the paper if something happens to him."

More than likely the event would be front page news no matter what the outcome. "I have Rachel's cell number. I can try to reach her."

Jess didn't look too keen on that idea. "I wouldn't want to disturb her."

He fished the phone from his pocket and hit the speed dial. "She's probably on her way to Jackson, if she'd not already there."

After two rings, Rachel answered with a harried "Hello."

"Hey, Rachel, it's Chase. Are you at the hospital?"

"Yes. How did you know?"

At least she didn't sound too distraught, a good thing. "I answered the call."

"Of course you did. I keep forgetting you're a deputy now."

Sometimes Chase wished he wasn't. Tonight happened to be one of those times. "How's your brother doing?" He tried to sound concerned but his tone was noticeably dry.

"He's undergoing tests right now and he's still unconscious," Rachel said. "Do you have any idea what happened?"

He had a few, but none he cared to share. "Jess says it was an accident, but that's all I know."

"Where is Jess now? I tried to call the home number and her cell but I didn't get any answer."

"She's here with me. Do you want to speak with her?"

"I'd like that. I'm worried about her."

Jess waved him away when he tried to hand her the phone. "Just talk to her for a minute," he said. "She's one of your best friends and she's concerned."

After a brief hesitation, Jess reluctantly took the cell and murmured a soft "Hello."

Chase waited and watched while Jess spoke with Rachel. She sounded meek, very un-Jess-like, but he could understand why she might. While he put away his gun in the locked cabinet in the corner, he listened as Jess repeated the accident scenario without any details. And after a few brief questions about Dalton's condition, she ended the conversation.

"At least he's still alive," she said as she handed him back the phone.

He could tell she found little relief in Dalton's status. "If he makes it through the night, he'll probably be okay."

"And if that's not the case?" she asked. "What happens then?"

Nothing good. He leaned back against the counter and crossed his arms. "Let's just worry about that if and when the time comes. Right now you need some sleep."

"I've already told you I can't sleep." Her irritable tone said otherwise.

"You can try." He pushed away from the cabinet and returned to the table. "I'll show you to my room."

"I told you I'll sleep on the couch."

"You'll be closer to Danny if you're in my room."

That seemed to get her attention. "I guess that would probably be better."

Jess took her time coming to her feet while he picked up her bag from the floor in the den. She slowly and silently followed behind him as he made his way down the hall and paused outside the guestroom.

"Do you think I can hear Danny if he calls me?" she asked.

"You'll be right next door," he said as he pointed out his bedroom.

After a slight hesitation, she entered the area and looked around before her gaze settled on the king-size bed.

He nodded toward the closed door to his right. "The bathroom's through there. After you're done, I need to take a quick shower."

She took the bag from him and clutched it like a lifeline. "Is this the only bathroom?"

"The only one with a shower," he said. "There's a half-bath next to the laundry room. I've just started framing out two more bedrooms and another bath at the back of the house."

"Why?" she asked, catching him off guard.

"Why not?" he answered back.

"I don't see why you'd need four bedrooms unless you plan on having a family," she said. "And since you're not a settling down kind of guy, well…"

Exactly what he'd told her all those years ago. "Extra bedrooms add to resale value."

"Are you going to move after you're finished with the renovations?" Her tone held an edge of alarm, like she worried he might desert her.

"I hadn't planned on it, but it doesn't hurt to prepare for the future."

She lowered her eyes. "Sometimes you can't prepare for what life throws your way."

He hated she couldn't look at him straight on, that she'd obviously lost her confidence, unlike the girl he used to know. But then her bastard of an ex-husband had played a huge role in that.

"We all make errors in judgment, Jess." He'd made more than his fair share, one that had been particularly serious. Two if he counted what had happened in her dorm room a decade ago.

She took a few steps back and pointed behind her. "I'm going to wash up now."

"Fine. I'll be right here."

"I won't be long," she said as she turned, hurried into the bath and closed the door behind her.

Chase sat on the edge of the bed and streaked both hands over his face. He should be dog-tired, but he wasn't. He should be convinced of Jess's innocence, but he had his doubts. He should disregard duty and demand the truth, but he couldn't…and not only because of job.

The truth could very well be more than he could handle.

After checking on Danny one more time, Jess climbed into the king-size bed, pulled the sheets up to her chin and surveyed the area cast in overhead light. The room had been painted neutral beige and the accessories were patently masculine, from the leather chair in the corner to the heavy pine furniture. Funny, this place had barely been four rickety walls and rough-hewn wood floors when they used to play here as kids. She smiled as she recalled their childhood games and her ongoing argument with Chase—she refused to play damsel-in-distress to his superhero just because she was a girl. Over and over she'd insisted she was quite capable of using her pretend powers to save him. But with a flash of his dimples and a few well-chosen words, he'd won the battle.

These days, he rarely smiled. These days, she had barely been able to save herself. Especially tonight.

As Jess settled deeper into the feather pillow, she absorbed the fresh, clean scent of cotton and a hint of Chase's favorite soap. She allowed the memories to take her back to a better time when she'd given him some fancy, manly shower gel one Christmas—which he'd promptly given back and said, "No offense, but no, thanks." She'd known all along he'd been a bar soap kind of guy but she'd reasoned that he could change. She should have known better.

People didn't change, at least not for the better. She'd learned that hard lesson from her ex-husband.

In response to a sudden, strong chill, Jess chafed her arms with her palms and felt the tender spot right above her elbow. She shuddered at the sudden surge of recent recollections. Horrible recollections of what had transpired only a few hours before.

The sound of the opening door startled Jess and thankfully thrust her back into the here and now. Chase came out of the bathroom wearing a pair of navy pajama bottoms and a seen-better-days gray T-shirt.

As she scooted up against the headboard, he headed to the closet, where he placed his boots beneath the neat row of jeans and shirts hanging on the rack.

"Nice place," she said, grasping for a topic other than why she had landed in his house.

"It's fairly simple."

"You have a whirlpool tub and granite countertops, Chase. I don't think that qualifies as simple."

He tossed a glance over his shoulder. "I had some help decorating."

Jess imagined he did. Female help, and she doubted his mom had contributed. Missy Reed was as country as country came. "I'm sure the county girls stood in line to help you out."

"Just Savannah," he said as he pulled out a khaki uniform shirt and hung it on a wall hook next to the closet. "She and Sam are redoing the farmhouse so she volunteered."

She experienced a little bite of guilt over jumping to conclusions. But considering Chase's legendary ladies-man reputation, who could blame her? "That was nice of her to help. I'm sorry to say I haven't seen much of her since she moved back from Chicago." She hadn't seen much of anyone for that matter.

Chase pulled some bedding from the top of the closet, closed the door and finally faced her. "You might want to give her a call when she's back in town."

Jess immediately understood the motive behind his suggestion. "Do you think I need an attorney?"

"I don't know, but it couldn't hurt."

A rock of nausea settled in Jess's belly. "I'll wait and see what happens tomorrow." If Dalton didn't survive, she'd definitely make that call. Or if the statement didn't go well, she might then, too.

Chase returned to the bathroom and only partially closed the door, allowing enough light to escape to keep the room from total darkness. Jess wasn't the least bit surprised by the gesture. He'd always been considerate and thoughtful, at least when it came to her needs.

"It's late," he said as he crossed the room. "Let me know if you need anything."

"I do need something," she blurted, driven by an overwhelming blast of anxiety.

He paused with his hand poised on the light switch and faced her again. "Ask away."

"I need you to stay with me tonight."

His gaze slid away. "Not a good idea."

She knew the root of his concerns—what happened the last time they'd been in bed together ten years ago. "I'm not going to touch you or ask anything more of you than your company. I just don't want to be alone tonight. I promise I'll stay on my side of the bed. And it's a big bed—"

"I tend to toss and turn these days. You probably won't get any sleep at all."

"We'll be restless together." Jess despised the desperation in her voice, but then she was desperate. Desperate not to be left alone with her horrible memories. "Please, Chase. Only for a while." The same plea from their past.

He released a sigh. "Okay."

While Jess silently celebrated her minor victory, Chase replaced the bedding in the closet and closed the door. After he turned off the light, he sat on the edge of the mattress and kept his back to her, motionless as if preparing to join her. Or reconsidering.

Jess recalled the last time he'd done that very thing—right after he'd told her they'd made a huge mistake sleeping together and it would never happen again. Since then, nothing had been quite the same.

They'd exchanged letters often during his time away, but not once had they ever talked about that one memorable night. Not once had she asked him if he'd regretted it, because in reality, she hadn't. She only regretted that she'd disregarded his advice and jumped into a marriage that was doomed from the beginning. At the time, she felt she'd had no choice.

A few minutes passed before he slid onto his back, his hands laced together atop his abdomen, his body as rigid as a steel beam.

"Thank you," Jess said. "For everything. I don't know what I would've done if you hadn't been there to help me. I appreciate it more than you know."

"No problem."

The razor-sharp edge in his tone told Jess everything she'd asked of him was a problem, and suspected he had more on his mind than he'd let on. She should probably drop it, but some soul-deep need to clear the air drove her to turn on the bedside lamp and gain his complete attention. "Go ahead, Chase, say it."

"Say what?" he muttered as he flipped onto his belly, his face turned toward the opposite wall.

She rolled to her side toward him. "Tell me I'm a fool

again just like you did after I told you I'd married Dalton."

He turned his head and stared at her straight on. "I never said you were a fool. I said Dalton had you fooled."

"You're right, but I can't take back my mistakes." Oh, that she could. "But I do want to make it right between you and me. We've never discussed that night in my dorm—"

"Not now, Jess."

She rose up on one elbow and supported her jaw with her palm. "When Chase? We've skirted that topic for ten years and—"

"I said not now." He turned his head again, making it all too clear that he was done with the conversation. Maybe even done with her.

Feeling weary and emotionally drained, Jess turned off the light and rolled away from Chase. Years ago, he would have held her close and reassured her. He would have been more than willing to provide a leaning shoulder. A swell of sadness overcame her as she silently mourned the loss of her best friend. She chastised herself for all the ways in which she'd ruined her life. Perhaps even her son's life.

Worse still, she might find herself without a job. The good citizens of Placid could be judgmental, and if any parent in town even suspected she'd intentionally harmed her ex-husband, they'd kick her to the curb without a second thought. Not to mention, her former father-in-law served on the school board. No job meant no way to support her child other than the money Dalton grudgingly gave her.

Everything seemed so hopeless and that only fed her remorse.

As the tears began to fall, she buried her face in the pillow, tried hard not to let Chase know that she was an emotional wreck. And just when she'd begun to honestly believe they would never be able to repair their relationship, she felt the mattress bend and Chase's strong hand engulfing hers.

"You're going to be okay," he whispered. "Danny's going to be okay, too."

Jess couldn't respond but she didn't need to. And although he only held her hand for a few moments, it seemed enough to get her through, at least tonight. Tomorrow would be another story.

The shrill buzzer jarred Jess out of sleep and her eyes snapped open. Confused, she took a few moments to survey the room in order to acclimate to the surroundings. As she finally recalled exactly where she was, and why, she resisted the urge to pull the covers back over her head and hide away from the world. She reached out and felt the space beside her only to discover that Chase had apparently left the bed before the annoying alarm sounded. How he could be up so early was beyond her. He'd thrashed about most of the night, taking the blanket with him and rousing her from sleep that had come in fits and starts. During those awake times, she'd checked on Danny twice and with great relief, had found him soundly sleeping. If only she could say the same for herself.

Recognizing what awaited her in a matter of hours—a trip to the sheriff's department to present her written statement—Jess decided to get up and get it over with as quickly as possible. She climbed from the bed, grabbed a robe and slipped it on as she made her way to the guest-room to tell Danny good morning. When she came upon only an empty bed, a swell of dread weighted her chest and robbed her breath.

Panic sent her on a fast clip into the kitchen where she thankfully found the missing deputy and her son. They sat at the breakfast table, both bent over a bowl of cereal—the kind with the fruity marshmallows that made her queasy just thinking about them. Neither seemed to notice her presence as she watched the pair for a few more minutes. She'd envisioned this scene many times throughout the years—her one-time best friend and her precious boy getting to know each other. Yet the picture-perfect scene was only an illusion. Her entire life to this point had been an illusion, and that wouldn't end today.

Jess approached her son from behind and ruffled his tousled blond hair. "Time for you to get a trim, Danny."

He didn't bother to look up from the bowl or offer a response. She sent Chase a forlorn look before checking the clock on the wall. "What time are we supposed to do this?"

He took a drink of coffee before pushing the cup aside. "I figure in an hour or so we'll head down to the department for the interviews."

"Interviews" meaning both she and her child. Not if she could help it.

Jess touched Danny's shoulder to garner his attention. "Why don't you go wash up and get dressed?"

He sent her only a fast glance before scooting back from the table and carrying his empty bowl to the sink. Funny, she usually had to ride him to clean up after meals. Then again, he didn't seem at all himself, and rightfully so.

Once Danny had left the area, Jess poured a cup of coffee from the pot on the counter and claimed the chair that her son had just left. "Did he say anything at all to you?"

Chase shook his head. "Not a word. I found him sitting in here staring off into space when I got up about an hour ago."

She closed her eyes and pinched the bridge of her nose with her fingertips. "I pray he'll come around in a few days."

"I think that depends on what he saw last night."

The long pause told Jess he wanted her to fill in the blanks despite his warning last night to keep her confessions to herself. "I don't think he saw anything except that Dalton had been injured." Lie number one. "That's why I don't see any reason for Danny to have to endure a lot of questions that will only upset him."

Chase inclined his head and fixed his gaze on Jess, causing her to look away. "Are you sure he didn't see it happen?"

"As sure as I can be." Lie number two.

"That might explain his silence," Chase said.

"As I told you last night, it was an accident. Dalton came to pick up Danny three hours late, he'd been drinking, and when I refused to let him take Danny, he grabbed my arm and I yanked it away. I guess he lost his balance but I'm not sure. It's all a blur."

Lie number three. She remembered every last detail, sickening sights and sounds included. She recalled Dalton's insistence they get back together, her refusal, his threats to take her son away from her permanently if she didn't do his bidding. His accusations. And then...

Feeling the need to escape, Jess downed the rest of her coffee and stood. "I'm going to get dressed now, unless you want to go first."

He leaned back in the chair and made a sweeping gesture toward the hall. "You go ahead."

"Okay. And after I've finished making my statement, I need to get my car and a few things from the house."

"I'll have to escort you until Buck clears the place as a possible crime scene."

Great. Nothing like being considered a hardened criminal. But then she had been guilty of more than her fair share of crimes, the first entailed marrying the wrong man. The second—not leaving him years ago. "Fine, but I want to find a place to rent today if at all possible. If I do, I'll need more than a duffle bag and one change of clothes."

"You're welcome to stay here as long as you like," he said without much conviction. "Once Dalton verifies your account of the events, you'll be free to move back into your house."

"It's not my house," she answered with more force than necessary. "Dalton made all the decisions when we had it built so I never considered it mine. During the divorce, he agreed to sell it and split the proceeds but unfortunately, people around here can't afford it. And Dalton's too damn stubborn to just buy out my half so he can move back in."

"He still wants to control you," Chase said, his tone etched with anger.

"You're right, but I refuse to let him control me anymore." Easier said than done. Even lying in a hospital bed, he was still controlling her life. If heaven forbid he died, that control still wouldn't end. "Do you happen to know of any place I can rent? Since we're on the holiday break, I'd have time to get settled before school resumes after the first of the year."

He released a cynical laugh. "Most of the rentals around here are owned by your father-in-law."

Jess hadn't stopped to consider that. "Surely there's some property available somewhere that Edwin doesn't have his hands on."

Chase kicked back in his chair and stretched his arms above his head. "I'll ask around. In the meantime, you can stay here."

She didn't see that as a viable option, especially after his obvious discomfort last night. "Thanks for the offer, but I can always go to the motel if I have to."

Chase shrugged. "Suit yourself, but your pride isn't going to benefit you or your son. Forcing him to live in a rat-hole motel won't help matters."

As usual, he was right, but that didn't make living in his house more appealing. "I'll just wait and see what happens today."

She had one more question to ask him, one she'd been purposely avoiding to this point. "Have you heard anything on Dalton's condition?"

"I called Rachel a little while ago. He's still in ICU but he's stable."

Jess experienced some measure of relief that she wouldn't be facing a murder charge—yet. "Then, he's going to be okay?"

"Looks like it. He's also awake."

Her relief dissolved into dread. "Did he say anything about last night?"

"He said he doesn't remember what happened. But that could only be temporary. They won't know for a few days."

"I'm glad his condition has improved," she added without a shred of sincerity.

Chase studied her as if he could see right through her deception. "I guess it probably is a good thing. Unless it's going to cause more problems for you in the long run."

Somehow Chase knew she was withholding information, but he could never know what really happened last night. No one would know if she could help it. Jess could only hope that Dalton's memory loss was permanent, saving both her and her son. If not, she'd deal with the fallout later. Right now she had to move on to the matter at hand.

"I'm going to check on Danny and then dress." As she started toward the bedroom, Chase called her name. She faced him and attempted a smile that fell short. "Yes?"

His gaze didn't waver from hers. "When you give your statement, don't forget all the misery Dalton's caused you and Danny. Consider what's best for you and not what's right."

Comprehension dawned slowly before Jess realized Chase had been telling her to cover her tracks. To do what she had to do to skirt any legal issues. Basically, to lie.

Without offering a response, Jess left the kitchen to seek out her child. She discovered the guestroom door partially ajar and pushed it open to find Danny seated on the edge of the bed, tying his sneakers. He glanced up at her with that same vacant look in his eyes, sending a pang of regret coursing through her soul.

She took a seat beside him, draped her arm around his thin shoulders and locked into his gaze. "Danny, when we get to the station, Sheriff Reed's going to ask you some questions."

A flicker of fear called out from his brown eyes, yet he didn't respond, leading Jess to continue. "It was an accident. That's all you have to say. Or you don't have to say anything at all. In fact, it might be better if you didn't say anything."

When fear turned into confusion in Danny's expression, Jess felt as if she was falling into a black hole of deceit and dragging her son down with her. Still, she saw no way around asking him to lie, if only by omission.

She tipped her head against his and whispered, "I promise you I'm going to take care of this. Nothing bad's going to happen if you'll trust me, sweetie."

He looked as if he didn't quite believe her, but he did nod his head in acknowledgment.

Jess kissed his forehead and came to her feet. "Try not to worry, Danny. It will all be over soon."

If only she sincerely believed that. If only she could convince her child of that when she wasn't convinced herself.

For the time being, Jess decided to follow Chase's advice and only disclose what she needed to get by, skirting the truth and in turn, shattering everything she'd been taught during her childhood. Everything she'd taught her only child about honesty.

Even if she continued her cover-up, she ran the risk that eventually her secrets would be revealed. Two very important secrets. The first she'd kept for over ten years, the second less than twenty-four-hours. Both were closely intertwined. That ten-year-old secret could drive an irreparable wedge between her and Chase as well as complicate her current problems.

But the second could cost her everything…including her son.

Chapter 3

"You look like hell, Deputy Reed."

Chase leaned over the counter and sent Sue Ellen Parker—the sixty-something Crowley County dispatcher—his best grin. "You look mighty pretty today."

A serious blush spread across the woman's plump cheeks. "I thought you outgrew that silver-tongued devil tactic years ago. Just goes to show, once a bad boy, always a bad boy. And I'm thinkin' your bad boy ways may be the cause of your fatigue."

He wouldn't argue that point. Having Jess in his bed had prevented him from getting much rest. Sometime during the night, she'd curled up against him and it had taken all his strength not to take up where they'd left off all those years ago. Repeating past mistakes never turned out well. And if he knew what was good for him, he'd scour the county and find her a place to live before he screwed up again.

He couldn't think of a better resource for rental property than Sue Ellen, who knew everything about everyone, just like the town gossip, Pearl Allworth. But one huge difference set the two women apart—Sue was discrete while Pearl shot rumors around town like a human AK-47.

Chase sent a glance toward the small conference room across the hall where Buck was probably bullying Jess, hoping she might break. Danny was sitting in the corridor, his legs in constant motion. He felt sorry for the kid on many levels, the first being born to a bastard like Dalton Wainwright. Now to be dragged into a mess that could land his mother in jail, that sure as hell wasn't fair. But then life wasn't always fair. He'd learned that through experience.

Chase walked around the counter and took a seat next to the dispatcher, determined to do what he could to help Jess and her boy. Keeping his back to Danny, he asked Sue, "Do you know anyone who has a house for rent besides Wainwright?"

She took a pen from behind her ear and tapped it on the desk. "Is the remodeling going down the toilet?"

He lowered his voice and said, "It's not for me. It's for Jess and Danny."

Sue raised a penciled-in brow. "What's wrong with that big old house she's been living in?"

Either Sue was playing ignorant, or she really didn't know about Dalton. "Hard to believe you haven't heard about what happened there last night."

She exchanged the pen for a paper clip that she began to straighten. "I've heard, but as soon as she's cleared, she should be able to move back in, right?"

If she was cleared. Chase hoped that would be the case

for both her and Danny's sake. "She doesn't want to live there, and I can't say that I blame her."

Sue leaned forward and in a hushed voice asked, "Do you think she did something to him?"

Chase refused to take the bait. "Now, Sue, you know I can't talk about an ongoing investigation." He wouldn't even if he could, especially not with Jess involved.

She patted her tightly-curled salt-and-pepper hair. "Sorry, but I can't help but wonder if he drove her to it. Not that anyone in this town who knows that sorry sapsucker would ever judge Jess if she did take matters into her own hands. Why, just the other day when I was driving downtown, I saw Dalton coming out of the general store and it was all I could do not to hit the accelerator and jump the curb in my Jeep."

Chase tried not to smile but couldn't stop himself. "I wouldn't repeat that around here. Buck might start questioning you."

Sue rolled her eyes. "Your daddy doesn't scare me, Chase. If he gives me grief, I'll pour a little salt in his coffee and he knows it."

Back to the matter at hand. "So do you know any places for rent?"

Sue tapped one temple like she was trying to dislodge a thought. "I know of a few on wheels that I wouldn't recommend to my worst enemy. But the Wooley's old farmhouse on the outskirts of town is vacant. I'm not sure Gabe has done much to it since his mama went into the nursing home about a year ago, so it might not be livable."

Chase knew the place well, and if it wasn't too run-down, it would be perfect. The house sat well off the road, giving Jess privacy and Danny a lot of room to roam. "I'll call Gabe and see if he's interested in renting it out. Thanks."

She gave him a toothy grin. "You're welcome, Deputy. Anything else?"

Chase shot another look at Danny over one shoulder. "Yeah. Could you take the boy into the break room and get him a snack? He doesn't need to see his mother upset."

"Sure," she said. "Are you going to answer the phone?"

Chase leaned around her to see Barkley seated at his desk not far away. "Only if Bobby Boy gets swamped with calls, and around here, that's not likely."

Sue rolled back her chair and stood. "You never know, Chase. We've had a lot of shoplifting calls lately."

That didn't surprise him in the least. When times were tough, people got by any way they could, even if it meant stealing what they needed.

Chase watched as Sue held out her hand to Danny and after a brief pause, he took it and allowed the woman to lead him away. A few seconds later, the conference room door opened and Jess stepped out, looking like she'd been run through the mill twice. She'd always been fair-skinned, but Chase had never seen her quite so pale.

After his dad emerged wearing his patent sheriff's scowl, Chase joined them in the hallway, ready to offer support and an explanation when Jess looked around, obviously concerned over her son's absence. "Where's Danny?" she asked, a touch of alarm in her tone.

Chase pointed down the corridor. "Sue took him to the break room. Third room to the right." After Jess hurried away, Chase faced his dad. "Is she free to go now?"

"Not until I talk to the boy," Buck said. "I need to hear

his version of the story because I'm not buying the bill of goods I just got from his mother."

Chase resented his dad for continuing to treat Jess like some hardened criminal. "The kid's still in shock. Maybe you ought to wait another day or two before you harass him like you did Jess."

"I'm just following procedure, son, like I would with anyone else who's involved in a questionable incident."

And that's what irked Chase—his dad viewing Jess like someone he'd never met before, not the kid who used to call him Daddy Buck. "Did she give you any reason to think that this was anything other than an accident?"

Buck rubbed his stubbled chin. "I don't know any more about what went on than I did before the interview. I do know she's holding something back."

Chase clung to his control before he blew a verbal gasket. "You've been in this business so long everyone starts to look guilty to you. Jess is only guilty of marrying the wrong man."

"And marrying into the wrong family. But she did marry into that family and that makes me wonder if she didn't learn a thing or two along the way."

"Like what?"

"Like how to lie to cover your ass."

Fact was, Chase worried Jess might be lying. Or at least not telling the whole truth. But he had no intention of letting on that he had his suspicions, especially around his dad. "Look, giving the boy a couple of days to calm down isn't going to hurt a damn thing. Besides, Rachel called this morning and said Dalton's awake and talking."

"I know," Buck said. "And as soon as I get the go-ahead from the doctors, I'm going to have a talk with the victim about his recollections of last night."

Chase couldn't think of Dalton as a victim no matter what had transpired. "He doesn't remember what happened, and even if he did, like you said, the Wainwrights know how to cover their asses. He might just point a finger at Jess for spite."

"And that's all the more reason to question the boy," Buck added. "But I'll make a deal with you. If Dalton regains his memory and he backs up Jess's accident story, then I won't involve the kid. But if he tells a whole different tale, then I have no choice but to question Danny. He could be the key to the truth."

Chase stuck out his hand for a shake. "Deal. In the meantime, I'm going to get Jess settled in. She's going to need some of her things from the house."

"Fine, as long as you escort her." Buck inclined his head and studied him a moment. "You gonna keep her at the cabin?"

His dad's tone sounded like he planned to hold Jess hostage. "No. I'm going to find her another place to rent."

"Good. I wouldn't want folks around here thinking you're in cahoots with a suspect. That wouldn't be proper behavior for a peace officer."

Chase gritted his teeth and spoke through them. "Best I recall, we don't name a suspect unless we know a crime's taken place."

Buck hitched up his pants. "True. You still don't need to be too friendly with her, just in case."

"She is a friend, Buck, and has been for as long as I can remember." Even though that friendship had suffered in the past few years, thanks to his stupidity.

Buck gave him a condescending pat on the back. "Look, son, people change. Jess just might not be that girl you used to know."

Chase wouldn't even make an attempt at denial because he acknowledged his dad was partially right—Jess wasn't the same. Neither was he.

Without further comment, he spun around and headed toward his office to take care of some pressing arrangements. He made a quick call to Gabe Wooley, who was more than happy to have someone renting the old home place until the family decided whether they wanted to sell it.

Satisfied he'd done something constructive today, Chase made his way to the break room to find Jess and Danny sitting at the small round table in the corner, looking like they could both use a friend.

And that's what he intended to be to them both—a friend. To hell with propriety.

"Let's go," he said when Jess looked up.

"Is it Danny's turn?" she asked in a voice barely above a whisper.

"Not today."

Her shoulders sagged from obvious relief. "We can go?"

"Yeah." Chase didn't have the heart tell her it might only be a temporary reprieve.

Jess stood and pulled out Danny's chair. "Let's go, sweetie. We need to look for a place to stay."

"I've got that covered."

Jess and Danny exchanged a look before Jess asked, "Where?"

"You'll see."

Jess could only see overgrown trees and knee-high, winter-dry grass as Chase maneuvered the department's SUV up the narrow road. But she'd recognized the area immediately as soon as they turned off the highway.

Many times she'd accompanied her mother to the place to deliver supplies to widowed Nita Wooley, whose health had declined in recent years. The same place where Nita and Gabe Sr. had raised five children on a limited income but a lot of love.

Once Chase stopped near the front door, Jess glanced back to see Danny staring out the window with curiosity. She could only imagine the thoughts running through his mind—his mother was taking him from a custom-built, modern multilevel semi-mansion to a small, weather-worn, single-story farm house.

As far as Jess was concerned, if the place was relatively clean, furnished and warm, they would make do. At least there was plenty of privacy and enough room for Danny to play. She even spotted a tire swing tied to an ancient oak in the front yard that would provide a much-needed diversion for her child. Yes, this would definitely do, at least for the time being.

Chase slid out of the driver's side and Jess followed suit, opening the door for Danny, who refused to take her offered hand. Maybe after they'd settled in, he'd be more himself again. Maybe he'd even talk to her again.

Chase lifted the dusty welcome mat and retrieved a key that anyone with any sense could have found and helped themselves to whatever remained in the house. But in Placid, crime was low and life was simple. Most people had very few possessions that anyone would deem valuable.

The minute Jess stepped onto the scuffed hardwood floors, she was overwhelmed by the musty smell and the amount of stuff scattered about the small living room. Numerous trinkets, along with portraits of children and their children, sat out on various tables and stationary shelves lining the walls. A family's legacy proudly on display.

Chase turned and handed her the key while Danny remained at the door. "Gabe said you'll find everything you need and then some."

She tucked the key into the pocket of her jeans while she continued to survey the living room and its personal treasures. "No kidding. I feel like I'm in a museum."

"He also said Millie comes over now and then to clean the place but she hasn't been here in a while."

Jess remembered Gabe's wife, Millie, very fondly. She'd worked in the high school cafeteria to supplement Gabe's farming income and she'd always sported a smile while serving questionable fare. Unfortunately, Gabe was about as crabby as they came. "As long as we have a roof over our heads, I can deal with tidying up. How much does he want for rent?"

Chase's gaze faltered. "Nine hundred a month plus utilities. No deposit or lease required."

Highway robbery as far as Jess was concerned, especially if her job was in jeopardy. She wouldn't know for certain until after the first of the year, unless she happened to be indicted. Even if she was cleared of all wrong-doing, some would want her contract terminated immediately, namely Edwin. Then she would have no choice but to leave her hometown. "Does Gabe know I'm the prospective tenant?"

Chase brought his attention back to her. "Not yet. I told him I was asking for a friend and I'd call if we're interested after we checked the place out. But he's going to want to know who's renting the house if you decide to take it."

What choice did she have? "The price is a little steep

but beggars can't be choosers. And as far as Gabe knowing I'm renting the house, I imagine everyone's going
to hear about what happened last night sooner or later."
More than likely sooner.

"Okay. I'll let him know and drop off the rent during my shift."

That posed another problem. "My checkbook's at the
house."

"I'll take care of it."

Jess already owed him too much. "I'll pay you back
as soon as I get the rest of my things. What about the
utilities?"

Chase dropped down on the shabby blue sofa. "The
electricity's still on but the heat runs on propane and the
tank's empty. I'll call Freddie and see if he can deliver
some tomorrow."

"It's not supposed to be too cold tonight. We'll manage." Jess pointed at the pot-belly stove in the corner. "Or
we could use that I guess."

"I'll see if I can find some wood before I go."

Jess didn't want him to go, but she also didn't dare ask
him to stay. "As long as we have blankets, we'll be okay
until tomorrow. What time are you on today?"

He came to his feet. "I work eleven to eleven."

"A twelve-hour shift?"

"That's what happens when you're short on man-
power."

That meant he had little time left before he had to
leave, and she probably wouldn't see him again today.
"I really need some extra clothes and my car from the
house."

"I'll have to accompany you and I don't have much

time. If you have enough to get by until tomorrow, we can stop by first thing in the morning."

"I guess we can make do," she said, though she hated not having control over claiming her own belongings. "But we will need food."

"I'll send Sue over with some lunch as soon as I'm back at the department. She can bring you some groceries after work."

Jess didn't particularly care for that idea. "Again, I don't have any cash and I really wouldn't want to inconvenience anyone."

"Sue won't mind as long as I promise to cover the cost, which I will."

"I have my own money, Chase."

"I'm sure you do, and you can pay me back by making me dinner sometime. I could go for some mac and cheese or tuna fish sandwiches."

He still thought she was the girl who couldn't cook to save her life. Little did he know, she'd learned a lot in his absence. "Fine. But I still don't want Sue to have to come all the way out here."

Chase inclined his head and studied her a few moments. "If you're worried she'll tell someone your whereabouts, don't. You can trust her."

Jess's concerns had more to do with shame than privacy. But her growing boy needed to eat and until she had her own transportation, she'd have to rely on the kindness of others. "Okay. As long as you promise I'll have my car back by tomorrow."

"I promise," he said.

Jess noticed her son had taken a seat in the yellow-striped chair near the door, still stoic and silent. "Do you want to pick out your room, Danny?" she asked, hoping to somehow engage him.

He shook his head no and studied the toe of his sneaker.

"Well, I'm going to take a look around and you can decide later," she said. "Don't go anywhere unless you tell me." Like that would happen since he still refused to speak.

Jess crossed the room into an adjacent hallway and came to the first door to her right—a small bathroom with a claw-foot tub on the opposite wall. When she heard heavy footfalls, she glanced back to see Chase filling the doorway. "This is great," she said as she examined the tub that appeared to be clean and in decent shape except for a few nicks here and there. "Unfortunately, no shower. Is there another bathroom?"

"Nope. But I can rig you a hand-held when I come back tomorrow."

Funny, she'd gone from four fully-equipped baths to one. "I'd appreciate that." She'd also appreciate it if he stepped back to give her some space.

When he failed to move, Jess brushed past him and continued her investigation of the premises. The first bedroom housed two sets of bunk beds, the second two double beds, all reminders that a large family had once lived there. At the end of the corridor, she came upon the largest room that held a dresser and another double bed with an iron headboard that looked to be as old as the house itself.

Again she turned to find Chase with a shoulder propped against the frame. "I assume this is the master bedroom."

He sent her a half-smile. "Yep. The place where the Wooleys made all the little Wooleys."

He could have gone all day without mentioning that. "Let's hope the mattress has since been replaced. And speaking of that, I noticed all the beds have been stripped."

"Gabe said there's clean linens in the hall closet."

At least she wouldn't have to bring those from the house. "Good. What about the washer and dryer?"

"Washer but no dryer. Nita hung her clothes on the line."

Jess felt as if she'd unwittingly stepped back in time. "I suppose that's why they invented coin-operated laundries." And the nearest one happened to be five miles away.

"The washer's in a small room off the kitchen," Chase said as he stepped into the bedroom, making the adequate space seemed too cramped for Jess's comfort.

She clapped her hands together enthusiastically. "Let's go see the kitchen, shall we?" When Chase laughed, taking her by surprise, Jess asked, "What's so amusing?"

"For a minute there I saw the head cheerleader coming out in you."

She hadn't had anything to cheer about in years. "That girl went away a long time ago. If you don't believe me, take a gander at my backside."

Chase raked his gaze down her body and back up again. "You don't look all that different, Jess."

"Try telling that to Dalton." She regretted the acid comment the moment it left her mouth.

Chase scowled as he always did whenever she mentioned his archenemy's name. "You shouldn't care what that bastard thinks."

Old verbal wounds were hard to heal. "I don't care about anything but seeing the kitchen."

He stepped aside and made a sweeping gesture toward the hall. "After you."

Jess once more passed through the living room where Danny was rooted in the same spot, still wearing his gray down jacket as if he had no intention of staying. As soon as she had some alone time with him, she'd explain this was only a temporary home. Yet she wasn't certain he truly cared one way or the other. And if his demeanor didn't change in the next day or two, she'd be forced to seek professional help for him. She prayed she could wait at least until the current legal storm blew over. If not, she'd have to trust that a counselor would be bound by patient confidentiality should Danny decide to reveal the events leading up to Dalton's injuries. Right now she had to concentrate on getting her bearings so they could begin to move in.

With that in mind, she found her way into the kitchen with a small dining area housing a wooden table, benches on both sides and a chair on each end. She began opening cabinets and drawers to discover myriad pots, pans, dishes, glasses and utensils. When she heard Chase approaching, she turned and leaned back against the well-worn butcher-block counter. "There's enough equipment here to feed an army."

"That pretty much describes the Wooley family," he said as he entered the room, dropped into one chair at the table and stretched his long legs out before him.

Jess was suddenly struck by his undeniable presence and authority, from the top of his cowboy hat to the tip of his boots. He portrayed old-West lawman to a T. Oddly, everything about him kept her off balance, as if she didn't really know him at all. In many ways, that was accurate.

She moved to the massive farm sink that provided a nice view of the pasture from the window above it. "This is really a pretty place."

Before Jess even realized he'd left the table, Chase reached around her and turned on the faucet, his body flush against her back. "The well's supposed to be working, but Gabe says to check the water since we've had a fairly long dry spell. I can sure relate to that."

Jess glanced back to see his half-smile and a hint of the consummate charmer he'd always been. "I have a hard time believing that." Even if for some strange reason, she hoped it were true.

"You know how it is around here, Jess," he said. "Not a whole lot of people our age in Placid."

She returned his smile. "Poor Deputy Reed. No one to irrigate his crops."

He brushed a strand of hair from her cheek. "Don't worry your pretty head over me. I get by."

Getting by seemed to be the recent story of her life. Getting away from Chase seemed to be the better part of valor. The innuendo had begun to take its toll on her composure, especially when he remained so close she could trace a line around his lips with a fingertip with little effort. The fact that his proximity, his words, could affect her at a time like this was beyond explanation.

Right when she started to move away, Chase stopped her progress when he said, "Will you take a look at that?"

Jess turned her focus back to the window to see Danny seated on the ground, holding his hand out to a young tabby cat that stood a few feet away, back arched and tail sticking straight up. Not only had she'd not heard him leave the house, she'd inadvertently allowed him to come face-to-face with a wild animal. "Oh, heavens. That thing is probably feral and hasn't had any shots. I need—"

"To leave him be," Chase said as the kitten skittered away.

She sent him a look of sheer surprise. "Are you crazy? He could've been scratched or bitten and ended up with rabies."

"But he wasn't and he's fine. Seems to me he just needs a little time to himself."

Jess silently admitted Chase was probably right, but her motherly instincts at times commandeered her common sense.

"You know what else he needs, Jess?" Chase said.

"A friend?"

"A dog."

Another memory, sharp as shattered glass, dug into her mind. "Danny had a puppy once when he was five. A Golden Retriever named Birdie. She chewed up a pair of Dalton's Italian loafers, so Dalton gave her away to some hunter two counties over. Then he told Danny that she'd run away because he wasn't a good boy."

"That sorry son of a bitch," Chase muttered, pure venom in his voice.

Jess had called him that very thing in her mind, but she'd never said it to his face...until last night.

Shoving aside the reminders, Jess planned to go to Danny just to make sure he'd been left unscathed, at least when it came to the cat. Yet when he took a stick and began drawing in the dirt, his mouth moving as if he were speaking to an imaginary friend, fascination kept her planted where she stood. At least that confirmed he could still talk, even if not to her. He could also still smile, she realized, when he grinned as he looked to his right to see the kitten had returned. A smile that always warmed her heart whenever his precious dimples came into view, the one on the left more prominent that the one on the right.

Overcome with the need to distract Chase, she side-stepped him. "I'm going to bring Danny in before he ends up on the wrong side of the cat."

Chase checked his watch. "And I'm going to head out."

Jess realized that after he left, she had no means to communicate with the outside world. "I left my cell phone on the charger at the house."

"I'd give you mine but I need it for work. I'll see if Sue can come up with a spare until we get yours in the morning."

If Sue didn't come through, that meant she'd spend the day wondering if Dalton's condition had deteriorated. "Thanks again. For everything."

"No sweat. That's what friends are for."

At least he still considered her a friend, or he could be playing nice out of pity. Only time would tell.

They walked side by side to the door and when they stepped onto the porch, Jess resisted the urge to throw her arms around him and ask him to stay a few more minutes. "Have an exciting day."

He barked out a cynical laugh. "Sure. About the only excitement I'll see is if I have to break up a bar fight."

She shuddered at the thought of Chase throwing himself into the middle of danger, though that wasn't unfamiliar territory. She'd had to live with that reality the whole time he'd been at war. "Tell Sue not to hurry on our account."

"Sue doesn't have any other speed."

He sent her a smile, displaying his dimples to full advantage, touched the brim of his hat and said, "See you tomorrow, ma'am," before climbing into the SUV and driving away.

As Jess rounded the house to join Danny, a cool breeze blew across her face and brought with it a sudden chill that had nothing to do with the mild winter weather. She longed to be around Chase, yet she realized the possible peril in that. The more time he spent with her child, the greater the risk that he might begin to suspect what she'd suspected—and denied—for years.

She'd ignored all the signs, just as she'd ignored Dalton's many fatal flaws. Yet in her heart she'd known all along that the quiet little boy with the dimpled smile, dark pensive eyes and sandy hair, could very well be the deputy's son.

And last night, during one fateful confrontation, the worst had come to pass when her ex-husband, who'd never been much of a father to her son, had voiced his suspicions, too.

Chapter 4

When the knock sounded at the door, Jess expected to see Sue Ellen standing at the threshold for the second time today, this time with groceries. But never in her wildest dreams had she predicted that Rachel Wainwright Boyd—her former sister-in-law and longtime friend—would be gracing the doorstep. Not with her brother still lying in a hospital bed and his ex-wife believed to be responsible for putting him there.

"What are you doing here?" Jess asked, painfully aware she sounded as if she didn't welcome the visit.

Rachel's smile looked somewhat self-conscious as she held up two pieces of familiar paisley luggage. "I come bearing gifts."

Jess opened the screen wide and told her, "Come in," around her surprise.

As soon as Rachel stepped inside and set the bags on

the floor, Danny sprinted across the room and wrapped his arms around her waist, nearly knocking her backward. "Whoa there, my little angel of a nephew."

Though Jess appreciated Danny's enthusiasm, she couldn't quell the tiny nip of envy. He'd refused any show of affection, at least when it came to his own mother. "Be careful, Danny. Aunt Rachel's got a baby on board."

Rachel leaned down and kissed the top of his head. "Don't worry. This baby is going to be tough as nails if he's anything like his father."

"He's been cooped up in the house all day with me and no TV," Jess said. "That's why he's so glad to see you." After she realized how that sounded, she added, "Of course he's always glad to see his favorite aunt."

Rachel ruffled Danny's hair when he stepped back and looked at her as if she'd come to save him. "I've got a few things for you out in your mom's car that should take care of some of the boredom."

Stunned over the revelation, Jess looked through the window to discover her beige hybrid sedan parked in the driveway. "How did you manage that?"

"The same way I managed this," Rachel said as she rummaged through her purse, withdrew Jess's cell phone and handed it to her. "The charger's in a bag with a few of your clothes."

At least she wouldn't be naked and since Sue hadn't brought a spare phone, she now had a way to communicate with the outside world. Provided she actually had service. "I assume you've been talking to Chase."

"He called me a few hours ago and he told me where to find you. I volunteered to retrieve a few of your things and deliver your car."

Jess couldn't believe her friend would risk entering

the enemy camp. Then again, they'd never been enemies, even after she'd divorced her brother. "How did you get into the house?"

"I used my spare key. Of course, that idiot Barkley followed me around like I was up to no good. I just ignored him when he acted like I was going to steal your car after I grabbed the keys off the hook in the kitchen. Other than that, piece of cake."

Thank heavens for girlfriends to rely on through thick and thin. "I can't tell you how much I appreciate this."

"Not a problem at all," Rachel said. "Matt's at the Stanfield farm not far away, treating a mare that came down with colic. He's going to pick me up when he's done." She hoisted a bag onto the sofa, unzipped it, pulled out a pair of red designer platform heels and held them up. "I just knew you couldn't live a day longer without these."

Jess had purchased those treasured shoes during a trip with Rachel to Atlanta six months ago. The trip where her sister-in-law had told her she was pregnant, and she'd told Rachel she was leaving Dalton. "Thanks, I guess, but I don't have any immediate plans to go out dancing."

"You can wear them around the house." Rachel tossed a lock of near-black hair over a shoulder in dramatic fashion, sheer amusement calling out from her dark eyes. "I think they'll look fabulous with your outfit, don't you?"

Jess glanced down at her gray sweatshirt and faded blue yoga pants, then frowned. "Oh, right. A wonderful fashion statement while I'm scrubbing the toilet."

They shared in a laugh before Rachel turned to Danny again. "Why don't you help me get the rest of the stuff out of the car, kiddo?"

Danny nodded and clasped Rachel's offered hand while Jess followed behind them. It took two trips to retrieve the numerous bags of clothing, groceries and Danny's toys. By the time they were finished, Jess felt as if she finally had the makings for a decent home for her child.

After Danny retreated to the bedroom with the bunk beds and closed the door, Jess invited Rachel into the kitchen to put up the food.

Her friend did a visual inspection of the area and smiled her approval. "Not bad at all."

"If you like yellow," Jess said as she began to rummage through a bag. "It's not exactly my ideal abode, but I'm afraid it's going to have to do since rental property is at a premium in Placid."

"And since my father has a monopoly on most of the rentals."

A subject she didn't care to undertake. "I wasn't going to mention that, but you're right. I doubt he'd want me as a tenant."

"My father only cares about how much of the town he can purchase at a bargain."

Jess had no reasonable defense for Edwin's actions so she chose not to respond.

They remained silent for a time while Rachel placed a few items into the freezer. "Most of this came from your refrigerator and pantry," she said. "I wasn't sure how long you planned to stay here and I didn't want anything to spoil. I also looked under the tree for Christmas presents, and then I remembered you've always been a last-minute shopper."

The upcoming holidays had been the furthest thing from her mind. "Yes, I'm a procrastinator, but my son is a snoop so I don't dare buy too early, otherwise he'll find the gifts. Besides, I still have time to shop."

Rachel frowned. "Christmas is one week from tomorrow."

"I thought it fell on a Sunday."

"That's right. Today is Saturday, Jess."

Heavens, a few hours of isolation and she'd lost complete track of time along with a good deal of sanity. "You're right. I'm a little fuzzy from lack of sleep."

She sent Jess a quick glance. "Do you think you'll be here Christmas?"

Unless she found herself incarcerated. "I don't have any definite plans about the living arrangements other than I don't intend to go back to the house."

Rachel hesitated a moment before sliding a can of soup into the cabinet. "I don't blame you."

Jess wondered if her friend did in fact blame her for Dalton's current condition. And on that note she said, "Chase told me Dalton's been awake."

Disregarding her pregnant state, Rachel hoisted herself up on the kitchen counter, a habit she'd developed in their youth. "The doctors say he's going to be groggy for a few days, but they expect the skull fracture to heal on its own without any surgery."

She swallowed hard. "Skull fracture?"

Rachel looked altogether perplexed. "Didn't Chase tell you?"

Most likely he'd been trying to protect her by withholding details. She couldn't fault him for that since she was guilty of the same. "He said Dalton probably had a severe concussion."

Rachel sent her a reassuring smile. "Hey, it wasn't as bad as it could've been. The hospital staff is pretty certain he didn't suffer any serious brain injury because he's responsive. He is rather confused and sometimes doesn't make a lot of sense when he speaks. Then again, I've seen him that way after he's been to happy hour."

So had Jess on the numerous occasions he'd come home under the influence. She'd seen him that way again last night. "So he's going to make a full recovery?"

"That's my understanding, although they're not sure he'll ever be able to recall the events that led to his hospitalization." Rachel topped off the comment with a meaningful look.

Jess welcomed that news for reasons she didn't dare disclose to her friend. "I'm glad he's going to be okay."

"You are?"

"Of course I am. No matter what's happened between us, I would never wish any harm on Dalton. You have to believe that."

"I do."

The lack of conviction in Rachel's tone drove Jess to further explain the situation, or as much as she could offer without providing all the gory details. "Look, Rachel, I swear to you that Dalton's injuries resulted from an accident. He'd been drinking and he stumbled." With a little help, a fact she opted to leave out of the mix.

Rachel's gaze drifted away. "According to my father, Dalton's tox screen was negative."

A surge of panic swelled in Jess's chest, making it difficult to draw a breath. She could see a criminal case against her building with every disclosure. "There has to be some mistake. I've been with Dalton a long time and I know when he's had too much to drink."

Rachel sent her a weak smile. "Well, I didn't hear the doctor say it, and it wouldn't be the first time my father made an effort to save Dalton's reputation, usually to no avail."

How well she knew that about her former father-in-law. He'd lie to a clergyman if it meant saving face.

Needing a diversion, Jess began rearranging the canned goods according to contents. "It really doesn't matter as long as Dalton recovers. Danny's completely torn up over this, so much so he hasn't spoken since it happened."

Rachel reached over and patted her hand. "If you're really concerned about him, I have a friend from college who's a child psychologist. She lives in Vicksburg and I'm sure she'd be more than willing to see Danny."

"I've thought about counseling," Jess admitted. "But I'd like to wait a few days until he's had more time to recover. I'm not sure turning him loose on a stranger would help matters right now."

Rachel hopped down from the counter. "Just let me know when and I'll give her a call. And one more thing."

She wasn't sure she could handle one more thing. "What?"

Her friend's expression went somber. "If something happened last night that caused you to lose your temper, I would never blame you for lashing out at my brother. I know how he operates. He spent our childhood deriding me for being Daddy's little girl because he's always been Daddy's tow-the-line target. He's never understood that after my mother died giving birth to me, our father was bound to coddle me a little more. To hear Dalton tell it, I got away with murder."

When mortification passed over Rachel's face, Jess was determined to reassure her. "I'm sure he'd say the same thing about me, but he would be wrong on both counts."

The sound of a blaring horn caused Jess to physically

jump while Rachel muttered, "My husband has no manners. The last time he honked to summon me, we were dating and he did it just to spite my father."

Jess tried hard to smile but it didn't quite take. "Men. Can't live with them, can't find anyone else to take them."

Rachel braced her hands on her hips. "Well he can just wait while I help you get the house in order."

"You've already done enough, Rachel. And there's not much else to do. I've spent most of the day clearing the cobwebs and dust and disinfecting the bathrooms with some cleaning products I found here and there. Of course, I still have to tackle the oven."

Rachel put a hand to her ear and pretended to listen. "I do believe I hear my husband calling my name."

Jess laughed. "I knew I couldn't count on you to clean the oven."

"You know me so well." Rachel leaned over and gave her a hug. "Hang in there, Jess. Dalton's going to be fine and then you'll be able to get on with your life."

If only she could share her friend's optimism. "Thanks for everything. And in the meantime…" She patted Rachel's belly. "Take care of junior and I'll see you soon."

"You better believe it," Rachel said. "We still have to go baby shopping before this little one makes an appearance in about eleven weeks."

Jess had no idea where she would be in eleven weeks. Preferably not in jail. "It's a deal."

After Jess saw Rachel off and waved to Matt, who obviously didn't feel comfortable enough to come in for a visit, she went back inside the house to check on her child and resume her cleaning.

Yet an all-consuming guilt plagued her when she considered the details she'd intentionally withheld from the people who cared about her the most. She'd begun to dig a hole so deep she might never find her way out of the abyss. If Dalton never regained his memory of the events that led to this mess, she might be able to keep that secret. What she did with the other secret still remained to be seen.

Chase had a right to know he could be Danny's biological father, but she worried her failure to acknowledge that possibility a long time ago could send him packing for good. He happened to be the only grounding force in her life at the moment, and she couldn't bear the thought of losing his support. Even now the temptation to see him was so great, she considered calling.

But he had a job to do and she had no right to prevent him from doing it because of her insecurities. At least she'd see him tomorrow.

He had no intention of paying Jess a visit until tomorrow.

But before he finished his shift, Chase decided to drive by the house to make sure it was secure. And when he noticed all the lights filtering through the windows, he signed off for the night and returned to his cabin to retrieve a spare TV to give Jess. If she was going to be stuck at home alone with a bad case of insomnia, he might as well provide her with some entertainment.

Who the hell was he kidding? He wanted to be with her, if only for an hour or so. He had to let her know he had no intention of deserting her, even if good sense said he should keep his distance.

As he pulled into the drive twenty minutes later, Chase was satisfied he'd done the right thing when he discovered the place was still lit up like a billboard. Of course, she could be sleeping, but he had his doubts about that. Enough doubts that he got out of the truck, hauled the thirty-six-inch console from the bed, and carried it to the front porch.

After he elbowed the bell, Chance glanced to his right to see Jess pulling the curtain back and peering outside. She opened the door in a matter of moments, sporting a look of surprise. "Is it tomorrow already?" she asked.

Chase didn't know if she was teasing or unhappy to see him. "Thought you could use this for a late-night diversion," he said as he raised the TV for her inspection.

"You could have waited until tomorrow," she said. "Danny's already asleep and I've been reading a book I found in a closet. Not to mention I imagine a satellite dish wouldn't work out here in the boondocks with all the trees. No service, no channels, no reason to have a TV."

He considered himself a fairly strong guy, but the outdated television had to weigh well over a hundred pounds and was top-heavy to boot. At this rate he was going to strain something before she made up her mind. "This set has a built-in DVD player and it's got a converter so you might be able to pick up a couple of channels out of Jackson."

"I guess that's worth something."

It wouldn't be worth a plug nickel if he dropped the damn thing on the porch. "Look, holding this thing is like bench-pressing your car, so I'd appreciate it if you'd decide if you want it before I get a hernia."

She tipped her temple against the partially-open screen. "Sure. I'd hate to think I gave you a hernia and also made you squander your own sleep to help me out with mine."

Like he didn't have his own problems sleeping. "Now

that we have that settled, can I come in or do you want me to toss this to you and leave?"

"Sorry," she muttered as she held open the door, finally allowing him inside.

He avoided looking at her attire—a short flannel nightshirt—and kept his focus on the few available surfaces to support an oversized TV. But the images of her bare legs stayed imprinted in his brain. "Where do you want it?"

"Where do you want to put it?"

That was a loaded question. He nodded toward the low wooden table in the corner near an electrical outlet. "Move that stuff and I'll set it up there."

Jess padded across the room in her sock-covered feet and bent over to clear the table of a candy dish and some cheap figurines. When the blasted shirt rode up her thighs, Chase was forced to lower the TV to preserve his dignity.

He didn't know what the hell was wrong with him. In all the time he'd known Jess, he'd never been turned on by her legs. Well, almost never. He could think of a few times he'd had some fairly male reactions during a swim at the pond together, but he'd always maintained control. And he couldn't forget that one night...

He damn sure didn't need to go there, otherwise he'd be forced to hang onto the television until the pain overrode his libido.

Jess fortunately straightened to give him some relief, her arms full of knick-knacks. "There you go. I'll just put these in the spare room and be back in a sec. In the meantime, make yourself comfortable."

Even if she returned wearing a black garbage sack,

he wouldn't be comfortable. "I've got to get the remote out of the truck."

"Okeydoke," she tossed over one shoulder as she headed away.

Chase put down the TV and stepped outside, hoping the frigid night air would help cool his overheated body. He braced both arms above the passenger door and drew in a few deep breaths while uttering a few choice oaths that would cause his mother to send him into the corner as punishment for his many sins.

Finally feeling more composed, he opened the door and took out the remote along with some DVDs he'd brought with him. He then walked back to the house, slowly, and opened the door to Jess seated on the sofa, her heels propped on the coffee table.

"It's pretty cold in here." Not that he didn't welcome the chill.

She pointed at the black iron stove in the corner. "I wasn't sure how to work that thing, but I did find a space heater in a closet. I put it in Danny's room."

"Do you want me to light your fire?" Damn.

She grinned. "How do you propose to do that?"

"In the stove. With wood and matches."

"I'm fine."

Yeah, she was. Real fine. "I brought a few action movies for Danny but this one's for you." Chase tossed her a DVD featuring a couple in the throes of passion splashed across the label.

After she made a two-handed catch, she surveyed the case for a few moments. "I've been dying to see this."

"I figured it was your kind of movie."

She turned over the unopened package before looking

up at him. "I appreciate the gesture, but you shouldn't have gone to the trouble of buying it just for me."

He didn't particularly like having to shatter her assumption for the sake of honesty but he saw no good reason to lie. "I bought it a while ago for someone else."

She frowned. "One of your Friday-night girls?"

No surprise she'd think that. "My mom, for her birthday. I noticed the R rating and gave her something a little less risqué."

Jess laughed. "It's a romantic comedy, not porn. I'm sure it just features some racy language."

"And nudity," he added. "Missy doesn't like naked people in her movies."

Her amber eyes went wide. "You've already seen it?"

"No. It says so on the label."

She tore open the package and her face lit up with excitement. "Let's watch it now."

No way would he watch a bunch of sex scenes with her, especially when he considered the way he'd reacted to her night clothes that most would deem more than modest, even his mother. "I probably should get going."

She patted the space beside her. "It's not even midnight yet, and you said yourself you have a hard time falling asleep."

He'd been having a hard time ever since he walked into the house. "I don't like chick flicks, Jess."

She looked thoroughly frustrated. "And I don't like violent, shoot-'em-up films, but I've watched more than my share with you in the past."

She obviously craved his company but she sure as hell wouldn't if she could read his mind. If he had any decency at all, he'd suck it up, stick around and watch the freaking movie. Decency was a huge problem at the moment. "Maybe later."

She pretended to pout. "Come on, Chase. If you stay, I'll make you some popcorn. Besides, you'll probably be asleep after the first fifteen minutes."

Maybe so, if the first fifteen minutes didn't involve any sex, and that was a big if. "Fine, I'll give you fifteen minutes, but if I'm not asleep or I hate it, I'm out of here."

"It's a deal." She hopped up from the sofa and went into the kitchen while Chase paced around the room with enough nervous energy to power Placid.

After a few minutes, Jess returned with a bag of potato chips and napkins tucked under one arm, a soft drink clutched in each hand. "I just realized I only have the microwave kind of popcorn and there's no microwave," she said as she gave him a can of cola.

He opened the tab and took a drink, wishing he had something a little stronger. "We can pick one up at the hardware store tomorrow when we stop by your house."

She sat back down on the sofa and tore open the bag. "I can live without a microwave. And Rachel brought everything I need so we can forget the house. By the way, thank you for sending her over."

He could only imagine how that visit went. "She wanted to do it."

"I'm glad she did. Anyway, I'll pick up what's left at the house, as soon as I decide where I'm going to permanently reside."

Chase figured she just wanted to avoid the bad memories. "Suit yourself." He set the drink down on the napkin she'd placed on the table and held out his hand. "Give me the movie and I'll start it, unless you want me to show you how it works."

That earned him a sour look. "I'm not a complete moron, Chase. I know how it works. Beside, you're already up so you can stick it in."

Everything she said sounded downright dirty, but then his mind—not her mouth—had taken a freefall into the gutter. "That coming from someone who called me to program her VCR back in high school."

"Shut up and play the movie."

She nailed him with a grin and those crystal-clear amber eyes that sometimes looked green, sometimes gold, like now. Cat eyes, he used to call them. She also had a mouth that the stuff male fantasies were made of. Put the package all together and you had temptation personified. A deadly combination, especially to a guy who didn't need a whole lot of encouragement to throw logic to the wind and climb all over her.

Forcing himself back into cautious mode, Chase plugged in the TV, inserted the DVD and started it rolling with the remote. He thought about claiming the straight-back chair, but it looked about as comfortable as cactus. He opted to join Jess on the sofa and slid as far to the left as he could until he butted up against the arm. Better a furniture arm than her arm.

He pointed the remote and turned up the volume while they watched the opening credits, complete with sappy music that made him want to cover his ears. "Too bad we don't have surround sound," he said with a whole lot of sarcasm.

Jess rolled her eyes. "Boys and their toys. Dalton was always about high-dollar sound systems and woofers and tweeters. The man loves big tweeters. Guess that's part of the reason why the marriage didn't work."

Chase tried to center his attention on the TV but his

evil eyes betrayed him, landing his gaze right on Jess's chest. "Your tweeters are fine."

She let go a sarcastic laugh. "Ha! That coming from the guy who told me in the seventh grade that he was sorry my training bra needed to be trained for better results."

Man, he thought she'd forgotten that. "Just a stupid remark from a stupid kid."

She popped a chip into her mouth. "If you think I'm going to buy into that excuse, think again."

"You could be pretty caustic with the remarks, too. I recall you throwing around dumb jock more than once."

"Don't forget tail chaser."

"Shrimp."

She hurled a potato chip at his head. "Dimples."

He'd hated that one the most and that called for bringing out the big guns. "Stop throwing food, Gertrude."

She narrowed her eyes and glared at him. "You know how much I despise my middle name. Now apologize."

When she poked him hard in the ribs, he grabbed her leg and pressed his fingertips in the sensitive spot above her knee. "Not until you apologize for the dimples remark."

She writhed and laughed until he released the pressure, then straightened and sent him a fierce look. "If you try that again, I swear I'll kick you off the couch."

He leaned closer. "You don't scare me, Gertie."

But with his hand still on her thigh and that lethal mouth only a few inches away from his, she did scare him. Correction. He feared what he might do to her if he didn't get away quick. He hadn't wanted anything or anyone this much since he'd come back to town. But he couldn't compromise their renewed connection all in the name of a quick roll on the couch. Provided she'd even go for that.

She would, he realized when she closed her eyes, drew in a slow breath, and inched her mouth closer to his. If anyone needed to be kissed, she did. If anyone could kiss her the way she should be kissed, he could. If the stakes weren't so high, he'd do it. Now. To hell with the consequences.

Instead, Chase moved back into his original spot and muttered, "We're missing the movie."

Jess adjusted her clothes, pulled the lone throw pillow from behind her back and hugged it. "Like you really care."

No, he didn't care, but at least the video provided a distraction. Too much of a distraction, he decided after the lead guy backed the gullible girl up against a wall and started tearing at her clothes. Pretty soon the clothes were gone and the action was on and that just about sent Chase completely over the edge.

He had two choices—steal the pillow from Jess to put in his lap or make a fast exit. He opted for the exit.

"I've got to go," he said as he pushed off the couch and headed toward the door.

Jess move lightning fast and thwarted his departure before he could even turn the knob. "What's the problem, Chase?"

He didn't dare face her and let her see his problem. "I can't do this."

"Can't do what? Watch a movie with me?"

He tipped his forehead against the door and sucked in a couple of breaths. "I can't pretend everything's the same between us."

"And I can't believe you'd let one night, that by your

own admission didn't mean anything, stand in the way of our friendship."

If she only knew how much that night had meant to him. How often he'd thought about it over the years. How much he still wanted her. "I'm not as strong as you think. You deserve better."

"Chase, look at me."

He reluctantly answered her command and realized how damn sexy she looked with her hair a complete mess. "What?"

"We both deserve to be happy, and nothing has ever made me happier than having you as my best friend. Sometimes you have to fight for the things in life you consider worthwhile." Her gaze and confidence wavered. "Unless you don't view our relationship that way."

He sighed. "Yeah, I do."

She took his hands into hers. "Then can we at least try to start over again and regain our trust in each other?"

He'd like nothing better than to start over, but easier said than done. Still, he owed her that much and more. "I'll try, but it's going to take time."

Her smile went straight to his heart. "We've got all the time in the world, at least for now."

Chase worried spending that time with her could lead to betrayal, if he didn't keep a chokehold on his desire. But she was right about one thing—their friendship was worth a second shot. He couldn't think of two people who needed each other more. And he could think of all the reasons why needing each other too much could be way too risky.

Chapter 5

She needed more sleep.

The sound of the TV prevented Jess from pulling the covers back over her head and hiding away from the world. That would mean hiding away from her son, who'd apparently left his room since the last time she'd checked on him.

She'd gone to bed not long after Chase had made his abrupt exit, yet she'd tossed and turned for what seemed like hours on end. That powerful spark of awareness between them had played over and over in her mind like a favorite poem. She'd come so close to falling into the same trap—wanting more from him than he could give her, other than meaningless sex. Meaningless to him, but not to her.

If they'd lost control, she would have been no better for the experience. After all, he'd said he'd been going through a dry spell, and if that happened to be the case, she'd be nothing more than the means to refill his well. She had too much upheaval in her life as it now stood. Becoming just another one of his emotional casualties would only make matters worse.

Sadly, that reality didn't prevent her from wanting to be with him, whenever or however she could.

She pushed aside the sheets that had wound around her body during the night and grabbed the cell from the nightstand. The clock indicated it was five minutes past eight, much later than she'd assumed, but only four hours since her last look. Regardless, she had to get up and face the day.

Jess left the bed, retrieved her robe and headed down the hall. As predicted, Danny had discovered the latest gift, compliments of the deputy. She hoped her child hadn't discovered the movie she'd left in the player last night.

She strolled into the living room and fortunately found that suspect film lying on the floor next to her son, a nice action-packed superhero movie playing on the screen. He was stretched out on his belly, elbows bent and cheeks supported by his palms. He didn't acknowledge her, but at least he appeared somewhat content. He also looked so innocent, so undeniably sweet, she wanted to sweep him into her arms and hold him as she'd done when he was much younger. He'd hate her if she tried, so she wouldn't. She'd simply have to settle for giving him a good-morning kiss.

Before she reached Danny, the doorbell sounded, echoing through the small space. For someone who lived alone in the middle of nowhere, she'd certainly had a lot of visitors over the past twenty-four hours. She assumed that Freddie the propane man had stopped by to replenish the tank and, in turn, save them from another day of ice cold water and a night with no measurable heat.

She discovered she'd been sorely mistaken in her assumption when she pulled back the curtains and peeked outside. The gorgeous guy standing on the porch had been the one responsible for her lack of sleep and, admittedly, her savior in many ways. He hadn't shaven and that only enhanced his unquestionable sex appeal. So did the unbuttoned, untucked navy flannel shirt covering a white tee, the sleeves drawn tight around the bulk of his biceps. The faded jeans, a small rip at the knee, did incredible things for his long legs and narrow hips. Not that he needed any help in that regard. With an axe gripped in one hand and a tool box at his feet, he could pass as one hunk of a handyman. And she knew how handy Chase Reed could be. So did at least half the women in the county.

Jess opened the door and masked her surprise with a mock smirk. "Well as I live and breathe, it's Daniel Boone on my doorstep."

His smile arrived as slow as the sunrise, traveling all the way to those delicious brown eyes framed with sinfully long lashes a little darker than his sand-colored hair. He had the audacity to hook the thumb on his free hand in his pocket, and she had the nerve to look a little left of that pocket. Obviously she'd been visited by the Hormone Fairy sometime during the night.

"That's Deputy Boone, ma'am," he said, followed by a salute. "At your service."

She wouldn't mind being serviced by him. "What's with the axe?"

"Just thought I'd chop some wood before I give you a makeshift shower."

Right now he was giving her some very heady chills. "I was just about to fix Danny breakfast. Have you eaten?"

"I had some coffee."

"Want some eggs and bacon?"

"I wouldn't turn it down. But first, I have a few things to get out of the truck."

Jess peered behind him and didn't see a vehicle in the driveway. "Where did you park?"

"Around the side. I have a surprise for Danny. It's in the truck bed." He leaned the axe against the column supporting the porch. "Come here and I'll show you."

She tightened the robe's sash around her waist. "In case you haven't noticed, I'm not dressed."

He gave her a long once-over. "I've noticed, but you're not exactly naked. And even if you were, I'm pretty sure there's no one else around to see you."

No use arguing with his logic. "Okay, but this better be good."

"It is," he said as he strode away without her.

Jess stepped down the two stairs leading to the yard and picked her way across the gravel drive in her sock-clad feet. She rounded the corner just in time to see Chase lowering the tailgate, preparing to release what she worried might be the surprise.

She'd imagined a new bike or fishing poles or maybe even a baseball bat. She hadn't imagined the shiny, coal-black monstrosity of a canine bounding from the truck's bed, its tongue hanging out and tail wagging like a windshield wiper. But the minute its paws hit the ground, Chase pointed at the gravel drive. "Sit, Bo."

The dog remarkably complied and seemed glad to do it.

Jess cautiously approached the pair, just in case Bo mistook her for an intruder—or a meal. "I didn't know you had a dog. After Rory died, you swore you'd never have another one."

"Bo's not my dog."

Her concerns had all but been confirmed. "Please tell me this isn't Danny's surprise."

"Yeah, he is. Something wrong with that?"

He had to be kidding. "First of all, he weighs at least one hundred pounds."

"I'd say about seventy, maybe seventy-five pounds."

Nothing like splitting dog hairs. "Secondly, I'm renting this place and if he tears anything up, I'll be—"

"He won't," Chase said. "He didn't do all that well as a hunter so Jim Creary's offering him as a pet. He's three years old, so he's out of the puppy stage, and he's housebroken. His shots are updated, he's a registered Lab, he's as smart as a whip and he minds better than most kids."

And he most likely ate like a horse. "I'm just not sure this is a good idea. Danny might be completely overwhelmed by him."

Chase streaked a hand over the back of his neck. "Listen, Jess, that little boy in there needs something to get his mind off his troubles. Pets are used all the time for therapy. Bo could be just the thing to draw him out. Nothing else has worked so far."

That made sense, but his insinuation also stung like a hornet. "You're saying that as his mother, I don't have the skills to do that."

He looked somewhat apologetic. "I didn't mean to insult you. I only meant that Danny could use a distraction."

She realized he could be right, but still… "Any chance Bo might be a watch dog?"

When Bo barked, Chase laughed. "Guess that's your answer."

One bark did not a guard dog make, especially with that tail still wagging. Yet Jess acknowledged Chase had made some valid points. Danny could use some companionship. School wouldn't be back in session for another two-plus weeks. Being so far from civilization, she doubted any other children lived nearby, and she didn't feel comfortable arranging play dates in Placid, particularly if rumors had already begun to abound.

If something as simple as giving Danny a dog could bring him back around, then she was game.

"Okay," she said. "We'll see how Bo does on a trial basis. If it doesn't work out, promise me you'll make sure he has a good home." And that in itself posed a huge problem. Once again Danny would be losing a pet, and this time she'd be responsible for the heartbreak, not Dalton.

Chase raised a hand in oath. "I promise I will take Bo myself if it doesn't work. But I'd bet my badge they'll do fine together. He's a great dog and Danny's going to enjoy having him around. You might even enjoy him, too."

We'll see, Jess almost responded but instead headed back toward the house, Chase and Bo following not too far behind. She entered first, thankful to find Danny still planted in front of the TV. Under normal circumstances, she would have encouraged him to go outside. But now she needed to know where he was every minute of the day for fear he might take off to escape her. Paranoid, yes, but his attitude toward her hadn't been at all encouraging.

"Danny," she said. "Chase has something for you and I think you're really going to like it."

As it had been for the past two days, Danny didn't acknowledge her.

Chase moved forward with the dog close on his heels. "Hey, Danny. You have a visitor."

Only then did Danny glance to his left, looking decidedly disinterested, until his gaze landed on Bo. His brown eyes widened and his smile illuminated the room as if Christmas morning had arrived early.

Danny sat up and stared at the dog with blatant awe. "Is he mine?"

She wanted to do cartwheels over Danny's verbal response, the first one since the accident. She had Chase's wisdom, and a dog named Bo, to thank for the breakthrough. "You have to feed him and make sure he has water. Can you do that?"

"Uh-huh."

"Then I guess he's yours."

Chase crouched down and signaled Bo forward. "Danny, this is Bo. Bo, this is Danny, your new owner."

When her son reached to pet the dog, Bo rewarded him with a sloppy lick in the face. Then suddenly Danny did something so surprising, Jess couldn't contain her own excitement—he laughed. She'd always loved that exuberant laugh and she couldn't remember the last time she'd heard it. She vowed to hear it more.

Her child's joy encouraged the dog to dole out more wet canine kisses. As soon as Bo let up, Danny leaned over and hugged the Lab, the grateful look on his face priceless. Chase came to his feet and sent Jess a satisfied look. "I believe it's going to work out just fine."

So did she, much better than expected. "Yes, I believe it will. Good plan. Thanks."

"Don't thank me," he said. "Thank Bo." He looked

around the room for a few minutes. "You know what else this place needs?"

"Hot water would be nice."

Chase frowned. "Have you lit the pilot light? Freddie called and said he filled the propane tank around seven."

She'd barely fallen asleep by that time. "I haven't tried that yet, but I hope it works. I had to heat water on the stove last night so Danny could bathe and I toughed it out."

"You took a cold bath?"

"Yes, I did."

"Join the club. I took a cold shower after I left here last night."

"Something wrong with your water heater?"

"Just the opposite. My heaters were working a little too well."

Jess considered that to be an apology. A strange apology, but an apology none the less. "Are they functioning correctly now?"

"So far, but the day is young." He sent her a wink that made her want to both slug him and kiss that cocky look on his face. The old Chase had clearly returned, quite possibly to her own detriment.

"You never said what you think the house needs," she added to move away from a conversation that could land them both in trouble the next time they were alone—if they were alone. "Maybe a good coat of non-yellow paint?"

"I'm thinking something that's a quick fix."

She shrugged. "I give up."

"A Christmas tree."

Jess had yet to be visited by the holiday spirit. Maybe a tree would help, and so would some presents to put under the tree. Too bad she didn't have either. "Even if I did have a tree, I have no decorations readily available and I'd rather not make a trip to the house to get some. I could string popcorn, but I still don't have that microwave."

"Not a problem," he said. "I'm sure Mom has some extra decorations in the attic. She's out of town right now but I could give her a call."

Jess frowned. "Where is she?"

"In the Smoky Mountains with her sisters for a Christmas craft fair and last minute shopping. They're staying at Rachel and Matt's cabin."

Good for Missy and her girlfriend getaway. Jess wished she'd made more effort to stay connected with her own friends. Only one of the many things Dalton had made difficult. "So Buck's having to manage everything alone, huh?"

"Yeah. That's why he's been in such a foul mood."

That and the fact he'd had to deal with a family friend's daughter whom he viewed as uncooperative—and more important, a criminal.

Chase regarded Danny who'd gone back to watching the TV, Bo lying beside him as if they'd always been fast friends. "Hey, bud, why don't you and me go to the tree farm over at Wilson and pick out a nice one?"

Danny looked back over his shoulder. "Can we take Bo?"

"You bet."

Jess couldn't quite believe that her baby boy had finally reclaimed his voice, all because of a four-legged creature. "You can go right after breakfast."

When Danny wrinkled his nose with disdain, Chase added, "We can pick up something at the diner and take it with us."

She'd been thrown over for a dog and suspect food from a greasy spoon. "Fine. Go get dressed, Danny."

He was off like a racehorse with Bo by his side, leaving Chase and Jess alone.

Feeling generous, she faced Chase with a smile. "I'm amazed and I'm very grateful. I was beginning to think I'd never hear him speak again."

"Not possible since he's your son."

She punched his arm and he let go an exaggerated wince. "That's a weird way to thank me."

Jess could think of a few ways she'd like to thank him, none that were advisable for the situation or appropriate for the setting. "You better be glad I'm out of shape."

"I'd have to disagree." He finished off the comment with a rake of his gaze down her body and back up again, shades of the old Chase, only he'd never been quite so attentive to her in the past.

Jess felt a major blush coming on and she couldn't do a darn thing to stop it. "While the two of you are off tree hunting, I'm going to stay here and make a to-do list."

Chase groaned. "For me?"

She patted his whisker-shaded cheek. "Of course. You have to put those tools to good use."

"Good point. A man's tools are meant to be used on a regular basis." The wicked sparkle in his dark eyes punctuated his suggestive tone.

"I'm not going to even justify that remark with a response." But, boy, did she want to. "I am going to see if my son is dressed and ready to go. And please make sure you return him to me in one piece."

His suddenly serious expression bordered on angry. "Any reason why you think I wouldn't?"

"You do have a habit of driving fast and—"

"I'm more than capable of being careful with a kid in the passenger seat."

She couldn't quite peg the extreme change in his demeanor. "I'm sure you are but I worry about him. If you had children, you'd understand."

His jaw tightened so much Jess thought it might break. "I may not have a clue about raising a child, but I value life as much as anyone. If you're that worried, maybe we should just forget it."

She didn't have the heart to disappoint her son, not when he'd made such progress today. "I'm sorry, Chase. I trust you."

"Fine. I'll have him back home by noon."

"Good. Now that we've established that, I'll go get him."

As Jess walked away, Chase called her back, forcing her to face him once more.

"I should be apologizing," he said. "It's just that over the past few years…" He drew in a deep breath and let it out slowly. "Never mind."

Jess did mind. She minded that she'd apparently exposed a nerve, and he seemed to be holding something back. Perhaps some bitter experience during the war. In light of her deception, she couldn't judge him for not coming clean.

Maybe someday in the near future, after they'd finally come full circle in their friendship, they could both confess.

With a seven-foot fir tied down in the bed, the boy and his dog in the front seat of the single-cab Ford, Chase set out for home. He checked the dashboard clock and realized they'd spent more time at the tree farm than he'd intended. He figured Jess was fit to be tied about now, but he hadn't been able to reach her on the cell. The small town of Wilson was forty miles away from Placid, which meant they had an hour's drive ahead of them, unless he ignored the speed limit. He'd be damned if he did that after making the promise to Jess to protect her son.

He'd done everything in his power to do that today, including watching Danny like a hawk when they were picking out the tree. He never let him out of his sight and at times that had presented a challenge. But he wanted to prove to Jess that he could be a proper guardian to her son. Maybe even prove it to himself.

As he traveled down the main highway, he glanced at Danny, half expecting him to be asleep. Instead, the boy stared out the windshield, looking like he might be returning to that internal refuge where he'd been for the past two days. Chase knew that sanctuary well. He'd visited often, before and after he'd ended his military service, and he learned it wasn't always a good place to be. Sometimes it was necessary for self-preservation.

But he'd made good progress today with Danny and he didn't want to ruin him by letting him withdraw again. "What kind of sports do you like?" he asked, although he knew the answer from the memorabilia in Danny's former bedroom.

"Baseball," he answered without taking his eyes off the scenery.

"What position do you play?"

"Second base. My mom says I'm good at it, but she's wrong."

Chase immediately picked up on the animosity in his voice. "I imagine you're good at it, otherwise you wouldn't play the infield. Besides, Mom's are usually right about those things."

"She's wrong," he said adamantly. "She's wrong about a lot of things."

He wasn't sure whether to move forward, or halt the conversation right there. If he did continue, he could be heading down a treacherous path leading right into what happened the night Dalton was injured. But if the kid wanted to vent, he shouldn't stop him. Any information passed between the two of them would have to remain private, the best thing for all concerned, especially Jess. Even if it meant he'd have to lie to her, and for her.

"Are you mad at your mom for some reason, Danny?" He took another quick look to gauge the boy's reaction.

Danny only responded with a nod.

"That's okay," Chase said. "Moms aren't perfect. Sometimes they make mistakes, but that doesn't mean they don't love us. If she did something you didn't like, maybe you should talk to her about it."

After a short span of silence, Danny declared, "I'm mad because she married my dad."

Chase shouldn't be all that surprised by his response. "Why's that?"

"Because my dad hates me," he said quietly.

If the bastard made his own kid feel unloved, that was sinking to an all-time low, even for Dalton Wainwright. For a brief moment, he regretted he wasn't Danny's father, until he remembered why that wouldn't be a good thing. At one time he'd questioned if that might be a possibility due to the timing. After his mother had told him Jess was pregnant, he'd almost went straight to the source and asked. Almost. But he'd believed that Jess would never withhold that kind of information from him, in spite of what he'd said to her the one and only night they were together.

Jess could be too spontaneous for her own good, and sometimes forgetful, but she leaned toward being brutally honest. Exactly why he had a hard time buying she had anything to do with Dalton's injuries. And as far as he could tell, her son couldn't implicate her, either.

Returning to the problem at hand, he grappled with finding some consolation to offer Danny. "My dad's always been pretty hard on me," he began. "At times we haven't liked each other very much." He could think of one instance in recent history—when Buck had questioned Jess's innocence. "But I'm still his son, and I know he loves me. He just doesn't know how to show it."

"My dad doesn't love me at all."

The boy sounded so certain, he was inclined to believe him. "Are you sure about that?"

He kept his eyes lowered, like he was ashamed. "He told me so."

Chase gripped the steering wheel tighter with the force of his fury. He didn't know how to respond, so he chose to say nothing.

They rode the rest of the way in silence, and when they pulled into the drive, Jess came out the front door. She didn't exactly looked pleased over their tardiness, but as soon as Danny slid out of the truck, that all changed. Her face instantly lit up over the sight of her son. Unfortunately, she didn't afford Chase the same enthusiasm.

She folded her arms over her chest, looking every bit the school teacher, except for the tight, long-sleeve, stretchy top and dark form-fitting jeans. "Did you forget how to tell time?" she asked.

He pretended to be the contrite student while trying

to keep his eyes off her cleavage. "It took longer than we planned, but feel free to stick me in the corner and make me write 'I will not be tardy' a hundred times." Or she could send him to bed early, which would be okay if she joined him.

And there he went again, acting like a man who'd been stranded on a desert island for months, lonely and lusting for his former best friend. A friend who had more problems than she could count.

Jess ignored him and peered into the back of the truck. "It's a gorgeous tree. You're forgiven."

"You can thank your son for the tree. He picked it out."

She turned to Danny, who stood beside the truck, kicking gravel while Bo sniffed around the yard, anointing every bush in sight. "You did good, sweetie."

Danny sent her a "whatever'" look before calling the dog and bounding back into the house.

Pure frustration showed in Jess's eyes. "Did he say anything to you during the trip?"

He'd have to play it by ear when it came to how much he disclosed of the disturbing conversation. "Yeah. He talked quite a bit on the way back."

"About?" she asked.

"Your sorry ex-husband. He told me Dalton said he didn't love him."

Jess's gaze slid away. "Not in so many words, but the insinuation was there. At first, I was the target for his verbal attacks. But when Danny got older, he ended up in Dalton's line of fire."

"Son of a bitch," he muttered. "There's not one damn excuse for that."

"I see it as the 'kick the cat' syndrome," Jess added.

"His father bashed him on a daily basis, and then he came home and bashed us."

Chase began to seethe inside over the thought of Wainwright belittling his wife and child—and wondered if there might be more to the story. "Did he ever hit you, Jess?"

She shook her head. "Not physically, but words can wound all the same. There were a few times I thought he might punch me, but fortunately he refrained."

Chase wanted to punch something, namely Dalton Wainwright. "I'm just glad you finally came to your senses and left him. But I can't understand why it took you so damn long."

"I tried to leave after Danny started school," she said. "I'd finished my degree and student teaching. I felt like I could finally make it financially. When I told him I wanted a divorce, he threatened to ruin my parents' business if I didn't do his bidding. I couldn't risk them losing everything they'd worked so hard for all their lives. Eventually Edwin bought them out and they had more than enough money to retire in style."

Chase knew her folks well and he had a hard time with their apparent abandonment. "They left you here to fend for yourself?"

She twisted the ruby ring around her finger. "I gave them my blessing when they decided to join Gary and his family in the Carolinas. They deserved a change of pace."

"And you deserved to have their support while Dalton was doling out all his crap."

She leaned back against the truck. "They didn't know how bad it was, Chase. No one really knew, except for Danny. Not a day goes by that I don't hate myself for subjecting him to a cold, uncaring father."

And not a minute had gone by when he hadn't shouldered some of the blame for her decision, too. "At least now he's out of your life for good."

She sighed. "Sometimes I think he'll never be out of my life."

He draped an arm around her shoulder. "Let's forget about the demon today and concentrate on decorating a tree."

Finally, she smiled. "You're on. And I'm going to make you fried chicken for dinner."

"No mac and cheese?"

Her smile faded into a frown. "If you're worried I can't fry chicken, don't. I learned a lot in your absence."

Yeah, she had. A lot about her ex's faults the hard way. "I'm impressed."

"Don't be until you eat it."

"That doesn't give me a whole lot of confidence in your culinary abilities." When she dropped his arm from her shoulder and started to walk away, he added, "I've got another idea, Jess."

She turned and continued to step backward. "Fast food?"

"No. Why don't we take Danny into town tonight for the Christmas tree lighting ceremony?"

She stopped cold. "I've already thawed out the chicken."

"We can pick up something to eat there, and you can save the chicken for tomorrow night. I'm working the seven-to-seven shift and I can fix your shower after I'm off."

He was walking a tightrope by inviting himself back over for dinner. In fact, she'd be better off if he stayed away from her. But he didn't see that happening any time soon. At least not until she was cleared of all wrong doing.

"I'm not sure walking around town is a good idea," she said after a few moments. "Word about Dalton has bound to have gotten around and who knows what people are saying about me."

She had a valid concern, but Chase had never known her to back down from a challenge before. He wanted to see a glimpse of the old Jess, the one who could tell everyone to go to hell so sweetly that they thanked her for it later. "Look, you and Danny need to get out of the house. We don't have to stay long and if anyone harasses you, I'll arrest them."

"Now that would make for a really fun night, especially if we run into my father-in-law."

"Edwin's probably at the hospital with Dalton."

Her face fell. "You're right."

Damn, he'd spun her mind back onto her troubles. "I hear the furniture store's going to have a train display this year and Mayor Crenshaw's going to be Santa."

"With that beer belly of his, he won't need a suit."

"And we can't miss cow-patty bingo."

She wrinkled her nose. "Speak for yourself."

"The volunteer fire department's auxiliary ladies will be serving pies."

"I can make a pretty good pie from the comfort of my own kitchen."

He saved the best for last. "They're going to have a silent auction and I believe I saw a microwave on the list of donated items."

She raised her hand. "I'm sold."

"Good." He pulled the work gloves from his back pocket. "I'll get this tree set up in the house, go home and clean up and I'll be back in a couple of hours with some decorations."

"Chase Reed, you should've been a used car salesman."

He shot a look over his shoulder. "I'll keep that in mind in case Buck decides to fire me." And he very well could if he showed up tonight and got into a fight to defend Jess's honor.

Not likely that would happen. People respected Jess and they hated the Wainwrights. He couldn't imagine anyone faulting her for Dalton's current predicament. Hell, they might even applaud her.

Chapter 6

She felt like a pariah.

From the moment Jess stepped onto the downtown street with Danny and Chase, she'd noticed people talking behind their hands. Some of her students' parents only murmured polite greetings and kept right on walking. Some of the older folks were blatant in their disapproval, doling out looks that made her want to climb beneath the nearest craft booth. Some simply ignored her. On the other hand, they treated Chase with admiration, offering up handshakes and general hero-worship.

Luckily, Danny seemed completely unaware of the snubs. He was too busy playing in the fake snow surrounding the giant, elaborately lit Christmas tree positioned in the center of the parklike town square.

As she and Chase stood on the sidewalk, Jess pulled her denim jacket closer to her body in response to the gust of winter wind. "I'm freezing to death," she said. "I think we should go."

Chase took a drink of coffee, wadded the paper cup and tossed it into a nearby bin. "It's not that cold."

"Easy for you to say since you've always been hot-blooded."

His responding smile was clearly cocky. "That's the rumor."

Once a bad boy, always a bad boy. He wore his baseball cap turned backward and a high school football letter jacket in keeping with the nineteen-fifties-themed Christmas festival. That attire clearly revealed he had the "boy" part down pat tonight. A very mature boy with a physique that warranted a second look, or ten, as evidenced by a nearby group of young women who couldn't seem to take their eyes off of him. They giggled and he smiled, displaying those darn dimples that made many a female want to be bad right with him. Jess included.

She tapped him on the shoulder in an effort to tear his attention away from the admiration society. "Do I have a third-eye growing in the middle of my forehead?" Her tone held enough sarcasm to offend the most practiced cynic.

He narrowed his eyes and surveyed her face. "Not that I've noticed. Why?"

"Because I could swear everyone's talking about me."

He leaned a shoulder against a tree and brought his attention to Danny. "Just ignore them."

If only she could. "Kind of hard to do when the whispering's so loud it makes my ears hurt."

"If you'd worn a poodle skirt, you would've blended in better."

If she saw another poodle skirt tonight, she'd hurl. "Sorry. I don't happen to have one lying around."

"What about your cheerleader uniform?"

Like she could actually get the thing over her expanded butt. "I have no idea where it is. Even if I did, and it still fit, I'd worry someone might ask me to do a back flip. I haven't been that limber in years."

He sent her a sideways glance. "You could try it when we get back to the house."

"And you can kiss my megaphone."

He cracked a killer grin. "Just stick with me, babe, and I'll do wonders for your reputation."

That deserved a serious sneer, which she gave him. "It appears you picked up an extra case of ego while you were out buying the tree."

"I'm just saying that if I have no problem walking around with you, then I obviously don't think you're guilty of anything other than poor taste in men."

She imagined people assumed he'd been assigned to guard her, in case she decided to run. "Present company excluded, of course."

"Damn straight."

She prepared to pose a question she'd been withholding all day for fear of the answer. "Have you heard anything more on Dalton's condition?"

He shifted his weight slightly, a sign of his uneasiness. "I talked to Buck earlier. He says Dalton's alert and they've upgraded his status to stable. He also said he plans to interview him tomorrow morning."

Jess shuddered and it had nothing to do with the weather. "Does he still not remember what happened?"

"Guess we'll find out tomorrow."

She dreaded tomorrow. "Guess we will."

"Look at it this way," he said. "Now that Dalton's out of the woods, and after he clears everything up, the rumors will die down, and so will all the speculation. Everyone will move on to the next gossip target."

Or those rumors could heat up, depending on Dalton's account of the night in question. "I hope Buck realizes that my ex-husband can be fairly vindictive. There's no telling what he's going to say about me."

"You've got enough to worry about without borrowing trouble."

Lately trouble just seemed to follow her around, like a recurring case of the flu. Yet obsessing over the impending interview tonight would only serve to ruin everyone's mood, including her son's if he picked up on her distress.

Jess checked her watch, amazed to find two hours had already passed since they'd arrived. "We really have to go. We still need to decorate the tree and Bo needs to be fed."

"Unless he's already raided the fridge."

Jess couldn't imagine the dog being that smart. "Or eaten half the contents of the house."

"I still have to show Danny the train," Chase said.

She wouldn't feel right denying her son that opportunity. "Fine, but let's make it quick."

Chase stuck both pinkies in his mouth and let go an ear-splitting whistle, then called Danny's name to gain his attention.

In a matter of moments, Danny raced across the park and joined them, cheeks rosy from the cold and eyes alight with excitement. Jess loved that he seemed so carefree, and prayed nothing would happen to crush his enthusiasm tonight.

Chase laid a large hand on his shoulder. "Let's go see the train, bud."

Danny sent the deputy a grin and like everyone else in town, disregarded his mother.

Jess kept a few steps behind Chase and Danny as they traveled the block to the furniture store, amazed at the similarities between boy and man. Both walked with hands in pockets in a slow, leisurely gait, their gazes focused straight ahead. To any casual observer, they'd definitely pass as a father and son spending quality time together. That could very well be an accurate assumption.

Once they reached brightly lit glass windows, Danny took on look of awe as the elaborate train traveled around the track through a storybook town decked out in holiday regalia. He turned that look of wonder on Chase. "Cool."

"Real cool," Chase added with a satisfied smile.

Jess almost laughed when she noticed the brass plate propped up in the corner of the display.

Made possible through the generosity of Edwin Wainwright.

Not a shocker that her erstwhile father-in-law would require his *generosity* be acknowledged. She was surprised he hadn't demanded a life-size portrait be included with the exhibit.

She started to comment on the miniature village, yet words escaped her as she glanced to see Chase crouched down on Danny's level, one hand resting on her son's shoulder. Her heart took a little tumble over the memorable scene—the tall, strong deputy and the soft-spoken, self-doubting little boy, connecting on a level she'd only dreamed about. The more she viewed the two together, the more she became certain that Chase, not Dalton, had fathered Danny. And she desperately wanted to tell them both. Right here, right now.

This wasn't the time or the place to make that revelation. Besides, she had no real proof aside from identical dimples, a mother's instincts and a good deal of wishful thinking. Maybe she wanted it to be true so badly, she'd let her imagination play tricks on her mind.

"I want another corndog, Mom."

He'd addressed her for the first time in two days. She recovered quickly from the shock and went into mother mode, even though she wanted to throw her arms around him and praise his effort. "You've already had two, Daniel. Don't you think that's enough?"

He actually smiled at her. "I'm a growing boy."

"Yes, you are." And a beautiful, precious boy.

Chase straightened, fished through his pocket, and withdrew a dollar bill. "I used to eat four or five when I was his age. Besides, they only cost a buck. That's a bargain these days."

Normally she might resent Chase usurping her parental power, but she was too thrilled over Danny's breakthrough to argue. "Fine. If he has a stomachache, I'll be calling you in the middle of the night."

He placed the money in Danny's open palm. "Knock yourself out, kid."

"Thanks, Chase!"

After her son hurried away, Jess's euphoria dissolved as several horrible scenarios began to bombard her brain. "Go with him, Chase, and make sure he's okay."

He countered her request with a frown. "The booth's just across the street, and the street's blocked off to traffic. He'll be fine."

She noticed the crowd gathered around the concession

stand and her panic began to escalate. "People don't always think before they speak, especially kids. I'd hate for someone to say something that might upset him after he's made so much progress today."

Comprehension finally dawned in his expression. "I'll make sure that doesn't happen."

"Thanks. I'll wait right here." Perhaps she was taking the coward's way out, but she also didn't want to subject Danny to anyone who might harangue her about Dalton.

After Chase left the sidewalk, Jess returned to train-watching for lack of anything better to do. For the first time in a very long time, she felt as if the tide might be turning in her favor. That maybe everything would work out after all.

"Hey, pretty lady."

She didn't have to turn around to know who owned that voice—Buster Eustace, the creep who'd made walking into the girls' locker room during high school a daily sport. He'd also spent a lot of time making verbal passes at her, and she'd spent a lot of time telling him where to shove his suggestions. Seeing no way out, she faced Buster with a smirk. "Fancy meeting you here, Buster." And most unfortunate. "I'm surprised Sally May let you roam the streets alone. Are you lost?"

His seedy smile revealed several missing teeth. "It's real good to see you, too, Jessa Belle."

That insulting endearment had almost cost him a few teeth back in the day. "Now you've seen me, and now I have to go." She'd rather face a group of gossip mongers than to spend another second with Buster.

When she took a step forward, he caught her arm, preventing her departure. "Not so fast," he slurred. "I gotta ask you a question."

The smell of smoke and booze on his breath caused Jess's stomach to roil. "I'm in no mood for questions, so please unhand me."

"I hear tell you hit old Dalton in the head with a baseball bat," he said, ignoring her command. "Is it true?"

She yanked out of his hold. "Don't believe everything you hear, Buster boy."

He inched closer, practically trapping her between his bone-skinny body and the display window. "Did Dalton finally grow a pair and try to put you in your place?"

Her last thread of composure snapped. If he didn't back off, he'd find himself in need of a new pair.

Jess put on a syrupy sweet smile and spoke through it. "Let me ask you something, Buster. Do you and Sally May want to have more children?"

That seemed to momentarily sober him up. "We already got three girls, but I'm aimin' to try for a boy."

Lovely. Like the world could use another little Buster. "Then I suggest you head back to your wife before my knee becomes personally acquainted with your crotch."

When he still refused to move, she tried to push him away, but he wouldn't budge. He might be only a few inches taller than her, and maybe twenty pounds heavier at best, but he was a lot stronger than he looked.

Buster swayed slightly before he invaded her personal space even more. He continued to stare at her like she was a glass of whiskey, and he was about to go through withdrawal. "I have a good mind to bring you down a notch. Show you what it's like to be with a real man. You were always too high and mighty for your own good."

The minute he grabbed her butt, Jess thrust her mighty knee high, jabbing it squarely in the intended target.

She tried to wrest away but Buster took an unexpected

swing, landing the back of his hand directly below her left eye. The force of the blow threw her off balance and she blindly grabbed for the brick ledge below the window. The pain shooting from the point of impact made her feel as if her head might explode.

After her vision came back into focus, she straightened and caught sight of Chase shoving Buster against the glass, a murderous look on his face. "You're under arrest, you son of a bitch."

To her mortification, a group of onlookers had gathered in response to the commotion. And to her horror, she looked to her left to see her son seated on the sidewalk, arms wrapped around his legs as he rocked back and forth, staring off into space.

After all the progress Danny had begun to make, Jess felt as if she'd lost him again. Maybe this time for good.

"Is he okay, Chase?"

After closing the door to the hallway, Chase crossed the room to where Jess had stretched out on the couch, a bag of ice pressed against her cheek. "Hard to tell," he said as she bent her knees, allowing him enough space to sit on the sofa. "He looked like he could use some company, so I let Bo stay in the bed with him. He was drifting off when I left."

"But he didn't say anything?"

"Not a word." And that worried Chase as much as it worried Danny's mom.

Jess raised the bag and touched the red welt below her eye. "I can't believe this happened."

Chase bore most of the responsibility for the disaster. If he hadn't pressured her to go to the festival, then she wouldn't be lying here, nursing a wound inflicted by a worthless jackass. And since he'd turned the official arrest over to another deputy, he didn't have all the details. He didn't like asking her to recount the events, but he needed to fill in the blanks. If she faced criminal charges, Buster could be called to testify, and he'd probably twist the story to make Jess appear to be the perpetrator. "Tell me what happened with Buster, beginning to end."

She blew out a slow breath. "He made a few snide remarks, I issued a few warnings. Then he grabbed my butt and I kneed him. That's when he slapped me senseless."

The thought of Eustace putting his hands on Jess made his blood boil. The image of the bastard slugging her was still fresh in his brain, refueling his anger. If he hadn't remembered where he was, or who he was—a deputy who'd sworn to uphold the law—he might've wrapped his hands around the guy's throat and applied enough pressure to make his eyes bulge.

"It's my fault," he said. "I should've known some of Placid's sleaziest would show up and give you grief."

Jess held the bag to her cheek and grimaced. "Buster's genetically predisposed for sleaziness. Buster Sr. is still serving a ten-year sentence for two home invasions and forgery."

And everyone thought Placid had a low crime rate. "Now they can have a family reunion when Junior joins him."

Jess shook her head. "That's not going to happen. Maybe if he'd backhanded his boss, dear Edwin, he'd find himself incarcerated. But because it was me, the ex-daughter-in-law who gravely wounded his son, Edwin will make sure he walks away. He might even give him a bonus."

Boss? "What does a scumbag like Buster do for the old man?"

"He does Edwin's dirty work." Jess lowered the bag and returned it to the table. "For instance, Edwin hired him to take pictures of Horace Breedlove walking into the motel with Janie Adams. The scuttlebutt has it he used those photos to blackmail Horace into selling him a prime piece of real estate adjoining Potter's Pond. As it turned out, Horace's wife found out and divorced him anyway."

Placid had become a regular hotbed for scandal, thanks in part to the wealthiest family in town. And the fact that Eustace worked for Wainwright could make matters even worse for Jess.

He retrieved the bag and pressed it against her face, causing Jess to wince. "You need to use the ice so it doesn't swell."

"You're going to freeze my mouth shut."

"That would take a glacier."

When she tried to smile, she flinched again. "Please don't make me laugh. It hurts."

It hurt him to see her in any kind of pain. "At least one good thing came out of the chaos."

"I caught you up on all the small-town drama?"

"You have a new microwave." After lowering the bag to give her a reprieve, he tipped her chin up to get a better look at her injury. "You also have a black eye."

She dropped her head back against the sofa's arm. "Great. I'd gladly give back the microwave if it meant not having the black eye. Better still, I'd give anything if Danny hadn't witnessed that horrific scene. I feel like he's take ten steps forward, only to be pushed back a mile."

Chase straightened her legs and draped them over his

lap. "I think it's time to consider calling that counselor, before he withdraws even more."

After she lifted her head, he witnessed a flicker of alarm in her eyes. "You're right. I wanted to give him a few more days, but after what happened tonight, I realize I can't wait. I'll call Rachel tomorrow and get the number. By then we should know how your dad's interview went with Dalton."

If Dalton didn't support Jess's story, or if he still maintained he had no recollection of the events leading up to his injury, then Buck would go after Danny for answers. All the more reason for Jess to find her son a good counselor.

After Jess yawned and stretched her arms above her head, Chase considered that his cue to leave, even if he didn't particularly want to. "You look like you could use some sleep."

"Not really." She sat up and shifted to face him, her arm resting on the back of the sofa. "I need a new life."

He brushed a lock of hair from her cheek and tucked it behind her ear. "You'll have that as soon as this garbage with Dalton goes away."

The first sign of tears welled in her eyes. "What if it doesn't, Chase? What if he makes allegations that aren't true?"

He had the same concerns. Dalton didn't possess one ounce of integrity, especially when he had an agenda. The Wainwright men always had an agenda. "Then it's going to be up to Danny to tell Buck what he saw."

"I can't put him through that," she said. "I'd rather go to jail than have him suffer more than he already has."

"You might not have a choice, Jess."

She tipped her forehead against his shoulder. "Maybe

it's time I accept the inevitable. If Dalton has his way, he's going to gain full custody of Danny."

Chase framed her face in his palms. "Don't you dare give up, Jess."

She looked as if she already had. "What's the point, Chase? I don't have the means or the clout to take on both Dalton and his dad, if it comes to that. You can bet Edwin's going to be right in the middle of it before this is all over."

He recognized how easy it would be to kiss away her concerns. To provide the means to make her forget, at least tonight. But that would only complicate matters more.

He dropped his hands from her face to maintain some distance. "The point is, when you see an injustice done, you just have to fight through it, no matter what the outcome might be."

"It's the possible outcome that worries me," she said.

She had the right to be worried. "Believe me, I know what you're going through. You wait for the other shoe to drop until you think you might go crazy. You know it's going to be bad, but not knowing is worse." And the reality was always much worse than anyone could ever predict.

The images came back to him, sharp as a switchblade, and that was all he could see. Unknown enemies. Children playing amid the violence. One minute, a normal day. The next, sheer chaos. Flashes of gunfire, civilians taking cover, weapons drawn. The bloodcurdling screams...

"Chase?"

Jess's voice thrust him back into the present. "What?"

She studied him with concern. "Are you okay?"

Not in the least. "Yeah. Why?"

"You looked as if you went somewhere else."

He should've known she'd see through him. Then again, he'd been fairly transparent, at least for a moment. "I was just remembering something."

"About the war?"

He could attempt to lie, but he probably couldn't fool her. "Yeah."

"Did something happen over there?"

"It was war. What didn't happen?"

She released a frustrated sigh. "It's more than that. I saw the same thing the other day. At times there's a part of you that's completely unreachable."

"I'm still the same old me." What a load of bull. Truth was, war claimed numerous victims, and not just fallen soldiers.

"No, you're not the same," she said. "No one expects you to be. But when you're with Danny, it's as if you understand what he's going through. I sincerely believe it's because you've been through something similar."

In some ways he had, but he couldn't provide any details. Disclosing the fatal mistake might be his undoing. So might the random flashbacks, if his father ever found out. "I watched a lot of people die, Jess. Men and women who had families waiting back home. Sometimes I wonder how soldiers ship out knowing they could be seeing their spouses and children for the last time. It's a good thing I wasn't cut out to be a husband and father. It made it a helluva lot easier to do what I had to do."

She touched his face. "You'd make a good father, Chase. Just look at the way you've handled Danny. I can tell he worships you."

The boy would do well to focus his misplaced admiration on someone who deserved it. "I'm just being a friend to him, Jess. That's not nearly as tough as being a father."

"I agree. Raising a child is a tough job. But the rewards are worth all the trouble."

"Again, I'm not equipped for fatherhood. I never have been."

"It breaks my heart that you really believe that," she said. "And I personally believe you're wrong."

He needed to turn the topic back to her issues. "The point is, you're a good mother. Don't let this mess with Dalton make you doubt that."

"I do doubt it, Chase, thanks to the ongoing war I've been having with Dalton for years. And now I'm facing one more battle that's chipped away at my confidence. A battle that I might not win."

Her dejection was killing him. "If you promise to stay optimistic, I promise to help you get through this." A penance he needed to fulfill. A promise he hoped he could keep.

"How can I stay optimistic if I might lose my son? He's all I have."

As he watched a lone tear slide down her face, he wanted to say, *You'll always have me.* But that commitment wouldn't benefit her in the long run. He'd returned home a broken man who'd erected walls for self-protection. Unfortunately, Jess had begun to see through his guise, and that could be dangerous. If she only knew what he was capable of, what he had done, she'd never view him in the same light again.

Chase tugged a tissue from the cardboard box on the side table and handed it to her. "You're a lot stronger than you realize, Jess." Stronger than him, at least on an emotional level. "You have to hang in there and fight."

She dabbed at the tears with the tissue. "How do you propose I do that?"

"I'm pretty sure that cheerleader's still in there somewhere."

She tucked the tissue in her pocket and raised her fisted hand. "Rah. Rah."

Her attempt at humor through her tears was classic Jess. "That was sorely lacking in school spirit. Maybe you ought to try that back flip."

She sent him a shaky smile. "I'd probably hit the floor facedown and give myself another black eye."

He glanced over his shoulder at the bare tree centered in the front window. "Want to put that microwave to good use? We could make some popcorn decorations to go with the ones I found in my parents' attic."

He turned to see her shaking her head. "I can't decorate a tree without Danny."

He should've known she'd say that. "Then that leaves you going to bed, and me going home. I'll come by tomorrow night for that chicken dinner and we can all decorate the tree together."

"I just hope I'm here and not in jail."

Just when he'd thought she'd made some decent strides. "Don't go there, Jess."

"All right," she said. "I promise I will think nothing but positive thoughts."

"Good."

After Chase rose from the sofa, Jess stood and followed him to the door. "Thank you for saving me from Buster, Deputy."

He barked out a laugh. "Best I recall, you saved yourself. You might want to register that knee as a lethal weapon."

She slid her arms around his waist and laid her head against his heart. "I don't know what I'd do without you, Chase."

There could come a time in the very near future when she'd be forced to find out, maybe sooner than he'd planned. But if her fears about Dalton came to pass, they'd wind up on opposite sides of the law.

Last night, he'd promised her a fresh start, but he realized that wouldn't last past the short term. He could continue to offer her support until she no longer needed it. Beyond that, he couldn't offer her anything but a lifetime of grief.

He pressed a kiss against her forehead and let her go before he lost his will and asked her if he could stay. "Try to get some sleep."

Jess tip-toed down the hall, muttering a silent oath every time the wood floor creaked beneath her feet. She didn't dare wake Danny, but she couldn't go to bed until she made sure he was okay.

When she opened the door, ribbons of light streamed across the bed, revealing the sweetest scene. Danny slept on his belly, his face turned toward the wall, one arm draped over the dog. Bo opened his eyes but didn't stir, aside from a slight wag of his tail.

Maybe Bo lacked in the watchdog department, but he obviously gave Danny the comfort she couldn't give him. And after the downtown debacle, she doubted her son would ever trust her again. Yet he did trust Chase.

After taking a seat in the chair at the foot of the bed, she recalled Danny's and Chase's interaction, and how many times tonight she'd almost told Chase the truth. But that truth had died on her lips when he'd insisted he wasn't father material. She wondered if his attitude would change if he did know Danny might be his son. Or would he simply walk away?

She couldn't afford to risk that now. She would need Chase's support in the coming days. Especially tomorrow.

Chapter 7

"He wants to see you ASAP, Deputy Reed."

Chase didn't have to ask the dispatcher who "he" was. Nor did he have to ask why he'd been summoned. "How long as he been back?"

"About ten minutes."

So far the morning had been uneventful—a couple of traffic tickets, chasing two heifers out of the road. He figured that was all about to change. "Did he say anything about how it went?"

"You'll have to ask him."

He shouldn't have expected Sue to offer any information, even if she did know what had transpired between Buck and Dalton. "I take it he's in his office."

"Yeah, and a word of warning. Be prepared."

He would if he knew what the hell to prepare for.

As he strode down the corridor, a million possibilities

tore through his brain, not a one of them favorable. Either Danny, or his mother, would soon be on the hot seat.

When he reached the closed door, he didn't bother to knock. Instead, he pushed his way in and found his father seated behind the desk, wearing his usual poker face. "Tell me what you know," Chase said, not bothering with formality.

Buck gestured toward the opposing chair. "Sit."

"I'll stand."

"Suit yourself."

Buck snatched a pen and began tapping it on the wood surface, a sure sign of trouble. "You know, for a guy who suffered a head injury a few days ago, Dalton Wainwright's doing pretty good."

He didn't give a horse's behind about Dalton's condition. "Just tell me what he said."

"The good news is, I won't be bothering Jess's boy. Not in the near future, anyway. Dalton tells me he's not going to be any help."

Chase braced himself for the bad news, because as sure as grass was green, bad news was coming. "Then he remembers what happened."

"Yeah, he remembers. Right down to the last detail. Pretty interesting details at that."

His dad seemed determined to try his patience. "Stop beating around the bush and get on with it."

Buck again pointed to the chair. "I still think you should sit."

He'd stand on his head if that would speed up the process. After yanking back the chair, he dropped into it and glared at Buck. "Okay, I'm sitting. Now get to the point."

Buck sat back in the chair and sighed. "Dalton says

Jess said she was going to kill him, then she attacked him, plain and simple."

There wasn't anything simple about it. "And you believe him?"

"No reason not to believe him."

Chase could think of at least a hundred. "You're saying that a woman who's a few inches above five feet could take down a man well over six feet? Not to mention he's got to outweigh her by at least eighty pounds. If you're buying that, then you're probably padding your retirement fund with swampland."

Buck's ears began to turn red. "You are about this far—" he held up his pointer finger and thumb an inch apart "—from finding yourself suspended."

Any other time, he might've told him where to stick the job. But he couldn't. Not if he wanted to protect Jess. "I'm only saying that I don't believe Jess is physically capable of inflicting that kind of injury."

"She could if she had a weapon."

A weapon? "I was the first on scene and I didn't see a weapon."

"I checked the log," Buck said. "You didn't get there until five minutes after Jess placed the 9-1-1 call. That gave her plenty of time to get rid of it."

Even if he didn't believe Buck's theory, he couldn't argue the possibility. "What was the object supposed to be?"

"Dalton's not sure. He just remembers her hitting him in the head with something."

He thought back to that night and Dalton's position. "That doesn't make any sense. I found him on his back."

"He could've rolled over. I'll have to ask Barkley if that fits with the crime scene."

Like that sack of manure had enough sense to analyze evidence. "Maybe you should run it past the county D.A. before you jump to conclusions."

Buck scowled. "I've been doing this job since you were a tadpole, son, so give me some credit. I stopped by the courthouse on the way back and reviewed the case with Millsap."

"And?"

For the first time during the meeting, Buck refused to look at him straight on. "A warrant's been issued for Jess's arrest."

Chase took a moment to absorb that information before coming to terms with the inevitable. He couldn't stop the system, but he sure as hell wasn't going to let Jess go through this alone. "I'll bring her in."

Buck tossed the pen aside. "It's too late for that. I sent Barkley to pick her up five minutes before you walked in here."

Chase sprung into action and headed out the door, slamming it shut behind him. He ignored the sound of Buck's warning to stay out of it. Ignored Sue, who also tried to stop him by claiming he had a message. He only knew he had to get to Jess.

He opted to take the cruiser instead of the SUV to save time. With lights flashing and siren blaring, he raced down a back street through town and increased his speed when he hit the winding country road. The ten minutes it took to reach the house seemed like thirty. Once he arrived, he discovered another cruiser parked in the drive, next to a plain navy sedan that he didn't recognize.

As he slammed the car into park and exited the cruiser, a strong sense of dread hit him with the impact of a gut punch. The same dread he'd experienced when this nightmare had begun to unfold. Only this time, he knew what to expect.

But nothing could ready him for the scene that played out before him. A scene that stopped his blood cold.

Jess came out the door in handcuffs, flanked by Barkley and a young deputy named Mike. A gray-haired woman followed, leading Danny away as he reached for his mother, calling her name over and over. Barkley recited her rights as Jess begged for a moment with her son, the pleas falling on deaf ears.

But Chase heard everything, from Jess's gut-wrenching attempt to reassure Danny, to the dog barking furiously behind the screen door.

He remained frozen for a moment, until he caught sight of her struggling against the restraints. "Don't fight the cuffs, Jess. And don't say anything."

The minute her gaze connected with his, and he saw the abject terror in her eyes, adrenaline kicked back in, sending him straight toward the trio. But he didn't get far before Barkley handed her over to Mike, and then headed Chase off at the pass.

Barkley raised his hand, palm forward. "Hold it right there, Deputy. I'm in charge of this arrest."

He wanted to knock the cocky look off the jerk's face. "Uncuff her, Barkley."

Barkley stroked his mustache like a pet. "Well, now, Chase, you know I can't do that, even if she is your girl-friend."

He saw no sense in correcting him about their relationship. His main concern was Jess's well-being. "She's not going anywhere, so take the damn cuffs off her."

Ignoring the demand, Barkley turned and headed toward the cruiser, while Mike pushed Jess's head down as she slid into the backseat.

Chase automatically followed him to the car. If Barkley wanted to stop him, then he'd have to do it with force.

When he tapped on the window to garner Jess's attention, she looked at him with tear-filled eyes and mouthed one word. "Danny."

"I'll take care of him," he said as the car began to back down the drive. "I'll take care of everything."

Chase glanced to his right and realized the sedan had yet to move. That meant he still had the opportunity to speak with Danny. His words might not offer the boy much consolation, but he had to try.

He walked to the driver's side to find the window halfway open. "Excuse me, ma'am."

At first the social worker seemed startled, until she noticed his badge. "May I help you, Deputy?"

He peered into the car and spotted Danny in the front seat, his head lowered and his shoulders shaking. Every broken sob shot straight to Chase's soul. "I'm a family friend. I'm just wondering what the next step will be."

She pushed her glasses up on the bridge of her nose. "Since Danny's father is currently hospitalized, I've contacted the child's aunt, a Mrs. Rachel Boyd. She's agreed to assume emergency custody until the time Mr. Wainwright is able to care for Danny. I'll be taking him to her home immediately."

He hoped Dalton's recovery took a long time. Living with a father who didn't give a damn about him was the last thing the kid needed. A lying, worthless father. "Mind if I have a word with Danny before you go?"

She looked almost relieved by the suggestion. "That might make the transition a little easier for him. Normally we ask a relative to be here, but there wasn't enough time."

Thanks to Buck, who couldn't wait to toss Jess in a cell. "I'll do what I can to calm him down."

"Wonderful. And if you can convince him to wear his seat belt, I'd truly appreciate it."

As soon as Chase heard the lock trip, he rounded the hood and opened the passenger door. Danny immediately flew out of the car and wrapped his arms around his waist. He stayed that way for a few moments, letting the boy cry and cling to him as long as he needed to.

Chase loosened Danny's grasp before lowering to his level. He rested his hands on his thin shoulders and waited for the boy to make eye contact. "I know this is bad, kiddo, but you're going to be okay. Your Aunt Rachel's going to take good care of you until your mother comes home."

Danny swiped at his nose and sniffed. "When is she coming home?"

He wished he had a more positive answer to hand him. "I'm not sure, but hopefully soon. I'm going to do my best to fix this." His best might not be good enough.

"Will you come see me?"

The boy looked and sounded so hopeful, no way could he refuse. "You bet. And as soon as you're settled in, I'll see if your aunt's okay with me bringing Bo over. In the meantime, I'll take him home with me."

Danny lowered his gaze to the ground. "It's all my fault."

He hated seeing a nine-year-old kid taking the blame for something completely out of his control. "No, bud, this isn't your fault. It's no one's fault."

"But—"

"Try not to worry too much, Danny. It's all going to be over soon." What *over* entailed was anyone's guess.

Danny didn't look like he believed him, but who could blame the boy? His life had been a series of disappointments. And lately, one trauma after the other.

Chase needed to give him something to look forward to. Something to get his mind off his troubles. "Tell you what. I'll come over in the next couple of days and play some catch with you. And if Aunt Rachel says it's okay, you can come to my place and I'll show you how to drive a few nails into wood. I could use some help building the new room on my house."

"Really?" Both his smile and voice reflected his gratitude.

He smiled back. "Really."

Danny's expression suddenly turned sour. "My dad never did that for me. He never did anything for me."

One day in the near future, Chase planned to confront the rat bastard over all the misery he'd caused Jess and Danny. If Dalton wanted to pick on someone, he'd give him a target his own size. Then Wainwright could see exactly how it felt to be on the losing end.

"You're going to be okay," he assured Danny again. "You'll be with your aunt and uncle real soon. Last I heard, they have a new foal in the barn."

The social worker emerged from the car. "We need to go, Deputy."

Chase gave Danny another solid hug and a pat on the back. "Hang in there, bud," he said as he straightened. "And buckle your seat belt."

Danny nodded, climbed back in the car and secured the belt without any argument.

Chase waved at Danny as he watched the sedan drive

away, and then started to turn to retrieve Bo. But another car caught his attention, stopping him dead in his tracks. A black luxury car parallel-parked near the end of the drive. He'd seen that vehicle around town, front and center at the bank. He recognized the silver-haired driver immediately. Arrogance in an expensive suit. He despised the millionaire almost as much as he despised the millionaire's son.

Chase wondered how long Edwin Wainwright had been there, and how much he'd seen. He also questioned how he'd found out about Jess's arrest. Then again, Wainwright made it a point to know everyone's business. He wouldn't be surprised if he had a mole in the sheriff's department. Enough money earned unlimited access to information.

Whatever the man's motives might be, he had no reason to be there, and Chase had no problem informing him of that fact. As soon as he strode down the drive, Wainwright pulled away, but not before displaying a sickening, satisfied smile.

Chase recognized Jess was about to undertake the fight of her life. A fight with the devil himself.

She now knew the meaning of true humiliation.

Dressed in county-jail orange and her hands bound by cuffs, Jess left the cracker-box hell with an armed guard at her side—a mountain of a guard named Bill, whom she'd known most of her life. Although respectful, he'd still treated her as if she were any other common criminal. In his eyes, she probably was.

She traveled down the cell-lined corridor to the sound of cat-calls and comments so crude, she wanted to cry. But she refused to cower. Instead, she walked with her head held high, keeping her gaze focused forward. They might have taken her dignity, but she wasn't going to let them take what was left of her pride.

Bill opened a steel door and escorted her into a small room containing a table and two chairs—as well as one of her very best friends. Savannah Greer looked every bit the successful attorney, from the sleek blond hair pulled back in a low ponytail, to the tailored, brown wool suit and diamond stud earrings.

Jess couldn't remember when she'd been so glad to see anyone. Had she not been shackled, she would have launched herself into her friend's arms.

Savannah came to her feet, gave Jess a smile and favored Bill with a frown. "Please uncuff my client."

Bill pulled out a chair for Jess and guided her into it. "Now, Miss Savannah, you know that's against the rules."

"Now, Mr. Bill," Savannah countered, "in case you don't remember, this is the former Jessica Keller. You know her folks well. I believe Ronnie Keller helped you dig a new well a few years back. And Cathy used to play bridge with your wife."

Jess was floored that Savannah remembered all those details, not that any of it mattered to Bill. He had yet to make a move to remove the silver bracelets that made her wrists ache beyond belief.

He rubbed the top of his bald head and sighed. "That's true. But I also recall that you and Jess and that group… What did you call yourselves?"

"The six-pack," Jess and Savannah said simultaneously.

"That's right," he said. "You two and Miss Rachel and the three boys, Chase, Matt and Sam. You were all responsible for me having to clean toilet paper out of my trees, and eggs off my front porch, after that Halloween a few years back."

Savannah tapped her chin. "Ah, yes. I also recall your son accompanying us that night, and the eggs were his idea. I still have the photos of Willy hurling those things."

Muttering under his breath, Bill fished the keys from his pocket, unlocked the cuffs and slid them from Jess's wrists.

She worked her wrists in circles, grateful for the temporary relief. "Thank you, Bill. I promise I'm not going anywhere." If only she could.

Savannah reclaimed her seat and folded her hands before her. "Now if you don't mind, I'd like a few minutes with my client."

Bill pointed a beefy finger at her. "My job's on the line, so don't you two do anything stupid."

She raised her hand as if swearing in. "I promise I don't have a file hidden in my shoes. I assure you Ms. Wainwright will be right here when you get back."

The guard muttered again and finally left them alone, closing the heavy door behind him.

Savannah leaned forward and studied her a long moment. "How are you holding up? Aside from the whole booking process, which I imagine is pretty dreadful."

Dreadful was a colossal understatement. Being poked and prodded, stripped of all personal effects and then finger-printed, ranked right up there with a root canal. "I'll be better when I know where they took my son."

"He's with Rachel," Savannah said. "She wanted me to send you her love and tell you that you have hers and Matt's full support."

"I appreciate that so much." She also appreciated her

pregnant sister-in-law taking care of her baby boy. "At least I know he's in good hands."

"Chase stopped me before I came back here," Savannah said. "Basically he told me the same thing, that he'll help in any way he can. He also said don't try any back flips because the cell is too small."

Jess stopped short of laughing. "He's been a godsend. I couldn't have survived these past few days without him." And she longed to see him again. "Is he still here?"

"No. Buck told him to go home and not to come back until the day after Christmas. Something about his lack of objectivity."

Her guilt increased. "I should have never dragged him into this mess."

"He's one of your closest friends, Jess. He'd never abandon you when you needed him."

"I understand that, but I still hate that he's going to take the heat for supporting me."

"Chase is tough. He can handle it." Savannah lifted a briefcase from the floor and pulled out a pen and yellow legal pad. "Time to get to the business at hand. I have a few questions I need to ask."

Exactly what she'd been dreading. "Ask away."

"First of all, I want you to know that I'll only be handling the arraignment since corporate law is normally my thing. But since I'm the only game in town, you're stuck with me for the time being."

"I couldn't imagine having anyone else represent me, Savannah."

"Again, I'm only going to take you through the initial proceedings. However, I've spoken with a defense attorney from Jackson, and he's agreed to take your case.

Unfortunately, he'll be out of town until the latter part of next week."

Her stomach clutched from anxiety. "I'll have to stay here until next week?"

"No, but you will be here overnight. The county judge only hears pleas twice a week, Tuesdays and Thursdays. I have you on the docket for first thing tomorrow morning. Depending on the bail, you should be out after lunch." Her gaze momentarily drifted away. "If all goes as planned."

She swallowed hard. "Are you saying something could happen to change those plans?"

"The judge could decide to remand you into custody until your trial, especially if he feels you're a flight risk."

Not only would she have to spend the night in a virtual cave, she might be incarcerated for months. "That's ridiculous. I have nowhere to go. My parents are on vacation and I don't even know where I put my passport. I would never leave my son and—"

Savannah laid a palm on Jess's hand, halting the tirade. "It's only a remote possibility. I just want you to be prepared if the D.A. argues that you're a threat to society, and your son, due to the attempted-murder charge."

Attempted murder? "I didn't attempt to murder Dalton. In fact, I didn't do anything to him."

Savannah clicked the pen and rested her hand on the pad. "That brings me to the night of the alleged attack. Tell me everything that happened to the best of your ability."

Though she trusted Savannah, she couldn't reveal everything. Not yet. "Dalton has Danny every other weekend, so he stopped by last Friday night. He was two hours late and he'd been drinking."

Savannah looked up from the notes she'd been taking. "Not according to Edwin Wainwright."

"Rachel told me Edwin claims that Dalton's tests were negative for alcohol. But I swear to you, Savannah, either he replaced his aftershave with bourbon, or he'd tied one on after work."

"We'll subpoena the medical records."

That might suffice under normal circumstances. Unfortunately, she hadn't married into a normal family. "What if Edwin paid someone off to alter the results?"

"That's highly unlikely," Savannah said. "Regardless, we'll worry about that later. Go on."

She'd had nothing to do but worry. "Anyway, I had no intention of letting my son get into a car with him. That's when he threatened me."

Savannah continued to jot down the facts without missing a beat. "What kind of threats?"

"He said that if I didn't agree to go back to him, he'd take me back to court to gain full custody of Danny."

"What did you tell him?"

"I told him no, and then he claimed that since Danny didn't look a thing like him, I must have cheated on him before we married."

Savannah stopped writing and released a caustic laugh. "That's so rich. Of course, it's been my experience that men who cheat usually believe everyone does, including their spouses. It's nothing more than a skewed justification of their own infidelity. Dalton knows you'd never cheat on him."

She could gloss over her friend's assumption, or she could tell her the truth. She desperately wanted to tell her the truth. For ten years, she'd never confided in one soul, and she was tired of carrying around the secret.

She drew in a deep breath and exhaled slowly. "He's right."

The shock took a while to subside from Savannah's face. "You cheated on him?"

"Not exactly, although he wouldn't see it that way. We broke up for a month. It happened then."

"When was this?"

"Ten years ago. Two weeks before we married."

She hadn't been struck by lightning, and the roof hadn't caved in. Yet she'd run the risk that by confessing, she could have lost her friend's respect.

Savannah put down the pen and laced her hands together atop the paper. "I realize it's none of my business, but do you mind telling me the identity of this mystery man?"

"As long as you promise not to tell anyone. Not even Sam."

"Anything you say to me in this room is protected by attorney-client privilege." She traded her serious demeanor for a smile. "Besides, you know how my future husband feels about gossip. The less he knows, the better."

The less anyone knew what she was about to reveal, the better for all concerned. "We were friends. The night before he left for Afghanistan, he came to see me at my dorm. We were both scared and sad, and we turned to each other for comfort. Neither of us intended for it to happen. It just did."

Savannah's mouth dropped open before she snapped it shut. "Are you telling me you slept with Chase?"

Jess could only nod.

She could see the calculations turning in Savannah's

mind. "If this happened ten years ago, then there is a possibility that Danny—"

"Could be Chase's son. But I'm not sure since the timing was so close. I haven't let myself believe anything other than Dalton was Danny's father."

"You didn't think Chase had a right to know the possibility existed?" Savannah's tone held no judgment, only sincere interest.

"I only knew he was away fighting a war," Jess said. "And I knew he might never come home. In the meantime, I'd already married a man I thought I loved. A man who was going to be around to provide for my son, while Chase kept volunteering for more tours of duty."

"And you thought that was best for Danny."

She paused and sighed. "Even after the marriage began to deteriorate, and it became apparent Dalton didn't care one whit for Danny, I was still stupid enough to believe any father was better than no father at all. Guess I was wrong about that."

Savannah remained silent for a few moments, as if weighing her words. "As your friend, I'd encourage you to tell Chase as soon as possible. As your attorney, I'd advise you to wait until after your legal issues are resolved. Otherwise, it could compromise your case. The D.A. could claim the paternity question served as your motive for attacking Dalton."

"I didn't attack Dalton. And how could he use that against me when I divorced Dalton months ago?"

"Easy. Dalton could claim he voiced his suspicions about Danny's paternity, and you decided to do away with him to retain any alimony or child support that would be challenged in court, if it's determined Chase is Danny's father."

All the more reason to keep her second secret. "I can't win for losing, can I?"

Savannah picked up the pen again. "Let's return to what transpired after the threats."

Now came the part where Jess could only tell a partial truth. "I ordered him out and he grabbed my arm. It's like I told Chase and Buck, after that, it's all a blur. I think he stumbled and fell backward and hit his head on the raised hearth."

"You didn't see it happen?"

She had. The images still haunted her. "I was distracted. I thought I heard Danny calling me."

"Dalton stated that Danny wasn't around. But if what you say is true, then Danny may have witnessed the fall."

She suddenly realized she'd said too much. She also realized that either Dalton didn't remember any details at all, or he was bent on ruining her. "I don't want Danny involved in this."

"In light of what you just told me, he could be called as a witness."

"And I hope you'll make sure that doesn't happen. He's so traumatized now, I'm not convinced he'll ever be the same again."

"I'll do what I can."

That was all Jess had to rely on. "Is that it?"

"I have one more question before we wrap this up. A very important question."

Nothing would surprise her at this point in time. "Go ahead."

Savannah retrieved a document from the briefcase and turned to the second page. "According to Dalton's most recent revelation, you hit him in the head with a fireplace iron."

Of all the ridiculous accusations. "He's lying. In fact, he's making this up as he goes."

"That could be, but that iron is missing."

Jess racked her brain to recall the last time she'd seen that tool, and then recalled she'd used it the night before Dalton's fall. "It had to be there when I left the house with Chase that night."

"Well it's not there now, and that's a problem. If it turns up, we can prove through forensics that it wasn't used to injure Dalton. But if it's going to show traces of his blood, then we don't want it to surface."

Her own friend sounded as if she doubted her. "I promise I did not whack Dalton in the head with anything." Not that the thought hadn't crossed her mind before. "But I can think of a number of ways that the iron could have gone missing. With enough money on hand, anything could disappear."

"I suppose that's true. Does anyone else have the key to the house?"

"Only Rachel and my parents. But that doesn't mean Dalton didn't have copies made without my knowledge."

When the sharp rap came at the door, Jess jumped like a jackrabbit.

"That means my time's almost up," Savannah said as she slid the notebook back into her briefcase. "But I need to ask you to do something, and you might not like it."

Right now she was so appreciative, she'd do anything for her friend, short of murder. "What?"

"Stop seeing Chase. I don't care how innocent your relationship might be, a rumored affair is the last thing you need."

Jess fought the urge to burst into tears. Chase had been her touchstone, the one person she could rely on to make her feel better. The only person her son seemed to trust. "If that's what we have to do, we'll do it."

"I'll let Chase know." Savannah took her hands and gave them a gentle squeeze. "I'll do whatever I can to help your new attorney win this case. Then you can get on with your life."

If only she could count on that promise, yet the future seemed ominous. She would probably lose her job. She would most likely go to trial. She could end up in prison—unless she revealed the piece of the puzzle that could free her, and possibly imprison her son.

When she thought back to that awful Friday night, Dalton's words echoed in her head.

The kid's a wimp. A whiny mama's boy. He's worthless. I'd wager my last dollar that he's not even my son....

No weapon had been involved, only an angry little boy who'd suffered enough verbal abuse to last a lifetime. A sweet, insecure little boy who, with all the strength he could muster, shoved the only father he'd ever known, sending him backward to suffer a blow to the head. A precious little boy who'd been born into a family that embraced lies and deceit. And revenge.

The world might forgive Danny for his actions, but Edwin Wainwright surely wouldn't—especially if he learned that his presumed grandson could be another man's child.

Chapter 8

He'd be damned if he let him get away with this.

Chase stormed into the department and went straight to Buck's office. When he didn't find him there, he retraced his steps and located him in the break room. As usual, he was seated at a round table, drinking his morning coffee and reading the Placid newspaper.

"We need to talk, Sheriff."

Buck continued to scan the page without bothering to look up. "I thought I told you yesterday to go home and not come back until Monday."

He still didn't care for that directive, then or now. "And I thought I told you Buster Eustace belonged in jail."

"Yep, that's what you said."

Buck's lack of concern only fed Chase's anger. "So why is it that he's still roaming the streets?"

He flipped to another page. "We only arrest 'em. We don't decide how long they stay."

He thought about Jess spending last night in a hellhole, while Eustace was free as a bird, having breakfast in the local diner. "How long did he stay, Buck?"

Buck folded the paper in precise creases and put it aside. "Not too long after you turned him over to Jones and he hauled him in. I was in bed when I got a phone call from the D.A.'s office. They said a couple of witnesses came forward, claimed it was a misunderstanding, and I was then instructed to let him go."

In all probability, bought-and-paid-for witnesses. "A misunderstanding? He slapped the hell out of Jess right there on the street."

"You probably should count your lucky stars that Buster didn't file charges against her. From what I hear, she started it. She's already in enough trouble already. You don't need to borrow more for her, so leave it alone."

He planted his palms on the table and leaned forward. "You can bet Wainwright had something to do with Buster's exoneration."

"Maybe so, but I learned over the years not to ask too many questions."

That had to be the sorriest excuse he'd ever heard coming from a peace officer's mouth. "And during all those years, you just bent over and took it."

Buck gave him a look as hard as steel. "I did what I had to do to put food on the table and keep a roof over your head. Some battles aren't worth fighting if you stand to lose more than it's worth. You'll learn that when you take over this job after I retire next year."

His own father had pretty much looked the other way to save his own ass. Disgusted, he straightened and backed away from the table. "I don't want this damn job. Not if it means turning my back on the law."

"Where are you going now?" Buck asked as Chase headed toward the door.

"To Jess's arraignment."

"You're already in too deep."

Chase turned, slowly. "I'm not going to desert her, so just lay off."

Buck inclined his head and narrowed his eyes. "Are you in love with her?"

The hesitation in his response was pretty damn telling. "I care about her." And he couldn't imagine not having her in his life, something best left unsaid.

Buck looked like he'd just caught a ten-pound bass. "It's more than caring about her. I can see it in your eyes. But you need to remember one important thing. She's been a Wainwright for a decade. She's bound to have learned something about lying."

"I don't have time for this," he said as he strode out the door.

He didn't have time for Buck's unwelcome advice, or to ponder his father's questions about his feelings for Jess. He'd have to take those out and examine them later.

Chase left the department the same way he entered, in a hurry. The hearing was scheduled to being in less than five minutes. Fortunately, the county courthouse was right next door.

Wearing civilian clothes and a baseball cap, Chase kept a low profile as he stood at the rear of the packed courtroom. The only courtroom. One-stop shopping for all things legal. He suspected a lot of bartering between the Wainwrights and the powers that be went on behind closed chamber doors.

Word of Jess's arrest had traveled like a wildfire

through town, drawing every Tom, Dick and Bubba to the proceedings. Including Edwin Wainwright, who was seated two rows back, studying his nails like he was contemplating his next manicure.

Chase had half a mind to plop down right next to the rich bastard just to see him squirm. Maybe get in a few digs while waiting for Jess's case to be called. Instead, he stayed rooted in the same spot in order to prevent a scene. He'd already landed on Buck's bad side as it was. Any job was better than no job at all.

The drunk driver he'd arrested two nights ago stepped forward, announced his innocence, followed by a very loud and drawn out explanation. Considering the jerk was slapped with the maximum bail allowed, the outburst apparently didn't set well with the circuit judge. Or maybe the judge was in a foul mood. The honorable R. J. Perkins wasn't always known for his good humor, or impartiality. He was known for his ties to Edwin Wainwright. And that might not bode well at all for Jess's release.

The bridge officer rattled off a docket number, followed by, "The People versus Jessica Keller Wainwright. Attempted murder in the second degree."

When the side door creaked open, all heads turned toward that direction, the crowd falling suddenly silent.

Savannah entered the courtroom first, with her cuffed client and the rail-thin bailiff trailing a short distance behind. Chase expected Jess to look battered and broken. Instead, she kept her chin raised and her eyes focused forward. "That's my girl," he muttered, thankful she hadn't lost her pride.

Savannah and Jess moved behind a table while the D.A., Jed Millsap, stood on the opposite side. After the judge flipped through the file, he glanced up over his glasses and looked squarely at Jess. "How does the defendant plead?"

"Not guilty, Your Honor," Jess stated, her voice clear and concise and confident.

She's been a Wainwright for a decade. She's bound to have learned something about lying....

Chase forced away the thoughts and concentrated on the proceedings.

"Your Honor, the defense requests that the accused be released on her own recognizance," Savannah said. "She has no prior record, she's a valued second-grade teacher, and she's well-known for her volunteer work with—"

"Might I remind the defense this is an attempted-murder charge, not a botched bake sale," Millsap chimed in. He waited for the chuckles to die down before he added, "Mrs. Wainwright's reputation doesn't take precedence over the fact that she tried to kill her husband. The People request remand."

"Ex-husband," Savannah corrected. "And might I remind the district attorney that the defendant *allegedly* tried to kill her *former* husband. Not to mention, your case has more holes in it than a ten-year-old pair of underwear."

Perkins rapped his gavel in sharp succession. "Might I remind you both, counselors, to save it for the official trial. Bail is set for four-hundred thousand dollars. Next case."

A collective intake of breath echoed in the courtroom and for the first time, Chase witnessed Jess's armor begin to melt. She walked out with her shoulders slumped and her head lowered, like she was just about ready to deflate.

Before the crowd moved toward the exit, he pushed

through the double doors and strode down the corridor toward the holding cell. He arrived just in time to meet Savannah head-on in the hall.

"Four-hundred grand?" he said before she even came to a stop. "What in the hell is that all about?"

Savannah gestured Chase over into a small alcove and set her briefcase at her feet. "It's higher than usual, but it could have been worse if she'd been charged with first-degree attempted murder, not second."

"And it might have been more reasonable if Wainwright wasn't a major contributor to Perkins's campaign."

Savannah took a quick visual survey of the area. "Be careful what you say, Chase. Accusing an officer of the court of misconduct is serious business."

He didn't give a damn who he offended. The truth was the truth. "Is Perkins going to preside over the trial?"

"No, he won't. That will be handled by a superior court judge."

Chase couldn't think of one judge in the county who'd qualify as superior. "Guess it doesn't matter who it is. Edwin prides himself on filling his pockets with local officials."

"That's why I intend to encourage Jess's new attorney to file a change of venue."

New attorney? "I thought you were going to handle the case."

She shook her head. "As I told Jess, I'm not experienced enough in criminal law to defend her beyond the preliminary phase."

He understood what she was saying, even if he didn't like it. "Who is this new attorney?"

"A hotshot named McDonough out of Jackson. I'm hoping we can move the trial there."

"She'd be better off staying in Placid." Closer to her friends. Closer to him. "If you throw her at the mercy of strangers, then she's as good as convicted."

She looked like she didn't appreciate him telling her how to run the show. "Sure, Chase. Let's put her fate in the hands of her peers who rely on Edwin Wainwright's bank to keep their businesses and farms afloat. A jury filled with folks who are terrified of him will not encourage a just verdict."

He wanted to debate that point but couldn't come up with a single argument. "Fine. Back to the bail. I have some cash in savings and I can put up my land. I can also draw on a line of credit through—"

"It's taken care of, Chase."

Unless Jess had a secret stash or a serious benefactor, he couldn't imagine anyone coming up with that amount on a moment's notice. "It's a hell of a lot of money, Savannah."

"Yes, and Rachel has it all, in cash. She received the balance of her trust fund when she turned thirty. She volunteered to use those funds and claims there's plenty more where that came from."

Chase rubbed his chin. "I'll be damned. That means—"

"Edwin Wainwright is indirectly paying for Jess's defense. Isn't that ironic and highly amusing?"

They exchanged a smile before Chase asked the most important question. "When will Jess be ready to go?"

Savannah checked her watch. "Probably in less than an hour."

"Good. I'll drive her home."

Savannah looked as stern as a spinster schoolmarm. "No, you won't. I'll drive her home."

"Dammit, Savannah, I need to do something for her."

"The best thing you can do for Jess is stay away from her."

Not acceptable. "No way am I going to abandon her when she needs all the support she can get."

"She has support from her friends, myself and Sam included. Your presence in her life might cause more harm that good."

"How do you figure that?"

"I don't have to tell you that this town thrives on gossip. If anyone misunderstands yours and Jess's relationship, that could open a huge can of worms. Besides, you're the law, and right now, she's on the wrong side of it."

Everything she'd said made sense, but Chase couldn't stomach the thought of leaving Jess high and dry. "We're just friends, Savannah. Everyone knows that."

Something about his words made Savannah frown. "Jess is vulnerable, and you're still too charming for your own good. Under the current circumstance, that could be a lethal combination."

She was basically accusing him of being a womanizer who couldn't control himself. "I'm not that same guy, Savannah. People change."

"Yes, people change. And so do relationships between people. That's what worries me."

Chase wondered if she knew about that night he spent with Jess. Nah. As far as he could tell, Jess had never mentioned that to anyone. If she had, the guys would've ribbed him about it a long time ago. "I'm not going to do anything to hurt her, if that's your concern. She's already been hurt enough."

"I don't believe you'd hurt her, at least not intentionally." Savannah picked up the briefcase and gave him a
quick hug. "Unfortunately, the hurt might not end today. I
just heard that Wainwright's called an emergency school
board meeting to determine what they're going to do
about Jess's teaching position."

Hell, that's all she needed. "I have a good mind to
barge in and try to convince them why they should hold
off on doing anything."

Savannah wagged her finger at him. "Now, now. Let's
control our temper and not make matters worse. I assume
the most they could do right now is temporarily suspend
her. If she's officially indicted, the contract could allow
the board to terminate her position immediately."

Only another phase Jess would have to endure. "Do
you think they'll have enough to return an indictment?"

"We won't know until the grand jury convenes after
the first of the year. Right now, it's not looking good
for her."

"Even if the case is built on the word of an expert
liar?"

"A wealthy liar with a father who basically owns the
town."

So much for an impartial justice system. "Maybe he'll
grow a conscience between now and then and clear Jess."

Savannah looked as skeptical as Chase felt. "And
maybe I'll strike oil in my front yard. In the meantime,
we'll just have to keep Jess as upbeat as possible."

"Kind of hard to do when I'm not allowed to see her."
When he was feeling anything but upbeat himself.

"I don't see any reason why you can't pick up the
phone and call her now and then." She pointed at him.
"But only phone calls."

Chase would agree to that, but only because he had no choice.

History definitely had a way of repeating itself. Once again, he was forced to leave her alone. Only this time, he'd be damned if he turned her away if she really needed him.

"You're not supposed to be here."

Not exactly the greeting Jess had hoped for when she appeared at his front door. Yet she shouldn't be all that surprised. In less than twenty-four hours, she had already broken the cardinal rule set out by Savannah—stay away from Chase.

"I know I'm not supposed to see you, but the house was so quiet, I just couldn't take it. I thought about watching a movie. I even considered going to bed, but it's not even nine o'clock. Besides, I'm too keyed up to sleep."

He remained as immovable as a boulder. A gorgeous rock of a man dressed in a navy T-shirt and a pair of camouflage pants, reminiscent of the time he'd made that surprise visit to her dorm. "I don't have to tell you what Buck's reaction will be if he sees your car."

She slipped her hands into her jacket pockets, feeling as contrite as a teenager who'd just blown curfew. But not so contrite she would turn around and leave before she had the opportunity to spend some time with him. "I didn't drive. I walked."

He looked completely incredulous. "That's got to be five miles."

"Probably only three, if you take a short cut through the Allworths' land, which I did."

"Not smart, Jess. That's rugged terrain. You could've

fallen and broken your pretty neck. Or found yourself on the wrong end of Frank Allworth's shotgun."

At least he thought her neck was pretty. "As you can see, I made it just fine, all in one piece. Don't forget I ran cross-country my sophomore year in high school. And I was one heck of a tumbler in my day."

"How many years ago was that?"

She shrugged. "Okay, it's been a while. I'm only saying my ability to walk several miles proves that I'm in better shape than I thought."

"And that you've lost your mind."

Close, but not quite. "Look, if you'll let me in, I won't stay long." Did it count that she had her fingers crossed behind her back?

"This is still a bad idea, Jess."

Time to play the guilt card. "After the day I've had, I just need to talk to someone. They won't even let me call my own child. And when you didn't call, I felt so isolated. I had to get out of that place."

The guilt card worked. He hesitated only a moment before stepping aside. "You've got an hour, and then I'm driving you home."

She didn't come here for an hour of his time. She wanted all night, right or wrong. But if his cranky attitude didn't improve, she might not last five minutes.

Jess brushed past him and walked into the den, where a floor lamp and a roaring fire provided the only light in the room. Only then did she notice how cold she really was. Slogging through ankle-deep water through part of her journey, in thirty-five degree weather, certainly hadn't helped. Her cross-trainers had dried. Her socks, however, had not.

She shrugged out of her coat and hung it on a spare

hook near the door, right next to Chase's jacket. "I would've been here sooner if Frank hadn't dug a trench right in the middle of his pasture." She turned and came face-to-face with his frown. "Wading through the slush slowed me down."

He glanced at the bottom of her frayed jeans now caked with mud. "Do you want to borrow a pair of my pants?"

She'd have to pin up the hem to keep from tripping. "If they fit, I'd be even more depressed than I already am."

His stoic expression softened somewhat. "That bad, huh?"

"I'm okay." And she was, now that she was with him.

"Are you sure?"

"I'm sure." She decided to share her latest accomplishment to prove she hadn't completely collapsed into a worthless puddle of gloom and doom. "I actually lit a fire all by myself in that old stove. I even chopped some wood with your ax. It's not as nice as your fire, but it warmed up the house fairly well." Yet it hadn't done a thing to rid her of the ongoing chills that had accompanied thoughts of her tenuous future.

"I knew you could do it," he said. "You can do anything if you set your mind to it."

Except keep myself out of prison. She halted the comment before it left her foolish mouth. She didn't want to spend these moments with Chase, drowning in self-pity. "Sam and Savannah stayed most of the afternoon after they brought me home. We had a nice visit."

"That's good. You probably needed the company."

She needed his company.

He gestured toward the sofa facing the fire. "Have a seat."

Using the back of the couch for support, she toed out of her shoes, stripped off her soggy socks, and set them near the door. She returned to claim a spot at the end of the sofa, discarding all decorum when she rested her heels on the edge of the coffee table to thaw her frozen feet.

Chase joined her, keeping a fairly wide berth between them. "What's going on with Sam and Savannah these days?"

She appreciated his attempt to avoid talk of literal trials and tribulations. "They're completely enamored of each other. In fact, they couldn't seem to keep their hands off each other." And she'd been stung by the jealousy bug just watching them. "I did appreciate having them around. But, honestly, I was glad when they finally left. I felt like an intruder in my own home."

He smiled, but only halfway. And it didn't last long. "You should've told them to get a room."

"I almost did. But I was afraid they'd end up in mine and I'd have to endure the sounds of heavy breathing."

Finally, he grinned, showing his dimples to supreme advantage. "I guess they're making up for lost time."

Jess truly couldn't fault the couple for that. Not after what they'd gone through to find each other again. But she couldn't deny she was jealous of the way Sam looked at Savannah, as if she were the most special woman on the planet. Dalton had never looked at her like that. No one had.

"Savannah did say they're moving forward with the wedding plans," she added. "They're going to wait until the spring so they can marry on that rickety bridge that joins their farms."

"I was beginning to wonder if they were actually going to do it."

She pushed up her sleeve and checked her watch. "They left my place several hours ago, so I imagine they've already done it. Probably more than once."

"I meant get married."

She faked confusion. "Oh, that. I certainly hope so. Then they can officially move in together and make-out in the privacy of their own home." She sounded like an envious harpy. "Don't get me wrong. I have nothing against public displays of affection. I'm just not used to it."

Chase rested his arm on the back of the sofa and shifted to face her. "Old Dalton wasn't into that, was he?"

She barked out a sarcastic laugh. "Dalton's idea of affection involved slapping me on the butt, right before he told me he needed his shirts ironed."

Chase's loathing for her ex-husband was palpable. "He's a real romantic guy."

"He can be, when he wants something."

"Like sex?"

The word went straight to her head like a shot of tequila. "What's that?"

His dark eyes looked even darker in the flickering firelight. "Do you want a summary, or the dirty details?"

Before she did something totally insane, like tell him she preferred a hands-on demonstration, she switched the subject. "By the way, do you have Bo?"

He shifted his weight, as if the query made him uncomfortable. "I took him to Matt and Rachel's this afternoon. They both agreed it might help Danny if I left Bo there for the time being."

She was starved for news of her son, and not altogether happy he'd withheld that information. "Why didn't you tell me you'd seen him before now?"

"Because I wasn't sure how you'd feel about it when you're not allowed."

She laid a hand on his arm. "I'm glad you checked on him. He thinks you hung the moon."

He pulled his arm back and faced forward, as if he couldn't stand her touching him. "I didn't have the chance to speak to him. He was taking a nap and I didn't want to bother him."

Her heart broke all over again when she thought about Danny weathering the storm without her. "He's probably exhausted. Did Rachel say how he was doing? Is he eating?" Had he asked about her, or had he'd written his mother off entirely?

"She told me he hasn't spoken much at all," he said. "She also said she's going to call that counselor she told you about. She'll try to set up an appointment, but it might be after the holidays. I need to let her know by Monday if you're okay with it."

She could barely think beyond the next few days. "Anything to help him through this." And she prayed her son didn't make any disclosures. That could present too many complications to count.

"Speaking of eating," he said. "Are you?"

She hadn't had much of an appetite, but she didn't dare mention that to him. She didn't want to encourage a lecture. "They fed me watered-down eggs and stale toast at the jail this morning. I can't remember when I've had such an interesting gastronomic experience."

"That doesn't account for the rest of the day."

"Savannah and Sam brought burgers from Stan's." And she'd thrown out over half the sandwich, another fact she would keep to herself.

"Just make sure you take care of yourself," he said. "You can't afford to get sick."

So much for avoiding a lecture. "True. I wouldn't want to miss work." She snapped her fingers. "Oh, wait. I no longer have a job."

Chase scowled. "Savannah told me about the board meeting, but she said they couldn't fire you unless you've been officially indicted."

Just more bad news to add to the rest. "They suspended me. Without pay. The principal called and apologized. It took her two whole minutes. But it's only a matter of time before they dismiss me for good, if Edwin has any say-so in the matter, which he does."

"Guess we're in the same boat. I'm on leave until Monday. Buck's orders. If I keep pissing him off, I might find myself without a job, too."

And she carried most of the responsibility for that. "Savannah mentioned that to me, right before she told me we couldn't be around each other."

"And that's why you shouldn't be here."

She wasn't so needy that she couldn't take a hint. Clearly he didn't want her, not in the way she wanted him. "If my presence is bothering you that much, I'll be glad to leave right now." She pushed off the sofa and stood. "And don't worry about driving me home. I prefer to get there the same way I got here, on foot."

He clasped her hand and pulled her down next to him. "You're already here, so you might as well stay for another hour. And I am going to drive you home, whether you like it or not. You don't need to be traipsing around all alone in the dark."

"I had enough light to see." She could also see she'd

begun to wear him down. With a little luck—and a lot of convincing—her plan might work after all.

"A word of advice," he said. "The next time you decide to go for a late-night walk, and you don't want to risk falling over a log, do what I do."

"Pack night-vision goggles?"

"I have a flashlight in my pocket."

She should keep her mouth shut, but she couldn't seem to contain the questionable thought. "I bet you say that to all the girls."

When he patted her thigh, she felt it all the way to her tingling toes, and all points in between. "Glad to see your smart-ass switch still works."

He'd turned on her libido switch with only an innocent touch and devilish smile. "Do you take a lot of walks at night?"

"Not since my Army days."

She decided to pose a question she'd wanted to ask for ages. "Exactly what did you do over there?"

His gaze drifted to some unknown focal point across the way. "I trekked through mountains and deserts, looking for bad guys."

"Did you find them?"

"Yeah, and they found us. Unfortunately, sometimes it's hard to identify the enemy. Mistakes are made when that happens."

Jess watched as Chase went to that place again. A place in his head that she couldn't go, unless he agreed to take her there. "If you ever want to talk about it, I'm here."

After a brief bout of silence, he came out of his momentary mental fog. "I'll make a deal with you. I'll talk about it, as long as you tell me everything that happened that night with Dalton. All the details."

A deal she couldn't—wouldn't—make. "I thought you said you didn't want to know details that you might be forced to reveal in court."

"If I do have to take the stand, I'll claim I don't know anything."

She couldn't believe he'd break his code of honor for her. "You'd lie under oath?"

"If that's what it took to save you."

She could be beyond saving. "Don't worry. You don't have to lie. I've already told you everything." Everything she was willing to tell him.

"Are you sure about that, Jess? Because I'm sensing you're withholding something."

For once in her life, she wished he didn't know her so well. "I didn't attack Dalton. I didn't touch a hair on his perfectly-styled head. And I have no problem saying *that* under oath."

He kept his gaze centered on hers for a few moments, as if searching for hidden truths. "I believe you." His lack of conviction said otherwise.

"Thank you," she told him anyway. "And now it's your turn to talk about what happened to you over there."

The sound of breaking glass brought the conversation to a standstill and sent Chase off the sofa to investigate. Jess stayed close behind him as he flipped on the light and opened the front door. Since his broad shoulders blocked her view, she leaned to her right to see a large, ornamental black vase in pieces on the porch.

"I told Savannah not to put the damn thing there," he muttered. "But she thought it gave the entry character."

"Not anymore," Jess said. "There's barely a breeze blowing. I can't imagine how something so heavy would just fall over."

"Probably a raccoon or a possum looking for food knocked it over."

That sounded plausible, but it didn't completely alleviate her fear that a human might be lurking in the shadows. "It had to be that. I highly doubt someone would try to break into a deputy's house. Unless they were incredibly stupid."

He faced her again, putting them in very close proximity since she'd failed to move. "I'll grab a flashlight and take a look around, just to be sure."

"Okay. But be careful. I'd hate for you to get ambushed."

"Yeah. Gotta watch those killer possums."

She would rather watch his killer smile. All night.

They returned inside where Chase retrieved a flashlight and put on his jacket. After he left out the front door again, Jess dropped into a nearby chair and contemplated her next move. She'd always believed in the "there are worse things than being alone" adage, but she'd never been in this situation before—without her son, and facing possible prosecution for a crime she didn't commit. She wanted the opportunity to escape her troubles, forget the tenuous future. To ignore the world in the arms of a man who could easily erase all her worries. Problem was, he could very well reject her request. She wouldn't know unless she tried.

"All clear," he said after he came back in the house. "Whatever knocked over the pot is probably long gone."

Jess came to her feet and walked to the window. She

pulled back the heavy brown curtain and peered into the night, needing some time to gather her courage, to implement her plan. "If you say so."

"Don't you trust me?"

She did. Otherwise, she wouldn't be here, planning to invite herself into his bed.

After she turned to find Chase hadn't removed his coat, she suspected he was ready to boot her out. "I trust you. I'm just a little jumpy tonight." For obvious—and not so obvious—reasons.

"Do you need anything before I take you home?" he asked, confirming her suspicions. "I have some extra cash."

She needed something all right, but strictly from a non-monetary standpoint. "I'm fine on that front. I used to sock away money when Dalton and I were still married. A rainy day fund." She hadn't realized she'd be swept up in a hurricane at the time, otherwise she would have saved more.

"Just let me know if you run short." He glanced at the clock hung over the bookshelves flanking the fireplace. "It's getting late. I better get you home."

Now or never had arrived. She opted for now. "I don't want to go home. Not now. Not tonight."

She'd expected a resounding refusal, yet he seemed to be mulling it over. "If you're that worried about being alone," he said, "I guess I can lend you my couch. But you'll have to be out of here before dawn."

"I'd rather be in your bed."

"Then I'll take the couch and you take the bed."

If he insisted on being obtuse, she'd simply have to be

straightforward. "I don't want you to sleep on the sofa. And I don't want you to sleep in your bed, either."

"You're not making any sense, Jess."

She wasn't making any progress, either. "You're really out of the loop if you don't recognize a proposition when you hear one."

He started to pace around the room, his hands laced behind his neck. "We can't do that, Jess."

"Yes, we can. If you recall, we already have. But then, you did tell me that night we should forget it ever happened. But here's a flash, Chase. I didn't forget, even if you did."

He spun around, frustration etched in his face. "You really believe I've forgotten?"

She leaned back against the door to block the exit, in case he decided to leave when she refused to go. "It wouldn't surprise me in the least if it never crossed your mind. After all, I was just one of your many conquests. A mistake you made along the way."

He stood right in front of her before she realized he'd moved. Bracing both hands above her head, he trapped her between solid wood and his equally solid body. "First of all, there haven't been as many women as you think. Secondly, not a day's gone by when I haven't thought about that night."

Years of pent-up emotional pain, prompted by his careless disregard, drove her to bait him. "Funny, you never mentioned it again. Not one time in all the letters we exchanged." Then again, neither had she.

"What did you expect me to do after you ran off and married Dalton? You're right. I've made mistakes in my life, but staking a claim on another man's wife isn't one of them."

She might not have been another man's wife if she'd meant more to him than a quick round of send-off sex. "I still have a difficult time believing you."

He pressed his body flush against hers. "Here's a flash, Jessica," he began, throwing her words back at her. "At night in the barracks, when there wasn't a woman in sight and I had to take matters into my own hands, do you know what I fantasized about?"

"Supermodels?"

He leaned closer, his warm breath a whisper on her ear. "You."

Jess had a difficult time composing herself enough to catch a breath. "Then you don't regret being with me?"

"I regret that I didn't take my time with you."

She felt remarkably empowered. Bold and brash. And sexy, for the first time in years. "You can make up for it now. I'm not asking for forever, just one night."

"I don't want to hurt you, Jess."

"You won't unless you tell me no. I assure you, I'm going into this with eyes wide open. You don't even have to pretend you care about me more than you do."

"If I didn't give a damn about you, I would've had you naked and flat on your back long before now."

His intense expression, the rapid rise and fall of his chest, told Jess she was about to taste triumph. "Let me stay, Chase. I'll make it worth your while."

"You're making it real hard to say no."

All a part of the master plan. She traced the indentation in his cheeks, then feathered a fingertip across his lips. "I gave you comfort that night before you left. This time, I need some comfort, too. I need you."

A storm of indecision reflected in his eyes, and she knew the very moment he conceded defeat. When kissed her.

After ten long years, she would finally get what she thought she would never have again. Another night with Chase Reed.

Chapter 9

He had Jess down for the count on the couch in a matter of minutes, one hand up her shirt and the other poised on his fly. And then he had a moment of clarity. A big one.

He raised his head and locked into her gaze. "Are you on the Pill?"

"No."

The next question was a long-shot at best. "You didn't happen to bring any condoms with you, did you?"

"No. They're at home in the cookie jar."

"I'm serious, Jess."

She looked seriously ticked off. "No, I don't randomly keep condoms in my pocket."

"Then we can't do this," he said as he climbed off her, leaving Jess looking as perturbed as he felt. But he wasn't mad at her. He was mad at himself.

She sat up and glared at him. "You mean you're just going to kiss me like that and then not follow through?"

He'd had every intention of following through, until he remembered something too important to neglect. "We don't have a choice. The last thing we need is for me to get you pregnant."

A strange, unreadable look passed over her expression. "Yes, that would definitely be inadvisable. But my question to you is this. Why in the heck don't you have a condom cache? You're the confirmed bachelor, not me."

Because he hadn't been with a woman in well over six months. "Like I told you before, I've been in a—"

"Dry spell. I know." She grabbed her hair with both hands, like she wanted to pull it out by the roots. "This is a fine time for you to ignore your Boy Scout motto."

How could he have prepared for her blatant seduction? Not that he wasn't willing to scratch her itch. But the cost was way too high to throw their clothes, and caution, to the wind. "Maybe this is a sign we shouldn't be doing this."

She came to her feet, looking as determined as ever. "It's not a sign. It's a minor inconvenience that can easily be remedied. That's why they invented convenience stores, hence the convenience part. There happens to be one this side of the county line, and it's open until midnight. I'd go, but by the time I walk there and back, I could be too tired to tango. And that, Deputy, just won't do."

She was definitely serious about seeing this through. No one ever accused him of not giving a lady what she wanted, even if this could be a catastrophe in the making. If anyone found out what they were doing—what they were going to do—they'd be instant grist for the rumor mill. Just like Savannah had predicted.

What the hell. No one would find out. The closest

neighbor lived over a mile down the road, and he doubted anyone was out driving around. Besides, if he backed out now, he'd have to live with disappointing Jess. Again. She needed him, and he needed her, and that was a good enough reason to go for it. Then he'd have to find a way to break all ties in order to protect her.

He put on his jacket, fished the keys from his pocket and faced her again. "I'll go. You stay here."

She sent him smile that was so damn sexy, he almost said goodbye to the store and hello to poor judgment. "Marvelous idea," she said. "My socks are still wet, and I don't do wet socks."

Old habits came home to roost. "Sweetheart, sometimes wet isn't a bad thing. I'll show you what I mean when I get back."

That seemed to shut her up, but it didn't stop her from tagging along behind him as he walked out the door. Before he reached the first step, she tapped him on the shoulder, drawing him back around to receive an all-out assault on his mouth. If she didn't let up soon, he'd never be able to walk into the store with his dignity intact.

"What was that for?" he asked when she finally broke the kiss.

"I just wanted to remind you what you'll be missing, in case you decide to keep going and not come back."

"I'll be back." She'd pretty much cemented that with her wicked mouth. "In the meantime, get naked and get in bed."

She saluted him like a drill sergeant. "Do you want any shirts ironed before I do that?"

Damn. She'd just pointed out he wasn't any better in the romance department than her sorry ex-husband. "Come to think of it, I'm going to take off your clothes, real slow, and then I'll carry you to bed. If we make it that far."

Without waiting for a response, Chase strode to the truck, unlocked it with the remote and slid inside the cab. For once he wished he had the cruiser at his disposal, but he'd been forced to leave that at the department after his temporary dismissal. Permanent dismissal, if Buck got wind of this little rendezvous.

He waited a few minutes to start the ignition, closing his eyes to reclaim some calm. When he opened them, he saw Jess standing on the porch, tapping her foot. Patience had never been one of her stronger virtues. Evidently the same held true for her modesty, he realized, when she shimmied out of her jeans. The oversize, long-sleeve T-shirt she still wore covered her enough, but also revealed a lot of bare leg. That sight was enough to ignite a fire that shot straight to his groin. So much for cooling his jets.

He backed out of the driveway in a rush, spewing gravel and dust as he hit the main road. As bad luck would have it, he'd only traveled a few yards when a beat-up, aged, tank of a sedan pulled out in front him. The driver had to be going a good ten miles under the speed limit, which made Chase wonder if the person behind the wheel had been drinking. But the car held steady to the curve of the road, which thankfully shot holes in that concern. Probably just some geezer with bad eyesight going out for milk at his wife's request.

The car finally pulled over to the shoulder, allowing Chase to pass him. He punched the accelerator and made it to the store in record time, fortunately finding the parking lot deserted. He sure as hell didn't want an audience when he made the purchase. Unfortunately, he recognized the clerk behind the counter. A tall, lanky seventeen-year-old who played guard for the high school basketball team.

Chase grabbed a cup of black coffee from the pot near the soda dispenser before heading down the candy aisle. After picking up a box of chocolate-covered mints— Jess's favorite—he made his way to the display near the front of the store. Might be nice if they put the damn condoms in a less obvious place, but he figured they had a lot of teenagers trying to steal the things. Right now he felt like a sneaky teenager. But he wasn't. Not even close. Maybe guilt had something to do with the return to his youth.

After snatching a couple of packets from the long metal hooks, he set them on the counter, along with the candy and coffee.

"Evening, Deputy Reed."

Chase looked up to meet the clerk's obnoxious grin. "Evening."

"It's party time, huh?"

He withdrew his wallet from his back pocket, pulled out a twenty and offered it to the kid. He also offered him a mind-your-own-business glare. "Why are you working this late on a school night?"

The kid looked like he could crawl under the counter. "It's the holidays, sir. Do you need a sack?"

He needed to stop being such a hard-ass, otherwise he'd end up just like Buck. "No thanks, and keep the change."

Chase pocketed the items, grabbed the coffee and then pushed through the double glass doors and walked into the frigid night. Before he stepped off the curb, he noticed a car sitting near a flickering guard light in the corner of the lot. A car that looked a lot like the one he'd passed on the road. He couldn't make out the driver's features that were set in shadow, but he did recognize his gender from the hairy hand holding a lit cigarette out the open window.

He could be lost, which would explain why he'd been driving slowly. Or he could be up to no good.

Chase thought about the boy in the store, alone and probably unarmed. Some mother's son who needed someone to look out for him. With that in mind, he opened the door, and leaned into the cab to retrieve his gun from the locked glove box. After he put the coffee cup in the holder and stuck the weapon in his back waistband, he straightened to see the car pull away. He didn't make another move until he watched the taillights fade out of sight.

Satisfied the clerk was safe, he climbed back in the truck, put away the gun and sped back to the house without encountering anyone on the road. He cut off the ignition and paused to down the last of the coffee. By the time he reached the front door, he was high on caffeine, adrenaline and a whole lot of anticipation.

The sound of crackling wood filled the otherwise silent den, the dying fire providing the only real light. Chase assumed Jess had decided to wait for him in bed, but that assumption was splintered when he caught sight of a lock of auburn hair draped over the arm of the sofa. He almost called her name, but decided to wait until he assessed the situation. As expected, she was stretched out on her side, eyes closed, a throw pillow supporting her head, and both hands curled beneath her cheek. The T-shirt had ridden up high on her thighs, exposing a lot of bare leg and the lace edge of a pair of jet-black panties. The ache way down south returned. An ache that only she could alleviate.

As badly as he wanted to wake her—as badly as he wanted her—he decided to let her sleep. Aside from making the three-mile walk to get to him, she'd been put through the emotional wringer over the past five days. She needed her rest, regardless of how bad he needed her.

He retrieved a white wool blanket from the bedroom closet, and after making sure she was sufficiently covered, he claimed the club chair adjacent to the couch.

She reminded him of the girl he once knew. The girl who'd played angel to his devil. When he'd defended her honor on the playground, she'd kicked him in the shin for disrupting her flirtation. After she'd suffered a number of break-ups with childhood boyfriends, he'd been in charge of bandaging her broken heart. And she'd been the one to scold him when he'd broken someone's heart. They'd been thick as thieves, and the best of friends— until Dalton Wainwright rode into her life in his shiny red sports car, sweeping her away with priceless gifts and promises the bastard had never intended to keep. To Dalton, she'd been nothing more than a pretty possession. The girl many a boy wanted, but could never have. Including Chase.

He knew the exact moment he'd begun to see her as more than a friend, and it had happened long before the eve of his first deployment to the Middle East. She'd come to the party his parents had thrown the day before he'd left for basic training. He remembered what she'd been wearing—a white sleeveless dress with black polka dots. He remembered the last thing she said to him, too.

If you ever get lonely, just think of me thinking of you and wishing you were back home with me.

In that moment, he'd viewed her as a woman worth waiting for. As someone he loved, and not only as a friend. He hadn't admitted it then, not even to himself, but he realized it now. And that scared the hell out of him.

When she stirred, he thought she might wake up and expect him to finish what they'd started. Instead, she rolled onto her belly and sighed in her sleep. He couldn't deny his disappointment, but he also couldn't deny that maybe this wasn't meant to be.

He pushed out of the chair, kissed her cheek, and set off to bed alone. But not completely alone. As sure as the dawn would come, he'd be visited by the horrors of war that often infiltrated his dreams—and the face of the little girl who had died in his arms.

The little girl who had died by his own hand.

Jess came awake with a start, jolted from sleep by a tortured voice filtering into the room from down the hall. After she got her bearings, she moved toward the sound. Toward Chase.

She felt blindly along the wall until she found the switch and flipped it on. The light allowed her to see the partially-opened door, and the bed where he thrashed about. She perched on the edge of the mattress and watched the anguish form on his face as he muttered unintelligible words. But a few were crystal clear—"save her" and "too late."

The dog tags resting on his bare chest glinted in the limited light, a symbol of what he stood for. A reminder of a war he clearly still fought in his dreams. She wasn't sure how to wake him. She wasn't sure she should. Yet she couldn't bear his torment any longer. But as she smoothed her hand over his damp forehead, he grabbed her wrist and bolted upright, almost scaring her out of her skin.

"It's Jess, Chase," she whispered softly. "It's okay."

He loosened his grip as his dark eyes finally focused on her, and awareness dawned in his expression. "Did I hurt you?" he asked, his voice grainy from troubled sleep.

"No, you didn't hurt me."

He collapsed back onto the pillow and stared at the ceiling. "I'm sorry."

"You don't have to apologize. I'm just worried about you."

He shifted toward the middle of the bed and opened his arms. "Come here."

He didn't have to ask her twice. She curled up close to his side on top of the covers, and rested her arm across his belly where the sheet barely covered his hips. She was content to just hold him. To be held.

But as he stroked her arm, back and forth in a steady rhythm, she was no longer satisfied with the limited contacted. She wanted more. She wanted everything he could give her. What he would have given her if she hadn't foolishly fallen asleep. The question was—would he still be willing?

She shifted restlessly against his side and an odd sound slipped out of her parted lips before she could stop it. He showed her that he understood her need when he framed her face in one palm and kissed her. Gently at first, before it deepened to the kind of kiss that told her he wanted more, too. He wanted her.

Without saying a word, she rose up and tugged her shirt over her head, then removed her bra, all under his watchful eye. Having a baby, and age, had softened her in places, widened her in others. She definitely wasn't as thin as she had been when he'd made love to her the first time. But amazingly, she didn't feel at all self-conscious or shy. She just felt…hot. Really hot after he tossed the sheet away, revealing that he was several steps ahead, as far the undressing went. He was also very aroused, but then so was she. And she became even more aroused when she returned to his side and he slid her panties away.

As they faced each other, he teased her with a kiss, then another, before he skimmed his palms down her body. He caressed the curve of her hip with a feather-soft touch, never taking his gaze from hers.

"You're beautiful," he whispered. "Did you know that?"

Not until now. But she actually did feel beautiful, and desired. All because of him.

She wanted so badly to touch him, too. She was dying to touch him. But when she reached for him, he caught her wrist again, more gently this time. "If you put your hands on me right now, it won't last long enough." He nudged her onto her back and rose above her. "And I want this to last a long, long time. Unlike the last time."

The reference to that long-ago night wasn't completely lost on Jess. Everything had happened so fast back then, she hadn't had time to really enjoy the experience. She'd also been racked with sadness and fear for his safety. Later, with more than a little remorse.

Right now, she couldn't consider anything beyond the downward path he was traveling with his lips. He paused to linger at her breasts before he moved to her belly, but he didn't stop there. As he approached his final destination, Jess knew exactly what he was about to do. She was powerless to stop him, even if she wanted to. She didn't want to.

This ultimate act of intimacy required a good deal of trust, and the willingness to let go, to follow wherever he cared to lead her. She did trust him, and she did let go as he brought her to the brink with his incredibly talented mouth.

As the climax began to build, a thousand heady feelings rushed through her. Her heart beat at a rapid pace. Every breath became an effort. She wanted to savor each sensation, wanted it to go on forever, but the release was so powerful, so quick, she could only surrender to it.

So lost in the afterglow that had eluded her for a long, long time, she hadn't realized Chase had moved, until she heard the sound of tearing paper. She looked to her left to see him seated on the edge of the bed, keeping his beautifully sculpted back to her. She waited eagerly for the all-important pay-off, although she'd already been paid in full. Now it was his turn to reap the rewards.

Yet instead of doing what she'd expected, he moved over her and braced on bent arms, leaving too much space between their bodies. "Tell me your fantasies," he said in a low, sensuous whisper.

She wasn't accustomed to talk during sex. Dalton had never made a sound, except to snore after the fact. She banished her insignificant ex-husband from her brain, and tried to come up with an answer to Chase's question that didn't sound totally off the wall. "I really don't have any fantasies."

"Sure you do," he said. "Everyone does. Maybe a place where you'd like to make love, but never have. A way you'd like to make love, but you've never been brave enough to do it."

One thing did come to mind. She should be embarrassed to share, but she wasn't. Okay, maybe a little. "Do you promise not to laugh?"

He kissed her forehead. "Babe, right now, laughing is the last thing I want to do." He rubbed his lower body against hers, sending a strong message, loud and clear.

"I've imagined having sex on top of Dalton's desk down at the bank," she rattled off. "But not with Dalton."

"Then with who?"

Oops. "With you."

He looked rather pleased by her answer. "Babe, I can't physically take you there right now, but imagine we're on that desk while I take you to a place you've never been before."

She managed a weak smile. "A little cocky, are we?"

"Just confident."

Chase had the skill to back up that confidence, she soon realized, as he finally slid inside her with an easy glide and built steady momentum with his powerful body. He practically blew her mind with very descriptive words that were somewhat crude but oh-so-sexy. As promised, he did take her to a place she'd never been before, right into the throes of another climax, the second equally as strong as the first. And he wasn't far behind her, she realized, during her slow journey to recovery. With one last thrust, every muscle in his body tensed, and a low groan escaped from somewhere deep in his throat. And then he collapsed, giving Jess all his weight after giving her the experience of a lifetime.

They stayed that way for a while, as closely joined as two people could be, until he moved away and took her back into his arms. She couldn't imagine anywhere else she wanted to be in those quiet moments. She couldn't imagine any man ever measuring up to him.

"Are you okay?" he asked, finally breaking the silence.

"I am, but are you?"

"Couldn't be better."

Oh, but he could. And as much as she wanted to stay steeped in bliss, she needed him to open up, now more than ever. After what they'd just been through together, maybe he would.

Covering herself with the tangled sheet, Jess leaned over and turned on the bedside lamp, then scooted up against the headboard. "I have something I need to ask you."

He honored her with his trademark dimpled grin. "Yeah, I bought another condom. Just give me fifteen minutes and we'll put it to good use."

As tempted as Jess was by that suggestion, she had a more pressing issue on the table. And as badly as she hated to ruin the mood, she had an urgent need to know the story behind his night terrors.

She drew in a deep breath, let it out slowly, and started down the path possibly leading to the truth.

"Who was the woman you couldn't save?"

Chapter 10

Right when he'd finally had a few minutes of peace, she'd forced him to remember.

Chase instinctively wanted to shut down. Shut her out. The need to guard his emotions overrode his need for absolution.

He draped one arm over his eyes to avoid her scrutiny, only to see the never-ending horrors. "Let it go, Jess."

"I can't, Chase. You need to talk to someone about this. Why not me?"

"I've already talked about it." But not all of it. Never all of it. "I've talked to doctors and counselors. I even took the pills they offered for a while, but I didn't like the way they made me feel. Or I should say, the way they kept me from feeling."

"I see. You want to relive it, whatever it is, because you have some absurd need to punish yourself."

She had that one nailed. "Just forget what you saw, and what you heard, and let me deal with it."

"How can I forget it when you obviously can't? And it's more than apparent you're not dealing with it."

Fine. If she wanted the gritty details, he'd give them to her. He'd been looking for a way to cut her off, to discourage this situation from happening again. Once he divulged the facts, and his downfall, she wouldn't hold him in such high esteem. An easy out. Not an easy story to tell. But one that had to be told so she would understand.

He climbed out of the bed, grabbed some clothes from the bureau, and went into the bathroom to clean up. He ran the risk she might take off before he was finished, but that wasn't likely. She was prone to digging her heels in when she wanted something. She'd proved that tonight with her proposition. And he'd given in to her wishes without that much thought. Sad thing was, if she hadn't witnessed his nightmares, or at least overlooked them, they might still be in bed, making some more real, sweet love. He needed that a whole lot more than a sorry trip back into the past.

When Chase returned to the bedroom, she was still in the same spot, looking as mad as a soaked hen. And sexy as hell. Her hair was a mess and her cheeks were flushed. She looked like she needed to be kissed again. Everywhere.

"Going somewhere?" she asked when he failed to move.

Yeah. He was about to board the insanity train.

He gathered her clothes from the floor and tossed them on the bed in front of her. "Get dressed."

Anger as turbulent as a tornado flashed in her eyes. "Oh, so that's it. Now that you've had your wicked way with me, you just pat me on the butt and take me home. Heaven forbid I want to be your friend, not just your one-night lover."

He sensed a tirade coming on. "Put your clothes on, Jess."

She didn't disappoint. "Perhaps, Deputy Reed, you believe keeping your emotions locked tight is the manly thing to do. That needing someone is a sign of weakness. In my book, that's darned arrogant. And dangerous. One day you might crawl so far inside yourself, you won't be able to feel anything. But I guess that suits you just fine, doesn't it? All a part of your skewed macho persona."

She didn't know the half of it, but she would. Provided she kept quiet long enough for him to have his say. "If you want to know the truth, you've got it. But if I'm going to tell you what happened, we're going to do it somewhere other than in a bed."

Otherwise he'd be too distracted. To tempted to persuade her to drop the whole admission thing. He had the means and the know-how to do it. But that would only be a temporary diversion. She'd eventually hound him about it again.

"Meet me in the den when you have your clothes on," he said.

Then without another word, he walked into the kitchen and went straight for the bottle of tequila someone had left during a card game back in the summer. He wasn't one to drink hard liquor. He'd seen the effects of too much booze on fellow soldiers and friends and even enemies, namely Dalton Wainwright. And he sure couldn't forget Matt Boyd's dad. But in this case, desperate disclosures called for desperate measures.

He poured a shot, drank it fast and then had one more.

The tequila burned his throat and left a foul taste in his mouth. As much as wanted to be numb, he didn't want to be drunk when he tore open old wounds, and that could be the case if he downed another shot.

After he dumped the rest of the tequila into the sink, he set the glass aside and returned to the den. The fire had gone out completely, but he didn't have the will to start another. The pile of ashes scattered in the hearth seemed like a proper backdrop for the confession.

He sat on the sofa and waited for Jess. Waited to drop the information bomb that could blow her opinion of him right out of the water. She came into the room a few minutes later, bypassing the space next to him, choosing the chair instead.

She sat straight as a stick, hands gripping the chair's arms. "I'm here, and I'm ready to listen. Feel free to begin when you're ready." The speech was so dry, no one would believe they'd been about as close as two people could be only a short time ago.

Chase had a hard time believing it himself. He also had a hard time believing he was about to let her in on his secrets. Let her in, period. But he'd come this far, he wasn't going to turn back now.

Leaning forward, he draped his arms on his knees and focused on the beige area rug beneath his bare feet. "It was near the end of my second tour of duty. It happened on a day like any other day." The air had been thick with dust and the usual tension. Weapons loaded and readily on hand. Everyone prepared to spring into action on a moment's notice. Everyone but him.

"We were patrolling the streets that afternoon, keeping the peace," he continued. "The open-air market was crowded with civilians. That's the first time I remember seeing her, at least on that day. She'd been around before."

"The woman?"

He looked up to discover Jess had scooted to the edge of her seat. "Not a woman. A girl. She was maybe a year younger than Danny."

He could tell that struck a chord with her, but she still remained calm and attentive. "Go on."

Consciously living those moments, step-by-step, was akin to walking across burning sand without shoes. He wanted to rush through the events to avoid the pain, but the terrain was too vast. "Anyway, she was a little thing with big brown eyes and a huge smile. She used to come around when we'd hand out treats to the local kids. As far as I could tell, she only knew one English word. *Candy.*"

He allowed a smile over the few good memories, and that didn't escape Jess's notice. "I guess the love of candy is universal," she said. "She must have been a special little girl if she stood out from the crowd."

"She was special. They all were in their own right. Survivors of a living hell. But they could still get excited over a gumball."

"Maybe we could both take a lesson from that."

He was too jaded to believe he could be that resilient. He'd proven it every night. "A lot of the kids were orphans. But that little girl always had her mother nearby. That day was no exception."

As the events unfolded in his mind, the visions were razor sharp, as if they'd happened only hours, not years, before. The fortress he'd built for self-protection began to crumble, one memory at a time. Ironic that for years, he couldn't talk at length about it. Now he couldn't seem to stop.

"She handed me a piece of paper," he said. "A drawing she'd done. I knelt down to take it from her."

Thank you, sweetheart. That's really pretty.

"She was smiling when the shooting started."

Mass chaos. Bullets ricocheting all around him. Sheer terror.

When Chase leaned his head back against the sofa, Jess came over and sat beside him. "Do you want to take a break?"

"No. I want to get this over with."

He waited just long enough to collect his composure before he began again. "People starting scattering when the gunfire erupted. I grabbed her hand, pulled her behind me. I could hear her mother screaming *Safa* over and over again. Funny, I didn't even know her name until that moment."

He paused to draw a breath, then let it out slowly. "I saw one of the insurgents shoot one of my men, then he tried to escape when he saw me. I don't know for sure, but I believe he was out of ammo."

His mind momentarily froze when the next images began flashing in his brain, like some freak slideshow.

"Go on, Chase."

Jess's voice thrust him out of his stupor. "I was so damn determined to stop him, I let go of Safa's hand. She ran into the street, trying to get to her mother. I discharged a round, and she took a bullet. Right in the heart."

Jess gasped and covered her mouth with her palm. "Oh, Chase."

The words kept flowing like water from a busted dam. "I dropped to the ground and crawled over to her. I picked her up and held my hand on the wound, but I couldn't stop the bleeding. She was still alive at the time, and I watched the life drain out of her eyes. And, God, her mother…"

He streaked both hands over his face. "Her mother kept screaming. I've seen a lot in my time, but I've never heard that much agony coming from another human being."

When he glanced at Jess and saw her tears, he thought for a moment he might just join her. But he didn't dare cry. If he did, he might never stop.

"And you know what's so damn unfair?" he said after a time. "The gunman I shot survived, while an innocent little girl died. Helluva world we live in, huh?"

She took his hand into hers and held it against her damp cheek. "This wasn't your fault, Chase. You couldn't have known what would happen."

He'd tried to convince himself of that for years, but so far it hadn't worked. "I could've held on to her hand. I could have let the bastard go. Then she'd still be alive."

She tipped her head against his shoulder. "I understand why you feel the way you do, but I don't understand why you won't give yourself a break."

"Because I can't. I took that child away from her mother, the same as if I'd intentionally turned the gun on her. And that's what I see at night, that moment I let go of her. The fear in her eyes a split second before she left this world. I hear her mother's screams." Sights and sounds that would never go away.

No longer able to sit still, he stood and walked to the fireplace where he gripped the edge of the mantel. On one hand, he felt drained of energy. On the other, he could punch the wall with the force of his despair.

"Why on earth did you go back again?" Jess asked.

That could be answered with one word. "Absolution."

"But you didn't find it, did you?"

He'd stopped searching when he recognized he didn't warrant it. "No."

"And why would you take a job in law enforcement? That has to make matters worse."

"Because I promised Buck I'd do it. Because it's always been expected of me." Being the best soldier. Being the best deputy. Eventually being the best father. He'd failed at two, he wasn't going to set himself up to fail at the other.

"Then Buck doesn't know about what happened."

He shot a quick look at her over his shoulder. "Hell, no. I couldn't tell him that his hero son isn't a hero after all."

When he felt the light touch on his shoulder, he tensed from the contact. "You are a hero, Chase. Just think of all the other lives you've saved. You're certainly Danny's hero."

He dropped his arms and faced her. "Danny needs to find someone else to admire. I'm only a man who made an unforgivable mistake."

"I forgive you."

He'd underestimated her compassion. Looking back, he wasn't sure why he had. "I don't deserve your forgiveness, Jess. I don't want it."

She tipped her chin up and glared at him. "Well you've got it, whether you want it or not. And you can either beat yourself up, or you can finally accept the fact that you're mortal. You never meant to hurt that little girl, and the fact that you're still mourning the loss only demonstrates you're a good man."

That brought him to a question he needed to ask her. "What about you, Jess? Have you ever done something you regret? Something that keeps you awake at night?"

She instantly looked away. "If you're talking about what happened with Dalton, I've already said all that I want to say about that."

He didn't know where the anger had come from. He only knew it hit him like a left hook. "Great. You force me to expose my soul, and you're not willing to do the same. That's kind of unfair, don't you think?"

That earned him her attention. "Everything I've done in my adult life, good, bad or indifferent, I did to protect a child. Maybe it hasn't turned out the way it should, but my intentions were good, and so were yours. I have to keep telling myself that to keep going."

That wasn't exactly a confession, but in Chase's opinion, it was darn close. "You know what they say about the road to hell and good intentions."

"They can shove it. I believe if your heart is in the right place, anything can be forgiven."

He wanted to adopt her optimistic attitude. He wanted to go to bed at night knowing he hadn't completely botched his honor. Right then, he wanted to sweep her back into his arms, carry her back to bed and forget everything aside from making love to her. But he had to stay away from Jess or risk failing her, too.

"I need to take you home," he said. "I'll go warm up the truck while you put on your shoes."

When she moved closer and cupped his jaw in her palm, he saw the sympathy in her eyes. "I can stay a little longer. It's still dark outside."

Now came the hard part. He clasped her wrist and took her hand away. "This is the last time we're going to do this, Jess. I don't want to be responsible for ruining your life, too."

She crossed her arms over her middle and sighed.

"Okay. We can't take the risk again. But I'm not worried about you ruining my life, because you can't. You don't have that much power over the cosmos, or me. I'll go home now, but as soon as this thing with Dalton is settled, I'm going to help you through this guilt. The same way you've helped me in the last few days. Even if I have to do it from jail."

The thought of her being thrown into a cell made him sick. "Most of the time, I'm not fit to be around."

She smiled. "Only when you haven't had your coffee, or you can't watch a playoff game. But in my eyes, you're still about the best thing going when it comes to being a friend."

He wanted to fight her on the issue, but he was too damn exhausted. In spite of what she'd said, he vowed to keep his distance, at least for the time being. If he had any sense whatsoever, he'd take a permanent hiatus from her life. But the fact that she knew his well-kept secret and still didn't think any less of him, made leaving her alone all the more difficult. And so did the feelings that had begun to surface. Feelings as hard to ignore as the night terrors.

Buck had been right—he was in love with her. He just didn't have a clue what to do about it.

He was clearly done with her.

Jess had come to accept that over the past three days. Chase hadn't bothered to call. Hadn't bothered to answer her calls, until a half hour ago. And he certainly hadn't paid her any surprise visits. Pride had prevented her from visiting him. That and the fear that, this time, he would turn her away. For good.

Yet the rain that had steadily fallen for a good part of

the previous night, and most of the day, had presented her with an opportunity to see him again. Thank heavens for backed-up plumbing, a leaky roof and a landlord who refused to pay a repairman's double rate during a holiday.

She stood at the window and waited for Chase, the overcast skies contributing to her melancholy mood. But her spirits lifted when she spotted the truck coming up the drive. They went into a free-fall when she became aware that it wasn't Chase's truck after all. His was silver with a single-cab, while this one had an extended cab. And as the mystery vehicle drew closer, she recognized the truck by the magnetic sign adhered to the door that read, Matthew J. Boyd, DVM. Rachel's veterinarian husband. Jess's former brother-in-law and recent surrogate father to her son.

At first she experienced a twinge of panic when she considered something might have happened to Danny. Then blessed relief arrived as Chase emerged from the passenger side. So did the heightened awareness that had become all too familiar. He looked so good, she had to wrangle the urge to run to him. Yes, he needed a shave. And yes, he wore a plain chambray shirt over his white T-shirt, along with his usual dark wash jeans. But since she'd recently seen, up close and extremely personal, what lurked beneath that non-descript clothing, she viewed him in a whole new light. Lately, she'd been seeing him unabashedly naked in her very vivid imagination.

Shaking off those thoughts, Jess walked outside and waited for the pair on the porch. Matt arrived first, tool box in hand, and gave her a quick peck on the cheek. "How are you holding up, Jess?"

"With both of my legs, Matt." Though her legs could

give out on her at any moment, thanks to the deputy's appearance.

When Chase didn't even bother to say hello, she turned back to Matt. "How is my son?"

"I'm pretty sure Danny misses you," Matt said. "But Chase has been coming over to play some catch with him. He took him over to his place yesterday, right, Chase?"

To that point, Chase acted as if he'd lost his voice. "I gave him a hammer and showed him how to pound some nails into a two-by-four. Didn't take him long to get the hang of it. He's got good hand-eye coordination."

She could use a couple of two-by-fours and a hammer to vent her irritation. She was grateful Chase had paid special attention to Danny. She wasn't so thrilled by his inability to look at her. "That's great," she said. "Thanks."

Still no eye contact, but he did say, "You're welcome."

Matt pulled at the collar of his shirt, as if he were a bit uncomfortable over the obvious tension. "Chase says you have a roof leak."

"Yes, I do. Water's dripping from the ceiling in the middle bedroom. I called Gabe and he basically said to put a bucket under it until Monday." And she'd wanted to tell him where to shove the bucket. Sideways. "To top it off, now the sink in the kitchen is overflowing, and after I bathed this morning, the tub wouldn't drain."

Chase looked directly at Matt. "You check out the roof, and I'll see about the plumbing."

"Good idea, Reed," Matt replied. "I don't like to deal with plumbing, and you're damn good at it."

Finally, a way to force Chase to engage with her. "You never told me you had plumbing skills."

When he answered with a noncommittal lift of his shoulders, Matt jumped back into the conversation.

"Yeah, he's real good at it. He knows his way around plumbing about as well as he knows his way around a woman." He gave her a wink. "But I'm not telling you anything you don't already know."

Jess's mouth dropped open and Chase practically sneered. "The roof is calling you, Boyd."

Matt hooked a thumb over his shoulder. "I'll be gettin' the ladder out of the truck now."

Jess planned to get Chase alone to play a game of twenty questions. And if she found out that he'd been playing kiss and tell, she'd give him a piece of what was left of her mind.

Without further acknowledgment, Chase picked up the tool box and walked into the house, practically slamming the screen door in Jess's face. She tried to catch up to him, but his legs were too long and his determination to flee her, too great. Well, too bad. She'd corner him eventually.

And she did, in the kitchen. He'd stopped to investigate the sink although he didn't appear to be doing anything, other than staring at the faucet.

Jess leaned a hip against the counter and let the frustration flow like a fountain. "Did you tell Matt about the other night?"

"Didn't say a word. He was just making a dig at my reputation."

His well-deserved reputation. She'd gained literal firsthand knowledge of that.

But that still didn't explain why he hadn't afforded her even a passing glance. "Then why won't you look at me?"

"Because if I did, then he'd know."

A ridiculous assumption. "Yeah, right. He's going to

know you got me naked and made a woman out of me, all because of a look."

"We can sense that kind of thing. We have a built-in radar when it comes to sex."

Men. "Look, I know this thing between us is a mess, but we're going to have to be adult about it. There's no need to stress over it."

He planted his palms on the edge of the sink and shifted his weight from one leg to the other. "About the only stress I'm having right now is the stress going on behind my fly. When I saw you standing on the porch, wearing those holey jeans, it took every ounce of strength not to tell Matt to get lost. I was ready to take you down right there on the front porch."

She shivered in some places, heated up in others. She hadn't given a thought to putting on her favorite rainy-day jeans. The ones with the rip across the upper right thigh, and another just below the back left pocket. How could she have known that a few tears would turn him on?

She should have known. The produce department at the grocery store could turn a man on. "Since having wild sex out in the open isn't wise, albeit tempting, you're going to have to man up."

He groaned and finally met her gaze. "Poor choice of words, Jess."

It took a minute for her to catch on to his comment. "Maybe I should have said down boy."

He went back to the sink-studying. "It's killing me not to be able to touch you."

He could join her celibacy club. "I'd hate to think I'd be the cause of your premature death, so I'm going to go now."

Before she could take one step, he had her in a body

vise against the counter. He had his hands on her butt and his mouth locked tightly with hers. The things the man could do with his tongue. The things he could do to her with just a slight tilt of his hips. Yes, he had definitely manned up, and she needed to stand down, before they took it way too far.

The sound of the slamming screen door effectively sent them to opposite ends of the kitchen. And Chase conveniently walked right out the back door, leaving Jess to face their friend.

She pulled a cloth band from her pocket and twisted her hair into a knot at her neck, hoping to appear a little more put together. Regrettably, she couldn't do a thing about the whisker-burn.

"Where's Chase?" Matt asked as he entered the kitchen.

Hiding out. "He went in the yard to check something."

"I found the missing shingle where the water's coming through," he said. "But he's going to have to help me fix it."

"Good." When she noticed Matt staring at her mouth, she had to come up with something to distract him. "Where's Rachel?"

"She took Danny downtown for the afternoon. Edwin's got her helping out with a blood drive."

"On Christmas Eve?"

"Yeah. They figured they could catch the last-minute shoppers and solicit donations. Edwin claims this is the family's efforts to replenish the blood they gave Dalton while he was in the hospital."

She just couldn't resist. "Dalton's always been somewhat of a bloodsucker."

Matt grinned, his teeth flashing white against his perpetually tanned face. "I agree, but I wouldn't have chosen the word *blood*."

Something occurred to Jess. An important question that could potentially be a paternity clue. "You know, after all the years we were married, I never knew Dalton's blood type."

"It's type O," Matt said, unknowingly taking the bait. "Same as Rachel's."

More important, the same as Jess. If her hunches were correct, the possibility that Dalton had fathered Danny was growing dimmer and dimmer.

Chase finally reappeared, looking quite a bit calmer than he had when he'd abandoned her. "The plumbing's going to require a backhoe," he said. "Looks like there's a big-time drainage problem."

"Sounds like a job for a professional," Matt replied. "Now you can climb on the roof and help me patch it."

"Not a problem."

Jess saw a huge problem. If the plumbing couldn't be repaired, she couldn't bathe. That was the least of her concerns. She had some sleuthing to do. First, she had to search for what could prove to be a pivotal piece of the puzzle.

Before the pair could leave, Jess addressed Chase. "Matt tells me Rachel's overseeing a blood drive for Dalton. I thought you might like to help. They specifically need type O. That's Dalton's type."

His expression turned lemon-sour. "I'm A. And even if I had the same type, I wouldn't give him a drop, unless I thought it would kill him."

Type A. *Danny's blood type.*

"Too bad you didn't know that before they gave Dalton the transfusion," Matt added. "I can start an IV. I would've hooked you right up."

"Actually, they're not looking for direct donations," Jess said, after she recovered from the stunning revelation. "They need to replace the blood bank's supply."

"By the time we get through here, it's going to be too late," Matt said. "We plan to have a nice dinner with Danny tonight and open a few presents."

"That reminds me." Reminded her that she wouldn't be spending Christmas with her son. "I went to the outlet mall yesterday and bought Danny a few gifts. Could you take them to him?"

Matt shook his head. "This isn't right."

She'd never known her former brother-in-law to be unreasonable. Just the opposite. "I can't see where it would hurt if I give him Christmas gifts."

"That's not what I meant," Matt said. "You should be with Danny during the holidays. And I far as I see it, you can deliver the presents in person tonight."

"That's risky, Matt," Chase interjected. "She's not supposed to contact him. I'll take them by."

Matt frowned. "The CPS workers have more to do than police our house. You can bring Jess over in your truck. You've already been there several times this week, so it wouldn't look out of the ordinary."

Chase turned his gaze on Jess. "If you're okay with the plan, I'll drive you over."

She was more than okay with it. She was thrilled over the prospect of seeing her baby boy. "It's worth the risk of getting caught."

She couldn't help but notice the meaningful look Chase gave her. He was mostly likely reflecting on the risks they took last night.

Matt cleared his throat. "We better get started on that roof. If I'm late getting home, Rachel's going to cook my goose instead of the one she bought for dinner."

After Chase and Matt walked away, Jess waited a few minutes before she seized her cell phone from the counter and sneaked into the bedroom. Since she had no Internet access, or a computer on hand for that matter, she'd go straight to the source.

She plopped down on the mattress and punched in a college friend's number. A nurse who happened to live in Alabama, so she shouldn't be privy to the recent legal issues.

The minute the woman answered, Jess launched into her query. "Libby, I'm sorry to bother you on a holiday, but I need to ask you something."

"Jess? How in the heck are you doing? It's been six months since we've talked."

She had no time for pleasantries. "I know, and I'm sorry. I've been very busy since the divorce. But I'm great. Danny's great. Merry Christmas. Now can you help me with a medical question?"

"Sure. I was just about to head to the in-laws, but believe me, I'd welcome the delay."

"This won't take long. I just need to know that if two parents have the same blood type, say O positive, could their offspring have A-type blood?"

"Have you been watching soap operas?"

Her life had certainly been one during the past few years. "Actually, I'm asking for someone else." Not a lie at all. This was for her son's sake. "It's a paternity issue."

"No, it's not possible for two parents with type O blood to produce a child with type A. I could go into the hows and whys, but I'd put you to sleep."

After hearing this particular verdict, she didn't expect to get much sleep in the immediate future. "You're absolutely sure?"

"Totally. My parents didn't pay for my education for nothing."

"You've been a great help, Libby. Give Johnny and the kids my love."

After Jess ended the call, she couldn't move. She just sat in the middle of the bed, steeped in shock.

Chase was Danny's father.

Short of an official DNA test, there was no doubt about it. And tonight, when she finally had the chance to see her son, she would do so knowing that today, he'd received the best gift he could possibly get—the opportunity to sever all ties, biological and otherwise, from a man who wasn't fit to be a father.

Problem was, she couldn't give her son that gift. She would have to indefinitely keep the news to herself until the time was right. She also couldn't tell Danny's real father. Just one more secret among many. And she feared that someday soon, at least one was bound to come back to bite her.

Chapter 11

The rain had stopped and the skies had cleared, revealing a sliver of moon and a host of stars. Jess appreciated the beautiful night in ways she never had before. And for the first time in ages, she felt almost giddy. In less than a minute, she would finally be reunited with her son.

Chase steered the truck up the drive leading to Rachel and Matt's place, an expansive stone ranch house with more Western flair than Southern charm. Jess had always thought it looked as though it should be in Texas, not the Mississippi Delta. Rachel had outdone herself this year with the Christmas decorations, from the team of horses and wagon composed of tiny white lights, to the life-size Santa, sporting a cowboy hat, set in the middle of the yard.

She could imagine Danny's delight over spending the holidays in such a beautiful home. He'd probably hung out in the barn with his Uncle Matt, and helped his Aunt Rachel make gingerbread men. If he couldn't be with her, at least he'd been in the presence of people who genuinely cared about him.

As soon as Chase stopped the truck, Jess reached into the backseat for the bag filled with gifts. Most were for Danny, but she'd managed to find a couple of items for her hosts. She'd also made a few impulse purchases, including the little black dress she wore with the red stiletto heels that Rachel had brought to her a week ago. In fact, she'd acquired several new outfits to replace those that still hung in the closet of her former residence. She was ready for a new beginning, and new clothes seemed to be a good step toward that goal. With any luck, she wouldn't have to wear those new clothes in court.

Determined not to spoil her rare good mood, Jess banished all negative thoughts as she walked with Chase to the front entry. Rachel opened the door wearing a free-flowing red silk blouse that complimented her long, dark hair. She possessed that proverbial pregnancy glow that reached all the way to her brown eyes.

After they stepped inside, Rachel gave out hugs to Jess, then Chase. "Merry Christmas, you two," she said. "I'm so glad you're both here."

Jess couldn't express how glad she was to be there. "Thank you so much for letting me come tonight. I know you're breaking the rules."

"Stupid rules," Matt said as he entered the room. He kissed his wife on the neck, and handed Chase a beer. "I thought you'd want this instead of eggnog."

"You thought right," Chase said, his first words since they'd arrived.

He'd been unusually somber when he'd picked her up,

and extremely quiet on the drive. She had no reason to believe she'd done anything earlier today to make him particularly angry. But she wouldn't even try to second-guess a man who still had many demons to conquer.

"What can I get for you, Jess?" Matt asked.

"I'm fine right now." Or she would be. She searched the great room for signs of her son. All she saw was taste-ful décor and a towering tree with myriad gifts surround-ing the base. "Where's Danny?"

After a grim look passed between Rachel and Matt, Jess sensed something was terribly wrong. "What is it?"

"Maybe you should have a drink first," Matt said.

"I don't want a drink." She hated that she'd sounded so snippy, and made an effort to temper her tone. "I'd just like to see him as soon as possible. We can't stay that long, and this may be the last opportunity I have for a while." Maybe even months, if the court decided she wasn't fit to raise her child. Longer if she was im-prisoned.

Rachel put an arm around Jess's shoulder. "He had a bad day. When we were downtown, one of the boys said something to him. He was very upset."

If only she could have been there to console him. She would have to settle for comforting him now. "What did they say?"

Rachel shrugged. "He wouldn't tell me. I wouldn't have even known if someone hadn't told me about the fight."

Fight? "Was he hurt?"

"It was only a scuffle," Matt said. "He doesn't have a scratch on him."

She could count her blessings for that. "Did anyone

talk to this boy's parents? He shouldn't be able to walk away without suffering the consequences."

"Danny started it, Jess," Chase said.

Her son had never been prone to violence. But he'd probably been beaten down so far, he'd decided to battle back. "I'll talk to him about it."

"He doesn't want to see anyone," Matt added. "After we told him you were stopping by, he went into his room with Bo, and he hasn't come out since, even for dinner."

Jess had never felt so helpless in her life. But when it came to her child, she refused to throw in the towel. She handed Chase the presents, took off her coat and gave it to Matt, then pushed up her sleeves as if preparing for her own fight. "I can't leave here until I speak with him."

Chase handed the beer back to Matt and set the bag on a marble end table. "I'll talk to him."

She'd rather handle it herself. Or at least try. "If he doesn't respond well to me, then you'll have my blessing."

"He's in the room across from the nursery," Rachel said. "You know the way."

She did. She'd helped stencil the wild horses along one wall of that nursery not more than a month ago. It seemed like a century ago. "Thanks. Just put his gifts under the tree, and I'll be back soon." Perhaps sooner than she planned.

After Jess reached the room, she paused with her hand on the knob. She didn't know if she should knock, or just make an entry without identifying herself. Knocking seemed the better part of valor, but he might not let her in. She compromised by rapping lightly on the door before opening it a few inches to peek inside. "Danny? It's Mom."

"Go away."

She might be deterred if she hadn't heard that before. "I'm not going away, Daniel. In fact, I'm coming in now."

She entered the room to find him sitting on the floor, legs crossed in front of him and an open book in his lap. At least the dog looked happy to see her. He was stretched out at Danny's side, his wagging tail beating a steady rhythm on the carpet. Her son, on the other hand, didn't bother to acknowledge her.

Oh, how she wanted to hug him. To kiss his sweet face and tell him how much she'd missed him. How very much she loved him. But since he still hadn't bothered to look up from the book, she would talk now and save the affection for later.

If she hadn't been wearing a dress, she'd join him on the floor. Instead, she perched on the edge of the queen-size bed. "What are you reading, sweetie?"

He stared up at her with soulful brown eyes. "Are you going to jail?"

If she answered no, she could be giving him false hope. If she said possibly, she'd completely shatter his security. She'd have to meet in the middle. "I don't know what's going to happen, Danny. I do know that I have a team of people working for me. They're going to do everything they can to keep that from happening."

He closed the book and tossed it aside. "I should be going to jail. I'm the one who pushed my dad."

How easy it would be to tell Danny that Dalton wasn't really his dad. Yet she couldn't lay that on him now. "Oh, sweetie, don't say that. You were just upset with him, and you had every right to be. You didn't mean to cause him any harm."

Pure defiance showed in his expression. "I did mean to hurt him. He hates me and I hate him."

Regret and fear pelted her like a hailstorm. If he ever admitted to anyone that he'd pushed Dalton with malice, he could face a term in a juvenile facility. And she could lose her custody rights.

Disregarding the dress, she pushed off the bed and lowered herself to her knees. But when she reached for him, he leaned back to avoid the contact. He might as well have slapped her. "Danny, I know you're really mad right now. And I also know a boy said something to you today that made it worse. Do you want to tell me about it?"

He lowered his eyes. "He said we were trash. He said you're a husband-killer and then he called you a bad word."

She could only imagine what that word might be. "Who was it?"

"Austin Prather."

The son of Edwin's second-in-command at the bank. "He doesn't know what he's talking about."

"He should've called me a criminal. You didn't do anything."

That brought about another major concern. "Did you tell him that?"

Thankfully, he shook his head no.

"Good."

He gave her a look so desperate, it stole her breath. "But I want to tell Chase. He'll make sure I don't go to jail."

She was mortified to think that he might follow through. "You can't tell him, sweetie. He doesn't need to be involved." Not any more than he already was.

Jess was torn over what to do. Had she given Danny too big a burden to bear in order to protect him? Should she finally let someone know the details, and hope that her son didn't suffer for his actions? She simply didn't know which road to take.

"You're going to have to trust me, Danny," she said. "Just give me a few days to sort this out. Besides, I understand your dad is doing okay, so that's a good thing. Right?"

His desperation turned to anger. "I have to see him tomorrow at Grandpa Edwin's house, and I don't want to."

The second shock of the day. "He's home from the hospital?"

He nodded again.

Jess accepted that Rachel would want to be with her father on Christmas, and that she would take Danny with her. But she hadn't dreamed that Dalton would be there. If only she could find some way to prevent it, but she had no control over the situation.

She gently tipped Danny's chin up, forcing him to look at her. "You don't have to be alone with your dad. You don't even have to talk to him if you don't want to. He's not going to say anything about what happened to him." And she could be giving Dalton too much credit.

But she still truly believed that Dalton didn't remember anything about that night. Otherwise, he would have implicated Danny. Or perhaps he did remember, and he was bent on punishing her, knowing she would never accuse her own son. It would be so like him to use the child to get to the mother.

She couldn't leave until she made one more attempt to make her baby boy feel better. "I have to go now, but I left you a few presents under the tree. It's not a lot, but I'm sure your grandfather will have some very special things for you." Edwin had never shown Danny much affection, but he'd always been generous when it came to gifts.

Tears began to form in his eyes, breaking Jess's heart. "When are you coming back?"

"I don't know, sweetie. It might be a while."

"Am I going to have to live with Dad?"

A very real possibility. One that made Jess ache with regret. "Let's just take it one day at a time."

She leaned over to hug him, and this time he didn't pull away. "I love you, honey. Never forget that."

"He hates me, and I don't blame him."

Chase took his eyes from the road to see that Jess was trying hard not to cry. "He doesn't hate you. He's a scared kid whose life has been turned upside down. He wants to blame someone, and you're a safe target. But if anyone's to blame here, it's that prick, Dalton."

"He's been released from the hospital," Jess said. "He'll be with the family tomorrow, and that means Danny's going to be forced to see him."

He tightened his grip on the steering wheel. The world was sorely lacking in justice when a jerk like Dalton Wainwright could spend the holiday with a son he didn't want, and Jess couldn't. "Maybe I should show up and invite myself in for Christmas dinner."

"I'd buy tickets to that."

He heard a hint of a smile in her voice, but he suspected she was only trying to cover her distress. By all rights, he should drop her off at the house and then go home. But he'd determined that morning she shouldn't be alone tonight. He'd also made plans to make the evening as special as possible.

After he pulled up the drive and turned off the ignition, he reached over the console and took her hand. "You know what you need?"

She pulled a tissue out of her coat pocket and dabbed at her eyes. "Right now, I need makeup remover. And two tickets to Bolivia."

If he thought he could get away with helping her escape with her son, he'd damn sure do it. "I was thinking more along the lines of a party. Just me and you in attendance."

The smile she sent him was soft and sexy. Maybe even a little suggestive. Or maybe he wanted her so badly, he was jumping to conclusions. "That sounds interesting. Are clothes optional?"

Okay, he wasn't imagining it. "That's entirely up to you, babe."

"Did you bring champagne?"

And he just thought he'd remembered everything. "That totally slipped my mind."

"That's okay," she said. "I have some orange juice and ginger ale, so we can fake it. And I could probably scrounge up some cheese and crackers, too."

"Why don't we just skip the refreshments and get right to the celebration?"

She smoothed a hand over her skirt. "You know, for two people who've been warned to keep their distance, we certainly aren't doing very well in that regard."

That had been his original goal, to stay away from her. But he didn't have the will or the want-to. "I just figured we both deserve to have a good time."

"You're not worried we're going to get caught?"

He should be, but he wasn't. "I can park the truck in the shed out back, if it makes you feel better."

"That's probably not necessary. I doubt anyone's going to be snooping around here on Christmas Eve, trying to catch me engaged in illicit behavior."

He grinned. "You forgot about Santa."

She returned his smile. "That's all I need, some rotund guy tromping around on the roof that you and Matt just fixed." Her smile suddenly dropped from sight. "I don't know what I'm worried about. Since there aren't any children here, he has no reason to come."

And that only bolstered Chase's reasons to stay. He could attempt to keep her mind off her son's absence, at least for a few hours. Beginning now. "I have a couple of presents for you." He also had a surprise in the house.

Her expression brightened. "I have something for you, too. It's not much, but it's cute."

Cute always meant trouble. "You didn't buy me another pair of reindeer boxers, did you?"

Now she just looked downright mischievous. "You'll have to wait and see."

"Then what are we waiting for?"

No sooner than he'd said it, Jess was out of the truck and onto the porch before he'd even unbuckled his seat belt. He came up behind her as she slid the key into the lock, and turned her around before she opened the door.

He rested one hand on her waist and pointed to the porch's overhang with the other. "You know what that means, don't you?"

She looked up and then her gaze snapped to his. "Where did you get mistletoe and when did you hang it?"

"It's some my mother had lying around the house."

She raised a brow. "She has mistletoe just lying around?"

"Okay, I stole it from the hall. I hung it when you were getting ready tonight."

"Since you went to all that trouble, let's put it to good use."

He slid his arms around her waist, lowered his head and gave her a quick kiss. "How's that?"

Her glare said it all. "That's probably the lamest kiss I've had since I left my ex-husband."

He saw a challenge, and he had no problem rising to it. But before he could prove his worth in the kissing department, the sound of squealing tires drew his attention.

He witnessed panic spreading over Jess's face. "We should have gone in the house."

She was right about that. "It's probably just some kid showing off for his girlfriend. But you're right. We should go inside."

"Good idea."

He reached around her, opened the door, and when he flipped on the light, he was pleased to see his plan had been perfectly implemented. Every inch of the once-bare tree had been covered, from top to trunk.

"When did you do this?" Both her expression and her voice told him she was pleased with the finished product, too.

"I didn't exactly do it," he said. "I hired a couple of elves to take care of it while we were out. I'm kind of surprised they got it done since they can't seem to keep their hands off each other."

"Sam and Savannah did this? I thought they were spending the holidays with her mother in Knoxville?"

"They are. Their flight doesn't leave until midnight."

She turned her attention back to the tree. "It's absolutely beautiful. I can't believe you pulled this off."

He'd do just about anything for her, and he'd tell her that later. "I know what you said about not wanting to decorate unless Danny was here, but—"

She stopped the commentary when she gave him a soft kiss. "You're here, and that's what matters."

He planned to be here all night. Most of it, anyway. He'd have to be gone before morning came, and that royally sucked.

He moved behind her and wrapped his arms around her waist. "It does look pretty good."

"It's wonderful. Are these Missy's ornaments?"

"Yeah. My mother's taken to decorating in line with the latest trend. She used purple and black this year, with a lot of bows and sparkly crap. I thought my dad was going to stroke when he saw it. Buck doesn't like prissy."

She lifted one ornament from a branch and examined it closely. A homemade ornament made out of a circle of cardboard, trimmed in foil, with a photo stuck right in the middle. His friends could have gone all year without including that one.

"I remember this picture," she said. "You were in the first grade. You wouldn't smile because your front teeth were missing."

"Yeah. My mother was fit to be tied. Serves her right for giving me that chili-bowl haircut."

"It's cute." She looked back at him. "Speaking of cute, I want you to open your present."

"And you can open mine." He released her and knelt to retrieve the two packages underneath the tree. When he straightened, she was nowhere to be found.

"Where you'd go?" he called out.

"I'm getting yours," she called back. "I'll be there in a minute."

He stepped to the side of the tree and looked out the window, still worried someone might be spying on them. With Dalton now on the loose, anything was possible. But he didn't see anyone around. No vehicle parked on the road. No movement aside from the bend of the trees in the wind that had picked up steam earlier in the evening. His gut still told him something wasn't right. Maybe he'd come down with a major case of paranoia.

"I'm ready if you are," Jess said from somewhere behind him.

He turned to discover she'd taken a seat on the sofa, a shiny red gift bag on the coffee table before her. She was still wearing that black, knock-'em-dead dress that fit every one of her curves to perfection. When she crossed her legs, the hem climbed up her thighs, and Chase's temperature climbed right with it. And man, those red high-heels. He could picture taking that dress off her slowly and making love to her while she still wore the shoes. If he didn't kill that fantasy real quick, he'd be ready, all right. Ready to ditch the gift-opening so he could take her straight to bed. That wasn't part of the plan. Not yet.

After setting his presents on the coffee table, he dropped down beside her. "You want to go first?" he asked.

"Of course I do." She sounded as excited as any kid would at Christmas. But she definitely wasn't a kid anymore. She was a woman through and through.

He offered her the larger of the two boxes. "I want you to open this one now, and then the other one after I open mine." Saving the best for last. He just hoped she saw it that way.

Jess tore off the wrapping paper with a vengeance and opened the lid. When she pulled back the white tissue, Chase wished he had a camera to capture the awe in her expression. He didn't realize that something as simple as a picture of him showing Danny how to hold a bat could have such an impact on her.

After she lifted the photo to study it more closely, her eyes begin to mist. "When was this taken?"

"Thursday at Rachel and Matt's. Matt took the picture, and Rachel had it framed. Believe it or not, I wrapped it."

Tears began rolling down her cheeks. "It's the best gift I've ever received, aside from my son."

He put his arm around her and thumbed away a tear. "I'm sorry, Jess. I didn't mean to make you cry."

She swiped at her eyes and sniffed. "These are good tears. I don't remember the last time I've seen him look so happy. And I have you to thank for that."

He should be thanking her for introducing him to Danny. "He's a great kid, Jess. And he's tougher than you think."

She sighed. "He's his father's son."

Dalton didn't deserve any praise for Danny's upbringing, and he was surprised she'd given him any. "He's your son, Jess. He's got that same strong will and determination. He's going to get through this, and so are you. And I'm going to do everything in my power to help." Even if it meant crossing over the legal line to do it. They both meant that much to him.

"I really do appreciate what you've done for Danny. You've paid more attention to him in the past week than Dalton ever did in nine years."

And during time spent with her son, Chase's eyes had been opened to things he'd taken for granted. "Being around Danny brought back a lot of memories of my dad. Maybe Buck was strict and made me tow the line, and sometimes he really pissed me off. He still does now and then. But he never missed one of my games, and he took me camping at least twice a year. We might still butt horns on a regular basis at work, but at the end of the day, I know he has my back."

"That's what good fathers do," she said. "And that's why I know you'd be a wonderful father. You've learned by example."

Yeah, he had. And for the first time in his life, he was starting to think he might be willing to give parenthood a try, somewhere down the road.

He was ready to move away from the heavy stuff, and get back to the party. "Can I open mine now, or are we just going to sit here until it opens itself?"

"I was just about to get to that." Jess propped the photo on the table and then handed him the gift bag. "Don't expect anything quite as good as what you gave me."

She'd given him her time and trust, and the opportunity to get to know her boy. That was enough.

He dug through mounds of paper, and some sort of curly strings, before he finally got to the actual gift—a pair of navy silk boxers, complete with flying, red-nosed reindeer. "You shouldn't have."

She laughed. "I'm sorry. When I saw them in the store, I couldn't resist. And they're much more fancy than the last pair. Besides, I assume that since I gave you those when we were in junior high, you probably outgrew them and tossed them out."

"Yeah, I've outgrown them quite a bit. But since you didn't know me the way you know me now, you'll have to take my word for it."

When he winked, she frowned. "You are so bad, Chase Reed."

She'd know exactly how bad when she opened his next

gift. On that thought, he handed her the final box. "Just so you know, this one's as much for me as it is for you."

"Did you buy me a power tool?" she said with fake enthusiasm.

"Not exactly, but it is a powerful tool."

Now she looked stunned. "I know they don't sell those in Placid, so you must have either ordered it online, or bought it in another town."

He was a little slow on the uptake at first, until he finally figured it out. "Sorry, sweetheart. It's not that kind of tool."

"Too bad."

"Just open it already," he grumbled.

She tore the paper away, one strip at a time, apparently just to see him squirm. It worked. By the time she finally opened the box, he was about ready to do it himself.

She held up the silky red, barely-there gown and then turned the empty box over. "Where's the rest of it?"

"That's it, babe. And you better appreciate it. The dress shop was already closed, so I had to sweet talk Polly into letting me have my own private shopping trip."

She dropped the gown into her lap. "Knowing Polly, she would have preferred to give you a private showing of all her wares. She used to service my ex-husband."

With the exception of Jess, Dalton had questionable taste in women. "If you don't like it, I can take it back." And that would be a damn shame. But if that's what she wanted, so be it.

"I love it," she said. "But I can't wear it. I don't have the body to wear it."

He was inclined to disagree. Strongly. "I don't know what Dalton Wainwright said to make you believe that, but he was dead wrong. Just thinking about your body makes me hotter than hell."

A blush started at her neck and spread to her cheeks. "Since you put it that way, I suppose I could try it on. But if it doesn't fit, you'll have to return it."

He had no doubt it would fit. He could judge a woman's size by touch alone, a talent he'd developed over the years. A talent not worth mentioning to her.

"Then go try it on," he said. "I'll be waiting for you."

"In here?"

As badly as he wanted to be waiting in bed, he also didn't want her to think that's all he wanted. "Let's just see what happens when you put it on."

"Okay."

When she left the room, Chase took off his jacket and draped it over the back of the sofa. On afterthought, he yanked off his boots and socks, but he stopped at that. Getting completely naked would send the wrong message.

He collapsed onto the couch, laced his hands together behind his neck, and waited for her return. And waited. And waited.

About the time he thought she'd reconsidered, two feminine hands with red-painted nails slid down his shoulders from behind him. He started to look back, until he heard, "Close your eyes and don't open them until I say so."

That was going to be torture, but he complied. He found himself waiting again, this time for permission to check out the merchandise.

"You can look now."

He opened his eyes to see that she looked exactly as he'd imagined she would wearing that scrap of silk that clung to her like he wanted to. But he didn't care for one thing—she couldn't look him in the eye. "Man, I'm good. And you're damn beautiful."

She afforded him only a fast glance. "Are you sure? Because I think it's a little tight. I'm not convinced it looks good on me at all. Maybe on someone else a little thinner."

Her attitude just wouldn't do. He came to his feet, walked right up to her, and lifted her face with his palms. "In all the time we've known each other, I've never been one to tell you what to think. But that ends now. I never want to hear you say you're not good enough, because you are." Probably too good for him.

She lowered her eyes again, looking shy and self-conscious. "You're just saying that because you tossed the receipt and can't return it."

"I'm dead serious, Jess. And now you have to promise me something else."

Finally, she met his gaze. "What?"

"In a few minutes, we're going to make love. And when we do, don't close your eyes. I want you to see me tonight. I want you to see us, together. We don't need any fantasies because the reality is better. Can you do that?"

"Yes."

He kissed her with more restraint than he thought possible. "Then that's all I need to know."

Taking her by the hand, he led her into the bedroom and set her down on the edge of the mattress. He didn't bother to turn off the light or wait until she climbed under the covers before he undressed. She followed every move he made, watched him release every button on his shirt and then take it off. Her gaze never wavered when he unzipped his fly and stripped out of his jeans. She did smile when he took off his briefs, but she didn't look away for even a second.

"Don't move yet," he told her as he retrieved a condom from his jeans pocket and tossed it on the nightstand. "So we don't have to raid your cookie jar."

She answered him with a shaky smile.

He sat beside her and took her hands into his. "You're in control tonight, babe. I'm leaving everything to you, so do what you will with me."

After he released her, he stretched out on his back and prepared for the best. But when she didn't immediately move, he wondered if maybe he'd gone too far. Maybe she wasn't ready to take command of the situation.

Man, was he wrong. She crawled onto the bed and slowly slid her sweet, silk-covered body up his body, pausing to pay a little special attention to certain parts with a wriggle of her hips. Then she kissed him like there was no tomorrow. By the time she finally took her mouth away, he had no doubt who was in control, and it wasn't him.

She utilized a lot of creativity, with her hands and mouth, while she took care of the condom. Good thing he was still relatively young. Otherwise, his heart could very well give out.

When she knelt beside him on the bed, lowered the gown and shimmied out of it, he automatically went for her breasts. And she clasped his wrists to halt him before he got there. "No touching yet."

Damn. "Are you trying to drive me crazy?"

"As a matter of fact, yes."

She made good on that promise when she straddled his thighs and took the lead. Took him on a wild ride straight into oblivion. She eventually let him touch her, on her terms, and he took full advantage. Not once did she close her eyes. He didn't close his eyes, either, because he wouldn't have missed this for the world, watching as she went from self-doubting to completely confident in her sexuality. He might have let her have all the power, but she had no idea exactly how much power she had over him.

He soon felt the pull of her climax, and saw the absolute pleasure in her face and eyes. That's when he gave up trying to hold back. He could only roll with the tide, and he didn't care if he drowned. He didn't care about anything but Jess.

After they were both spent and winded, she collapsed against him and rested her cheek on his chest, right above his pounding heart. He could think of few instances when the sex was better than he'd expected. He couldn't think of one time when he'd been so blown away that he wasn't sure he could move. So he didn't.

As his body began to calm and his respiration slowed, Chase realized the time had come to kiss Jess good-night, get dressed and take off. His sex life in a nutshell. Meet a girl, have a good time, say so long and cut out before the dust settled. He'd never had a relationship that lasted more than a couple of months, because he'd never found what he'd been looking for. Until now. Funny thing was, she'd been right under his nose all along. And it was high time he told her.

He couldn't deny that putting his feelings into words scared the hell out of him. Words that he'd never said to another woman. He'd best do it now, before he lost his nerve.

"Jess, I have a few things I need to say."

Nothing but silence. He realized why when he lifted

his head. She was out like a light. He reached for the sheet at the foot of the bed, covered them both and dropped his head back on the pillow. Normally he didn't sleep for more than a few hours at a time, so he could afford to stay awhile longer. And that's if he could sleep with her in his arms without wanting to wake her for something other than a conversation.

But his eyes soon grew heavy, and he knew it was only a matter of time before he drifted off.

Just a little while, he told himself. Then he would go.

What was he still doing there?

Jess had woken a few minutes ago to find Chase sleeping soundly in her bed, and the morning sun streaming through the window. At some point, he must have turned off the light and turned over onto his belly. And she hadn't turned on the alarm.

When she looked to her left and noted the time, she hopped out of bed, retrieved her robe from the bathroom and slipped it on. She returned to find he hadn't moved an inch.

She leaned over and shook his arm, right above the sexy barbwire tattoo encircling his amazing bicep. That tattoo—and many remarkable details about his incredible body—had captured her fancy when they'd made love with the light on last night. "Chase. Wake up."

"Hmmm."

"It's 7:00 a.m. and it's light outside."

He finally rolled onto his back, but he didn't open his eyes. He did send his palm down his sternum and paused right below his navel. She truly wanted to follow that same path with her own hand, follow that happy little trail and keep going to see what lurked beneath the sheet draped low on his hip. But darn it, she didn't have time for that.

She sat on the edge of the bed, leaned over and kissed him lightly. "Get up, sleepy boy."

His grin slowly arrived and then he opened his eyes. "I already am up. But I guess I should probably get out of bed. Then again, maybe you should get back in the bed."

He caught her by the arm and pulled her down, taking her totally by surprise. When he started showering her neck with kisses, she started laughing. After she finally untangled herself from his hold, she sat up and moved as far from him as she could without falling off the bed. "Stop it. You have to go."

From the sour look on his face, he clearly took exception to her command. "I don't have anything better to do, and neither do you."

"Oh, yes, you do. It's Christmas, and I know Missy and Buck's routine. They'll be expecting you at the house in about an hour to open presents. If you don't show up, they'll come looking for you."

"I'll just tell them I met a she-devil last night and I couldn't tear myself away from her. Buck will understand."

"And your mother will send you to your room for the remainder of the day."

"Wanna come with me?"

He'd clearly lost his mind. "That will go over real well with the folks, me spending the day in your room with you."

He scooted up against the headboard. "I meant come to the house for all the traditional festivities."

At one time, she'd readily accept the invitation. But

not now. "You know I can't do that, Chase. Your father will have a total meltdown if I show up unannounced."

He rubbed a palm over his jaw. "You're right. Duty calls, even if I'd rather hang out here."

Without an ounce of shame over his nudity, he left the bed and gathered his clothes. He did turn his back as he worked his jeans up his long legs. And she had no qualms about admiring his attributes until they disappeared beneath the denim.

Once he was finished dressing, she followed him to the den where he sat on the sofa and put on his boots. After that, she expected him to leave, but he surprised her by saying, "Have a seat. We need to talk before I go."

His serious tone had Jess gearing up for the same old speech about how they couldn't do this again. How he needed to stay away or risk damaging her case. She sat beside him anyway.

He stared at the ceiling for a moment before regarding her again. "After this is over, and we're free to do as we please, I want to continue to see you. And I don't want to sneak around."

Time for the million-dollar question. "What exactly is our relationship?"

"I don't want to be without you, even for a minute."

Jess was totally floored by his assertion. "You want us to be a couple?"

"Yeah. Or a trio. You, me and Danny."

The moment was so surreal, she didn't know what to say. "There's still so much riding on the indictment, I don't think we can plan on anything right now."

He draped his arm around her shoulder. "If you're cleared, and this all goes away, would you be willing to try to make a go of this?"

She didn't have to think twice to come up with that answer. "Yes, but—"

"Then that's all I need to know. Dalton's story isn't adding up. I plan to dig a little deeper and see if I can punch some holes in it."

The "digging deeper" part worried her. "I doubt you'll get very far. He's going to stick to it even if it's fabricated." Which it was.

"Just let me worry about that," he said. "In the meantime, if I'm not around, don't believe for a minute it's because I don't want to be here. I can't think of anywhere else I'd rather be than with you."

He deserved a kiss for that, and she gave him a good one. Once they parted, she sensed he wanted to say something else. Instead, he came to his feet. "I'll call you later."

Jess walked Chase to the door, her mind still reeling over the conversation. But before he turned the knob, he faced her again, a solemn look on his face. "I have one more thing to say, and I'll try not to screw it up."

If what he had to say was as wonderful as what he'd already said, she was more than willing to hear it. "Go ahead."

"I might not have known it until recently, but I've been searching a long time for someone I can spend the rest of my life with. That someone is you." He kissed her softly, sincerely. "I love you, Jess."

And then he was out the door before she could even respond. She stood and gaped as he drove away, and continued to stare long after the truck disappeared. After she finally came back around to the real world, she ran through the house like a silly, smitten schoolgirl, considered a cartwheel but settled for a jump instead.

Chase loved her. She couldn't imagine a better Christmas gift.

The thought kept running through her mind during her bath, as she sorted laundry, when she made her breakfast that she didn't even mind eating alone. Everything was looking up, and hope was definitely springing eternal today. All because he loved her.

When the doorbell rang, Jess said a little prayer Chase had come back so she could tell him she loved him, too. Yet when she opened the door, another man stood on her porch. A man with slick black hair and an even slicker smile. His suit was tailor-made, his shoes designer quality, the platinum watch on his arm worth thousands of dollars. His near-black eyes could draw a woman into his web of deceit, before she realized she'd been duped by his charm. He was a chameleon, a charlatan, the consummate devil in disguise.

Her hope no longer sprang eternal, but her hatred did.

"Merry Christmas, darlin'. Did you miss me?"

Chapter 12

"What do you want, Dalton?"

His smile was the epitome of condescension. "Is that any way to greet your husband?"

He should feel fortunate she didn't kick him down the porch steps. "Ex-husband. Again, what do you want?"

"I want to have a little chat with you."

Of all the unmitigated gall. "What makes you think I ever want to speak to you again?"

He winked. "Because I have a deal you can't refuse."

He always had a deal, all of them suspect. "Look, you basically had me thrown in jail and now I'm possibly going to prison. I don't have my son and I don't know what the future holds. But I still have enough sense not to let you anywhere near me."

He put on his all-business face. "If you don't hear me out, you'll never have the kid with you again."

He'd found her Achilles' heel, and stomped on it. "Fine. You have five minutes."

She didn't hold the screen door open for him. She just let it slam shut and waited in the middle of the room for him to enter. He strolled inside, hands in pockets, and immediately made himself at home on the couch.

He leaned back, crossed his legs, and looked around with obvious disdain. "I see you've returned to your white-trash roots. How did it feel to go from the top of the mountain right into the sewer in a week?"

How would it feel if I slapped that arrogant look off your face? "You now have four minutes, Dalton. If you don't say what you need to say and get out, I'm calling the sheriff and I'll have you arrested for harassment."

"The sheriff, or his ass of a son?"

Red flags began to wave madly in her mind. "Leave Chase out of this."

"My dear," he said, "I can't do that. Not when he's screwing what's rightfully mine."

Jess thought she might be sick. Her nausea increased when Dalton stood, reached into his jacket's inner pocket, and tossed several photographs onto the table.

"Don't be shy, Jessica," he said. "Take a look at your sex-ploits, captured in living color."

She felt as she were watching some freakish horror film. She wanted to look away for fear of what she might see, but she couldn't.

When she leaned over to get a better look, she experienced blessed relief. She saw nothing but a blurry image of two people in an unknown location. "I don't know, Dalton. These are so out of focus, this could be anyone. Maybe even the mayor colluding with the city secretary, for all I know."

He released a dramatic sigh. "I agree. Buster means well, but his photography skills leave a lot to be desired. That's surprising since he's delivered good product before. Maybe it's that knee-jab to the crotch you gave him that's affected his brain."

Buster's limited brain could probably be found in that immediate vicinity. She suddenly thought back to that night at Chase's house. A possum clearly hadn't been responsible for the broken vase. More like a sleazy snake in the grass.

She folded her arms across her middle and stood her ground. "Again, you can't prove anything with these photos."

"But I can prove something with these." He reached in his side pocket, withdrew more photos, and spread them out like a pornographic deck of cards next to the other pile. "Unlike Buster boy, I have a quality camera with telephoto lens, and a much better knack for capturing the shot at just the right time. One of my many talents. Speaking of that, I didn't know you had so many."

Jess shuddered over the clarity of the pictures. Her and Chase holding each other on the front porch last night. Her modeling the gown Chase had given her. And worst of all, her and Chase making love in various stages, obviously shot through the bedroom window.

"Anyway," he continued, "I went to a lot of trouble to have these made available to you. I had to drive forty miles in the middle of the night to find a twenty-four-hour pharmacy, and I also had to shell out a hundred bucks to get the kid behind the counter to develop them. However, he did have the added bonus of getting off after seeing you in all your glory."

"For some strange reason, he actually liked having you as a daughter-in-law, even in light of your sad, working-class background."

That certainly made perfect sense, at least the part about pissing off Edwin. "Oh. I thought maybe your latest girlfriend dumped you after she discovered the rumors of your assets were a complete exaggeration. The manly assets, of course."

He glossed right over the insult. "As far as us remarrying, I missed having you around. You aren't a bad cook and you do a good job ironing my shirts. The sex wasn't great, but I can take care of that outside the comfort of our home."

He always had. "Well, I don't miss having you around. I don't miss being made to feel like I'm worthless. And I certainly don't miss you deriding my son."

"But you do miss him now. And even if you manage an acquittal, which I seriously doubt you will, I'll sue for full custody and I'll get it. Either way, you'll never see him again, unless you agree to my offer."

The thought of never again being with her son was so painful, she almost gave in. Almost. "Why would you even want custody of Danny when you've all but said you can't stand the sight of him?"

"Because I've invested a lot of money and time in him, and I don't like to lose on an investment. I'm also tired of Edwin riding me about being a crappy father, like the bastard has any room to talk. As far as having Danny around, that's why they invented boarding schools. I'm thinking he'd do well in a military academy. He could use a good attitude adjustment."

Don't cry... Don't cry... "I don't know what happened

to you, Dalton. I only know that you're not the man I married."

"Maybe that's true, but I am the man who holds your future in his hands. So what's it going to be? A life of luxury and raising the brat? Or a possible life behind bars and never laying eyes on him again?"

If she agreed, she would be trading one prison for another. She would be doomed to a life with a man she couldn't bear to be around. A life without Chase. But she would still have her precious son, and no one would ever have to know the role he'd played in his father's injuries.

Yet she still wasn't completely powerless. She could accept Dalton's terms and send Danny to live with her parents. She could visit him frequently since Dalton wouldn't care, as long as he could continue his exploits. He only cared about finances, and his father's opinion. She would also be taking him away from his biological father. But then, she couldn't reveal that, either. How unfair that Chase would never know he had a son.

She needed time to think, to weigh her options. In the meantime, she would pretend to go along with Dalton's plan, until she could come up with her own.

"All right," she said. "I'll do what you say. But I'll need proof that you're dropping the charges, and I won't make a move until Danny's with me again."

He patted her bottom, gathered the photos and put them back in his pocket. "I knew you'd come around. As far as proof goes, I can't do anything about that until tomorrow when the city offices are open again. But I'll be back around three with the kid. In the meantime, you pack up your things."

She couldn't wait to see Danny, but she dreaded Dalton's return.

He spun around to leave before he suddenly faced her again. "Oh, and when we're back in our own bed tonight, I expect you to give me the same attention you gave your boyfriend."

Over her cold, dead body. "Anything you say, honey pie."

"One more thing. If I ever see that ass-wipe anywhere near you again, the deal's off."

He left her with another seamy smile and an over-whelming sense of anxiety. But what was done, was done. She had one last important thing to do. A heartbreaking task.

Tell Chase it was over, before it had barely begun.

"What did you just say?"

"I said I'm going back to Dalton."

He'd been shocked as hell to see her standing on his porch in broad daylight. But that didn't compare to the shock of hearing her utter those unbelievable words. "Did the bastard threaten you?"

She dropped her gaze to the ground. "He promised to drop the charges and return Danny to me."

"And you agreed?"

He saw absolute desperation in her eyes. "I don't have a choice, Chase. He has pictures."

"What kind of pictures?"

"Of us, making love. He managed to turn something special into something ugly and sordid. I've never been so humiliated in my life."

And he had never been so ready to kill someone in his life. He should have listened to his gut last night. He should have stayed away from her. "If he even dares to show anyone those pictures, I'll arrest him for trespassing."

"And he'll claim that he hired Buster Eustace to do it, which he did. Only Buster's photos weren't quite as clear. I assume they were taken at your house, but I couldn't really tell."

The broken vase. The squealing tires. It all made sense. Every risk they'd taken to be together had blown up in their faces. "Come inside and let's talk about this."

"I can't come inside," she said. "He'll be at the house with Danny in less than an hour. I need to pack my things and be ready to go when he gets there."

He felt like he'd been dumped in the middle of a living hell. "I'll find another way to get you out of this, Jess. You don't have to give in to blackmail."

"There isn't another way, Chase. He's threatened to claim that you and I conspired to kill him for the life insurance policy he had to purchase in accordance with the divorce terms."

The fact any life insurance policy existed only strengthened the prosecution's case against her. "Don't worry about me. I'll handle him. We know he's lying about the plot, so he has to be lying about you forcefully injuring him. We just need some way to prove it." When she refused to look at him, he grew more concerned. "Dalton is lying, isn't he?"

She started to back away. "I have to go. I can't do this right now."

"And I can't let you do this to us. I can't let you do this to Danny. You send him back into that house and you may lose him for good."

"If I don't, I'll lose him. I have to go."

When she tried to leave, Chase caught her hand and reeled her into his arms.

She placed her palms against his chest and tried to push him away, but with only minimal pressure. "You have to let me go."

"I love you, Jess. I can't let you go. Not when it's taken so long to find you again."

As her tears began to stream down her face, he nudged her head against his chest and held her while she cried.

After a time, she raised her tear-stained face and gave him a soft kiss. "I love you, too. But I love my son, as well. I have to find a way to protect him, the same way I've been protecting him for the past week. You have to trust me when I say I'm doing this for him."

Then she wrested out of his grasp, sprinted down the steps and slid into the car. Before he could make it into the driveway to issue one last plea, she sped away.

He dropped down on the porch step and scraped his brain for some way to stop her from making the second biggest mistake of her life. The first had been marrying Dalton Wainwright to begin with.

He replayed the conversation over and over in his head. Then something suddenly occurred to him. Something she'd said about her son. A possible path to the truth.

I have to find a way to protect him, the same way I've been protecting him for the past week....

She'd been protecting Danny his entire life, not only the past week.

He'd been too stupid to see it, too worried about what she might have done to Dalton. But now it all made sense. She hadn't been lying to save herself. She'd been lying to save her child.

Going straight to the source would be the only way he'd know for sure. And he had no time to waste.

"May I help you, sir?"

Chase didn't recognize the maid who evidently served as the first line of defense against intruders trying to breach Edwin's inner sanctum. She might be tall as a timber, and had a linebacker build a lot of men would envy, but at least she wasn't a three-hundred-pound armed guard. Still, this would have been a whole lot easier if Danny had gone home with Rachel and Matt after the holiday dinner, instead of staying behind with his no-good father at the Placid Palace.

He flipped open the folder containing his badge and held it up for her inspection. "I'm Deputy Reed with the sheriff's department. I need to speak with Danny Wainwright."

She perused his credentials but continued to block the entry. "Master Daniel is having his afternoon snack. He can't be disturbed at the moment."

Master Daniel? He felt like he'd taken a wrong turn and landed in some uppity estate in New England. Regardless, he didn't have time to wait until after snack time was over. He wouldn't wait, even if he had all day. "I need to speak to him now. It's important."

Before the hired help could level another protest, Danny ducked under her arm and ran onto the stone porch.

He threw his arms around Chase's waist and hugged him hard. "Did you come over to play catch with me?"

Too bad that wasn't the case. He ruffled Danny's hair and set him back a bit. "Not today, bud. I came over to have a talk, man-to-man."

The maid finally stepped aside and gestured toward the entry. "You may come into the parlor to do that, sir."

Not a chance. If Dalton happened to be seated in said parlor, he'd lay him flat on his ass. Danny didn't need to witness another violent scene. "It's a nice day outside," he said. "I believe I'll just take a little walk with Master Danny."

"But, sir, I cannot allow—"

"You can, and you will, because I'm the law." He wasn't going to let any snobby mountain of a maid tell him what to do. "I don't know where you're from, but around here, that means something."

With her nose in the air, she turned around and closed the door behind her. He'd lay money that she was about to summon the real master of the house, Edwin Wainwright. Normally that would be okay. Old Ed didn't scare him, and he'd eventually have to deal with him anyway. He just didn't want to do it today. Not until he headed Dalton off at the pass, before he forced Jess to sign a devil's pact with the devil himself.

Chase circled the back of Danny's neck with his hand and walked him toward the corner of a lawn as massive as the city park. He almost laughed when the kid swiped a huge white flower from a perfectly-groomed bush. That ought to go over well with the landscapers. He just hoped the head gardener didn't come after him with a hedge clippers.

Before they'd traveled more than a few steps, Danny stopped and looked up at Chase. "Can I go get Bo? He's out back because Granddad won't let him in the house. He says he'll pee on the rugs."

Probably nothing Dalton hadn't done before in a drunken stupor.

He hated to disappoint Danny, but he needed his full attention. The dog would be too distracting. "Tell you what, kiddo. I'll come back tomorrow and we'll teach Bo how to catch a Frisbee. How does that sound?" If all went as planned, Danny wouldn't be there tomorrow. He'd be at Chase's house, with Jess, and they'd all be free to do as they pleased. Just like a regular family.

"That sounds okay, I guess."

So much for not disappointing him.

Chase spotted a stone table a few feet away, right beyond a row of low hedges that would provide some privacy. Maybe even afford them some time before Edwin called out the guard—or called the rest of the household staff—to have him extricated from the estate.

He sat Danny down on a chair and took the opposite seat. "Danny," he began, "the questions I'm about to ask you might be hard to hear, but you have to be honest with me. Okay?"

Danny began pulling petals off the flower and dropping them to the ground. "Okay."

He took some time to gather his thoughts and let Danny prepare for the next step. "The night your dad was hurt, did you see what happened?"

His eyes grew wide and he nodded.

Here came the tough part. "Can you tell me what you saw?"

Danny crushed the flower in his hand, but didn't respond.

"You can trust me," he said. "I'm not going to let anyone hurt you, no matter what you tell me."

Just when he was about to give up on getting answers, Danny blurted, "I didn't mean to do it. I swear I didn't."

He began to cry tears that shot straight to Chase's soul.

"It's okay, kiddo. I know you didn't mean to hurt him. But you have to tell me exactly what happened."

Danny drew in a ragged breath and let it out slowly. "He kept saying mean things about me. He called Mom bad names. Then he grabbed her arm and I thought he was going to hit her. I ran at him and I pushed him as hard as I could." He sobbed then sniffed. "He hit his head on the fireplace. There was blood everywhere."

No wonder the kid was so messed up. "What did your mom do after that?"

"She told me it was an accident, and not to say anything to anyone. Then she told me to go upstairs. That's where I stayed until you came."

He understood all too well why the boy had been so traumatized. He didn't understand why Jess hadn't come clean in the first place. She was too smart to believe that anyone in their right mind would fault a nine-year-old boy for trying to protect his mother from a known tyrant. Even Edwin Wainwright, with all his connections and pious airs, wouldn't punish his own flesh and blood. He'd proven that by letting his son get away with murder for years. Maybe not murder literally, but Dalton had "borrowed" the preacher's car once to take a joy ride. And he'd painted graffiti on the outside of their rival high school's gym. Each time he'd come away without a fine or even a slap on the wrist.

He didn't have time to ponder Jess's motives now. He had to get to her before Dalton did.

After coming to his feet, Chase rounded the table and knelt eye-level with Danny. "You're going to be okay. As soon as we get this cleared up, you'll be with your mom again."

"I'm not going to jail?"

Chase grinned. "Not unless you want me to give you the grand tour."

Danny's expression brightened. "Cool."

"Daniel, come here to me now!"

Chase looked to his right to see Edwin quickly approaching, the guard-maid lumbering behind him. Trouble had arrived.

When Danny hopped up from chair, Chase stood behind him, hands on his shoulders. He'd be damned if he let Old Man Bag of Bucks intimidate the boy.

Edwin stopped short of the hedge, his normally neat silver hair flapping in the breeze like an aging heron's wings. "Deputy Reed," he said, his voice sounding winded and weary. "I'm going to have to ask you to unhand my grandson and leave immediately."

He made a show of looking behind Edwin to the maid. "If I don't, is she going to attack me with a ladle? If so, that'll earn her fifteen to twenty for assault on a police officer. Then who would wash your gold-studded shorts?"

After Danny giggled, Edwin grimaced like he'd eaten a jar of pickles. "I'm warning you, Deputy. If you're not out of here in sixty seconds, I'll call your father."

That was supposed to scare him? "Fine. He's at home watching the game. I'd call him for you, but I have to leave and take care of another problem." A problem old Ed had created. Literally.

"See that you do it immediately," Edwin said as he approached the table.

Chase turned Danny around and smiled. "Just hang in there for me, bud. I'll get you out of here as soon as I can."

Edwin hovered over Danny and tried unsuccessfully to look intimidating. "Go with Zelda, Daniel."

Zelda. That fit.

Danny obeyed, but when he looked back at Chase with a frightened expression, he gave him a thumbs-up to reassure him.

After Danny was out of earshot, he turned his ire on Edwin. "Before I do leave, there's just one thing I have to say to you, old man."

His face turned so red, Chase though his head might blow off his neck. "Do you know who you're talking to, Deputy?"

Yeah. King of the Bastards. "I'm talking to someone who doesn't have control over everyone, including me and your former daughter-in-law." He pointed a finger directly at his face. "I'll go now, but you can bet I'll be back. We have a score to settle." Beginning with convincing him to give Jess her job back.

Without waiting for Edwin's reply, he took off across the lawn, satisfied he now had the information that would finally stop Dalton Wainwright's reign of terror.

Chapter 13

Jess had a plan to stop Dalton from forcing her back into his dysfunctional world. A plan that relied on a special device. A teaching tool that had saved her life on many occasions. She prayed that held true today.

Dalton had arrived on her doorstep a few minutes ago, looking every bit the pompous cat who'd dined on the canary. She didn't know what made her angrier— that he'd come an hour early, or that he didn't bother to bring her son.

As she reached up to retrieve dry goods from the cupboard, Dalton scowled at her from the seat that he'd taken at the dinette table to her right. "I thought you'd be through packing by now."

She'd purposely dragged her heels in that regard. "And I thought you were supposed to bring Danny."

"I told you he wanted to stay and play with the train

set my father gave him. He wasn't nearly as enthusiastic about seeing you as you are about seeing him."

She'd bet her last nickel Dalton hadn't told Danny about the arrangement.

While she placed a package of pasta in a canvas bag, she glanced at the pen barely peeking out between two canisters on the counter. A silver pen that had recording capability—her secret weapon. Every time they spoke, a red light came on, indicating it was working. She'd strategically placed it where it would pick up the sounds, yet it was sufficiently concealed from Dalton. Or so she hoped.

"Leave the damn groceries, Jess, so we can get out of here."

She didn't miss a beat with the packing. "I don't like to waste food. Besides, there's not much at the house, and what's there is probably spoiled."

"You can go to the grocery store tomorrow."

He could go to hell for all she cared. "I deserve some patience. You didn't give me much time to get everything together." And of course, he hadn't offered to help. He just sat there, watching her every move like a hawk about to pounce on its prey.

He released an irritated sigh. "It shouldn't be taking you this long. Most everything you own is at our house."

She would prefer never to step foot in *his* house again. And that led to a question. "I haven't been allowed to go in there since the accident. If you can't clear up the charges against me until tomorrow, how do you plan to explain my presence if someone from the sheriff's department happens to stop by? Deputy Barkley seems to have made it his goal to guard the place."

"I've already taken care of Barkley. No one will be stopping by."

Jess suspected that meant he'd probably bought Barkley's cooperation. She took another covert look at the pen, and prepared to proceed with the plan. "I've been wondering about something. How are you going to get the charges dropped against me without revealing you have no recollection of the night's events?"

"Let me worry about that. You just worry about getting your stuff together."

Every time that red light illuminated, Jess felt one step closer to victory. "Tell me something else. Did you have anything to do with the missing fireplace iron?"

She glanced over her shoulder to see his self-satisfied smile. "I didn't take it," he said. "But I know who did, and I know where it is."

She put forth her best guess. "Buster Eustace?"

"Nah. I wouldn't trust that idiot with something as important as manufactured evidence. Barkley was more than happy to accommodate me with that, too."

Her suspicions had been confirmed. "How did you convince him to do your dirty work?"

"He's up to his eyeballs in debt at the bank, and he has a kid about to go to college. That made him an easy mark. And he didn't even cost me that much."

She almost laughed. Her dear ex-husband was confessing to the woman he'd accused of trying to murder him. Now who was the idiot? "I still don't know how you're going to explain the fireplace iron."

"Not a problem. It will magically show up in the corner, or it might work better if it rolled under the sofa. That's a less obvious place."

She was so close to the finish line, she could almost see the checkered flag. "You've thought this all out, haven't you?"

"Yeah, babe, I have."

She'd never minded Chase using that endearment. In fact, she loved hearing him say it to her. But coming from Dalton's mouth, it sounded totally patronizing.

"By the way," he said. "I want you to meet me tomorrow at the courthouse. We can apply for a marriage license and have a small ceremony at my father's estate next weekend. I thought it would be a good way to ring in the new year."

Right now, she'd love to ring his neck. "I don't see why we have to remarry when we could just live together."

"I want you to be legally bound to me."

Little did he know, by tomorrow, he could be entangled in his own legal issues. Of course, in all probability, Edwin would find a way to rescue his son from the system. Again.

Jess moved onto the cabinet housing the canned goods, satisfied that she had enough information to prove her innocence, as well as Dalton's own machinations. "I'm almost done here, so you can run along and I'll meet you at the house."

"That's a good one, Jess. I'll follow you there, just to make sure you don't decide to take off for parts unknown."

She frowned at his lack of insight. He truly didn't know her at all. "I've waited a long time to be with Danny again. Do you think I'd actually leave him behind?"

"I don't know what you'd do these days, Jessica. After what you did to the deputy, anything's possible."

She had a feeling he wasn't going to drop that topic for a long time. One more thing to use to her advantage. "I'm really surprised we didn't hear you sneaking around in the bushes while you were playing voyeur and taking pictures."

"You were too busy screwing your boyfriend to hear me." His tone hinted at barely-contained rage.

"You are going to destroy the pictures, aren't you?" she asked.

"I'll tear them up after I get what I want."

When he pushed away from the table, came up behind her and ran his hands underneath her shirt, Jess new exactly what he wanted. She couldn't stop the bone-deep shiver, and it wasn't because his touch turned her on. Just the opposite. "What are you doing?"

He formed his palms around her waist. "I'm trying to decide if you've lost a few pounds, and I believe you have. Try to keep it off. I don't like being seen with a fat wife."

She was trying to decide which weapon she should use to knock him over the head—creamed corn or beef consommé. To prevent landing back in jail on charges that would be justified this time, she side-stepped him and turned around, a can in each hand and sarcasm on her lips. "Why certainly I will do everything in my power to please my master."

He took on a look of determination, right before he moved in front of her and pinned her against the counter with his body. "You know, since you don't care for waste, and you've already wasted rent on this dump, we could just use that bed one last time. That way you'd get your money's worth."

She would most likely get deathly ill. "Good try, Dalton. But you don't get the goods until I get my son."

When he kissed her neck, she cringed. "Come on now, Jess. It used to be real good between us, before you turned into a frigid bitch."

And he'd turned into a cheating creep. "It might have been good for you, but not so much for me. You just climbed on, got off and went to sleep. Not my idea of a stellar time."

"That was before I knew you'd be interested in taking a walk on the wild side." Bile rose in Jess's throat when he rested his palm on her belly, right above the waistband on her jeans. "Don't think for a second Chase Reed can give you what you need."

He already has. He'd given her a son and his love, something Dalton would never understand. She wasn't even sure he was capable of loving anyone but himself.

When he took the cans from her grasp and set them on the counter, his eyes narrowed. "What in the hell is this?"

Her heart began to race as Dalton reached around her and held up the only thing that could earn her freedom. "It's an electronic pen," she said, clamoring for a believable explanation. "It records the time and temperature."

"Do you really think I'm that stupid?" He flung the pen to his right and it landed with a *thunk* against the back door. "You *bitch!*"

Seeing her one and only chance to escape, Jess grabbed a can, aimed for his temple, and hit him as hard as she could. She saw the stunned look on his face right before she shoved him backward, and then ran for the nearest exit. But her hands were shaking so badly, she fumbled with the lock that refused to give, wasting precious time.

Her head suddenly jerked back when Dalton grabbed a handful of hair. Then he twisted her arm behind her waist, sending an electric shock through her shoulder, as he spun her around.

He trapped her against the back door and sneered. "Where's your boyfriend now, Jessica?"

If only Chase were around. But he wasn't, because she'd sent him away. "Give up, Dalton. It's over."

"It will never be over, Jess. You're mine. You always will be."

She didn't dare let him see her fear. "I don't belong to anyone."

"Yes, you do. I sealed us together for life when I gave you that kid."

"He's not your son, Dalton," she said, without regard for her safety. "He's Chase's son, and I thank God every day that he is."

He slapped his palm against the door, right by her head. "You're lying!"

She should be quiet, but she couldn't think beyond all the hatred she'd been harboring for years. "I'm not lying. When you were busy issuing ultimatums to me ten years ago, I was making love with Chase. He gave me Danny, not you. And he can give me what you never could—his unconditional love."

She witnessed the minute Dalton went over the edge, felt it when he wrapped his hands around her neck. She clasped his wrists and tried to dislodge his fingers now pressing against her throat, but he was too strong.

The photo Chase had given Jess flashed in her mind, followed by a host of regrets. If she had told him Danny was his, she could die knowing that her son would be safe with his real father. But she hadn't. And she would die, if she didn't find a way to flee.

As she stared into the eyes of a madman, she experienced terror in its purest form. And then the fight-or-flight reaction kicked in. She used the only thing available to ensure she would live. Live to spend her life with her son and the man she loved.

Her trusty knee.

As Chase rounded the curve on his way to Jess's temporary house, a county cruiser sped past him, lights flashing. And when he heard the sound of another siren, he looked in his rearview mirror to see a fast-approaching ambulance.

He didn't have his radio turned on, so he had no idea what could be happening. But his gut told him he had to get to Jess.

Instead of pulling over, he punched the accelerator to the floor, relying on the turbo-charged engine for enough speed to go around the cruiser now in front of him. He might have hell to pay for failure to yield, but that was the least of his concerns at the moment.

He stopped the truck in the driveway, shoved it into Park and tore out of the cab, right before the cruiser turned in behind him. His heart pounded in his chest, and every worst-case scenario ran through his mind as he raced toward the porch at a dead run.

Relief washed over him when Jess came out the front door. Fury replaced the relief when he saw the angry welts on her neck.

After he took her by the arms, she flinched. "Are you okay?"

"I think he broke my shoulder, and aside from the fact he tried to choke me to death, I'm fine."

His need for revenge began to build to the boiling point. "Where is he?"

"In the house," she said. "Doubled over in the kitchen.

His head's probably hurting, and his voice might be a little higher for a while, but he'll survive."

Under normal circumstances, he would appreciate her attempt at humor. At the moment, he only had one goal in mind—to find Dalton Wainwright and finally give him what he deserved.

Chase glanced to his right to see his father exit the car, which meant he had no time to spare. He turned back to Jess. "Wait here and tell Buck what happened."

Before she could respond, he yanked open the screen door and strode through the house to the kitchen. He found Dalton exactly as Jess had said he would, sitting in the kitchen floor, looking dazed.

He grabbed him by the collar, lifted him up and shoved him against the wall. "Give me one good reason why I shouldn't kill you with my bare hands right now."

Dalton tried to appear calm, but he couldn't mask the alarm in his eyes. "Hey, man. It was just a misunderstanding. No harm done."

"No harm done? She has the imprint of your fingers around her neck, you miserable son of a bitch."

"She started it," he said, sounding like the coward he was. "She whacked me up the side of the head with a can. I think she might have even given me a concussion. I had to defend myself."

Chase got right up in his face. "Let me tell you what we're going to do. I'm going to take you out back, and we're going to settle this, man-to-man. And while I'm beating the hell out of you, I want you to remember how Jess felt when you were *defending* yourself."

"Let him go, son."

He glanced at Buck in the doorway, but he didn't release Dalton. "I'm not on duty. I can do whatever I want with him."

"And you'll be doing it in front of a peace officer, because I'm not going to turn you loose on him. That means you'll end up behind the cage in the car, right next to him. You might want to keep in mind that Jess needs you."

Buck had said the magic words. He turned back to Dalton. "Today's your lucky day. But you never know what tomorrow's going to bring, so watch your back."

After Chase freed his hold from Dalton's collar, he took him by the arm to hand him over to Buck. But his father surprised him by holding up the cuffs. "I'll let you do the honors," he said. "I figure you deserve that much for not taking him out while you had the chance."

He grabbed the cuffs, yanked Dalton's arms behind his back with a little more force than necessary, and snapped the metal bracelets closed. "Dalton Wainwright, you are finally under arrest."

"I'll handle it from here," Buck said. "You go see about Jess. The paramedics are checking her out."

He would gladly relinquish his duty for that reason alone.

Chase found Jess seated at the back of the ambulance, a blue sling fashioned around her arm. He walked up to her, saw that bruises had begun to form around her neck and got mad all over again. "Is your arm broken?" he asked.

"Dislocated shoulder," she said. "I have to go to the hospital for X-rays before I know how bad it is. At least it's my left arm, not my right."

It was already bad enough. He suddenly remembered something he should have never forgotten. "Where's Danny?"

"Fortunately, still with Edwin. If Dalton would have brought him, this might not have happened."

"Or he might have seen it happen," he said.

She pinched the bridge of her nose. "You're right. That would have been horrible."

He should probably give her a break, but he needed to know exactly what had transpired to that point. He sat down beside her and rested a hand on her leg. "Can you tell me how this all went down?"

She sighed. "I decided to play along with Dalton's conditions that we remarry, and then defeat him at his own game. I used a digital pen to record the conversation, and got him to admit he didn't remember anything about that night. He'd concocted the entire story, and he paid Barkley to steal the fireplace iron."

He'd known all along something wasn't right with that sack of manure, Barkley. He'd deal with him later. "Go ahead."

"Anyway, Dalton saw the recorder," she continued, "and he went ballistic. I tried to get away, but he managed to catch me. If I hadn't kneed him in the jewels, he would have killed me."

"That's why you should never have tried this by yourself. Dalton's been heading toward this kind of violence for years."

"I realize that now," she said. "But I had to do something to clear my name. The pen's on the kitchen floor, near the back door. Hopefully he didn't break it and the confession is still there."

They might not even need the confession, now that he knew the real story. "I talked to Danny right before I drove over here. He told me he's the one who pushed Dalton, not you."

Her gaze shot to his. "I never wanted to keep that information from you, but I had my reasons for doing so."

"For the life of me, Jess, I don't know what they'd be. Danny's a beat-down kid who wanted to protect his mother from a worthless father. You should have realized he wouldn't be punished for that."

She folded the hem of her shirt, back and forth. "There's another reason I didn't say anything."

From the serious tone of her voice, he wasn't sure he could cope with the reason. But he still needed to know.

The sound of the slamming screen drew their attention to Buck leading Dalton down the porch steps. Since they'd have to pass by the ambulance on the way to the cruiser, Chase gently took Jess's right hand into his to give her support.

Dalton sent them both an evil glare as he approached. "Does he know what he's in for, Jess?" he asked.

Chase had learned to ignore the ramblings of a captured perp, but something in Jess's eyes sent up warning flags. "What's he talking about?"

When she didn't respond, Dalton started laughing. "You didn't even tell him the little bastard is his kid? That's great, Jess."

Buck yanked Dalton forward. "Move it, Wainwright," he said, without even showing one iota of shock over the revelation.

But Chase was shocked. And confused. "Is he saying that Danny is—"

"Your son," Jess said.

That sent Chase to his feet to face her. "Is it true?"

"Yes, it's true." She looked up at him, tears in her eyes. "I can explain."

Before she could begin, the EMT rounded the ambulance. "The ER's been notified we're coming, ma'am. We have to go now."

"I need another minute," she said. "I have to talk to Deputy Reed."

Filled with a sudden sense of resentment and anger, Chase backed away. "No, she doesn't need to talk to me. We're done. Go ahead and take her."

"Chase, please hear me out."

Ignoring her plea, he turned and started for the truck, a million thoughts racing through his mind, as well as the words Buck had said to him a few days ago.

She's been a Wainwright for a decade. She's bound to have learned something about lying....

His dad had been right. Chase had only seen what he'd wanted to see—the girl who'd been his best friend, the woman he'd always loved, couldn't be capable of something so damn cruel.

Betrayal, as sharp as shards of glass, cut him to the quick. If what she'd said about Danny was the truth, then she'd robbed of the chance to know his own child. She'd subjected her son—their son—to a contemptible man who didn't know the first thing about being a father.

He did have a lot of questions, and she did have a lot of explaining to do. But he needed time to think, time away from her. Time to grieve everything he'd lost. Including her.

She'd lost him.

After three days with no word from Chase, that reality had finally set in.

Jess had remained in the rental because she had nowhere else to go. With each passing moment, her hope for a normal life had begun to fade.

And the silence in the empty house…

That had been the worst part of all, and the reason she now sat at Rachel's kitchen table.

"What are your immediate plans?" Rachel asked as she set a glass of wine in front of Jess.

To get out of bed every morning. "I don't know. That depends on if and when they drop the charges."

"Savannah is certain they'll drop them," Rachel said. "With the nifty little pen confession, and Danny's statement, you'll be free and clear by the end of the week."

Maybe clear, but not necessarily free. "Buck said something about possible perjury charges."

Rachel's solemn expression didn't give Jess any substantial confidence. "Savannah mentioned you might have to deal with that in the future." She laid her hand on Jess's forearm, right below where the sling ended. "Look at it this way. Dalton will be rotting in jail a long, long time. That should give you cause to celebrate. Makes me want to jump for joy."

Jess was completely taken aback by the comment. "But he's your bother, Rachel."

Rachel shrugged. "I've never been one to believe in the 'blood is thicker than water' thing. Dalton deserves to be locked up and I'll be glad to throw away the key. Then we can be assured he'll never be around you or his son again."

Jess realized she had to come clean with her former sister-in-law, before she heard it from someone else. But it was going to be tough, telling her that Danny—the nephew she'd been caring for in Jess's stead, was still caring for—wasn't her biological nephew at all. "How long do you think Danny will be at Matt's clinic?" she asked, just to be sure she could speak freely.

"I don't expect them for another hour."

"Good." Jess rimmed the wineglass with her fingertip. "I have something important to tell you. Something I don't want him to hear yet."

"You've been sleeping with Chase."

Her gaze zipped up from the glass. "How did you know that?"

"Matt told me he figured it out when he was helping with the roof that day. I personally think it's great. Even if neither of you realized it, the chemistry's been there since high school. I've always thought the two of you should have been together years ago."

"We were," Jess blurted. "Actually, only once."

Rachel raised a brow. "Really? When?"

"The night before Chase deployed to Afghanistan."

"Two weeks before you and Dalton married?"

Jess assumed that, like Savannah, Rachel had already taken out the mental calendar. "Yes, and before you ask, Danny could have been either Chase or Dalton's son." Now for the bittersweet truth. "As it turned out, he's Chase's."

She let Rachel digest the information before she spoke again. "This doesn't change anything. He'll always be your nephew, just not biologically."

"Of course it doesn't change anything between us." Rachel made a face and touched her belly. "Does Danny know?"

"Not yet, and are you okay?"

"Just a little twinge," she said as she shifted in her seat. "This baby boy loves to curl up in just the wrong spot. Now back to your baby boy. When are you going to tell him? After he goes to college?"

At the right time. In the right place. "After he's back

with me, and I can convince Chase to tell him with me. That might be a problem since the good deputy is not speaking to me right now."

Rachel frowned. "Then Chase knows."

"Yes." She didn't have the energy to explain how he'd come by that information. "He's angry because I didn't tell him sooner."

"Well, he can just get un-mad," Rachel said. "He should be thrilled he has a son as great as Danny. I'm thrilled Danny won't be inheriting the Wainwright cut-throat gene."

Thank heaven for good friends. "Then you're not mad at me?"

"No, Jess, I'm not mad," she said. "I will be if you and Chase don't work this out. Danny deserves to have a real father. A good father. And you deserve to be with the man you love. You do love him, don't you?"

"Yes, I do." More than she could ever express.

Whether she loved Chase, or deserved to be with him, didn't really matter. Not unless he decided to give her another chance. Or to forgive her.

And that possibility was beginning to look bleak.

Chapter 14

Five days had gone by since Chase had last seen Jess. Five long, terrible days.

He'd returned to work, spent his nights in seclusion, thinking nonstop. The nightmares involving the war had begun to subside, but two nights ago, they'd been replaced by another that had been equally as bad. He'd dreamed of Jess coming toward him, smiling in the way he'd always loved. But as he reached for her offered hand, she'd suddenly disappeared. When he'd awoken to find she wasn't there beside him, that had been the greatest torture of all.

And that was the first time he'd allowed himself to cry.

His emotions were still raw, and his mind still wrapped in confusion. He had a lot to consider, and decisions he had yet to make. He hadn't stopped loving her. He probably never would. But he wasn't sure if he had the strength to forgive her.

Right now, he just needed to keep moving forward, get on with his life, even if he couldn't imagine not having her in it.

Today, he decided to finish his business with Edwin Wainwright. At least he could ensure that Jess had a job waiting for her, enabling her to give Danny what he needed, even if he couldn't. He also wouldn't mind seeing how the old man had handled the news that his son had been remanded without bail. Maybe old Ed couldn't buy every judge in the county after all.

Chase had chosen the bank as the place for the confrontation for the sake of accessibility. He'd phoned ahead, so he knew Wainwright would be there until noon, before the place closed for the New Year's holiday.

He walked into the lobby and looked around. When he saw the gold nameplate on a nearby door, he started in that direction. He didn't even bother to check in with the receptionist. And she didn't bother to flag him down, proving some advantages did exist when you were the law.

He did rap on the door for his mother's sake. Missy Reed was a stickler when it came to politeness, and she wouldn't take too kindly to him not minding his manners. But that was the last courtesy he planned to show the rich man today.

After he heard, "Come in," Chase entered without hesitation. He'd expected to see Wainwright seated behind the massive mahogany desk, maybe smoking a pipe while he played with other people's futures, like they were pawns in his private game of chess. Instead, the man stood at the window, looking out on the downtown street.

He didn't intend to beat around the bush. "I promised I'd be back, Ed."

Wainwright dropped the curtain and turned around. He leveled a weary gaze on Chase, and didn't appear to be that surprised to see him. "Have a seat, Deputy," he said, indicating one of two nearby chairs.

He wasn't in the mood for small talk. "I don't plan to stay long. I just wanted to stop by to say that when the school board meets next week, I expect you to reinstate Jess. It's the least you can do, considering the hell your son put her through."

"You may consider it done."

That was way too easy. "You'll convince the board to lift the suspension, just like that? No argument?"

"I give you my word." Edwin lowered himself into one of the chairs and folded his hands in his lap. "You don't have any children, do you, Deputy Reed?"

What a question to ask when the answer had so recently changed. But he still had no real proof Danny was his son, only Jess's claim. And even if it turned out to be true, Wainwright apparently hadn't heard the news. He wasn't about to enlighten him. "No. I don't have any kids." Not officially.

Edwin shifted slightly in the chair. "If you do decide to take that step, you'll eventually learn that you will go to great lengths to protect them. You believe their lies. You will lie for them. And no matter what you do, they will make their own mistakes. You only hope that those errors in judgment won't predict their future. And then you wake up one morning and realize that you're to blame for their failures."

The mogul before him wasn't only the callous business man everyone feared. He was a broken old man who'd just taken responsibility for his son's transgressions. Funny, Chase almost felt sorry for him. "I don't think you should carry all the blame for Dalton's actions. He's an adult in charge of his own fate."

"He's weak," Edwin said. "And I wanted him to be tough. I drove him to prove his strength. I didn't believe he would go this far. But now that he has, I've washed my hands of him. Still, there's no greater pain a father can experience than when he cuts a child out of his life."

That could explain why Dalton hadn't made bail, and why Edwin hadn't visited him. But unbeknownst to Wainwright, he'd solved one of Chase's dilemmas. If the past few days had taught him anything, he'd learned he had what it took to be a dad. And he couldn't desert Danny, whether he had a biological tie or not. "Do you think you'll ever forgive Dalton?" he asked out of curiosity.

"I already have, Deputy. His mother would have wanted it that way. She always said that if you rely on your heart to guide you, there is nothing that can't be forgiven."

Chase was immediately reminded of Jess's words on the night he'd told her about the war. Words everyone should learn to live by, including him. Especially him.

I believe if your heart is in the right place, anything can be forgiven....

And when he stopped to consider what Wainwright had been through after losing his wife, he had to respect the man on some level. "It must've been hard, raising two kids on your own."

He glimpsed unmistakable sadness in Edwin's expression before he composed himself again. "Yes, it was difficult. Ellen was a remarkable woman, and Rachel is a lot like her. That's why I know she'll make it through this latest crisis."

Chase wasn't aware of any crisis involving Rachel or Matt. "What do you mean?"

"I received a call right before you arrived," he said. I've not only lost my son, I've lost a grandson. Rachel went into early labor, and the infant didn't survive."

This week could go down in history as one of the worst for the members of the six-pack. The thought of Matt and Rachel losing the baby they'd waited so long to have, made him sick. "I'm real sorry to hear that."

"So am I," Edwin said. "I'll be going by to see her at the hospital as soon as the bank closes."

He planned to do the same, only he wasn't going to let the job stand in the way of checking on his friends. Wainwright may have displayed some humanity, but he was still a hardnosed businessman, first and foremost.

And that reminded Chase he still had one more item of unfinished business. "Before I go, I have another request."

Edwin came to his feet. "And what would that be, Deputy?"

"Jess could be facing perjury charges for not revealing Danny's role in Dalton's injuries. You still wield a lot of influence around here, so I'd appreciate anything you could do to take care of that. As long as it doesn't involve money exchanging hands."

"I'll see what I can manage," Edwin said. "Jessica doesn't deserve to be punished more than she already has. And I'm living proof of what a parent will do to protect their child. That's all she's guilty of, protecting Daniel."

Wainwright was making perfect sense. He'd be damned if he ever saw that coming. "Thanks. I appreciate you taking the time to talk with me."

"One more thing," Edwin said. "I hope you continue

to take care of my former daughter-in-law. She's one of the few people who can make me smile."

Chase could absolutely relate to that.

After he left the bank, he started for the cruiser parked at the curb, then changed his mind and crossed the street to the city park. He planted himself on a bench and went over everything Wainwright had said to him about forgiveness and parents protecting their children. Every bit of it had hit home. Too close to home.

He had to remember that Jess had forgiven him when he'd told her about Safa. He couldn't forget that until he'd reconnected with Jess, he hadn't been able to forgive himself. If she'd been willing to grant him grace for his sins, didn't she deserve the same from him? And didn't Danny deserve a father who'd be there for him? The answer to all those questions was a resounding *yes*.

Now that he finally felt grounded enough to sit down and work things out with Jess, he couldn't wait to find her. And he knew exactly where she would be.

What did you say to a woman who'd just lost a child?

Jess had no idea. Even though she'd recently faced a similar situation, Danny had been returned to her yesterday, healthy and relatively content. They still had a long way to go to rebuild their relationship, and plenty of time to get there. Rachel, on the other hand, would never have the joy of watching her child grow, and that made Jess incredibly sad.

As she sought out her friend, she passed a few rooms filled with joyful family members, the sounds of crying babies echoing in the corridor. She could only imagine how torturous that must be for Rachel.

She finally located the correct room, and when she

came upon the slightly open door, she pushed it open and peeked inside. Rachel was lying on her back, her dark hair forming a halo on the pillow, her eyes tightly closed.

Since she was obviously sleeping, Jess wondered if she should leave and come back later. She opted to sit in the chair next to the narrow bed and wait. But she didn't have to wait long until her friend opened her eyes.

"Hey, Rachel," Jess said quietly. "How are you feeling?"

"Groggy." She rested her hand on her belly. "Empty."

She felt Rachel's pain as keenly as if it were her own. "I saw Matt walking across the parking lot when I pulled up, but I didn't have a chance to speak with him."

"I told him to go home."

Something in Rachel's tone disturbed Jess. "I'm sure he's exhausted, and he sounded so upset when he called me this morning. Of course, he has every right to be."

Rachel rolled slowly to her side and reached for Jess's hand. "We decided to call him Caleb. He was such a beautiful baby. He was so small, but he had these perfect little feet and hands and a lot of dark hair. They only let me see him for a little while before they took him away. And then he was gone. I asked to hold him, but Matt thought it would be too upsetting for me. No one cared how I felt about it."

Maybe that explained why Rachel had seemed almost angry with her husband. "Do they know why the baby came early? I hope it wasn't the stress of what happened with Dalton, and then you had to take care of Danny—"

"It's no one's fault, Jess. That's what they told me. But I can't help but think that I... Never mind."

Jess squeezed her hand. "If they said it's no one's fault, then I hope you believe that, too. You took good care of yourself during the pregnancy. You got plenty of rest. You ate well. Me, I practically ate everything in sight when I was pregnant with Danny."

"How is Danny?" Rachel asked. "I've been thinking about him since he left our place."

Jess marveled over her unselfishness. "He's doing okay. He's still quiet, but he's opening up more. I did talk to your counselor friend yesterday afternoon. She's going to see Danny next week. I gave her a brief history but we'll go more into depth then."

"That's good. And your arm?"

"It's going to heal on its own." She wished she could say the same for her broken heart. "I had a hard time getting used to the sling at first, but I'm learning to function with only one hand."

"Just one more thing we tend to take for granted, I guess."

When Rachel's eyes began to look heavy, Jess took that as her cue to leave. She came to her feet and released Rachel's hand. "I'm going to let you rest now. Do you know when you'll be going home?"

"Tomorrow," she said. "But I'm going to Dad's for a few days since Matt will be working."

That made little sense to Jess. "Surely he'll forget about work until you're feeling better."

Rachel shook her head. "Not Matt. When things go badly, he buries himself in work. He's a lot like my father in that respect."

Jess would never think to compare Matt Boyd to Edwin Wainwright. They were as different as midnight and morning. "I'll call you tomorrow to see how you're doing. If you're up to it, I can bring Danny by. I know he'd like to see his favorite aunt."

Rachel attempted a smile. "That would be nice. I'll let you know."

"Is there anything I can do for you before I go?"

"Yes, there is." Rachel punched a button on the remote and raised the head of the bed. "If you and Chase still haven't worked things out, then go find him and make him listen to reason. That's an order."

Jess was so happy to see Rachel smile, but she wasn't sure she had the courage for a confrontation. "I'll think about it."

"Don't think, Jess. Just do it. Life is too precious to waste, even for a minute."

She leaned and kissed Rachel's cheek. "You're absolutely right."

And she was. If Jess wanted to resolve her issues with Chase, she couldn't wait for him to come around. Otherwise, she could be waiting another ten years.

She left Rachel's room, bent on a mission. She would track Chase down and make him talk to her. Make him see they belonged together. How she was going to find him remained to be seen. Buy a police scanner? Put out an APB? Jaywalk in hopes that he would be the one to give her a ticket?

Making a trip down to the department seemed a much more logical course of action.

But as she pushed through the double doors and entered the lobby, she discovered she didn't have to look far to find him. Chase stood right there, leaning over the information desk, obviously flirting with the volunteer, if the silver-haired lady's schoolgirl smile was any indication. The bad boy had returned. But he was still her bad boy. Or that's what she hoped.

He wore his uniform, and he wore it well. Khaki shirt,

dark jeans, brown rough-out boots and the cowboy hat Buck insisted his men donned during duty. A throwback to the Old West, even if Placid was much farther east.

As he moved away from the desk, he sent a glance her direction, then did a double-take. She couldn't escape now, even if she wanted to.

They crossed the waiting room at the same time and met in the middle.

"I thought I'd find you here," he said.

And he hadn't avoided her. A good sign. "I just left Rachel's room."

"How is she?" He looked and sounded seriously concerned.

"As well as can be expected," she said. "She was about to drift off when I left her."

"Then I guess I'll wait until later to see her."

Okay. Now what? Time to get with the program. "If you have a few moments to spare in the next couple of days, I'd like to talk to you. Of course, feel free to wait until Monday, after the holiday."

"I have time now," he said. "Maybe we could find a place around here."

Jess couldn't imagine where. The county hospital was small, basically an emergency room, a maternity ward—which seemed to be the most popular place—and two other medical floors. They did have a small lounge with vending machines, but people would be going in and out. As far as the lobby went, she surveyed the area and saw only two available chairs, each located on opposite sides of the room.

"Do you have any suggestions?" she asked him after exhausting all possibilities.

"There's a courtyard not far from the front door, with

tables and chairs. We could sit there. I'd offer my place, but I only have about an hour before I have to get back to work."

She'd vote for his place, but she understood he had a job to do. Besides, any setting would work, as long as she had the opportunity to speak to him. "I have to pick up Danny at a friend's house in a while, so the court-yard it is."

They left out the sliding glass doors and claimed a table and chairs in the corner of the small patio.

Once they were settled in across from each other, Chase took off his hat and set it on the table, brim up. He slicked his hand through his blond hair that glinted in the sunlight, just like Danny's hair. "It's warm today," he said. "Especially for December."

"It's almost January."

"Yeah, you're right."

For two people who used to talk about everything, it seemed strange that they could only discuss the weather. Back to square one.

After a time, Chase finally broke the uncomfortable silence. "How's the kid?"

She was pleased he was interested in Danny. "He came home yesterday, and he's doing all right. He starts coun-seling next week."

"That's good."

"He asked about you several times."

That brought about his dimpled smile. "Oh, yeah?"

"Yeah. He mentioned something about you teaching Bo how to catch a Frisbee."

"I forgot about that. Maybe I'll have a chance to do that soon."

She decided to put him to the test. "I spoke with Mom

yesterday and filled her in on what's happened. Needless to say, she's shocked. She also suggested that Danny and I move close to her and Dad."

His expression went somber. "Are you going to do it?"

That depended on how this conversation went. "I've thought about it. Danny doesn't want to leave, even after everything that's happened. But I think he'll eventually warm up to the idea."

"What about you, Jess? Do you want to leave?"

Not really. Not at all. "I don't have much reason to stay. I don't have a job and—"

"That's been resolved. You should be reinstated next week."

She could only gape for a few moments. "How do you know that?"

"Because I just came from Wainwright's office to plead your case, and he's agreed to convince the board that it's the right thing to do. It's his way of making up for what Dalton did to you."

He could have gone all year without bringing up her ex. "Thank you for going to bat for me. The question is, why did you?"

"I care about what happens to you and Danny."

"Because I'm the mother of your son?"

When he didn't immediately respond, Jess feared she already had her answer.

"That brings me an important question," he finally said. "How do you know Danny is my son when you've never asked me for a paternity test?"

She launched into a brief explanation about the blood type issue, and finished by saying, "But if you're not convinced, you are welcome to request a DNA test."

He released a rough sigh. "I don't have to. I know he's mine."

An acknowledgment she'd waited a long time to hear. "In my opinion, the dimples are a dead giveaway."

"That, and he's a switch-hitter, just like me when I played ball."

They shared a smile until Chase grew solemn again. "Why didn't you tell me about him sooner, Jess? If I'd known about him, I would've left the Army earlier. I sure as hell wouldn't have signed on for three tours."

Yet he wouldn't have afforded her the same consideration. "And I spent all those years in denial. I wouldn't let myself believe you were his father because I was so afraid you would never come home alive. You just kept going back, and every time you'd write and tell me that, I'd cry for days."

"Why? You had Dalton."

"Yes, and I loved you. I realized it the night in my dorm. But then you said it was a mistake, so I settled." And that was the first time she'd truly admitted it to herself.

"It would have been a mistake back then," he said. "I wasn't ready to settle down and have a family. It hasn't been all that long ago that I figured out I would never be ready for it."

Well, that was that. He'd all but said that their futures were heading in opposite directions.

Before she broke down and bawled, Jess scooted the chair back and stood. "Now that I know where you stand, I need to go. Call me if you want to see Danny. If you don't, then let me know that, too. I'll try to explain it to him as gently as possible."

As she turned to leave, Chase caught her wrist. "Don't go, Jess. I still have a lot to say to you."

"I believe you've already said it all. I had every intention of trying to convince you that we should be together. That what we have is so rare, we'd never find it with anyone else. But you obviously don't feel the same."

"You're wrong. That's exactly how I feel. You just didn't give me a chance to say it."

Jess dropped back into the chair for fear her legs might betray her. "Then you still love me?"

He took her right hand and brought it to his lips for a soft kiss. "I couldn't stop loving you, even if I tried. I just had to have time to sort out all my feelings. Then Wainwright said a few things that helped me understand why you did what you did. You were only trying to protect Danny. And I'm willing to forgive you for withholding the fact that I'm his father, if you'll forgive me for not giving you the benefit of the doubt."

She'd never understood what it meant to have your heart soar, until now. "I forgive you for everything you've ever done wrong in your life. Except for maybe those hideous slippers you bought me on my sixteenth birthday."

The sun had nothing on that beautiful smile. "I think the reindeer underwear more than makes up for that."

"Agreed." She felt it was time to put all teasing aside and consider her son. Their son. "When do you think we should tell Danny that you're his father?"

"We should probably ask the counselor her advice about that. In the meantime, I want you and Danny to move in with me."

This was all happening so fast, it made her head spin. "And leave my lovely abode with the questionable plumbing and dilapidated roof? Of course, you never did install that shower. Do you know what it's like to lower yourself into a tub with only one arm?"

The sexy devil shone through his dark eyes. "Believe me, babe, when you're at my house, I'll be glad to help you bathe."

She had another serious consideration. "As much as I want to move in with you, I'm not sure that's a good idea right now. Some people around here still don't approve of cohabitation before marriage. Danny's been exposed to enough scandal already."

"Actually, I thought about that." He fished through his pocket, pulled out a gorgeous diamond solitaire and held it up. "I saw this in the window of the jewelry store next to the bank. I just walked right in and bought it."

The moment was so surreal. Unbelievable. Wonderful. "Is it for me, or were you going to give it to the lady at the information desk?"

He grinned. "It's for you." He moved into the chair beside her and lifted her left hand without moving her bum arm. "Jessica Keller, would you do me the honor of being my wife?"

A tear slid down her cheek, and the words she'd never thought she would have the chance to say, flowed out of her mouth with ease. "Yes, Deputy Reed, I will marry you."

He leaned over and kissed her like he meant it, without any regard to the people milling about the area. Finally, she could make others uncomfortable with a serious public display of affection.

"I've been thinking," Chase said after he broke the kiss. "It would be great to ring in the new year with a wedding."

Jess laughed. She couldn't help it.

And Chase clearly didn't see the humor in the situation. "What's so funny?"

"It's just that I've been proposed to twice in the span of six days, and both of you said almost the same thing."

Chase sent her sour look. "Who else proposed to you?"

"Dalton."

His features relaxed. "I'm glad you turned him down."

"So am I." She rested her bent elbow on the table and propped her cheek on her palm. "Now you were saying?"

"Let's get married on New Year's Day. I happen to know a man who has the power to get the marriage license rushed, as long as we go apply for it now."

"What man is that?"

"Edwin Wainwright."

She couldn't imagine what had transpired between Chase and her ex-father-in-law, but she didn't care, as long as it had brought the love of her life back to her. "I don't know, Chase. Today's Friday, and that means we only have two days to get ready. I have to call my parents to see if they can fly in. I have to find a dress and—"

He stopped her protests with another kiss. "You've always been a jumper first, and a thinker later. It's time for us both to jump."

A leap of faith worth taking. "Okay. But we do need to tell Danny together. And it might be nice to decide on a place to have the ceremony, although I have no idea where that would be."

He cracked a crooked grin. "I happen to know a man who can take care of that, too."

"Don't you think it's kind of weird, getting married at your soon-to-be wife's ex-father-in-law's house?"

Chase glared at his best man, Sam McBriar. "Look

who's talking," he muttered. "You're about to get married on an old bridge."

He returned his attention to the small crowd that had gathered for the hurry-up wedding, held in the Wainwright estate's massive living room. It had all come together without a hitch. Jess's parents were in the first row, still looking somewhat shell-shocked. His parents were on the opposite side, and seated behind them, Edwin Wainwright and his maid, Zelda. The woman had starting sobbing the minute the string quartet had begun to play.

Sam's fiancée, Savannah, serving as Jess's maid of honor, started down the makeshift aisle, and when she reached the flowered arch, she winked at her future husband. Jess had planned to include Rachel as an attendant, but she hadn't felt like coming downstairs for the wedding. And Matt had declined to be a groomsman if his wife couldn't take part in the ceremony. That was the only glitch they'd encountered so far. A disappointing glitch.

When the music began to build, and Jess appeared on Danny's arm, Chase found it pretty hard to breathe. She was dressed in an off-white gown, with matching sling, and held a bouquet of white flowers from the garden. She looked as beautiful as he'd ever seen her look, and in a matter of moments, he'd willingly agree to see only her for the rest of his life.

After she reached his side, Jess handed the bouquet to Savannah and took Chase's hand, while Danny stood by Sam.

"Friends and family," the justice of the peace began. "We're gathered here today to join this man and this woman in holy matrimony. And at their request, they'll take it from here."

Chase had felt a little self-conscious about reciting his own vows, until Jess had called him the night before and they composed them together. He cleared his throat and focused into Jess's eyes, the place where he'd always found strength. "Jess, I promise to be faithful to you and to trust you for the rest of my life. I promise to take care of you and Danny, and to make sure you always have a solid roof over your head, as well as an appropriate shower. And I'll never ask you to iron my shirts." He waited for the chuckles to die down before he continued. "I also promise to always be your best friend, and to give you a part of myself that I've never given to anyone else. My heart. I love you, babe, and I always will."

He noticed Jess's lips quivered a little, but she didn't cry. Not yet. "Chase," she began, "I promise to be faithful to you for the rest of my life. To give you another child, but no more than three. And I will try to deliver the occasional back flip, as soon as I'm out of this blasted sling." The chuckles turned to laughter that quickly subsided as Jess continued. "I promise to hold you when bad dreams disturb your sleep, and to be completely honest with you from this day forward. I accept you for better or worse, knowing that our worst times have already passed. And as the day comes when I draw my last breath, your love will be the one true thing I take with me."

Chase realized she hadn't mentioned the last vow, but that made it all the sweeter.

They stood there smiling at each other, until the justice of the peace interrupted the moment with the exchanging of the rings. By the time the kiss came around, Chase was more than ready to seal the deal. And he did, maybe for a bit longer than some would deem appropriate. That was just too bad.

"Ladies and gentlemen," the JP announced, "I present to you Chase and Jessica Reed, and their son, Daniel."

Chase took Danny's left hand, Jess took his right, and they walked back down the aisle, this time as a real family. The family Chase never knew he wanted, until he met the son he never knew he had. And his life had finally come together through the love of one sassy, spontaneous and determined woman—his very best friend.

When the crowd began to gather to offer congratulations, Jess turned and smiled, then let go of Chase's hand. But that was okay with him, because he knew he wasn't really letting her go.

And he never would again.

* * * * *

We hope you enjoyed the
Small Town Christmas collection.

If you liked these stories, then you'll love
Harlequin Special Edition!

You know that romance is for life.
Harlequin Special Edition stories show
that every chapter in a relationship has its
challenges and delights and that love can be
renewed with each turn of the page.

Enjoy six *new* stories from
Harlequin Special Edition every month!

Available wherever books and ebooks are sold.

HARLEQUIN®

SPECIAL EDITION

Life, Love and Family

www.Harlequin.com

HTHMS1014-1A

***

She exhaled noisily and collapsed on the other end of the couch. "Casey—"

"I just wanted to see you."

She slowly closed her mouth, absorbing that. Her fingers tightened around the glass. She could have offered him one. He'd been the one to introduce her to that particular winery in the first place. The first time she'd invited him to her place after they'd moved their relationship into the "benefits" category, he'd brought a bottle of wine.

She'd been wholly unnerved by it and told him they weren't dating—just mutually filling a need—and to save the empty romantic gestures.

He hadn't brought a bottle of wine ever again.

She shook off the memory.

He was here now, in her home, uninvited, and she'd be smart to remember that. "Why?"

He pushed off the couch and prowled around her living room. He'd always been intense. But she'd never really seen him *tense*. And she realized she was seeing it now.

She slowly sat forward and set her glass on the coffee table, watching him. "Casey, what's wrong?"

He shoved his fingers through his hair, not answering. Instead, he stopped in front of a photo collage on the wall above her narrow bookcase that Julia had given her last Christmas. "You going to go out with him again?"

Something ached inside her. "Probably," she admitted after a moment.

"He's a good guy," he muttered. "A little straightlaced, but otherwise okay."

She didn't know what was going on with him. But she suddenly felt like crying, and Jane wasn't a person who cried. "Casey."

"You could do worse." Then he gave her a tight smile and walked out of the living room into the kitchen. A second later, she heard the sound of her back door opening and closing.

He couldn't have left her more bewildered if he'd tried.

***

Find out what happens next in
New York Times *bestselling author Allison Leigh's*
A WEAVER CHRISTMAS GIFT, the latest in
THE RETURN TO THE DOUBLE C *miniseries.*

Available November 2014 from
Harlequin® Special Edition.